D1243989

FROM WHENCE
WE COME

FROM WHENCE WE COME

Maurice W. Dorsey

FIC
Dorsey

CONTENTS

PART THREE
Seymour's Young Life

PART FOUR
Seymour in Adulthood

In Memory

Dr. Robert James Battjes
Mr. William H. Curry Jr.
Mr. and Mrs. William H. Curry Sr.
Mr. and Mrs. James Roswell Dorsey Sr.
Mr. and Mrs. Leander E. Dorsey
Ms. Rosalie Dorsey

ACKNOWLEDGMENTS

I am so fortunate to have been blessed with many people who guided me through the most difficult periods in my life, and I am deeply grateful.

My parents—James and Zelma Dorsey, who rose from lesser heritage than I—helped me throughout my life, but especially in the formative and teenage years. My love for them is eternal.

Being the only African American in my high school class of four hundred and sixty students, Robert E. Lee Ross placed me beneath his wing and mentored me through the trauma of integrating a racially segregated class during the 1960s, the height of the civil rights movement.

After four years of not taking undergraduate studies seriously at the University of Maryland, College Park, Dean Marjory Brooks guided me to rigorous academic study habits, graduation, and teaching me to understand the gift my parents had given me. She insisted, taught, and never gave up on my attaining a college education where many students did not have my opportunity. Pedro Ribalta, a visiting professor from Barcelona, Spain, who in addition to teaching me world-class commercial design also advised and counseled me in understanding and accepting my homosexuality.

Silas Roscoe Young, my only lifelong friend, was my anchor after leaving home and graduating from college. He listened to and endured my young adult insecurities and unhealed childhood wounds. He was a third parent in many regards.

Dr. Evelyn Pasture Valentine, Dr. Virginia Roeder, and Dr. Benjamin Whitten (Baltimore City Public Schools) were the first to offer me employment commensurate with my education and offered unlimited opportunities for professional growth and advancement. They built the foundation to my career in higher education and government.

Dr. George Johnson, University of the District of Columbia, personally recruited me for an opportunity to experience and work in a historically black university in the nation's capital.

Dr. Archie Buffkins personally recruited me for the Other Race Fellowship that allowed me to earn a PhD from the University of Maryland, College Park. Dr. Dan Huden was my graduate school advisor. He met with me weekly at his home in Columbia, Maryland, to get me through the rigorous dissertation process and graduation.

Dr. Robert Battjes exposed me to a world that I would have never seen without him. He taught me the value of stewardship over money, the meaning of commitment, and how to open the doors to my happiness.

Mr. Curtland Deville, Dr. A. J. Dye, Dr. Robert Koopman, and Dr. Daniel Kugler navigated and promoted me to a career in federal government. This experience changed the whole trajectory of my life.

A special thanks to Dr. Frederic Breed Mayo Jr., reviewer, and Michael Gold, photographer—both are coauthors of *Modern American Manners*. They helped me to improve and advance my writing skills.

These individuals and many others have helped me get to where I am today.

Know from whence you came.
If you know whence you came,
there are absolutely no limits
to where you can go.
　　　　　　　—James Baldwin

INTRODUCTION

This is the story of an orphaned girl who—as a result of her mother's death—is left to assume the role of surrogate wife to her father and mother to her younger sister and brother at the age of ten years old. Most of her childhood she lived in poverty, but she dreamed of having a career that would take her out of her impoverished condition. However, during this era, it was not customary for women to obtain a college education or a career. She marries and gives birth to two children of her own and raises them while her husband is overseas for the military. Ten years after the birth of her first child, she is pregnant with a third child she does not want. She tells the child throughout his life that she did not want him. Against numerous odds, she works her way out of poverty, and with immense difficulty, she attempts to understand the son she did not want, who is also gay. She helps elevate him to his dreams but never accepts his sexual orientation. This story is fictitious but based on a true story.

PART ONE

Estelle's Youth and Young Life

CHAPTER ONE

King and Anna

Washington, DC, was a bustling city in the early 1900s. The seat of the nation's government was erected in all forms from the Capitol, the Washington Monument, the Jefferson Memorial, expansive Pennsylvania Avenue, and the beautifully landscaped circle parks with corresponding statues commemorating Rear Admiral Samuel Francis DuPont, Major John A. Logan, and George Henry Thomas. These statues and many others symbolized the lives of the national and city leaders. Residents of means and influence were invited and welcomed in the homes of governmental representatives, senators, cabinet members, and the White House. The idea of desegregating the public schools was one of the topics of the day.

White citizens enjoyed great prosperity, and the society section of the *Washington Post* announced debutante balls, heads-of-state dinners, and grand receptions. Washingtonians who resided in Murder Bay and alley dwellings were not associated with the high-end affairs of the bustling city. They were then called colored people who lived in an area bounded by M, N, Ninth, and Tenth Streets. The homes were primitive and often with no running water. This was where immigrants and coloreds resided and was considered forbidden to whites. Many of the residents were sons and daughters of freedmen who had migrated from the South after the Emancipation. The conditions were nevertheless horrendous. Outbreaks of tuberculosis and cholera occurred.

With the failures of Reconstruction and the discrimination colored Washingtonians faced every day, the educated colored class maintained their pride although regularly insulted and ridiculed to their faces and behind their backs. Education, controlling their temper, and working beyond the required minimum was the way to get ahead. The concerns or troubles of immigrants and the coloreds were of no concern to the leaders of the city.

Harrison Cory was born to a respectable colored family. His mother gave birth to him late in his life. She was so happy to have given birth to a healthy baby boy that she loved, adored, and spoiled him. He was of fair complexion and became a good student in school. As he developed, his mother noticed he was becoming selfish. She decided to adopt a child with the hopes that Harrison would learn to share and socialize well with others. His mother later adopted a little girl near Harrison's age. Harrison never liked the little girl and taunted her every opportunity that he could. He did everything he could to make his adopted sister feel unwelcome in their home.

In later years, when Harrison's father died, his mother married for a second time to a man named Turnipseed. Harrison rebuked him as he did his adoptive sister. Subsequently, when his mother died, she stipulated in her will that her home was to be left to her son, Harrison—but her husband had lifetime residence. His mother was thinking her second husband would be dead long before her son, and thus her son would own the house. She wanted to be considerate of her second husband and the marriage they shared. In her mind, it was a simple and considerate thing to do considering she loved both men; thus Harrison and his stepfather lived together in the house.

Although Harrison never accepted his mother's second husband, over time, he eventually hated his mother for placing a stipulation in her will giving him lifetime residence in the home. As it turned out, after his mother's death, Turnipseed lived much longer than Harrison or his mother expected. Insult was added to Harrison's injured feelings when he learned his stepfather remarried. He and his younger wife eventually had multiple children. Turnipseed and his new wife and children literally squeezed Harrison out of his own house. Harrison repeatedly tried to force Turnipseed out of the house, and when he refused, Harrison would shout to Turnipseed, "You are a nasty man, and you have a nasty slave name!" Harrison was furious because, legally, there was nothing he could do as his mother stated that her husband had lifetime residence in the house. He hated Turnipseed and his mother. "Got dam her!" he would say.

Harrison was not only feisty at home, he was feisty in the workplace as well. His white employers would call him "Tom," and Harrison would retort, "I am not your Tom, and I am not your Uncle Tom. My name is Harrison Cory, and that is spelled C-O-R-Y. And I expect to be addressed as such!" It was not long after a few of these outbursts that Harrison was fired by his white employers. With building temper and fury, Harrison started his own handyman business. The business thrived.

As a young man, Harrison was known to be a sweet talker to the ladies, and they called him King. He would take the trains from Washington, DC, to New York and Philadelphia to the red-light districts to cavort with the ladies of the night in an attempt to hide and deceive his family and friends to the kind of proclivities he enjoyed. He thought his activities would go unnoticed if he was not playing around in his orchard—thus he played around in other orchards. He thought that he was pulling the wool over the eyes of his family and friends.

Harrison did not decide to marry until he was forty years old. When his body was not performing as they once had in his youth, he decided to give up the nightlife with women of the night. At this age, he remained self-centered, arrogant, and righteous. Although he never smoked tobacco or drank alcohol, he attended church every Sunday. Unknown to him, he repelled many people because of his pompousness, and some were not ignorant to what he was doing when he traveled to places where he had no family or friends. Some members of the church and community thought he was a hypocrite.

Anna, the young woman Harrison selected to be his wife, was twenty years of age when Harrison, age forty, persuaded her into marriage. Anna was from a prominent colored family in South Carolina. She was a sweet, kind, innocent young woman. She was extremely beautiful, educated, and poised as any white woman who was introduced to high society. She was of very fair complexion but still considered colored. She was a devout church leader and aspired to be a Christian missionary. She had a twin sister. Anna was the weaker of the two babies and was always susceptible to illness. Their parents were partial to non-African names and gave each of their children European names, a snobbery that distinguished them from the field colored from the Deeper South.

When Anna accepted Harrison's hand in marriage, she had never lived in a city before and was totally naïve to the kind of life Harrison was living before she accepted his proposal. All she knew was that he went to church and did not smoke tobacco or drink alcohol. She found these characteristics acceptable in a man. She did not realize just how worldly he really was or what his insatiable desires were for women. His bachelorhood life was a secret to her. Harrison wanted to keep it this way. He was told by his gentlemen friends in the cities that if he wanted to marry and get an untouched woman, he needed to go to the South, where the girls were more moral. Harrison took their advice. With Anna's sweetness and innocence, he could control and manipulate her to his desires. She was not hardened and tough like the women of the red-light districts.

Shortly after Harrison married Anna, they moved to a very nice row house in northwest Washington, DC. This was considered very upscale for colored people to own a home on the west side of the district. Together, they had three children: Estelle, Anise, and Harrison Jr. Anna loved her children and deeply revered them. She used delicate hands and showered them with all the love and affection she would have offered others while conducting the missionary work she performed in the church. They all lived as comfortably as colored people lived during the era. Harrison's handyman business was thriving, and he was bringing home a more-than-adequate sum of money, and Anna could stay at home with the children and not work outside of the home. Harrison owned a car, and he allowed Anna to furnish the home to her taste and desires. They attended church services commonly, and Anna could continue the community missionary work she loved. Harrison gave up his trips to New York and Philadelphia and lived a Christian life with his family. The children attended public schools that were rated among the finest public schools in the country for colored children. They were segregated schools, but their neighborhood was not.

Estelle was the firstborn of Harrison and Estelle's three children. She was born to a very stable colored family. Estelle was bright and very sturdy for a girl. She was every bit as feisty as her father and learned how to brag about her station in life. As a young child, she knew she was living better than most of her peers. Harrison and Estelle distinguished themselves as a born-free colored with no slavery in their heritage. They both had been spoiled and had fair complexions to boot. To be fair-complexioned in the color heritage was a commodity. Being of fair complexion as a colored provided a few more privileges not available to their darker counterparts.

Anise, the second child, was like her mother—very domesticated, thin, and sickly. She was extremely well-read but unbelievably naïve. She too was also of fair complexion, tall, and reserved. Although naïve, she, in her head, had a mind of her own; but as a child, she was obedient and did as she was told.

Harrison Jr. was the third child. He was handsome, almost pretty. He had the darkest complexion among the three children and was considered the least bright. Harrison Sr. severely punished his son for not being as bright as the girls, for after all, he was going to be a man someday and needed to have the wit to take care of a family. Harrison Sr. did not like his son representing the male species in a lesser manner than the girls. He would say, "What kind of man are you going to be?" He also applied a little extra pressure and punishment to his son for having a darker complexion too.

After ten years of marriage to Harrison Sr., Anna became very ill and died. It was suspected that Harrison—through all his bachelorhood sexual escapades—transmitted a disease to Anna that she did not know she had. The death certificate never made such a mention. Anna was a highly Christian woman, and such a revelation after her death would have disgraced the family—the devoted daughter, wife, and mother. No evidence was ever brought forward.

Deathbed requests were strictly adhered to in families during this time. Anna's deathbed request to her husband Harrison was this: "If one of my three sisters do not accept all three of my children, I want you to care for them. I do not want my children separated."

As Harrison and the three children stood around Anna's deathbed, Estelle listened to what her mother was saying. As her mother was whispering her last words, Estelle simultaneously thought about the implications to her if her mother died. She knew her father to be lazy, both at work and at home, and he would relegate as much as he could to somebody—anybody but himself. He would pawn off any work to keep from doing it himself. She knew for sure that all the work of running the house would fall to her after her mother died. At ten years old, Estelle knew how to get things done; and as it turned out, that is what came to pass.

Even the gods in heaven knew that at the age of fifty, Harrison Sr. did not want to raise three children alone; but it would have been sacrilege not to honor his wife's request. In the eyes of his Christian peers, he would have been outed as a horrible husband and father. With all his arrogance and boastfulness, he relented within himself to follow his wife's desires since neither of Anna's sisters would accept all three children.

He did not wait a whole day after the burial of his wife to dump Anna's household work on Estelle. When the family returned home after the church services, he took off his coat and hat and looked at Estelle and, with the sweetest of smiles, said, "Daughter, what do you think we will have for dinner tonight?" Estelle knew her father was sweet-talking her, and she hated it. She was the oldest and the girl. Men didn't know how to cook, she was always told. Estelle's attitude was this: "If they get hungry, they will figure how to cook or they would just die!" She always thought her mother was too naïve and fell for everything Harrison said to her while he worked the frail woman to the bone. Estelle thought her mother should be stronger, stand up, and speak up to her husband. Anna would have replied that it was not permissible or proper for a lady to be insolent.

Estelle knew that regardless of what she thought this meant, she had to go to the kitchen and figure out what they were going to eat. She had learned in Sunday school that children were to honor their mother and father. As her Christian duty, she did as she was told; but within, she did not like it. She vowed that if she ever married, she was speaking up to her husband come hell or high water. She was not going to be played as a sucker as most men treated their women. She would complain to her sister Anise, "Yeah, they are all lovey-dovey when they are dating you. And after they get you, they work you halfway to death! No. I am not going to let some man treat me that way!"

As the days passed, she found ways of managing the household chores of cooking, washing, ironing, and taking care of Anise and Harrison Jr. She was not as well organized as her mother, but she got the job done. Anise was so frightened of every little thing and remained sickly; she was of little help to Estelle. Harrison Jr. was frightened too and grieved the death of his mother. He was too young to be of help to Estelle. Further, Harrison Sr. would have forbidden Estelle from giving Harrison Jr. what he thought to be women's work. In a short period, Estelle saw Anise and Harrison Jr. as her children. In the beginning, she liked being the grownup and telling her sister and brothers what to do; but eventually, the many household tasks were becoming overwhelming for a child so young. In addition, Harrison Sr. made them all go to school.

Harrison Sr. saw just how well his daughter was managing the household. He thought just like a white slave master and squeezed as much out of his daughter as he could get out of her young body. He called her downstairs one day and told her to go change the flat tire on the broken-down old truck. Classmates and neighbors could see Estelle from their windows struggling to change a tire. After watching her struggle for some period of time, a gentleman from the neighborhood would come out and help her. This was Harrison Sr.'s intent. He knew she could not change the tire, but he was shrewd enough to give her the chore, knowing somebody would come along and help her. He would look on from the living room window with a smile of victory. Harrison always felt victorious when he get one over on somebody. Just as long as he did not have to do it, he was fine. He operated his business the same way and paid meager wages to his employees.

At the end of each day, Estelle was dead tired. Harrison Sr. was insensitive to Estelle's fatigue. When the next morning arrived and it was time for more work, school, or church, Harrison Sr. would yell through the house for the children to get out of bed. Anise and Harrison Jr. would awaken and get dressed, but they would not leave the bedroom until Estelle awakened and told them what to do next. They too looked at Estelle as their mother and protector against this harsh old man.

Estelle was so tired she could barely move her body most mornings. After Harrison Sr. yelled out a second time and got no movement from the children, he would simply go to the bedroom they shared, and on the coldest winter mornings, he would open the windows wide to let the bitter cold air in the room. Then he would pull all the covers off Estelle's bed, close the door, and leave the room. He would say to Anise and Harrison Jr. as they stood dressed but now cold and frozen with fear. He would laugh and say, "I bet Estelle will get her little butt up now!" Harrison Sr. showed no sympathy to Estelle's fatigue or the children's feelings. He was a cold and angry man.

Anna, upon her death, never could have foreseen that the fate of her children would be left in the hands of a cold and insensitive man. She was beautifully laid to rest. Harrison—also known in his bachelorhood as "King"—was on the road to raising three children on his own. This was a role he could never have forecasted for himself. This was his new reality.

CHAPTER TWO

Motherless Children

The comfortable life that Estelle, Anise, and Harrison Jr. had known before Anna's death was gone. Harrison Sr. had put all of them to work before they were teenagers. Their childhood had been stripped away. Estelle had control of the household. She managed the money, grocery-shopped, cooked, and cleaned. Anise washed and dried all the dishes and washed and ironed all the clothes. She also made sewing and clothing alterations to their hand-me-down clothes. Harrison Jr. had to learn to push the manual lawn mower, shovel snow from the steps, and shovel coal for the coal stove during the winter months.

Estelle worked as hard as she could to restore family life just as her mother had done. As critical as she was toward her mother, she knew she was no comparison to her mother's patience with the children, her fine Southern cooking, or hand-finishing the laundry to perfection. She knew she was just like her father in strength and durability. She was opinionated, loud, and had poor nerves when there was too much commotion around her. Estelle's meals were not as tasty, the laundry not as clean and bright, and assistance with the children's homework was skipped when Harrison Sr. attended his nights out at the men's club.

He was a dutiful third-degree Mason. Anise was always whining that she never felt good. Harrison Jr., the youngest, cried, continuing to grieve the loss of his mother. He was too young to fully understand where she had gone. Harrison Sr. was in a poor disposition most of the time and was harsh with all the children, but especially Harrison Jr. because he expected the boy to step up and assume the heavy work he wanted to relegate to him as soon as possible.

If one of the children was out of line, all three of them got a whipping. Estelle thought that was asinine. She was stronger, so she took what was coming to her and moved right along. Anise was so frail, Harrison did not whip her has hard. But what Anise did not get, the balance was added to Harrison Jr. When Harrison Sr. planned to punish his children, he would send one of them to the backyard and tell them, "Go outside and get me a switch for your whipping, then come on back in here, take off your clothes, and call me when you are ready." Anise and Harrison Jr. started to cry before the switch was brought. They feared their father, but Estelle did not. She was smart enough to know that the little thin branches left welts, so she would pick a dry branch. They did not hurt as bad and would sometimes break. She was shrewd like her father.

Estelle was the child that was most often out of line because she spoke up about her displeasure about having most of the responsibility while Anise got little or nothing to do and Harrison Jr. was much too young to even know what was going on. Anise got the lightest of the whipping because she was frail and sickly like her mother. Harrison Sr. was fearful of harming her. Harrison Jr.—the youngest, most obedient, and least deserving—got the heaviest hand of all the children because he was a gentle spirit. He purely hated his father. Harrison Sr. could see through his son's attitude that his son disliked him, but he did nothing to make it right. Harrison Jr. was too young to defend himself from his father's torture.

Although Estelle felt sorry for Harrison Jr., she would say to him as he cried, "I can stop what I am doing and pamper you, or I can cook this food and give you something to eat. So do you think you can stop crying? Eating will keep you alive—crying about whatever you are crying about won't." Some days, Estelle, like her father, lacked compassion for Harrison Jr. She was of the opinion that she had enough to do and he was not the only victim. She and Anise got whippings too. And after they arrived at school in the mornings, the students ostracized them too. Most days, she did not have time to feel sorry for him and pamper him. Nobody was getting Anna's love now, and she did not have the time to perform all the household chores and love them too! On various occasions, Harrison Jr. would try to charm a hug or a kiss from his sister as he had his mother. Estelle would look at him and give a halfhearted hug and afterward say "Look, boy, you are asking for too much sugar for a cent!"

Neither of the two girls had clothes that fit like the clothes Anna had hand-sewn for them. Anna sewed her children's clothing to fit as if tailored. After Anna died, Anise would take old newspapers and cut a pattern to sew a dress as Anna had taught her. Estelle, on the other hand, would take the hand-me- down clothes given to them by compassionate

11

lady neighbors, affix a large safety pin in the waist, and go to school. She did not have the time to be prissy like her sister. Estelle thought Anise was much neater in her dress and was just as good a seamstress as their mother. While Estelle conversed with her sister while she sewed on their clothes, she would say, "Anise, child, all that work you put into those hand-me-down rags and we still look like homemade sin!" Most of the time, their hair was not properly combed. They did not have money for toothpaste, so their teeth were dingy and stained. Their shoes were worn to one side and needed a good polishing. The neighbors would look out their windows and say, "Look at those poor motherless children." Classmates would shout out in the school hallways, "Catch-it, catch-it, those children have chinches. Catch-it!" And they stamped their feet behind Estelle and Anise, laughing out loud as they made fun of the two girls.

The struggle being motherless children was daily. There school lunches were meager, so they were hungry. Their winter coats had holes that barely kept them warm. After they arrived at school, they still looked poorly dressed and unkempt. Through it all, Estelle kept the strength of the family for both Anise and Harrison Jr. It was very difficult. She taught them all she knew on how to survive the cruel aspects of the school environment. Harrison Sr. managed his handyman business as the children struggled side by side.

CHAPTER THREE

The Great Depression

As if things were not bad enough for Estelle and the Harrison Cory household, the Great Depression arrived with all its gloom and desolation. The once bustling Washington, DC, was also in for a shock for both the rich and the poor. For the wealthy families who had their money invested in high-risk equities, many were losing it all due to the collapses of the stock market. For those who had very little money, many of them were losing their jobs. There was a sharp increase in unemployment that drove up the rate of homelessness. The *New York Times* and the *Washington Post* posted stories of men shooting themselves in the head and pictures of millionaires who were jumping out of windows twenty stories high because they had lost everything. Photographs of the homeless standing in soup lines were being taken all over the country.

The Harrison Cory family was no exception. Harrison lost a great number of customers who had hired him to make handyman repairs on their spacious homes and embassies in the upper northwest quadrant of the city and had patronized him for years. Eventually, he lost the prestigious home he and Anna purchased in the northwest for nonpayment of the mortgage, forcing him to sell the house at a loss and losing all the equity he had paid. Harrison had to take the little money that he had and scramble to find more affordable housing for his children in the southeast quadrant of the city—an area of the city relegated to low-income colored people. This was such a blow to his arrogant nature and feelings of superiority.

Estelle knew she was doing her part in running the house, and it was up to her father to figure out how the money was going to be generated.

She was not worried, and her modeling this behavior stilled and calmed Anise and Harrison Jr. Whatever she said or did, Anise and Harrison Jr. followed like puppy dogs behind Estelle. She had become their mother. She had noticed, however, that Harrison Sr. was bringing home less and less money for her to pay the milkman, the bread man, and the insurance man who came to the front door to collect payments and premiums on a weekly basis. Estelle had the common sense to just tell these men that her father was not home and she did not have the money. Although she was strong and bold, the collectors did not taunt or harass her because they knew that she was just a child and a girl too. Women were not expected to earn the money for the household—but the milk and bread deliveries stopped, and the insurance lapsed.

Some nights, Estelle and the children would go to bed hungry. Harrison Jr. would sometimes cry with hunger pangs. Estelle would say to him, "Hush crying. Go drink a glass of water and go to bed! In the morning, I will have something for you to eat!" Estelle was lying to calm her brother. She also lied because she could not tolerate his crying. She had no idea where she was going to get any food. It was late, and the stores were closed. Harrison Sr. had not returned home from work with any money, so she really did not know what she was going to do.

Early the next morning, Harrison Sr. finally arrived home. He awakened Estelle and had her run to the corner store to get four eggs and four potatoes. Estelle was hungry, so she hurried to get out of the bed and dressed to get to the store just as soon as it opened. When she returned home, she swiftly got to the kitchen and prepared the potatoes and eggs. Estelle had begged the man to throw in a few slices of bacon. The grocer knew the Cory family was struggling. He gave her several slices of bacon and made her swear to keep her mouth shut because he could not feed the whole neighborhood. When Harrison Jr. awakened, Estelle had prepared the best breakfast they had in several months. In Harrison Jr.'s mind, Estelle told him the truth the night before.

The next day, Harrison Sr. would return home at the end of the day or late in the evening with just some change, telling Estelle to go the local food market to get something to eat. Estelle would look at the inadequate money, knowing that she would not be able to get a meat, starch, and vegetable to make a full meal. She learned to haggle with the market merchants, and they would sell her day-old bread and a bushel of greens with the money she had. When she returned, she served the bread and greens. Everyone missed the meat, but nothing was said. Each day, they ate whatever the merchants had left over and could not sell. They would take Estelle's pit tens, and Estelle took the day-old food. The family would eat that same food for three meals—greens for breakfast, greens for lunch, and greens for dinner.

This continued until the economy recovered and Harrison could get increased day labor. It was a struggle, but they survived. Harrison was very proud of Estelle and would say after a meal, "Daughter, you did a good job today keeping body and soul together!"

Anise and Harrison Jr. were never recognized. Anise was mute. Waves of profound resentment flowed through Harrison Jr.'s bones, but he learned to keep his mouth shut. His father's punishments for insubordination were severe. The punishment for his slow learning was harsh enough; and in addition, he did not want Estelle and Anise to get whipped too. Thus he learned with agony to keep his mouth closed.

Estelle did not really think anything of her father's compliments or much of anything he had to say; she just did her job and kept her mouth shut too. Under her breath, she called her father "Grandpa" because she saw him as too old to be anybody's father. He was close to sixty years old. His head was bald, and he moved slowly from aches and pains he had not earned from working hard. Estelle did not like having an old father. In addition, she thought of him as mean and lazy, but she respected that he at least honored her mother's request and allowed them to go to school. Some families prohibited their children from attending school so that they could help out around the house.

Estelle, on the other hand, would have preferred to have the three children separated. She thought they each would have had a better life. Their aunts were far better off economically and educationally. Anna's side of the family was from a better crop of colored people. They each could get new clothes, and Harrison Jr. could get a haircut. She and Anise could get a hot comb every once in a while.

However, not one of the three aunts was willing to take all three of Anna's children. They said they would take one each, but this was not what Anna wanted. Since neither of the sisters would take all three children, Harrison got provoked and restricted the aunts from visitations or giving their nieces and nephew anything. Nothing! He wanted to make them look like the villains for making him (a man) take care of his three children. Neither Estelle, Anise, nor Harrison Jr. was able to visit or accept anything from Anna's sisters. Any assistance from the three sisters was truncated.

When Estelle thought about her father's attitude toward this situation behind his back, she would say to Anise and Harrison Jr., "He is acting just like an old fool. Now you know that does not make a bit of sense to stop your children from visiting their family." On many occasions, Estelle thought she had more common sense than her father.

When the economy improved and Harrison was gaining new customers, he recognized that the tiny house that they lived in was getting too small and the girls needed space for their bodily changes. Further, he thought Harrison Jr. too handsome for a boy and that he was becoming too timid and prissy sharing a room with the girls.

Although Harrison had given up the nightlife, he continued to date and charm the ladies after Anna's death. The lady friends Harrison brought home tried to educate the girls on feminine care, but there was only so much they could do considering Harrison refused to marry any of the ladies, and they were not there full time. Sometimes he was dating two or three ladies at a time. But regardless of whatever excuse he had made to the ladies for not marrying them, the real reason was because in Anna's final days, she informed her husband that there would not be a stepmother for her children—which implied Harrison could not marry again, or at least until the children were grown and on their own. Stepmothers had the reputation of being mean to children from a previous marriage. She did not want her children to experience such horrors.

Harrison Sr. did not want to marry again anyway. He had learned after his marriage to Anna that he liked bachelorhood better. He used Anna's request and other excuses to placate his lady friends, just to put them off in a gentlemanly way and maintain their company.

The Great Depression came to an end. The Cory family resumed— one widower and three motherless children.

CHAPTER FOUR

Mrs. Astor

A few years later, Harrison returned home as happy as Estelle had ever seen him. He had received word that a white businessman, for whom he had provided handyman repairs, needed a staff of in-resident house and groundskeepers. He had heard that Harrison Sr.'s wife had died and he was struggling to raise his three children, so he offered the job to Harrison. The businessman lived in upper northwest Washington, DC, near the National Cathedral. Harrison jumped at the opportunity to move to the best location in the city and in the nicest home he and his family had ever lived in. He had worked for rich white folk for years, but he knew, as a colored person, he would never live in such a neighborhood. For him, it meant no longer having to scuffle to pay rent or a mortgage, utilities, and other bills associated with operating a house. He was in his middle fifties, and the children would be leaving home in a few more years. This would be an opportunity to catch up on bills that he had no ability to pay during the Great Depression.

Although Estelle was a teenager, she knew how to rule the operations of a household. The tragedy of being forced into domestic work at such a young age, she could now use these same skills to earn money. When he informed Estelle of this opportunity, she, more than Harrison, jumped at the chance to live in the plush and stately furnished environs of upper northwest Washington, DC. This was the exposure and expansion she had hungered for. Estelle wanted to once again live as a privileged colored child, as they did before her mother died. Estelle admired even more the rich dark mahogany furnishings, fancy draperies adored with swags and jabots, and the vibrant colored oriental rugs.

Anise was more uppity and would have preferred remaining poor than have the title of a servant or housekeeper in a white family's home. Harrison Jr., a minor, simply followed Estelle's lead. She was his protector. He held on to Estelle for direction, guidance, safety, and his life.

Harrison was hired as household driver and butler, Estelle was the first-floor maid, Anise was the second-floor maid and managed the children, and Harrison Jr. shoveled coal and managed the grounds. Harrison Sr. supervised all his children and made sure they were paid a fair hourly price, although he made them give him their earnings. Estelle was outraged. She thought having her money taken was unfair. She was looking forward to buying a few dresses for school and getting her thick head of hair coifed, but Harrison Sr. took that thought out of her head. He told her she was here to work, not to look pretty.

Mrs. Astor was aware the children were motherless and saw to it that the girls were suitably dressed and performed necessary feminine hygiene to perform their duties in her home. She also made allowance for the girls to go to the colored beauty salon as well. Estelle was grateful for the mistress's compassion and worked extra hard to yet gain more benefits. She thought if she only had her own money, she would not have to depend on her father for every little feminine necessity. Harrison Sr. told her when she complained that women did not need money. Once they get money, they want to start telling a man what to do, and he would not tolerate a woman telling him what to do. He said, "When you get paid each week, I want you to give me your earnings. I will decide how it will be spent."

As Estelle washed the crystal and polished the silver to a glimmering shine, she thought someday she would like to have items like these in her home. From early mornings before attending public school and upon her return after school, the entire family worked for the businessman, his wife, and their two daughters. There was always something to be done. And though the businessman and his family went to the same denomination of church the Cory family did, the Astors attended the white church and the Corys attended the colored church.

For two weeks in the summer, the Astor family would vacation in Bethany Beach. Harrison was the driver, and Estelle was the maid. Anise and Harrison Jr. stayed behind to continue working and oversee the Astor home. Estelle hated the beach and the hot sand on her feet while watching the children. She thought Anise and Harrison Jr. got the longer end of the stick. She would rather have had the escape from her father and the labors of children. When the work was relegated to the family, Estelle chose to be first-floor maid simply because she did not want to be bothered with any more children. Her sister and brother were enough for her. In addition, she was the more social of the two girls, and she looked forward to and was impressed with the type of guest that traversed the threshold of the Astor home. Being on Bethany Beach was no vacation for her.

Estelle developed the greatest admiration for Mrs. Astor. She simply loved how Mrs. Astor dressed with nicely tailored ladies' suits in conservative colors with matching shoes and handbags. Estelle thought the coordinated underblouses were tasteful, and her jewelry was of high quality, small and refined. Every Sunday, she wore seasonal hats for the spring, summer, fall, and winter. Estelle aspired to this type of wardrobe as she aspired for similar home furnishings.

Estelle admired how she talked to her daughters with such love and affection and spent so much time with them in selecting their clothing. The girls were always so pleased with the generosity of their mother, and Estelle thought that if she ever had a daughter, she would like to have such a relationship.

More than anything, Estelle adored the fact that Mrs. Astor, a woman, always had plenty of money in her handbag; and with discretion, she doled out money to her daughters liberally. Estelle liked the idea of having her own money. Although Mrs. Astor did not work outside of the home, Estelle knew that when she married, she would need to work outside of the home. This working outside of the house did not bother her. She just wanted her own money. She hated the thought of being controlled and dependent on a man. He father had controlled her all her life, and she was not going to put up with this from any man if she ever married. She was taught by her church that money was the root of all evil. In Estelle's mind, she thought money was better than poverty.

After a few years of living better than she had ever lived since her mother died, Estelle was approaching dating age. Estelle had helped the Astor daughters in preparing for their coming-out parties and teenage events, but Harrison forbade Estelle and Anise from dating. He enforced strict rules on all his children. Estelle thought her father was unreasonable and just wanted to keep his children working for his benefit. He was thinking only of himself, she thought. Mrs. Astor softened Harrison Sr. in this regard.

Chapter Five

Estelle's First Date

Between Harrison's lady friends and Mrs. Astor, they coerced him to let Estelle have her first date. She was eighteen years old. Harrison finally relented and let Estelle have a date with a young man who was the only young man in her school that showed interest in her. He was extremely handsome and well groomed. Harrison told both his daughters that you can judge the character of a man by the collar of his shirt and the condition of his shoes. This meant a starched white shirt collar around the neck and shoes that were polished with new to slightly worn heels. With all of Harrison Sr.'s faults and shortcomings, he was a clean man and dressed extremely well. He expected no less from any man who dated his daughter.

The young date aspired to go to college and become a doctor, and his name was Christopher. Harrison looked the young man over to approve of his appearance. Then he looked at the young man with sharp examining eyes. He proceeded to interrogate him and directly told him there was to be no hanky-panky of any kind with his daughter. He said, "My daughter is a good girl. I have worked her hard and kept her busy, so she has not had any time for foolishness. Do you understand?"

The young man took the interrogation well and replied, "Yes!"

Harrison said, "What? What did you say to me?

The young man said, "Yes!"

"Well, it is 'yes, sir!' You don't just say yes to me. You address me as 'yes, sir!'"

The young man then said, "Yes, sir!"

"Now the way I am giving my daughter to you is the way I want you to give her back to me!"

"Yes, sir!" the young man replied.

Estelle was so embarrassed because she knew that her father's real motive was to bring her back home so he could squeeze more work from her. Estelle thought he just wanted to force her to work more hours so he could take her money. He was not pulling the wool over her eyes. She really was growing sick and tired of her antiquated father.

After Harrison looked the young man up and down and sized him up one more time, Harrison agreed to let Estelle go on her first date. The only hitch to his agreeing was that Anise had to join them as a sort of chaperone. Estelle actually did not mind for this first date because she could stay out on the date a little longer with Anise. Harrison Sr. was always more lenient on Anise. In addition, Anise did almost everything Estelle told her to do. As Estelle's date opened the door for her, she got in the front seat and sat on the passenger side. Anise was seated in the back seat.

Not long after the car turned the corner from the Astor house, Estelle moved toward the center of the front seat to sit closer to her date. Her date took them to a movie. After the movie, he asked if they had time to go to a popular soda fountain and dance hall. Estelle replied yes, and Anise replied no. Estelle said, "Come on, Anise! You know this is the first time we have ever been alone with a boy. Let's have some fun."

Anise said, "Estelle, you know that Father is not going to like us staying out this late. You know we are going to get in trouble."

Estelle directed her date to take them to the dance hall, and they danced together for a few more hours before Estelle came to her senses and decided that she and Anise had better get home. She and her date talked a lot and enjoyed each other's company.

When the three of them arrived home, Anise was shaking with fear for she knew that she and Estelle had stayed out too long and they would be punished. After the young man walked them to the front door, he stole a kiss from Estelle. He said he wanted to see her again.

After the young man drove away, Anise chided Estelle, "Why do you always disobey Father? You know he is going to be angry with us for staying out this late at night."

Estelle replied, "Shush before you awaken him."

When the two girls placed the key in the door, Estelle whispered to Anise, "I wonder if Father is home. He may not be home yet. He may be with one of his women friends."

A loud voice from the front room roared, "Yes! Yes, I am home!" Anise was in total fear of a whipping. Harrison simply said, "Estelle, I knew you were not going to follow my instructions to return home on time. That is specifically why I sent Anise with you! Until you learn to do as I tell you, there will not be a next time!"

The date went very well for Estelle and her beau. She was considered a poor girl by her middle-class classmates. However, she possessed a smooth, fair complexion and a thick head of flowing shiny black hair. She had very nice facial features but not much bust or hips. Her buoyant personality compensated for anything she may have been missing because at a very young age, she had common sense well above her years. She readily spoke up if something did not make good sense to her. She was funny too. She did not care what the other children said about her because, in her mind, she knew she was going to make something of herself someday. She did not know how, but she was going to make it. She would say to Anise and Harrison Jr., "I know how to take care of myself. You had better learn how to do the same thing, because nobody is going to take care of you in this world we live in. When your mother [Estelle] is gone, everybody is gone!"

Christopher was totally enamored with Estelle and wanted to marry her after they had dated for six months. However, when his mother learned of their talk of marriage, she convened the two and said they were too young to discuss marriage. She said after her son had completed college, they could discuss marriage; until then, there would be no marriage. She also said that if Christopher did not obey her request, she would not pay his college tuition and medical school expenses.

Estelle was crestfallen when Christopher succumbed to his mother's request. She had decided she did not want to marry a man who was so easily swayed by his mother. She was used to being in control of her father's household since ten years old, and she did not want to be married to a man who could not stand up to his mother. After all, if she was the proposed wife, she did not want to be associated with an interfering and meddling mother-in-law, and she told Christopher just that.

Although Christopher made promises of his devotion to Estelle and that he would marry her just as soon as he finished college, Estelle was unmoved by his words. She decided she was finished with him. She informed Christopher that she had lived under the domination of her father all her life and she no longer wanted to be in a situation where the two of them were dominated and controlled by his mother. This experience strengthened her resolve to get a job and take care of herself. She wanted to steer free and clear of controlling husbands and mothers-in-law. With this outburst, from the first date to the last date, she ended their dating. Estelle released herself from the situation.

CHAPTER SIX

Anise and Estelle Promenade

During the following summer, Anise was eighteen and decided she had had enough of being a servant for a white woman and her daughters. She decided to run away to Baltimore to live with her father's half-sister Clara. Harrison Sr. did not like Clara. He considered her a "fast woman," never considering he was a fast man too. He had also heard that she had married several times and had henpecked each of her husbands until they mysteriously died.

Harrison Sr. thought she was lazy woman and a filthy housekeeper. He also thought a lazy, nasty woman was far worse than a lazy, nasty man. He resented his daughter for not giving him notice of her departure and, moreover, for the loss of income she produced for the household. Harrison refused to speak to his half-sister or his daughter for years after she made this move. He never forgave Clara for accepting his daughter into her home without consulting with him. He was furious with both of them. Harrison felt they should have negotiated such exchanges through him, just as men have gentlemen's agreements. He did not like crafty women, especially if they got one over on him. If Anise had been in his sight, he would have whipped her. "And whipped her good!" he said.

Estelle continued to work for Mr. and Mrs. Astor. Their daughters had married respectable men and moved out of the house. Harrison continued on as driver, and Estelle assumed all her sister's chores, which were few. Harrison made sure Estelle got an increase in remuneration for the additional work she assumed with Anise's departure.

Harrison Jr. continued his before- and after-school duties. Harrison Sr. continued to discriminate against Harrison Jr. because he showed no interest in women, and he continued to dislike his son's darker complexion. For some reason, Harrison Sr. could not move past the color barrier for his child, who was also too handsome to his liking. At this point, he just did not like his son.

Estelle continued to receive two weeks of vacation time each summer from the Astors. Anise, who was still living with her Aunt Clara, wrote to Estelle and told her to come to Baltimore for her vacation. She wrote: "There are so many men over here ready to date. It is time that you get away from Father. He is mean and lazy; he has taken advantage of us long enough. It is time for you to get out of there."

After Estelle had dated Christopher, no one else showed interest in her. Although she now had all the wardrobe and finishing necessary to attract young men, she was viewed as a servant girl and was thus not viewed as the cream of the crop among her former classmates. Harrison Sr. would not allow her to go to college. He thought it was ridiculous for women to work when they were never going to make enough money to pay for the cost of the tuition. The young ladies and men looked down on Estelle as not good enough.

She decided to visit her sister in Baltimore for her two-week vacation, and sure enough, Estelle was more popular than she had ever been in her entire life. She had more offers to dates than she could imagine. The young men of Baltimore had no idea of the poverty Estelle and Anise experienced in Washington, DC. Estelle was on cloud nine with all the flirtations and attention. She thought this could be a new beginning for her in a new city.

The young Baltimore men were impressed with Estelle being a Washingtonian. Washington was the nation's capital and considered a tad more elite than industrial Baltimore. The young men were impressed with Estelle's attractiveness and intelligence—moreover, she was a virgin.

Mrs. Astor had taught both Estelle and Anise social graces and refinement just as she taught her daughters. These teachings showed up in both of their deportment. By the two girls having lived in the home of the white family, their vocabulary and speech patterns were distinctively different. This gave them an air of being highly elevated and more educated than they were. Estelle played up to the high-end lifestyle she had been exposed to in the Astor home. She relished every minute of the attention she was receiving. It was a new freedom for Estelle. She loved being noticed. She was above par in her self-confidence and style. Her smooth and fair complexion, thick dark shiny hair, and sense of humor were crowning glories that compensated for her not being able to attend college as she had desired. She felt desirable by the young men in Baltimore.

Within the two weeks, three young men were asking Estelle out for dates. Aunt Clara put a stop to it. She told Estelle that she had to choose one of the young men because she did not want the neighbors to think she was running a whorehouse. Estelle did as she was told and selected one man but enjoyed being acceptable to so many young men. It felt good and was excellent for her self-esteem. Estelle was gloating in her mind as she recalled the middle-class boys from her hometown laughing at her, throwing spitballs, and accusing her of having chinches. "Catch it, catch it!" they would shout.

Estelle thought, *Look at me now!*

Anise and Estelle both walked away from their father to make a life on their own terms.

CHAPTER SEVEN

Estelle's Gentleman

Estelle decided to stay in Baltimore. It took her a while to adjust. She adored all the attention from the young men, but she had to quickly find a job to pay her Aunt Clara rent. She hated living in Aunt Clara's house because it was unsanitary. If Estelle knew nothing else, she knew a clean house when she saw one. Her Aunt Clara's house had been neglected for years, and it was going to take some time to get it livable. Aunt Clara's house was by all means rock-bottom compared to the beautiful home she had lived in with her father and brother and the Astors.

She also had to get used to the smells of Baltimore. When she went downtown to apply for jobs, she could smell the spices from the spice factory; and then there was the smell of the harbor, which was the site of many small cargo and fishing vessels. These boats brought in the catch from Chesapeake Bay. She did not like the looks of the sugar factory that appeared to float on the harbor waters. She did not understand why the row houses looked so unfinished compared to the ornate and elaborate finishing on Washington, DC, row houses. She was used to the white marble monuments and the manicured parks and circles with orderly streetcars traversing the wide Pennsylvania Avenue. It was all so different, but she reconciled that she needed to start her life at this point. She could not live with the Astors forever, although they were more than satisfied with her work and did not want her to leave their service. She was a hard and diligent worker.

The man Estelle selected was a tall, handsome, well-groomed brown man who was quiet and reserved. He was educated in Christian schools. Estelle saw his education as equivalent to private school versus public schools she attended. Estelle did take pride in her education. Her public schools were considered very fine schools for colored people. Although she earned average grades in school, she knew she could have done a lot better had she had the opportunity to study after school and study at the library and to participate in extracurricular activities. Working for the Astors before and after school prevented her from advanced learning. Her father was of no help in that he believed women did not need an education. Nevertheless, Estelle thought Washington, DC, had a style of its own. The young man she chose was named Albrecht Rose. Albrecht was very kind, extremely intelligent, well-read, and studious. He approached Estelle in a gentlemanly manner and treated her with respect. He was somewhat shy and insecure in his ability to please such an educated and polished girl from Washington, DC, as Estelle.

When Estelle's two-week vacation was drawing to a close, she extended her visit for another two weeks then decided to quit her job in DC and stay on in Baltimore so that she could date Albrecht. Harrison Sr. was totally brokenhearted and saddened when Estelle informed him she was not returning to Washington. In his heart, she was his favorite child. She had cared for him as good as a wife and took excellent care of her sister and brother just as if she had given birth to them. Harrison knew he could count on her in the long run to take care of him in his old age. He wanted Estelle to stay with him forever. He was far more attached to his daughter than he had ever imaged. He had never felt the intenseness of affection for his other two children. He learned Estelle was his heart.

Estelle knew her father would take her not returning to Washington hard. She felt she had done the hardest work for the longest period of time of the three children. She knew she was a surrogate wife to her father. She raised his children. She attended school and worked as a child laborer. She had discharged more than her share of his responsibility, and she was ready to start a life of her own. Her father had taken all her money for as long as she could remember. At this point, she felt less of her father and more for herself. She had to break away.

Further, Estelle knew she was her father's favorite child. Through the years of her childhood, he never said a kind word or rewarded her to validate all she had done for him. It was all work and no time for play, niceties, affection, or love.

When the church ladies would commend Harrison Cory Sr. on what a fine job he was doing raising three children with no wife, he would say to the ladies, "Well, my children are all good Christians. They don't smoke, drink, or speak in foul tongue. I don't tolerate that from any of them. Yes! Thank God 'I' have done a good job! I never had to carry a cookie to a one of them in jail!"

Harrison always took 100 percent credit for how well he was managing and never gave his children one iota of the credit. Estelle saw herself as the adult in the family. In her mind, her father was her child too.

Albrecht Rose was the man she wanted to date. She made a decision. She moved forward.

Chapter Eight

Harrison Sr. and Harrison Jr.

Anise was the first of Harrison's children to leave home. Unfortunately, Estelle's departure left Harrison Sr. and Harrison Jr. together to fend for themselves. They would be on their own to figure out how they were going to manage their meals, laundry, and cleaning of their living quarters. Up until this time, Estelle and Anise had performed all the household functions. This new arrangement was a father-and-son pairing of mutual hatred brought face-to-face into the light.

Harrison Jr. never liked his father from his earliest childhood days. He blamed his father for his mother's death. He loved his mother and every memory he held of her. He had completely bonded with her before her death. He recalled all the memories of the cruelty expressed to his mother by his father. His mother was fragile and weak, and this youngest boy-child disliked his father for taking advantage of her.

Harrison Sr. would leave her alone at night in the house with the three children, knowing she was frightened and scared to be in the city by herself. She had grown up in the rural South and was not accustomed to city living. Anna would beg Harrison Sr. "Please stay at home with me!" she pleaded. In an exasperated tone, he would simply say, "I will get you a German shepherd next week to stay with you so you won't be afraid."

Anna would cry and sob, begging and pleading, "But, Harrison, I don't want to be alone in the house with the children." Harrison would reply, "You will be all right, Anna. I am just going to the temple for my meeting!" Harrison would just walk out the door, leaving Anna crying and alone. Harrison Jr. would try and comfort his mother until she settled down. He hated his father for neglecting his mother. He saw his father as cold and cruel. His dislike for his father had turned into hatred with each passing year.

He recalled in his mind over and over how Harrison Sr. would punish him by forcing him to stand in the living room bay window wearing one of Anise's dresses. This was punishment for not having outstanding grades in school or simply out of pure meanness. This was to embarrass and humiliate him in front of all the neighborhood children. Both the boys and girls that played in the streets in the front of their house laughed at Harrison Jr. They all watched Harrison Jr.'s punishment in the late afternoon and evenings. The next day in school, they told all the children who were not present of the spectacle. They laughed at Harrison and called him a girl. He was persecuted throughout the school day. The boys called him a sissy and a mother's boy.

Harrison Sr. did this deliberately because he wanted his son to show more manly qualities. He was embarrassed to have a mother's boy as his son. Harrison Sr. never considered that his son had grief issues surrounding the death of his mother. Nor did he consider that Harrison Jr. had little to no help with his studies and homework assignments. All Harrison Jr. could think of was how deeply he hated his father for such punitive and damaging punishments. He thought his father's punishments were insensitive and unreasonable.

He hated that his father would whip his girl children. Harrison Jr. was simply too young and too defenseless to stop it. Now that Estelle and Anise had moved to Baltimore, Harrison Jr. was stuck to pick up the pieces for a man he hated.

Being subjected to a man like Harrison Sr. was stressful for his mother, sisters, and him. Harrison Jr. needed to blame someone for his mother's death, and his father was the most logical person to blame in his mind. He had grieved his mother's passing year after year. He believed she would have protected him from his father's evil hands. He never made peace with her death or his father's brutality toward her, the children, and especially toward him.

Shortly after Estelle announced that she was not returning to Washington, DC, Harrison Sr. had a heart attack and could not work. This left Harrison Jr. with the weight of the household. Although Harrison Jr. had numerous reasons to hate his father and deep sadness that his sisters had left him one by one, he admitted to himself that Estelle had done more than her part in holding the family together. He did not blame Anise for escaping her father. She was like their mother, who was frail and sickly. She could no longer endure her father. Harrison Jr. had no choice but to drop out of high school and volunteer for the military to have an income to take care of his father. This would get him away from his father and a man he despised. With this choice, he could send an allotment to his father to ease any guilt he may have felt.

Harrison Sr.—in his old age, temperament, and poor health—was still getting someone to take care of him. He never seemed to be responsible for taking care of himself or to allow his children to grow into their own persons. He always had his wife or his children to take partial care and responsibility of him. Estelle and Harrison Jr. looked out for their father in spite of his cruelty toward them. Anise did nothing and felt nothing for her father. She was unconscious toward her father. They rarely spoke to each other after she left home. Her attitude toward her father was if he wanted to be obstinate, she would be obstinate toward him. In her mind, turnabout was fair play.

These were the beginnings of very difficult times for the two men.

PART TWO

Estelle as Wife and Mother

Chapter Nine

First Baby, Second Baby

Albrecht and Estelle continued dating in Baltimore for one year; then she discovered she was three months pregnant. Neither was happy about this news. Fireworks went off in their heads. Albrecht wanted to go to college, and Estelle needed three credits to complete the requirements for her high school diploma. When she did not return to Washington after her summer vacation, she missed summer school class, whereby she would have been an official high school graduate. Estelle knew Harrison Sr. would blow his top and be completely disappointed in his daughter for getting pregnant after all his harsh teachings on abstinence and virtue. What would Mrs. Astor think after spending so much time teaching and grooming the young girl throughout her teenage years? Most importantly, what would her mother think if she were still alive? Estelle was embarrassed for herself. After the reality set in, she decided this was her responsibility as much as Albrecht's, and she was going to face whatever the consequences were with her child.

Albrecht knew his devout Christian mother would be distraught to find he was not celibate and not following the orders of the church. He did not care what anyone thought as Estelle had. He had been taught to accept responsibility for his actions. He too had been just as naïve as Estelle, and he loved her. His mother would have told him in a stoic tone, "Well, you have made your bed now, so I guess you are going to have to sleep in it."

To avoid harsh criticism from both sides of their families, Albrecht and Estelle—quickly and without pomp and circumstance—married. They became Mr. and Mrs. Albrecht Rose. After the courthouse marriage, they spent one night in a downtown Baltimore hotel for their honeymoon. They shared a bag of seedless white grapes in wonderment of what they had done. Albrecht stared out the window as he thought of how he was going to be a man and make his change in life situation work to his advantage. For a few moments, it all seemed so daunting to him; but after some deliberation, he resolved he was going to have to dig in and be a husband and father. He was very intelligent and found happiness in the thought of becoming a father.

He had graduated high school two years earlier. He had only dated Estelle for one year. At moments, he floated back and forth between his single years that he was going to miss and the family life he created. In many ways, he thought it was a sad time, starting a marriage with a woman he hardly knew. Together, all they had in common were church teachings and moral training. Love and romance was suddenly superseded by responsibility for Albrecht and Estelle. His twenty years suddenly became the onset of his manhood. For Estelle, the girlhood she never had suddenly became womanhood and motherhood. She really did not want to get pregnant before getting married; nor did she want to have a child before she had gotten a good job whereby she could have money of her own. More importantly to Estelle was that she was tired from raising her mother's children, so she really did not want a child this soon.

Albrecht got a job as a bartender at a grand hotel, and Estelle got a job at a local bakery. They lived with Albrecht's parents. Theopolis and Bessie Rose lived in an apartment building in the city, where colored families lived. Bessie was a devout practicing Catholic. She had ten pregnancies and eight live births. Catholics did not believe in birth control, and Bessie saw herself as pious, devout, and following all laws of the church. The living quarters were not as spacious or elegant as the house where Estelle had once lived.

Although the living quarters were close for both Albrecht and Estelle, they both knew how to cope with unpleasant situations and discomfort. They both had poverty in their backgrounds. After having ten children of her own, Bessie was not thrilled to have her son and new daughter-in-law and a new baby living in her home; but there was no other place for them to live but in the streets, so she reluctantly opened her door to them.

Several months after completing her high school diploma at night school, Estelle received a letter from federal personnel. She had applied for several federal jobs and had been turned down. But on this day, she was being offered an interview for the position of clerk-typist, one of the entry-level positions for colored women who had not completed college.

Estelle was elated and accepted the interview. She took a train back to Washington, DC, where the position was being offered. A few weeks after the interview, she received another letter offering her the position. Estelle thought this was her big chance to secure a federal job in an office setting and leaving behind the memories of domestic work and having her father siphon off her money for the upkeep of the family. She could not wait to accept the position.

When she returned to her hometown for the interview, she remembered how beautiful Washington was in springtime. She missed seeing the tulips, the azaleas, and the cherry blossoms that flanked the government buildings and the homes of the affluent. The streets were wider and lined with trees, giving a look of promenades on the Champs-Élysées. She recalled playing on the steps of the Capitol as a child, the clean white marble, and the pristine white office buildings.

She thought maybe Albrecht would be willing to move to Washington. With his Christian school education, he could find a job easily. The big issue was who was going to take care of their baby. When she approached her mother-in-law to see if she would care for her expected child, Bessie said, "No!" She said, "I have given birth to ten children and raised them, and I am tired of raising my children. You and my son have made this child, and you are going to take care of yours as I have taken care of mine. Furthermore, I don't see why you want to work when Albrecht does not want you working anyway. You are pregnant!"

Estelle thought, *Well, she has made herself very clear. She is not taking care of my child.*

Bessie wanted Estelle to be content, as women were supposed to be. If a man did not want you to work, you should be grateful and do as he says. Bessie did not see the necessity of Estelle bringing her hoity-toity Washington, DC, ideas to Baltimore. No, she was not keeping any babies.

Estelle wanted Bessie, as a woman, to be happy for her and accept that now that the war was over, women were being allowed to work. Estelle cried when she informed the federal office of personnel she could not accept the position. Estelle was destroyed that she had to lose the opportunity of her dreams—a job in federal service.

Albrecht worked evening shifts as a bartender and took classes at business school during the daytime hours. He excelled in all he did, and Estelle got promoted to manager at the bakery but continued to grieve the loss of her federal job offer. In her mind, this was an opportunity that only came once.

When Estelle's father, Harrison Cory, caught wind that his daughter was married, he hopped a train from Washington, DC, to Baltimore to see what was going on with his favorite child and meet the man she had married. After she decided to leave Washington, DC, he had come to accept that she was grown and had to get her life started. But he did not see what the big hurry was to get married and certainly not to invite him to the ceremony.

Upon his arrival at Theopolis and Bessie's home, he was jovial and charming to his new in-laws; and in turn, they were cordial and hospitable. They invited Harrison into the kitchen for something to eat and a libation. Albrecht and Estelle had not returned home from their jobs, and thus the new in-laws sat around the kitchen table and chatted. Neither Theopolis nor Bessie said a word about Estelle being with child. A short time later, Albrecht and Estelle arrived. Albrecht always met Estelle at the bakery after his shift as bartender, and they walked home together.

Harrison greeted his daughter and new son-in-law. Harrison, during his bachelorhood, had been a man of the world. In his youth, he had consorted with women up and down the northeastern seaboard, so he felt he knew women. Harrison looked his daughter up and down in the kitchen, just as he did when she was living with him and dating Christopher. He looked her over this day thoroughly, examining her waistline. Today was no different. He squinted his eyes and uncouthly blurted out in front of everyone, "Daughter, are you with child?"

Estelle was totally horrified that her father would embarrass her in front of her new family. She had spent months trying to impress Albrecht's family of her worthiness, but she knew with her father you got it, where you did it in the parade. Estelle quietly and respectfully replied while simultaneously trying to temper and control the outrage that she felt. She was accustomed to her father's no-nonsense communications, charging headfirst into an immediate answer. Estelle said, "Yes, Papa, I am with child."

Albrecht broke out in a sweat when Harrison continued, "Well, this is mighty quick. When did you and this young man elope?" When Estelle replied, Harrison said, "Well, by god, daughter! It did not take long before the rooster got into the henhouse! You know that if you lived with me, this would have never happened. And if it did, you know I would have killed you!"

"Yes, Papa. I know," Estelle replied, embarrassed and ashamed in front of all.

Bessie, Theopolis, and Albrecht looked on as Harrison Cory finished his lecture to his daughter. He concluded in a much lighter tone, "Well, you are grown now, and you and this young man are going to have to figure all of this out." He looked at Estelle, saying, "And I hope that you have thanked his parents for accommodating the two of you because I am sure neither of you have a pot to pee in nor a window to throw it out of! Money does not grow on trees!"

Estelle respectfully listened to her father's lecture but wished he would hurry up, shut up, and return home.

When Harrison Cory finished his business with his daughter, he looked at Theopolis and Bessie and thanked them for their kind hospitality, stating, "Well, now I guess I had better be on my way." He looked at Albrecht and said, "You have my blessings, son." Pointing his index finger in Albrecht's face, he continued, "If you ever feel the need to lay a hand on my daughter, you send her back to me!"

Albrecht was frozen with Harrison's brutishness but replied, "Yes, sir!"

Harrison Cory looked at Theopolis and Bessie, who remained quiet, and said, "You did a good job raising this young man! I will be on my way."

*   *   *

Aries Rose was born healthy to Albrecht and Estelle. He was growing nicely, but a few months later, Estelle found she was pregnant again. She was not a happy camper, and she thought, *Got diggity dog!* Her doctor told her that she would be back again next year. He knew Estelle was a woman with very low mileage who was just beginning to enjoy her nuptials.

After Estelle married Albrecht and settled in her new environment, Bessie pulled her aside and informed her that when she married a Catholic man, the wife must take classes to convert to Catholicism and agree to raise the children Catholic. Estelle loved her Christian church and did not know that marrying Albrecht meant she had to convert to Catholicism. To get along with her new family, she agreed to convert to Catholicism and to raise their children Catholic, but she did not know what she was getting into.

After attending Catholic Church services, Estelle did not like the church because the masses were spoken in Latin and she never understood a word of what the priests were saying. She figured, *What is the point of going to church if you don't understand the message?* She thought the masses were too solemn and the choir was lifeless; it was sheer torture for her to attend. She much preferred the black church, where she could understand the message of the pastor and feel the spirit of God and the liveliness of the choir.

Estelle was in love with Albrecht, and for the children's sake, she would convert to Catholicism. But in her heart, she thought the church's views on celibacy, confession, birth control, no consumption of meat on Fridays, self-sacrifice, and consumption of alcohol was a bunch of malarkey.

When Estelle missed her period and later found out she was pregnant for the second time, she said to herself and without consultation with

Albrecht or Bessie, "Catholic Church or no Catholic Church, I am getting on birth control." It was not in her plan to start raising children so soon after rearing her sister and brother. She had already turned down the job of her dreams because of her own stupidity. She wanted an education and a career. Her dream of higher education was tossed out the window because her father would not allow her to go to college. Instead, he made her work for the family household. The career of her dreams was tossed out the window with the first pregnancy, and now here comes a second pregnancy interfering with her ability to get ahead. She thought back to her dating days. She was angry with herself because whenever she and Albrecht went out on a date, he carried a miniature of gin and would insist on having sex with her when she was not prepared. She knew better but weakened to his touch and the anticipated pleasure.

Estelle accepted that women were expected to have children when they married; but in her mind, this second child was her final baby. "No more!" she said. Neither Albrecht nor Bessie needed to know that she was not going to follow this Catholic Church law; nor did they need to know what was going on in her body. She had learned from the Great Depression that she did not like living with little to no money; nor did she like being totally dependent on a man. She always felt insecure living with her father because she had to be condescending to his wishes when she did not wish to be condescending. With her own money, she could do as she damn well pleased.

Although she ran the house as early as ten years old, she hated having to be at her father's beck and call. She wanted a career to insulate herself from being obliging to anyone. She never wanted to experience the poverty she knew as a child. She thought of some of her female classmates, both single and married, who had gotten federal jobs and were getting ahead and doing well. She wanted to get ahead and do well too. Her father repeatedly instilled in her: "Daughter, get a title to a car and a deed to a house, and you will be successful." Estelle wanted to live this reality but was not seeing it as possible with one child in hand and one on the way.

"Two back-to-back babies—I am so disgusted," she said to herself.

CHAPTER TEN

Enlistment

When Estelle told Albrecht she was pregnant again, he gave serious thought to how he was going to provide for her and two children working at a hotel as a waiter and bartender. His income was not going to be enough. He wanted to finish his business school classes, but he needed more money, and he was still living with his parents. He and Estelle wanted to get out of their house.

Theopolis was happy with them living all together. Bessie was getting irritable with thoughts of a second grandchild. As it was, three additional people were eating her out of house and home. Aries was a screaming and crying baby. She thought, *Who wants another screaming and crying baby in this house?*

Albrecht approached Estelle after the baby girl was born and said he wanted to enlist in the military. He wanted to enlist in that he needed more money to raise his two children. He had not been able to attend college as he desired. He thought the military would at least give him a career ladder to climb, and if he worked hard, he would be allowed to move up the chain of command to the rank of officer. He promised her that he would send her the maximum allotment check to raise the two children. Estelle hated to see him enlist, but she too could see the need for more money. Both of their higher education plans had now gone south with two back-to-back pregnancies. She too wanted to move from her in-laws' apartment. She gave her approval to Albrecht's request to enlist in the military. She knew full well that she would once again have the responsibility of raising two children—and this time, totally alone. The upshot for Estelle was she would not have to worry about getting pregnant again because Albrecht would not be at home. She was happy about this part since he refused to use birth control.

Albrecht was feeling inadequate as a man and thought the military would help make him more of a man. Estelle, in her heart, really did not know what Albrecht was referring to when he described himself as not enough of a man. This sounded like some flimsy excuse to her. She did not appreciate his leaving her alone with two children, but in disgust, she simply said, "Well, go ahead, Albrecht. If that is what you feel you must do." Albrecht was elated that she consented and to give him the freedom he felt married life had deprived him. Estelle recalled her father saying repeatedly, "Daughter, never stay with a man who does not want to be with you. Never force a man to your ways." Estelle did not push his staying home, and in thirty days, he was sent to Georgia for basic training.

After joining the military, Albrecht was entitled to subsidized housing at the base outside the city. The housing was a segregated project for any military families that were non-white. This included military mixed-race families that were produced as a result of a foreign war. Before being shipped overseas, Albrecht rallied around Estelle to set up their small three-bedroom apartment.

Although Bessie was anxious for Albrecht and Estelle to leave her home, she thought Fort Anderson was too far away for Estelle to live alone with two children. She knew that she was unable to drive, and the bus would take a few hours. To her, it did not make sense that a pregnant woman would venture off to a place where she did not know a soul living around her.

Bessie asked, "Estelle, you mean to tell me you want to move all the way out there by yourself with two children while your husband is overseas and not able to help you at all? And I won't be able to help you?" All Estelle knew was she was tired of living in a crowded house with so many people, and anywhere would have been better than living in all the commotion in Bessie and Theopolis's house.

Theopolis and Bessie had been very accommodating to Albrecht and Estelle. However, Estelle wanted a place of her own. She knew she was not rich like Mrs. Astor, but she wanted to start living independently. She accepted the military housing. Estelle told all her city friends and relatives that yes, this was what she wanted to do. It could not have been any more difficult than what she had been through at ten years old trying to raise her sister and brother, working for a white family, and caring for her father to boot.

The military apartment at Fort Anderson was three bedrooms and had two wood stoves, an icebox, and a standup shower with no tub. Albrecht chopped and stacked wood to store in the wood box for the two wood-burning stoves. The wood was to be used for the winter months. He would return on furlough to cut wood for the next season. He opened a checking account for Estelle where he could deposit his allotment check so she could manage the household expenses and the children's needs. He ordered bread and milk for delivery twice each week. He also purchased life insurance for the two children.

After he left home for the last time and got situated in the military, Albrecht kept his promise and sent Estelle a generous allotment each month. And he wrote to her often, expressing his gratitude and love. Estelle thought the allotment was very generous, and she was happy to move out of her father- and mother-in-law's house. She was also happy because it was her first living space she did not have to share with her family or Albrecht's family. And for the first time in her life, she had a room of her own, and her two children had a room of their own. This produced a good feeling for her; at least, it was a beginning.

After Albrecht was shipped overseas, Estelle took great pride in decorating her first habitat. She had retained all the skills she had learned as a first-floor maid for Mrs. Astor. She was confident in cleaning and maintaining a proper home. She was organized and created schedules for the children. Estelle remembered her father telling her over and over again, "Daughter, if you make a nickel, save a cent." Although she made the nickel, she could not save it because he took it away from her, but she received his message. Estelle accepted his lesson and was putting a little money aside in the savings account each month. Saving was a practice she had developed prior to her father's constant reminders because she always remembered being scared of being hungry during the Great Depression.

She stopped and thought back to the time when Mrs. Astor would give Anise or Harrison Jr. a tip for their weekly chores. Her father would take not only their earnings but the tip too! Estelle was getting sick and tired of her father taking her money, so she would lie and say, "Papa, Mrs. Astor did not give me a tip today!" Harrison Sr. accepted Estelle's tale for a while until he thought it unfair that Mrs. Astor tipped Anise and Harrison Jr. and not Estelle.

When Harrison confronted Mrs. Astor about not tipping Estelle, he would say, "Now, Mrs. Astor, I ask you, did my daughter perform a satisfactory job for you today?" When Mrs. Astor replied "Yes, Mr. Cory, Estelle did a very nice job today," Harrison would then say, "Then don't you think if you tip both Anise and Harrison Jr., you should tip Estelle too?" Mrs. Astor said to Mr. Cory, "Why yes, Mr. Cory! I always tip each of your children the same."

When Estelle returned home from school, Harrison Sr. would ask Estelle once again, "Did Mrs. Astor tip you as she tipped Anise and Junior?" Estelle lied again. Harrison Sr. said, "Daughter, you are lying to me, and I will not have that!" He grabbed Estelle by the arm as he pulled his leather belt from his waist, and he whipped his teenage daughter for lying to him.

Estelle screamed and cried, "Papa, stop! Get off of me." Her chants did little good once Harrison got a firm and solid grip on Estelle's arm.

Harrison asked Estelle, "Where are you hiding the tip money that Mrs. Astor gave to you?" When Estelle told her father where she had hidden the money, he said to her, "Go and get it right now and give it to me."

Harrison took all the money she had stashed away. Harrison would say to all his children after he had severely whipped them, "If I can't talk honesty in your head, I am going to beat it in your backsides! You are going to learn to be honest one way or the other! You cannot lie to me!"

Estelle did not like being forced to depend on someone else. She wanted to be responsible for taking care of herself. Since Albrecht was overseas, she did not lie to him, but she took in ironing and babysitting to have her own stash of money. Estelle saved some of her money, but she also purchased heavy curtains for the windows with sheers, a new Tappan range, a new refrigerator, linoleum for the kitchen floor, and a green wool carpet for the living room. These were all items she knew Albrecht would not approve of, so she spent her own money for these items.

Estelle wanted money too because she saw firsthand, while living alone on the military base, how perfectly good soldiers returned to the States and abused their wives and children due to being shell-shocked, alcoholics, or mentally depressed. She saw men punch their wives in the face, and she could hear through the thin apartment walls as wives were being raped or pushed down a flight of stairs by their husbands. She did not want to land herself in this kind of situation and always wanted to be ready to flee if the circumstances presented themselves.

As a teenager living with her father, she learned how to fight off men who were inappropriate and tried to whisper sweet nothings to her as she and Anise walked to and from the grocery store. Men did not know or care how most women dreaded and suffered having to fight off men who wanted their pleasures fulfilled. She knew men liked sex, and she knew she was not going to be abused or forced into something she did not want. She made her own common sense. This was why she wanted a job—a career for her meant being prepared for the worst. She wanted material things too, but she wanted to be able to take care of herself if "push came to shove!"

Albrecht came from a poor family and was not materialistic. When he returned home on furlough, he would marvel at how well Estelle had managed the money he sent home. He did not want her to take in ironing or babysitting, and neither did he want all the material possessions she was purchasing. It was much too showy, and he would have been content with less.

Estelle would postpone her response until Albrecht finished expressing his displeasure with the home furnishings Estelle had acquired. At some later time, she would say, "Now, Albrecht, just listen to yourself. This place is no bigger than a matchbox. There is just one single-pane window in each room. If you open the front and the back doors at the same time, you can look straight through the house! I don't know how you sound. You mean, you would begrudge a woman her feminine frills?" Estelle was not angry, but she would stand her ground. She failed to understand a man who could be so content with nothing. They both were adjusting to military life and being responsible parents.

CHAPTER ELEVEN

The Brightest Child

Estelle raised Aries Rose, her first child, in a rote fashion. He was born healthy. She fed, clothed, and bathed her son and cared for him as she had done her younger sister and brother. He was a child that did not appear to need much nurturing or a lot of attention. He appeared to entertain himself well with the toys she provided, and once he learned to walk, all he wanted to do was to go outside and play in the yard, get dirty, and do things she thought appropriate for a boy. He was nothing like her brother, Harrison Jr., who was attached to his mother. Aries was not attached her, and she did not care she enjoyed seeing his independence. She was tired of raising children. With the exception of inexplicable crying, Aries was a low-maintenance child.

Albrecht was still overseas, and she continued babysitting and taking in ironing to procure all the extras she wanted, and she continued to do a great job managing her house. She settled into the peace and quiet from not having anyone in the house. She liked not living under her father's roof. She liked not having to work so hard for Mrs. Astor, and she liked not living with her Aunt Clara, who kept a filthy house. And although Albrecht and Theopolis were very nice to her, she preferred not living with anyone except her family. When Albrecht came home on a furlough, they purchased a used car that she could drive to the post exchange, commissary, and church. She was content for the moment.

When her second child was born, Estelle named her Claudia Rose. Albrecht was home again on furlough, and as he was with Aries, he was pretty afraid of infants. He feared their fragileness and vulnerability. He let Estelle take care of their needs. The military had built him up pretty good, and he was strong and durable. He looked good. If Estelle placed either Aries or Claudia in his arms to hold, he would become as still as a statue. He never had time to be with his children enough to get comfortable with them or to show them affection.

As Claudia Rose was healthy, she grew and developed beautifully, almost without flaw. Estelle noticed that her daughter was an extremely bright child. She had exceptional grades in school and was a quick learner. When Estelle attended parent-teacher meetings, the teachers at her school all commented about Claudia and recognized that a more advanced school would have been better for her academic growth and educational performance.

Estelle agreed and thought it best if her daughter was enrolled in private school, but a Catholic school was about as much as she and Albrecht could afford. Albrecht had attended Catholic school from grades 1 through 8 and was an extremely bright man academically. He had received an outstanding classical education. Claudia was like her father. Estelle thought she could benefit from such and experience until she and Albrecht could afford a better school.

Throughout the marriage, Albrecht and Estelle compared notes on world religions. Estelle had lamented to Albrecht, expressing her displeasure at having to attend Catholic services, and she gave her reasons. Albrecht was beginning to glean from what Estelle was telling him and considered some of the hypocrisy of the church. From his comparison with the other Christian churches, he was beginning to question the Catholic Church and its laws. Soldiers with whom he shared space in the barracks also pointed to faults within the Catholic Church and other organized religions too.

When Albrecht came home on the next furlough, Estelle brought the subject of how bright their daughter was and that she thought a private school would help her in achieving higher goals for herself. And in the future, she might become a world leader. Estelle had seen and heard of many black women who were entering the institutions of higher education and earning high-paying jobs. Albrecht flatly refused, stating he did not see the need for the girl to get a classical education when all they do is get married, stay home, cook, clean, and have babies.

What was unspoken in Albrecht's gut was the fact that he had been an altar boy in the church and attended Catholic school, and he saw firsthand boys being taken advantage of by priests and nuns coming up pregnant within the diocese. Some of the nuns abruptly disappeared from his classes without explanation for months, and a few never returned. He did not share this with Estelle.

Like Bessie, Albrecht took the teachings of the church very seriously, and to have a priest defile the name of Jesus Christ offended him. He was losing faith in the church. He was learning in the military that men did have premarital sex and masturbation would not make you crazy. Albrecht thought the church had misguided him after he had taken all of the sacraments and teachings of the church to heart. He was angry and conflicted. His educational reality in the military contradicted things he learned in school. He felt cheated by the church, and he did not want Claudia to be subjected to the teachings that kept him so naïve and ill prepared for the world. At least that is how he saw himself. Albrecht thought the idea harmful and a waste of money.

Estelle disagreed and was disheartened with his attitude toward Claudia, his child, but the conversation ended. Claudia attended a segregated one-room school with Aries, along with all the other colored children. They were called the Rosenwald Schools, named after a benevolent Jewish man. Estelle would think to herself and say, "Men! It is a sin and a shame! Every child needs a moral education. Claudia didn't have to attend the Catholic school for the rest of her life, but she could get the classical education Albrecht had received in her educational foundations. It's just foolish!" But Estelle let the subject go. She could not afford the school tuition with her babysitting money, and it meant taking Claudia off the base each day, and she would have to do this while Albrecht was still overseas. If he had supported her idea and showed some interest, she would have made the daily sacrifice; but in that he flatly refused, she did not want the uphill argument. So she just let the dust settle and moved on, but she thought it was the dumbest thing she had ever heard.

Estelle's ambition was not solely for financial security and material acquisition. She had ambitions for herself and her children, if they decided they wanted to be anything or make something of themselves. She did not understand how Albrecht could deny a better education for a child that was his.

Albrecht was rising quickly through the entry ranks of the military since induction. He was honest, reliable, and efficient. Eventually, his commanding officer encouraged him to apply for Officer Candidate School. He did apply but was denied three times due to his poor vision. After the second rejection, he filed for an appeal but was still denied. This was a second major disappointment for him in his young life. The first was his lost opportunity of a college education. This rejection from the military had denied him the opportunity to rise to the higher ranks. His poor vision was a circumstance beyond his control. He was deflated.

CHAPTER TWELVE

Child Never Wanted

After several years in the military, Albrecht unlearned some of his Catholic teachings regarding sex. Albrecht realized he had a voracious appetite for sex and wondered why Estelle was not getting pregnant after he had returned home on furlough several times. He had made plentiful deposits. He would say to Estelle, "I like things natural, and I don't care how many children we have."

To have ten children was familiar to him in his upbringing, and he did not see any problem with procreation. Albrecht's masculinity was associated with making children, and for him, it was the markings of a man's man. After years attending an all-boys Catholic school and being an altar boy, he needed to regularly reassure himself of his manhood, and making babies was his answer.

Estelle finally confessed to Albrecht that she was on birth control. She told him she did not want to have any more children. The hassle of caring for her sister and brother and now two back-to-back children was wearing her down. She explained to him that she wanted to get ahead in life, and having more babies was not what she wanted to do. Furthermore, he was overseas and not available to participate in his children's lives anyway, so her question to him was "Why have all these children and you are not here to take care of them or be engaged in their lives?"

After her second child, she was wary of engaging in sex for fear of getting pregnant again. She thought sex was highly overrated. She told Albrecht, "Sex is for men anyway. It is not for women. Women have to clean up before sex and again afterward while the man is lying over there somewhere sound asleep! There is no romance, no affection for the women. I tell you, being a woman is being a sorry creature!"

Albrecht was not happy with Estelle's reasoning for her disinterest in having sex and giving birth to more children. So to get his way, he promised Estelle if she had just one more child, he would come out of the military, be more affectionate and romantic toward her, and play a more active part in raising this third child.

He agreed with Estelle that by being away in the military, he did not see his first two children growing up, and he wanted to have the experience of watching this third child grow up. But within, this was not his true motivation. He had a personal story he was concealing from Estelle.

Estelle loved Albrecht and thought he was a good provider and deserved whatever he wanted since his request of her were few. She rationalized and it was true that he had spent very little time with the first two children. She asked herself, *Should I deny him this opportunity?* Estelle was very clear in her heart that she did not want more children, and she wanted to start working just as soon as the second child was in first grade.

With agony in her heart and soul, she simply did not want another child. "I do not want it!" she would say to herself. But since she was not completely honest with Albrecht about her use of birth control, she agreed to have another child for him, but she was fully reluctant. He had vowed to come out of the military and help raise this child. She got off the birth control and was soon pregnant with a third child she did not want.

Estelle regretted being pregnant. She thought it was a man's world, and women were expected to condescend to a man's wishes because he was a man and the breadwinner. She longed for more money to buy a new car, to purchase larger living quarters, and put aside enough money to educate the two children she had. As far as she was concerned, this is what middle-class Washingtonians did, and for the life of her, she could not understand why Albrecht was so complacent and comfortable with so little for himself, his wife, and his children. He never wanted to own a car or a house, and in Estelle's thinking, these were the basic needs and normal desires when you marry and have children. "And now here comes another child!" she would say to him.

Still residing in military-subsidized housing, they were eligible for a newer three-bedroom apartment, and thus they moved to Chamberlain Street. Albrecht did not know his first two children very well, and childrearing was foreign to him. His son Aries was always in some kind of mischief at home, in school, or in church. Albrecht tried to understand his son but did not seem to get to the heart of his son's behavior problem. Aries never accepted authority, and Albrecht used military discipline tactics on him to keep him in line, but Aries kept him busy.

His daughter, Claudia, was much like Albrecht—very studious, did her homework, was quiet and reserved. She was independent and self-directed but distant and nonchalant. She held no affection for anyone in the family—at least it was not visible. She had been acknowledged academically for so many years during primary and secondary schools, she thought of herself as smarter than everyone, including her mother and father. She did not know she was naive to think this way.

As Estelle got larger and larger with the pregnancy of her third child and her attitude toward having it had not changed. She was thirty years old. She thought her life would not have the education or career she aspired.

One day, while walking down the street with Albrecht, he blurts out, "Woman, you have gotten as big as you are going to get walking the streets with me!"

This statement reawakened her fury about having this child in the first place. She was now even more regretful she was having this baby for him, and she angrily retorted, "Listen, buddy boy! I don't need to walk the streets with you either. And why would you make a statement like that? It is hurtful and insulting."

Albrecht seriously and unaptly replied, "Well, why would you get upset over something as simple as that when women have been having babies for centuries!"

"Yes, but they are not having your baby. And this is the baby you said you wanted to have, not me!" Estelle replied as she turned around and walked back home in fury and disgust. She was thinking, *When is this baby coming out? I am sick of it already! I never wanted to have it! I never wanted it!*

Chapter Thirteen

Reenlistment

When Albrecht returned to his post overseas to request a military discharge, he is informed that there is a reenlistment incentive. Eager to receive the extra money, he forgets his promise to Estelle. He accepts the incentive package and recommits to the military for another two years, thinking the extra money would help his family. In that he had been rejected from officer's candidate school, he wanted the extra money to help Estelle get ahead.

When he notified Estelle by letter what he had done, she was so angry she was seeing stars. She ranted and raved throughout the house, saying out loud to herself, "Here I am out here giving this man what he asked for, and what does he do? He re-ups for another two years, leaving me with another child to raise." Estelle was hot! She did not want this child from the get-go and decided right then and there she was going to do everything in her power to get rid of it.

When all her attempts to get rid of this third child failed, Estelle called Albrecht's commanding officer and requested he be discharged from the military on a child dependence clause. She had read about this policy while looking through the military wives newsletters. She would be dammed and hell-bent if she was raising another child alone. He had gotten all the playtime he was getting. She thought of the letters he had sent to her from overseas, telling Estelle of his sexual escapades along with pictures of him standing on the beach with European women. He would write to Estelle saying that he would be a better lover when he returned home.

Albrecht was nowhere near as mature as Estelle, but she thought, *He is a fool! What wife wants to hear this kind of news?*

"No, his playtime is over," she said to herself. She was liberal about his wanting to go into the military and wanting to develop himself as a man. She was aware their lives as young adults had been truncated by pregnancy and marriage, but she thought, at some point, he had to grow up. She had to grow up when her mother died, and there was no playtime and no introductory period for her. And Albrecht was going to grow up now!

This was one reenlistment that was going to be rescinded.

Chapter Fourteen

Civilian Life

Albrecht was honorably discharged from the military, and he returned to Fort Anderson and landed a civilian job working as a chemical engineer and a laborer. The money was good, but working as a laborer was not a part of Theopolis and Bessie's plan when they paid to send their son to private school; nor was it Albrecht's. It paid more money, and he was the type of man who could make himself content wherever he was. This was his work life now.

He reflected on his military years and thought Estelle was dead-on about his coming home. Estelle made no bones about telling him about the letters he had sent to her, for she kept each and every one. He was unfaithful to Estelle. He had made the promise to her, and out of the need of providing for his family, he thought the extra money would be useful. He had not one ounce of difficulty providing food, clothing, and shelter for his children. He gave Estelle the reenlistment bonus as some type of awkward apology for not paying attention to his decision and being sucked in by the incentive money. He sincerely wanted this child for his reasons. He was home now, and he was going to love this child that Estelle was carrying for him.

When Albrecht thought about his association and experiences with the other soldiers in the military, he recalled how they all laughed at him for trying to remain faithful to Estelle or his guilt feelings for being unfaithful to Estelle. They knew he was conflicted. They questioned why he was letting some woman rule his life. They made remarks: "Man, you are henpecked!" or "Man, monogamy is not normal. A man has got to have his women! Where did you get those ideas from?" They would laugh and ridicule Albrecht punitively. The peer pressure was great to conform to men's norms, and Albrecht wanted to be viewed and accepted as a man. He thought back to the first and second time he was unfaithful. The third and fourth were easy. He eventually reconciled his infidelity with his moral training in the church. He decided to honor Estelle during her pregnancy.

It took Albrecht quite some time to come to his conclusions. The Catholic Church did not believe in premarital or extramarital sex. Albrecht was taught that it was a sin similar to masturbation, which made you crazy or insane. All his life, he had believed and followed the Catholic teachings. The military soldiers from various orientations and religions had different views and exposed him to their thinking. In rare cases, men were having sex with other men if they thought they would not get caught. Those men still saw themselves as straight and good military soldiers. These views and beliefs collided with his teachings.

Albrecht and Estelle made the readjustment to his return home, and life resumed as husband and wife. Estelle was accustomed to being in charge of the house, but with Albrecht's return, she had to tone down her loud and controlling manner to accommodate Albrecht's need to be head of the household. Things were running smooth for Albrecht and Estelle.

CHAPTER FIFTEEN

Broken Leg and Labor Pains

Two days before the Estelle's baby was due, Albrecht drove the old Chevy to the service station to ensure it was prepared when Estelle was ready to deliver the baby. Once at the service station, the attendant informed Albrecht that he was backed up with other customers. He needed to keep the car overnight. Albrecht called a neighbor to pick him up from the service station and bring him back home.

On the way back home, the neighbor said to Albrecht, "Let's stop for a pint of gin to drink on the way back home." Albrecht had been drinking gin since his senior year in high school. Alcohol was not an offense as far as the church was concerned. As the neighbor sipped on his gin from a brown paper bag, it appeared to Albrecht that his foot got heavier and heavier on the gas pedal. This gave Albrecht a scare. When he asked his neighbor to slow it down, the neighbor said, "What's wrong, Albrecht? Are you scared?" And he mashed his foot harder on the gas pedal, causing his car to go faster.

Albrecht thought the man was going off his rocker, so he jumped from the speeding car. His body slammed to the curbside, and he tumbled down an embankment, removing the skin from his face, arms, shoulders, and back and, in the same course, broke his leg.

An emergency vehicle was called, and Albrecht was rushed to the hospital to get bandaged and his leg set in a cast. After the procedure, they took him to Theopolis and Bessie's house, which was the closest drop-off. Albrecht called Estelle to let her know where he was and told her the whole story of jumping out of the car. He thought he did the right thing trying to save his life, but Estelle was thinking something different. She was thinking, *I am nine months pregnant, twenty-three miles away from the hospital, no husband to transport me to the hospital and no car to drive myself.* And she said to herself, "What a mess."

At the time Albrecht called with his bad news, Aries and Claudia were fighting with each other, running back and forth to Estelle with a tale of "Ma, he hit me" followed by "yeah, but she called me a name!" Estelle was not in the disposition to hear Albrecht's news or to have sympathy for him. After settling the fight Aries had started with Claudia, she turned her attention back to Albrecht, who was waiting on the telephone, and retorted, "Albrecht, firstly, you should have known not to wait until the last minute to get the car serviced. The car should have been serviced two weeks or a month ago. Secondly, you should have had better sense than to get in a car with Charlie Willie anyway! You know he is an alcoholic, plus it did not help that you stopped with him to pick up gin? What kind of sense does that make? The children are here setting me crazy. Now I have to figure out who I can get to watch them and figure out how I am going to get to the hospital."

When Estelle hung up the telephone, she thought, *I love Albrecht. I acknowledge and accept he is a good, kind man. But sometimes he doesn't make any sense.* Estelle had been managing her father and felt she knew how things should be handled. Albrecht was just immature in her thinking. Even at thirty years old, he should have known to take care of business first.

Not long after the upsetting telephone call from Albrecht, Estelle noticed what she believed were the onset of contractions. The children needed to have dinner and a bath, she needed to find someone to watch them, and she had to make a bus reservation to the city. The military hospital was segregated and she did not want a midwife, so at this time of evening, the bus was her only choice of transportation. As she started preparations for her journey alone to the hospital and packing the children up, she thought, *Women are sorry creatures.*

Estelle arrived at the Greyhound bus station in Baltimore on time and very pregnant. She flagged a Yellow Cab to transport her to the hospital. The ride was so bumpy, she thought she was going to drop the baby in the cab. She was controlling the pain associated with her contractions but noticed the frequency—they were coming closer and closer together.

As she maneuvered her pregnant body out of the cab, she proceeded to the hospital entrance. A uniformed hospital guard informed her that she could not enter. Estelle said very politely, "Well, kind sir. I am having a baby here, and my doctor has made an appointment for me."

The uniformed guard paged a nurse to come to his desk to explain to Estelle why she was being denied access. "Why am I being denied access?" she asked the attending nurse.

Mrs. Rose, the nurse, said, "I am very sorry to inform you that there has been an outbreak of polio in the maternity ward, and we cannot risk you and your baby contracting the disease."

"But what shall I do?" Estelle replied. "I am experiencing contractions now."

The nurse said, "Well, that is up to you. But I cannot admit you to this hospital this evening. Now you are wasting time. Run along before you and your child are exposed."

Well Jesus! Estelle thought.

Estelle took a moment to compose herself and breathed in disbelief of what was happening to her this evening of all evenings. In a low voice, she said to herself, "This baby of all babies. The one I didn't even want to have is causing me all this trouble. Albrecht is laid up at his mother's with a broken leg, and I am out here in the street by myself, trying to deliver a child he wanted! Ump, ump, ump!"

The hospitals were segregated in Baltimore as well, and there was only one place to go, and that was to her mother-in-law's house, where she and Albrecht once lived. When she told the story to Albrecht and her mother-in-law what happened at the hospital, she opened her mouth and said, "I guess I will have my baby here."

Bessie quickly retorted, "There will be no baby born in this house tonight!"

"But Ma!" Estelle said. "What am I going to do?"

Bessie said, "Go on over to your sister's over there on Streeter Avenue."

Streeter Avenue was a beautiful street with a lovely median stripe that had fountains of water and beautiful flowers planted along the paving. White families lived on the east side of the street, and Negros lived on the west side of the street. Bessie knew that Estelle's sister was living high on the hog and had more space for Estelle and the baby than she had, so she sent Estelle along with two of her younger children for escorts. Bessie thought, *I can't take care of Albrecht, Estelle, and a baby too, along with my children. Estelle had to go!*

Bessie was a devout Catholic and never wanted to marry. She wanted to remain single. Theopolis, her husband, dated her very aggressively and sincerely wanted to marry Bessie. He thought she was a good woman for him. For many years, she would say to her family and friends, "I had to marry him to get rid of him!"

When they married, Bessie never gave up her childhood church, and Theopolis never gave up his childhood church. Bessie never believed in birth control and had ten pregnancies and eight live births. On Sunday mornings, Bessie and her children walked in one direction (to her childhood church), and Theopolis walked, puffing on his cigar, in the opposite direction (to his childhood church).

Theopolis deeply loved Bessie. Bessie was nonchalant about her marriage and her children. She longed for the day when the children would be grown and be out of her house. The thought of Estelle having her baby in her house was, in no uncertain terms, out of the question. Bessie was also sick and tired of Estelle lamenting about not wanting this child. Bessie thought, *It is done! You are pregnant. The church will not allow abortions. So get on with it and stop complaining!*

Bessie summoned two of her younger children to walk Estelle to her sister's house on Streeter Avenue. Estelle was much too distraught to analyze why her mother-in-law put her out of the house. She was thinking instead why she did not want to go to her sister's house to have her child and how Albrecht sat mute as Bessie blessed her out, and he did not say a word to support or defend her.

This is the child he wanted, she thought.

Broken leg or no broken leg, she was not happy about the child or Albrecht at this moment.

CHAPTER SIXTEEN

Birth Abode

Anise left Washington, DC, two years before Estelle. She was of fair complexion and attractive, as was Estelle. She had quickly married the man of her dreams. He was an ambitious man with big ideas. She was desirous of this kind of man, who would take her away from the life she knew with her father. She knew how to sew meticulously—a skill she had learned from her mother. She acquired a taste for fine home furnishings and good taste in clothing while living with the Astors. Although terribly knock-kneed, she could camouflage this defect by dropping the hemline of her skirts and dresses below the knees. She knew how to make a very nice presentation for an ambitious man. Anise and Estelle assisted with the planning of the Astor daughters' coming-out parties and cotillions and were exposed to proper etiquette and decorum. Both girls learned proper feminine care and grooming from Mrs. Astor, and they modeled all they had learned once they became self-sufficient.

Anise's husband was an arrogant man who desired the rank of lieutenant in the army. He told Anise before he married her, this was his dream, and he did not want any children until he had accomplished this dream. Although she and her father had not spoken to each other for well over a year after her abrupt departure from Washington, DC, she did call to inform him of her marriage. She explained she had done well and married a man who wanted to become a lieutenant in the military. Her father was shocked. He thought this was such a quick marriage to a man she scarcely knew. He knew he was hard on his children, but he thought he had taught them better sense than to marry someone so quickly. Harrison Sr. thought to himself, *I was forty before I decided to marry. I can't understand the child's hurry.*

Her father inquired, "Well, daughter, what is his name?"

Anise answered, "Sequester Toms."

He was aghast and authoritatively replied, "Sequester what? Daughter, when a Negro has a name like Sequester Toms, he is bound to be no good!"

Six months into the marriage, Anise happily found she was pregnant. Sequester Toms was not. And just as soon as he found out she was pregnant, he packed his suitcase and he deserted her and was never heard from again.

When Estelle finally arrived and settled at Anise's apartment, in labor, having traversed from Fort Anderson by bus to Baltimore, then to the hospital by a cab, then bounced from the hospital by the guard and nurse, then to a city transit bus to her mother-in-law's, and finally at her sister's place, she was fit to be tied.

This was the last place she wanted to be because she knew her sister would be just as useless to her as she was as a child and teen. She had always been the sickly whining type, and frivolous too. Estelle knew Toms had deserted her, and Anise was now seven months pregnant. She was constantly on the verge of tears with sorrow and regret with the desertion of her husband and the loss of the lifestyle she had hungered for.

Estelle was not prepared to hear another sad story or to offer compassion to her sister's aching heart. Estelle wanted, more than anything in the world, to unload herself of this child she was carrying. She was dreading the six years ahead, having to care for a child, when all she wanted to do was get a job and go to work. She had just gotten Claudia in first grade, and she was more than ready to go to work. She did not want to stay home and be "barefoot and pregnant again!" as she believed most men wanted of their women. She thought this was a man's way of holding a woman down and in place.

Estelle's wanting to work had nothing to do with the women' suffrage movement that was in the news those days but more that she never wanted to ever be hungry again, as she was during the Great Depression. She thought like Ms. Scarlet O'Hara in *Gone with the Wind*.

Estelle lay silent in Anise's double bed and felt the pain from the contractions coming closer and closer. She had delivered Aries and Claudia in a hospital. She felt safer there and got more attention and coaching. She was afraid to have this baby alone and without Albrecht, with no attending doctors or nurses. She told Anise to call the doctor to come to the house because it was time to deliver this child.

The doctor arrived and examined Estelle and told her the baby was not due for eight more hours and that he must return to the hospital due to the polio outbreak in the maternity ward. Estelle pleaded with the doctor not to go, but he firmly said, "Estelle, I must go back to the hospital. There are other patients who need my help, and there is nothing I can do for you for eight more hours. I will return to you." Estelle's doctor was considered one of the best in his field. He delivered both of her other children. She had hoped he would stay and comfort her, but he did not. Estelle lay in the bed, resigned to her reality.

Anise wandered around her apartment, not knowing what to do or say—like the behavior of Missy, also in *Gone with the Wind*. To make conversation, she said, "Estelle, why do you think Sequester deserted me?" Estelle was not in the mood for her sister's question and replied, "Anise, you had no business getting pregnant. Toms told you up front that he did not want any children until he became lieutenant. If you loved him so much, you should have taken the precautions necessary and just waited to have a child. Instead, you just wanted to have a child because I had two and you had none. I tried to tell you raising children is more than a notion. It is a lot of hard work. You know you were too weak to have a child anyway. You are sickly like Mama!"

Before Estelle realized it, she had given her sister a mini lecture. She hated herself afterward because she could hear the impatience of her father coming out in herself. Her father was the last person she wanted to be, but Estelle continued, "Look, Anise, I apologize. I just want to have this baby right now, raise it, and get it out of the way so I can get a job and go to work. Our mother is gone. Albrecht ran off to the military and left me with two children to raise alone. He wanted this child, and where is he now? Here I am again with another child to raise. Right now, I am not interested in Toms, and you need to figure out how you are going to raise your child alone. I just cannot help you now. I raised you and Harrison Jr. the best I could. I am trying to raise my children, and I am tired. Can't you understand?"

Anise was never offended or insulted by Estelle's' acidity or concise responses; nor did she want to add more stress to her sister. She just sat in a wingback chair at the foot of the bed and said, "You are right, Estelle."

A few hours later, the doctor called to check on Estelle. He instructed Anise by telephone to measure Estelle's dilation. But after she followed his instructions, the doctor instructed her to call him when the contractions were twenty minutes apart. Then he would leave the hospital and deliver Estelle's baby.

Estelle asked to speak with the doctor. She was getting increasingly more anxious, and she begged him to come back now. He repeated to Estelle that it was still not time for the baby. He repeated that the contractions were not twenty minutes apart. Estelle asked the doctor for pain medication. She was not a woman who was good with tolerating pain.

The doctor said, "Estelle, if I give you something for pain, it is going to slow the delivery process, and you don't want to do that."

Estelle said, "Oh! Yes I do! I want something for this pain."

The pharmacy delivered a mild sedative to quiet Estelle.

Estelle was weary and drugged from the sedatives she took to relieve the contraction pains and to quiet her down. Her sister and brothers-in-law who escorted her from Theopolis and Bessie's home sat in the living room. They stayed awake the entire time, awaiting delivery of Estelle's baby. They had not seen a baby delivered before.

Anise was sleeping in her bedroom side chair when two intoxicated couples who were returning from the Ebony Club at 2:00 AM came. When they saw the lights on over Anise's transom, they knocked on the door. They knew she was pregnant and had been deserted by Toms. As caring neighbors, they kept an eye on Anise since they knew she was living alone. When Anise opened the door, she frantically told the intoxicated couples that her sister was having a baby but she did not know what to do. The four intoxicated people pushed through the door and offered to deliver the baby.

When Estelle opened her eyes after a brief sedative-induced doze, two drunk ladies were looking up her dressing gown to see if the baby was anywhere near coming out.

Estelle screamed so loud and insisted the ladies get away from her. She said that she was all right and resting now. "Just leave me alone for now!"

Estelle's scream shocked them from their alcohol-induced stupor, and they said, "Oh, miss, we did not mean to frighten you. We just were checking to see if the baby was coming yet."

Estelle stated firmly, "No, the baby is not coming yet. I will let you know. Now please get out of this room and let me rest!"

And after an evening of drinking all night, the two couples went to the living room and waited with the two in-laws.

When the doctor showed up, everyone was sprawled out around the apartment, sleeping in upholstered armchairs and on the plush carpeted floors.

At 8:30 AM Daylight Savings Time, the baby was finally born. When the doctor smacked life into the eight-pound boy child, the child kicked his legs and smiled for life but never shed a tear. Estelle had not witnessed such a thing with her other two children. Aries had screamed and made all kinds of noise. Claudia would not make a sound. The doctor had to stick a needle in her side to get her to cry, and only then, it was barely a whimper.

As the doctor completed the delivery procedure and cleared the afterbirth and was about to sign the birth certificate, he said to Estelle, "Name? What do you name this child?"

Estelle looked at her sister-in-law and said, "Name the boy. I don't care what you name him."

At this point, she did not care. She just wanted to get this over with and get back to her apartment and pick up Aries and Claudia from the neighbor's house, where she had left them the evening before. She had to pick up the pieces of her situation and move on. The baby was here now, and there was nothing she could do.

Her sister-in-law named the boy after her brother, who stood right there beside her. He was patient and responsible throughout the delivery ordeal. They named the baby Seymour Rose. He was born on Mother's Day.

CHAPTER SEVENTEEN

Seymour's Conundrum

Estelle was back home with Seymour, but her disposition had not changed very much. She was upset about having this baby. As she moved about her chores for the day, she thought, *I have one more child to take care of, and I have to take care of Albrecht and serve his meals since he is still on crutches.*

Albrecht was healing from his broken leg and was home for a brief period with Estelle and Seymour before returning to work. Albrecht was happy with Seymour and spent more time with him than either of his other children. He would spend hours holding, coddling, and talking to Seymour. When he placed Seymour back in the crib, he would say "I will be back soon." When Albrecht watched Estelle feed or bathe Seymour, he would instruct Estelle to be careful with Seymour. He would critically say to Estelle as she moved about the kitchen making a bottle of milk for Seymour, "Estelle, now hold his head up. You look as if you are going to drop him."

Estelle paid Albrecht little attention because he did not know anything about caring for a baby. Estelle simply replied, "Well, Albrecht, I raised two babies while you were overseas, and I did not kill either of them." The implication was that she knew what she was doing and did not need his advice on taking care of the children. On a different thread, Estelle could not believe her eyes because Albrecht had never paid her or anyone else that much attention. She became slightly jealous of the attention this new baby was receiving.

When Albrecht got up for work each day, he made breakfast for Aries and Claudia and got them out to school. Estelle had given them a bath the night before. She did not like sending the children out to school wet from a morning shower. She wanted them completely dry, especially on winter mornings. She also laid out Aries's and Claudia's book bags and ensured they had their books, paper, and pencils needed for school. She also made Albrecht, Aries, and Claudia brown-bag lunches the night before, so all they had to do in the morning was to reach in the refrigerator and pull them out and rush out the door.

Once the house was cleared each morning, Estelle would sleep as long as she could to recover her nerves from hearing Aries and Claudia squabbling. As the months passed, she thought Seymour was a good-natured child. After awaking in the morning, he watched from his crib while Estelle slept. The neighbors could see Seymour playing in the window underneath the venetian blinds each morning as they were driving off to work. Estelle would throw a toy in the crib every fifteen or twenty minutes to keep Seymour quiet so that she could get a few extra minutes of sleep.

She expressed to Albrecht before marriage that she was never cooking breakfast for him. She justified her statement by telling him she had cooked for her father and siblings all her life and she wanted to sleep later in the mornings. Albrecht accepted the terms and prepared breakfast for the children and himself, never missing a day.

After a few hours of watching Estelle sleep and a wet diaper, Seymour tired of his toys. He was also feeling hunger pangs. He would then take the toys Estelle had thrown in the crib to keep him entertained while she slept and throw them back at her to wake her up. For a baby, he learned to aim at her head a couple of times to make sure she moved. Estelle was grateful Seymour was such an easy baby. She described him as a good baby. She would say to her friends, "All you have to do with this child is feed him and change his diaper, and he is all right." She would rise from the bed in a raggedy nightgown, go to the bathroom to freshen up, then prepare a breakfast for the two of them—usually eggs, bacon, toast, and applesauce, with hot tea for Estelle and milk for Seymour.

Seymour calmed himself after Estelle got out of bed. He sensed food would be coming his way shortly. He felt secure, and his appetite grew as he smelled the mixed aromas of the breakfast foods. Bacon sizzling in the pan as the grease popped all over the stove, eggs scalded as they dropped in the sizzling grease, and the smell of the cinnamon and sugar as Estelle stirred it in the applesauce.

During the weekdays, Albrecht worked, and Aries and Claudia were in school. Estelle and Seymour had a quiet breakfast in a calm and still house. The wood stove crackled and heat filled the small kitchen, where he sat in a high chair for his meal. After breakfast and with a full belly, Estelle would look at Seymour with a smile and say, "Seymour, child, God really wanted you to be here because I sure didn't want to have you!" Seymour had no idea what his mother was talking about. He was much too young, but he thought that whatever she was saying had a tone of not being completely good. It did not sound like "I love you." To his ears, it was a sound like "I never wanted to have you."

Estelle had a number of things on her mind as a young woman. She often thought of the loss of her mother and what her life would have been like had her mother lived. She thought of the childhood she missed. She thought of the work she had to put into raising Anise and Harrison Jr., the hardness of her old father, the worked she performed for Mrs. Astor, and now her marriage and three children. Psychologically, she felt tired because she never seemed to have enough time to think about and examine her life before something else entered her mind.

Estelle would sometimes go about her chores and talk aloud to herself; and sometimes she would talk to Seymour, thinking, at his young age, he would not know what she was talking about. One day, Estelle had become upset with thoughts of Albrecht's infidelities while overseas in the military. Out loud, she was chastising him for his past transgressions. She thought of the letters he sent to her with photographs of women he was having affairs with. His justification to Estelle was that when he returned stateside, he would be a better lover to her. She was thinking, *What a crock.*

Estelle went on with her conversation to herself, saying, "Albrecht should have known better. He could have been exposing me to all kinds of sexually transmitted diseases."

As she continued talking to herself, she never considered Seymour understood what she was saying. She went into her bedroom and retrieved the letters and the accompanying photographs. She showed them to Seymour.

Suddenly, out of nowhere, Seymour said, "Why don't you leave him?"

Shocked and stunned that Seymour possibly understood what she was saying, she snatched the letters and pictures from him and sharply retorted, "Shut up, boy! You don't know what you are talking about. You know too much. What do you know about leaving anybody?"

She paused for a few minutes from sheer embarrassment and continued, "Yeah, and if I leave, who is going to take care of you? Just shut your mouth! You don't know whose sash shay shy tut you are going to have to eat before you leave this earth. You may have to eat doodley!"

The only words Seymour heard from his mother's angry chastisement were "and who is going to take care of you?" He learned, in that moment, that Estelle was the hand that was feeding him. He also learned that he was not exempt from her harsh tongue and that Estelle wanted Seymour not to interfere in her conversations. She often repeated "Children are to be seen and not heard" or "Children are to speak when spoken to—otherwise keep your mouth shut!" These were the words she had learned from Harrison Sr.

From then on, Estelle continued to talk to herself in private but never again in front of Seymour. Still enraged, she thought, *That boy. I tell you! You don't ever know what is going to come out of a child's mouth!*

Seymour's feelings were hurt, and he barely said a word to Estelle unless she asked him a question, and then he came up with a minimal answer. And other times, he would just shake his head in reply.

For six years, Estelle bided her time until she could get Seymour in first grade. As she cleaned house and conducted her chores, she would incessantly tell Seymour stories about how poor she was in her childhood. She would tell him how her mother had died when she was ten years old. In Seymour's mind, Estelle was telling him these stories so he would feel sorry for her and to let him know just how lucky he was to have a mother. "I want you to be a grateful child and don't cause me as much heartache as my other two children. I have a near juvenile delinquent son and a cold, nonchalant daughter."

While beautifully caring for her home, Estelle never took Seymour to the playground or for a walk in the park or even took the time to read him a book. Seymour didn't know any different; he was no trouble for Estelle. He would sit still and listen to every word she had to say.

Albrecht would buy Seymour expensive tricycles, wagons, and other toys designed for play outside in the yard; but he remained in close proximity to Estelle. Estelle wondered why Seymour would not go outside to play with his toys. She would say to Seymour, "Don't you want to go outside and play with the other children?" Seymour would shake his head, indicating no. Estelle would shake her head and say, "You are not like my other children. They would be gone, and I would have to run up and down the streets looking for them." In a nonverbal way, Seymour discerned Estelle got pleasure from his wanting to be around her. She thought her other children paid her no mind. On the other hand, she did not want him to be a mother's boy like Harrison Jr.

Mother's boys could turn out to be sissies, she thought. *I do not want a sissy child.*

Estelle did not insist that Seymour go outside and play on his own. To compensate, she would give Seymour a coloring book and some Crayolas. He would sit and entertain himself with the coloring book or a puzzle for hours. Between chores, she would tell him to color within the lines. Sometimes Seymour would put the same puzzle together over and over again, but Estelle could not cajole him to play outside. She felt she did not have the time to play with him. She would say to him, "I can't play with you, boy, because I have roads to go down and too much I have to do!" Taking care of a house was what she was trained to do, and domestic chores were far more important to her. She raised herself independent of a mother, and she thought all children should learn independence. Seymour did not; he was a codependent child. Furthermore, her eye was looking forward to the day she could go to work.

Albrecht never wanted Estelle to work, but since that she was so insistent, he made her agree to stay at home until the children were in first grade. Estelle reluctantly agreed with Albrecht since the little money she would earn could not pay for a babysitter for two children. However, she never gave up her dream of getting a career and having her own money. She never wanted the fear of death associated with going to bed hungry, as she did as a child during the Great Depression. She also knew there were no guarantees on marriage.

She and Seymour peacefully coexisted until it was time for him to go to school.

PART THREE

Seymour's Young Life

Chapter Eighteen

One Family

Estelle was a beautiful housewife. She prepared lovely meals and made a weekly schedule of chores, including laundry in the Blackstone wringer washer, ironing everything from handkerchief to bedsheets, polishing furniture, and washing and waxing the kitchen and bathroom floors on her hands and knees. She even found time to plant zinnias along the front walkway, embellishing the entrance to the front door. Each spring, she also planted a small vegetable garden in the backyard. During the autumn months, she would stand over the hot stove and can string beans, fresh peaches, and bread and butter pickles and bake the most wonderful yeast breads. Albrecht gave her his payroll check, and she managed the house very well, saving a "cent" as Harrison Sr. taught her.

She never gave Albrecht chores to do inside or outside the house that he didn't step up to perform. He would cut the grass, wash and maintain the car, and make all the household repairs—whether electrical, plumbing, or general handyman. In her mind, Estelle thought that if she was a good housewife, Albrecht would someday be willing to buy a house—something she wanted and something he said he never wanted.

On Saturday mornings, Albrecht would sing along with songs from his extensive collection of Broadway musicals. He would sing from *Porgy and Bess*: "I got plenty of nothing, and nothing is plenty for me!" Estelle would keep her mouth shut but would roll her eyes and shake her head. This selection made no sense to her at all. She would think, *I got plenty of nothing! Who ever heard of such a thing?*

As Estelle continued to maintain the house, Seymour was always nearby. He sometimes watched her perform her chores, and sometimes

Estelle would give him little chores so he would have something to do. He performed each of these outstandingly well. Unbeknownst to him, he was being trained in domestic skills.

On weekdays at noon, Estelle would stop her housework to prepare lunch and watch the soap opera *Search for Tomorrow* while heating a can of Campbell's chicken noodle soup for the two of them. She would make a small green salad and serve some saltines. But just as soon as the soap opera was over, the television was turned off. She would then continue with more chores. She would go outside and take down her freshly washed clothes, work the vegetable garden, or cut some fresh zinnias to arrange and place inside the house. She would start dinner and anticipate Aries and Claudia's return from school. Seymour would hear her say, "It is always something to do around this joint!"

Her morning rest and daytime serenity was destroyed when Aries and Claudia arrived home from school at four o'clock. For some reason beyond her thinking, they were always squabbling between themselves. She tried without fail to teach them to get along and explain they were brother and sister, but they never quieted down until Albrecht returned from work. They paid Estelle little or no attention, but they were scared to death of Albrecht.

Aries was fearful of his father but would still try to rebuff Albrecht when he thought he could get away with it. Albrecht was time enough for him. Estelle would yell, scream, and shout like her father to maintain order. She could be strong and assertive with Aries too, but she would tire trying to keep up with his relentless challenges toward her and his childish antics.

One day, Estelle had instructed Aries to take a shower when he returned from school because she could smell his body odor. He had taken physical education classes earlier in the day but had not showered at school before returning home. She said to him as soon after he walked in the door, "You smell awful! Doesn't your physical education teacher make you boys take a shower after playing all those sports?"

Aries, not wanting to take a shower, replied to Estelle, "Yes!"

Estelle then said, "Well, you need another one. Go take a shower!"

Aries always gave Estelle a hard time about taking a bath, and she was getting sick and tired of telling him over and over again about his bathing. He was thirteen years old, and on this day, when she told him to take a bath, he shuffled in the bathroom turned on the water for a shower but did not get underneath the running water.

As Estelle was taking dried clothes off the clotheslines in the backyard, she could see from of the corner of her eye that Aries was not taking a shower as she told him. Instead, he was standing in the bathroom window watching her take down her freshly washed clothes.

She—unnoticed by Aries—quietly stopped what she was doing, returned to the house, and got one of Albrecht's leather belts. She proceeded to the bathroom and opened the bathroom door. Aries was still standing naked in the window, looking out, and the shower water was still running. This was when she commenced to beat Aries across the back, the front, and any place on his body she could hit until he was in the shower with soap and the water was running over him. Aries cried, "Okay, Ma! Okay, Ma!" But Estelle continued to swing the leather belt across his body until she was exhausted.

At the same time, she shouted, "When I tell you, boy, to do something, I mean for you to do it. Stop playing me for a fool. I was not born yesterday!" When she finished whipping Aries, Estelle's instructions were carried out.

When Aries exited the bathroom, he was fresh and clean. She would say to him afterward, "Now don't you feel better now?" But she continued to scold him. "You think I don't mean business when I tell you what to do? I will kill any one of my children if they disrespect me! And I don't plan to tell you this again! When I tell you to do something, I mean for you to do it. You don't pay any rent around here. You are not paying any rent or buying any food. So the very least you can do is cooperate! I am doing my part, and your father is doing his part! And all we want you to do is go to school and get some education in your head! Do you understand?"

Aries replied in one half of his full voice, "Yeah, Ma!"

But Estelle just kept on talking.

When Estelle was in this mood, Claudia would retreat to her bedroom to do her homework; and when she finished, she would remain there and read romance magazines until the air cleared. Seymour would get out of the way too! Seymour could tell that Estelle's mood changed when his brother and sister returned home from school.

Soon thereafter, Albrecht would return home from work. Estelle would have set the table by then and finished completing the dinner. She called the family to the table to eat. Albrecht and Seymour would be there on the spot, but on some occasions, she would get no response from Aries and Claudia. She would make a second attempt with a louder voice to gather Aries and Claudia to the table, and if there was no response, she would shout to the pitch of her voice in loud piercing screams as she marched to the hallway that adjoined their respective bedrooms, saying to them both, "It is bad enough that I have to go to the store and pay for this food, bring the grocery bags in the house, shelf it, cook it, set the table, and then have to beg you niggers to eat it!"

She was steaming hot!

Aries and Claudia hustled themselves to the kitchen table, Claudia moving first and Aries pacing behind. He was still pouting from his bathing lecture. It helped that Albrecht had come home from work to gain a little cooperation for Estelle. She was livid with having to repeat herself with these two children. Seymour, who said nothing, was saddened to see his mother in this state. He had watched her work hard all day around the house with little time for herself. Aries's and Claudia's attitudes registered to him as unappreciative and ungrateful. It also appeared that the two of them would stick together to deliberately agitate Estelle.

Being so close to Estelle and at home all day, he almost always agreed with his mother, even when she was loud and angry. He thought his sister and brother should have complied. They knew she was not going to tolerate insubordination and would become argumentative, but they persisted as some teenagers do. Seymour enjoyed the peace and quiet of the house before they returned home from school.

As the years passed and Seymour was closer to going to first grade, a used black Royal typewriter appeared on the red chrome and vinyl kitchen table. Estelle had purchased the typewriter with money she had saved. She practiced typing during the day, when Albrecht was at work and Aries and Claudia were at school. She needed to type sixty words per minute to pass the government typing test. It had been some years since she had taken typing in high school. Seymour was five years old now, and he could go to school next year. It took some time to procure a government job, and she wanted to be assured she could walk out the door to work on the same day Seymour started his first day of school—or if not then as close a time as possible.

The vacancy announcements for clerk-typist came in the Fort Anderson mail. She wanted to get a head start. Albrecht was not going to be happy, but she had determined for herself that she had sacrificed all she was going to for Albrecht's primitive ideas of women staying at home to care for him and the children. She was from Washington, DC, where women were going to college, working, and being good housewives too. She would practice her typing in the afternoon after completing her household work. Attention to her gardens and other nonessential household touches had to wait until the weekend, if they got done at all.

Estelle took the first typing test and failed. She took the test a second time and failed. On the third and final attempt, she passed and was offered a job immediately. This was her chance to go to work as she had planned. She had plans to save for a new house in Kirkland Park, where the Kirkland College faculty and staff resided, as well as upwardly mobile blacks and schoolteachers from the public schools.

Although Estelle did not have a college degree, this was the kind of environment she aspired to. This kind of neighborhood was the type she was exposed to while living with the Astors. With her fair complexion and Washington, DC, exposure to high-end whites and blacks, she thought this was where she wanted to live. She figured her proposed friends and neighbors did not know of her family background, and she thought she had enough (if not more) common sense as anybody. She had hopes of Aries straightening up, and her first- and second-born could go to college—an opportunity she never had. As a teenager, she had dreamed of going to college locally, but her father made her work to supplement the household income. He, like Albrecht, did not believe women needed a career other than domestic work. At that time, she was a child. She was saddened, but what could she do? This was her lost opportunity for a college education, but she would give her children a chance.

On the same day that Estelle was offered the job as clerk-typist at Fort Anderson, she received a telephone call from a mental hospital informing her that her sister, Anise, had a nervous breakdown and was admitted. They further informed Estelle they wanted to prevent Anise's son, Antwan, from being placed in foster care. They were reaching out to family members who could care for the young child while his mother was in treatment.

They informed Estelle that they first attempted to reach his father, but they failed to find him. Then the hospital traced Harrison Sr., but he was recovering from a second heart attack. They then reached out for Harrison Jr. and learned he was away in the military to subsidize his sick father. The voice on the other end of the telephone asked, "Will you accept this child, Mrs. Rose?"

Estelle lived fifty miles away; she was married with three dependent children and was unemployed. She was the next of kin. And with heartbreak in her soul, she knew this meant that she had to decline another job offer she had prepared for and which she had waited seven years to obtain. Further, she did not want to place the added responsibility on Albrecht and the children in the tiny apartment they shared. Although the apartment had three small bedrooms, they were already cramped. She did not want to accept this responsibility, but then the voice on the telephone again asked, "Will you accept?"

Estelle covered the telephone receiver and explained to Albrecht the situation, and he, without hesitation, said it was okay. Estelle's eyes were tearing, but she replied to the caller, "Yes, I accept." She hung up the telephone, went to her bedroom, and cried. She thought of how hard she had practiced to type sixty words a minute and how difficult it would be to retain this skill level.

The next day, she called the personnel office to inform them that she could not accept the job she was offered, crying and explaining her situation to the personnel officer. The personnel officer said to Estelle, "Well, I have heard of women crying because they had to go to work, but I have never heard of a woman crying because she wanted to go work!" She continued, "Since you passed your typing test, we will keep you on the eligibility list for one year, and if your circumstances change, you may reapply and not be required to take the typing test again. How is that, Mrs. Rose?"

Estelle wiped her eyes and said, "Okay! Thank you!" She hung up the telephone with defeat in her soul. She thought to herself, *I am still taking care of Anise. She is a grown woman. I am telling you, you never get finished with children.*

She was not happy, but she did what she thought was the Christian thing to do. Two generations of family are inextricably tied.

Chapter Nineteen

Mental Breakdown

After Sequester Toms deserted Anise, she could not cope with the loss of the man of her dreams, the loss of her beautifully furnished apartment, and the need now to get a job to take care of herself and raise a young child on her own. She lost it.

Estelle was compassionate toward Anise's helpless child, but she was not as patient with her sister's decisions, immaturity, and being so naïve. Although Harrison Sr. was hard and sometimes downright cruel to his children as far as Estelle was concerned, at least his sternness made common sense to her. But with Anise, it did not appear she had heard anything he had said; and rather than listen to her father, she rejected everything he said out of her dislike of him. Estelle thought everybody has something that is good. Anise did the direct opposite to be contrary, and when the shit hit the fan, she and Harrison Jr. always looked to Estelle for resolution.

Estelle's first thought was that Anise had no business running away from home at the age of seventeen. She was not prepared to make such a move. Estelle thought she left home "half-cocked." Secondly, it was foolish to voluntarily choose living in unsanitary conditions with their Aunt Clara, who had a notorious reputation for being a dirty housekeeper. Mrs. Astor had provided a perfectly good home, even if they were called domestics. Third, by moving in with Aunt Clara, she contracted tuberculosis even when warned by Estelle, Aunt Clara, and her father to stay away from the home of her best girlfriend, where TB was found. Fourth, she should have never married a man she did not know. It was way too soon. And fifth, why would she get pregnant when her husband specifically says to her up front, "I don't want any children until I make lieutenant." She wished Albrecht had said that to her. *No children!* Instead, he wanted as many as would make him feel manly. Anise frustrated Estelle as an adult at this point; she thought Anise should be getting some sense.

Estelle would preach to Anise, "Why do you continue to make poor choices when you know better? Yes, Father was mean to us, but that is no excuse for you to behave senselessly. He taught us better than that, Anise." Estelle did not know it, but in her heart, Anise and Harrison Jr. remained her responsibility. She would get as frustrated with her sister as she would with her own children. She was getting tired of helping Anise clean up the messes she created. Estelle thought she and Albrecht were struggling to get on their feet, and she no longer had the time to keep helping her sister, but she did. She made the time.

Estelle never realized while she was pregnant with Seymour and had lamented constantly about not wanting to have this child that Aries and Claudia were also lamenting the baby too. In expressing her unhappiness for the unwanted unborn child, they too felt the impact of the new baby to their lives in what they felt was an already completed family. They did not want Seymour either. Estelle tried to give Aries and Claudia everything she never had as a child and would have wanted for herself, but they had become spoiled, selfish, and self-centered. They were the first two grandchildren: Aries the first boy and Claudia the first girl. Claudia was the baby and a girl. They both knew that with this new baby, it would take away some of the attention they enjoyed. Claudia would no longer be the baby. Aries would have to share a bedroom. Estelle would let them rub her stomach while she was pregnant, but in their minds, this was an unwelcome child.

When Anise's son, Antwan, was moved into Albrecht and Estelle's apartment, Estelle moved Seymour out of the bedroom he was sharing with Aries and made him sleep in the bedroom with his sister. Although Claudia did not like the arrangement and wanted her room to herself, Seymour, on the other hand, was happy to be separated from his brother. Aries was a holy terror toward him, who abused and ridiculed him in every way he could. Aries was already upset when Seymour outgrew his baby crib that had been in the bedroom with Estelle and Albrecht. Estelle purchased bunk beds to place in the bedroom that was once Aries's alone. It also made Aries jealous that Claudia got to maintain a room of her own when he did not have equal. Aries didn't like sharing with his baby brother, Seymour. He hated even more the thought of sleeping in the room with his cousin Antwan. Aries thought his baby brother was the better of the two, but now it was too late.

Aries was spoiled and had behaviors identical to Harrison Sr., his grandfather. Estelle had to referee the situation with Antwan's arrival. This arrangement was the best she could do for the time being. She had attempted to break Aries of his selfishness, but it was too late in the game for him. Albrecht remained calm through it all and admired Estelle's management of the new circumstances. He believed families should take care of each other during difficult times.

Now that Antwan had moved in, Aries hated him more than Seymour and tormented him mercilessly. Every word that came out of his mouth, Aries imitated with sounds like a whiny baby. Antwan was a whiny child.

Anise had spoiled her son to compensate for his not having a father. Aries—knowing that Estelle did not tolerate whining from her children—took it upon himself to imitate him to encourage Estelle to chastise him as she had done with her own children. Estelle saw Antwan as a temporary guest and would let him be himself. Estelle did not want it said that she was unkind to her sister's child. She said nothing to Antwan. This did not bode well with Aries, and thus he continued to bully Antwan when Estelle was not around.

Seymour being assigned to sleep with his sister did not work out as well as he thought. Claudia was now thirteen and beginning to become aware of her sexuality. Seymour would be awakened in the middle of the night with his sister gyrating the center of her body against Seymour's buttocks and making a desperate sound. He did not know what was happening to her or him, but she was holding him tight, and eventually, the sounds would disappear as quickly as they had come.

Estelle would fill the car with gas and visit Anise every two weeks at the mental hospital. Along the way, she stopped for the purpose of putting water in the radiator and checked the tire pressure. She referred to the car as "this old heap!" She did not mind taking this outing to the hospital. It was an opportunity to get out of the house and away from the children. She would enjoy the car radio and the quiet time.

Aries and Claudia were teenagers now and had their own friends, but every time the car moved, Seymour was in it with Estelle. She would ask, hoping to discourage him from going with her and to force him to make friends. She would say, "Don't you want to stay at home and play with children your own age? You know they are not going to let you come into the hospital because you are too young. You will have to sit in the car by yourself." Seymour did not care. He would not let go of his mother and would reply, "No, I want to go with you."

Estelle hoped he would soon grow out of this stage he was going through, but for the time being, she would give in and say, "Well, put on some presentable clothes and get ready. I will be leaving shortly." She would drop Antwan off at his godmother's house, who was more than kind to give Estelle a few hours of relief from him during the weekend. She did not have children of her own. She had hoped Anise would have let him live with her rather than Estelle.

Anise recovered after six months of treatment. The hospital assisted her in getting a job as a stenographer, whereby she could take care of herself and her child. Estelle continued to visit Anise at her small two-room apartment after her treatments. She visited Anise like clockwork. She tried to keep her calm and focused so that she would not suffer another breakdown. Estelle would also try to be reasonable with her and try to talk some sense into her head. Whenever Estelle visited, she would tuck a few extra dollars in her hands as she departed, just as she had seen Mrs. Astor do many times for her daughters. She would tell Anise, "This is money I had pinched off the food money from Albrecht's pay. You know I am not working yet." Anise would say "thank you" but remained a whinner, frail, and sickly, just as she was as a child. Although Estelle helped out when she could, she remained impatient with her sister at times, but she never gave up her devotion.

Getting her children adjusted was difficult; the new household circumstances were difficult. She had compassion for the mentally ill.

CHAPTER TWENTY

Seymour to First Grade

Fort Anderson retained Estelle's passing typing score for one year. She reapplied and was offered a position with the medical labs. The happiness and glee she felt when offered the job initially was not the same as it was when offered now, but she rallied her spirits and started to work as she had longed for since leaving home and marrying. She began with an entry-level job; however, a medical lab was not her first choice since he hated blood and guts, but she took the first thing she could get since she could transfer later. She only had to type about blood and guts; she did not have to engage in medical testing.

Transitioning Seymour from being at home all day with her to first grade was traumatic for him, but Estelle knew he could make it. He had to make it because she was going to work whether he made it or not. The poor child, she thought, had been at home with his mother all of his little life. He had been up under her feet with every move she made. She had not taught him the basics for entering the first grade. All he knew was his coloring books, puzzles, and housework. He was not close to his father or siblings and had no childhood friends. He was not academically or socially prepared for first grade. He had never been around other children his age.

Before school started, Estelle took Seymour to the pediatric clinic to get his immunizations. She looked Seymour in the eye and said, "Now you are going to get two needles in your arm, and it is going to hurt. But I don't want you falling out, crying and acting like a fool like some of these other children in the project. I want you to be a big boy and take your shots like you have good sense, like I taught you. You are Estelle Rose's child." She hoisted Seymour to her lap as the nurse injected the shots one after the other. Seymour flinched and the nurse said, "Don't move!" Then she stuck the first needle in his arm, wiped it with a cotton gauze, then applied the second shot, wiped with a cotton gauze, and placed a Band-Aid over it and said, "Next!" Just as the day of his birth, he did not cry, but it was the most painful thing he had ever experienced.

As Estelle walked her little boy back to the house, she said, "You are a brave little fellow. I did not want you acting like some of those crazy children who are screaming and hollering like they did not have a lick of sense! You were a good boy! Now I am going to take you home and we will have some hot lunch, and you will take a nap until the pain wears off. When you wake up, it will be all over."

A few days later, Estelle drove Seymour to school for the first two days of first grade; but she kept telling him repeatedly each day that on the third day, he had to take the school bus with the other children. She said, "They are not going to harm you, so don't be afraid. Just sit in your seat and look out the window and look at the trees and cars along the way." Estelle knew Seymour was sheltered and without a friend in the world except her. She wanted him to grow up because it was past time for him to move on to the next stage of his development, but it pained her as much as him when the time arrived.

Estelle escorted Seymour to his classroom and introduced him to his first-grade teacher, Ms. Albright. Seymour turned to his mother with tears in his eyes and an expression on his face. "Don't leave me?" But Estelle knew she had to do this for her sake and his sake and turned him back toward the teacher and pushed him gently to his teacher and said, "Go ahead now. I am just going to be down the hall, and I will be waiting for you when your classes are completed." In Seymour's soul, he knew he had to do this for his mother. He knew she had practiced her typing and really wanted to work, and he knew she was tired of being at home with him. He knew he had to do this, and so he let go of her hand and went with his teacher.

Ms. Albright had never witnessed such a separation in her years of teaching. Usually, her children were always happy to come to school and get away from home. She was not happy with Estelle for sheltering her child this long and not creating some form of socialization for him. He was much too codependent for a boy this age.

In the few days of the school year, Ms. Albright divided the class into three reading groups: A, B, and C. Seymour was assigned to the "B" group. The assignment was a compliment to Estelle because Ms. Albright also taught Aries and Claudia years earlier. Seymour belonged in the "C" group because he had not been prepared for the first grade as she had instructed Estelle to do before bringing Seymour to school. This meant she had to devote more time to Seymour than some of the other children who were prepared. Ms. Albright was not pleased with Estelle because it meant more work for her.

Estelle had not taken the time with Seymour because she thought all her children were smart. Claudia was an honor student, and Aries was smart also; but she knew he was lazy, just like her father, Harrison Sr. "Just like my father!" she would say. She thought Seymour would catch on quickly, but instead, Seymour remained paralyzed most of the school year, showing little interest and minimal improvements. Ms. Albright thought Seymour was spoiled. She would call him to her desk and severely crack him in the palms of his hands for simply opening his mouth to another student in class during quiet time.

Seymour did not like Ms. Albright, and he would tell Estelle every time he was cracked on the hands with the yardstick. Estelle did not like Seymour being hit by the teacher. It reminded her of her father's punishments to Harrison Jr. Ms. Albright was frustrated with Estelle for not preparing the child for first grade. Estelle continued to dislike the thoughts of someone hitting her Seymour because he was the most unlikely child to cause her any serious problems.

Ms. Albright asked the class to go outside to the playground and divide up into two groups. When the two groups were formed, Seymour was standing with the girls. But before Ms. Albright came to the playground, one of the girl students said, "Seymour, I think you belong over there with the boys." This saved him humiliation from Ms. Albright, but he was labeled that day in first grade as a mother's boy and a sissy. Just like his mother telling him she did not want him, he knew the comments from the boys were not compliments. He did not know what his mother had meant, nor did he know what the first-grade boys meant. He was certain it was not a compliment, and it did not make him feel very good.

Seymour stood out in school for other reasons too. Estelle dressed him as if he was going to private schools that required uniforms. She dressed him in white shirts and gray flannel slacks. His hair was closely cut every two weeks without fail, his slacks had fresh creases, and his skin was shiny from cleansing and skin lotion. Aries teased and ridiculed him each morning before going to school with comments like "You look like Little Lord Fauntroy" or "You look like a greased pig." This hurt Seymour's feelings, but he just learned to ignore his brother. Estelle had taught him to kill his enemies with kindness, so this is what he thought he was doing, but his feelings were still hurt.

It did not help to report these hurtful comments to Estelle for the long haul because when she got tired of hearing Seymour complain, she would say, "Well, you don't want to grow up and be a tattletale." In reality, Estelle did not want to take the time to discipline Aries again and again. He was her most problematic child, and she did not have the time to keep pace with his persistent annoyances. Further, she thought it was time for Seymour to learn to stick up for himself. Aries was his brother and a good starting point. As a poor girl with no mother to run home to, she had to learn to defend herself from far worse. Seymour understood Estelle but never understood or forgave Aries for his persistent bullying insults that grew with each passing year to a level of childhood hate.

It did not help that the military school bus Seymour would ride on to school was green camouflage, and his classmates said, "Your school bus looked like baby-shit green!" It was the first bus in the lineup of all yellow school buses. The military children received first priority. First-priority busing made the other students feel less than equal. To even the score, they ridiculed the color of the bus and the students who boarded the bus.

As Seymour was promoted over the years in school, his classmates continued to tease and mock him about his mannerisms and attire. It became increasing more difficult to take the childhood abuses from his classmates. The children would say, "Hey, Matt! Look at Seymour switching up and down the hall like a girl."

When Seymour's art teacher would hear the students picking on him, he would chastise Seymour. The teacher would say, "Seymour! I don't see how you can take all of that bullying. Maybe you should try walking on your heels instead of your toes." Between the students and the teacher, Seymour somehow endured the taunts and comments without becoming the jackasses he thought they were.

Seymour was just a sore thumb and had learned all of Estelle's feminine speech and gestures. In some ways, Seymour was socially ahead of the rural children in that both of his parents were urban and were exposed to a broader cross-section of life and culture. Albrecht's exposure to Catholic schools and Estelle's exposure to Washington, DC, resulted in them thinking with liberal attitudes. His parents gave Seymour a better edge in school in many respects. He was tall and easy on the eyes. Estelle kept him dressed in the best department store clothes, and these distinctions provided some insulation from the hurt he felt inside. Aries and Claudia wanted to fit in with the rural children, but Seymour liked being distinctive.

Seymour eventually learned to stick up for himself. In addition to being tall, he was strong and held a physical advantage over children his size. But he remained physically disadvantaged to his older brother, and he maintained his fear and disdain for him.

Although Seymour learned he looked good and was overdressed for the school he attended, he never asked Estelle to change anything about the clothing she selected for him. He was comfortable with his appearance. If, by chance, he weakened from the practical jokes for a day and complained, Estelle would just simply say, "Sticks and stones will break your bones, but words can never hurt you!" She never supported Seymour's hurt feelings regardless of how slighted he felt. She responded in kind to Seymour as her father had responded to her. She had learned from her childhood that those experiences toughened you up for the real world, and a boy needed to be tough. She would say, "Nobody feels sorry for you in this world. This is a dog-eat-dog world. You just have to toughen up! My father used to say to us, 'Lay me down and bleed a while, and get up and try again!'" She laughed at what her father taught her, but she saw the wisdom in his antiquated aphorisms.

Seymour managed to get promoted from first grade to second grade and beyond, although Ms. Albright wanted to hold him back one year. Estelle and Ms. Albright's friendship ended over the dispute.

CHAPTER TWENTY-ONE

Cake Cutting

Every Sunday, Estelle made two cakes to serve as dessert after dinner for the week. Since it did not make any difference to Albrecht what kind she made, she would make a special cake for Aries and a special cake for Claudia.

In that the two older children always fought over which cake was to be cut first, Estelle knew Aries and Claudia would be squabbling over the two cakes, so she made Albrecht responsible for serving the dessert. To compromise, Albrecht would alternate the cakes every other day so that each child could have a slice of cake to their liking.

Aries was consistently the first of the three children to start begging to cut the cake before the dinner was finished. He would rush through eating his meal and rush Claudia and Seymour to hurry and finish their meals so that the cake could be cut sooner. Since he was the oldest, he felt entitled to cut the cake and have the largest slice. He attempted to nag Albrecht to take the cake from atop the refrigerator, but Albrecht would simply reply, "Aries, if you don't sit down, shut your mouth, and let the rest of us finish dinner, you will get nothing!" Aries would jerk around in his kitchen chair and, halfway, sit still, waiting. Albrecht's words did not subdue his desire to cut the cake. He would dance around in his seat like a happy clown in his anticipation to cut the cake.

Albrecht knew his son, and if allowed, Aries would cut the cake, and Claudia and Seymour would get little or nothing. Finally, after everyone completed their meal and there was a reasonable period of time for digestion, Albrecht decided to see if his son had changed his selfish ways. He allowed Aries cut the cake.

Albrecht planned to oversee the cutting. Aries, in typical fashion, cut an extra-large slice for himself, a medium slice for Claudia, and a sliver for Seymour. At the conclusion of Aries's cake cutting, he would reach for the largest slice of the cake, but Albrecht would calmly say, "Aries, put down the knife and take your hands away from the cake."

Aries would get furious and say "but, Dad."

Albrecht said, "Aries, sit back in your chair." Then he'd say to Seymour, "You have first choice of which slice you want."

Aries froze as Seymour quickly selected the larger slice, the slice Aries had intended for himself.

Then Albrecht said, "Now, Claudia, you select the next piece."

She smiled and selected the middle slice. She was never a greedy child and liked to maintain her weight, so she was happy with the middle slice.

Then Albrecht said, "Now, Aries, you get the piece that is left."

Aries was heart-broken that he did not get the slice he intended for himself.

Albrecht then said, "The next time I let you cut the cake, you will learn how to cut it fairly!"

Aries was totally deflated with his father's command and the sliver of cake he received. In his defeat, he said, "I don't see why Seymour gets the biggest piece when he is the littlest."

Albrecht swiftly snatched the sliver of cake from Aries and said, "Well, now you have nothing. And maybe the next time, you will also learn to keep your mouth shut! Leave the table!"

Albrecht was a leader to soldiers in the military, and Aries was no contest to him, ever. Although Albrecht was teaching Aries a lesson, Seymour always got the resulting repercussions from Aries's anger and hostility at a later time. He would knock Seymour alongside the head when no one was looking or wake Seymour in the middle of the night by rubbing feathers over his face or pulling the blankets from the foot of the bed. With Aries, there was always a price when he did not get his way, and it was regularly taken out on Seymour or Claudia.

Seymour, for a moment in time, thoroughly enjoyed the chunk of cake and thought to himself that Aries's greed worked to his advantage for a few minutes.

CHAPTER TWENTY-TWO

Career Launched

Estelle had known work all her life—both at home with her father and with her husband and children—but she never had money of her own. She wanted her own money! Now thirty-five years old, she landed an entry-level job at Fort Anderson. She had struggled through opposition after opposition to get a job where money landed in her pocket and would not be taken away as her father had done or dished out by her husband. Her father had kept the money she earned. When she first got married, Bessie would not keep Aries when he was born so that she could work. Albrecht didn't want her to work. Her pregnancies kept her from working, and her sister's mental health forced her to keep another child. Estelle's employment had been limited to the bakery, babysitting, and taking in ironing. It all boiled down to domestic work.

When Estelle was offered the job at Fort Anderson, Albrecht refused to allow her to ride with him to work, although Estelle's new work was just a few minutes away from Albrecht's work site. His denial of transportation was his protest to Estelle's working against his wishes. Estelle was determined to work regardless of his opinion. She had decided to board the military bus designated for civilians. She traveled each day to and from work on the bus due to Albrecht's dislikes. She thought, "Men!"

Estelle did not give a hoot or a toot about Albrecht's refusal to give her transportation. It would have been easier for Estelle to ride with her husband; but in her mind, she wanted her own money. And in the back of her mind, she considered she had put up with Albrecht's wayward ways and never knew if one day he would come home and tell her he wanted to be with another woman. From an intelligent angle, she thought he was being totally asinine. She decided she was not going to put up with that from any man. If his disapproval meant she had a price to pay for going to work, then so be it. She had been a good wife, and she had made enough sacrifices over the years to accommodate his desires. It was her turn, and she was taking it.

She took the bus each morning and returned and never asked Albrecht for a ride, although they departed home at almost the same time each day. The car she purchased with his allotment money was parked in front of their apartment. This was the car he scolded her from purchasing, stating, "We don't need a car." Albrecht was not known to be an unreasonable man, but his insecurity made him feel less of a man. Having "his" Estelle work outside of the home made him feel less than a man and gave the appearance he needed his wife to work because he could not take care of his family. Men in the neighborhood and at his job would assuredly have warned him: "Before long, she is going to think she is wearing the pants around the house. Wait and see." Albrecht remembered the ribbing he received from the military guys regarding infidelity, and this new ribbing did not feel any better.

To gain sympathy for himself, Albrecht voiced to Estelle what the men on the job were saying about him. Estelle felt no sympathy. Estelle dismissed the comments the men were making because it was not her intention to wear the pants in the house. She had come from a place where the people were still living in the dark ages. She thought Albrecht's insecurities were ridiculous because he should have had good enough sense to know that he was a good husband and provider and that she was a respectable wife and mother. Why on earth should he give a tinker's damn about what some unconscious, timeworn old men had to say? She told him just that!

Estelle started her new job and hoped her days of nightmares of being hungry or homeless would be put to rest, alongside the thoughts of being deserted as her sister had been. She remembered her childhood and the death of her mother, the days of the Great Depression, and her father putting her out to do the days' work before and after school to help keep a roof over the family. Estelle became matriarch when her mother died. This federal job was a mental relief for her because not only would she get a salary, she would get health benefits and a retirement annuity. This was an insurance in and of itself and in the event Albrecht decided to divorce her, as she had seen happen many times. She and her children could make it on their own. Love and marriage simply did not offer guarantees, and she wanted to be prepared.

Every morning, before sending the children to school, Estelle would have them in a line from youngest to oldest, and she would give each child a generous dose of Scott's Emulsion and cod liver oil. She wanted to ensure that they would not get sick, which would cause them to miss school. And, moreover, she would need to take leave from her job to come home and take care of them. She was in a probationary period, and she felt lucky just to get the job. Seymour got out of school an hour earlier than Aries and Claudia; thus she had to make arrangements for someone to watch him for a few hours until she got home.

As Estelle progressed in her position, she got in the full swing of accumulating the material possessions she had longed for. And between her income and Albrecht's income, they lived a solid middle-class lifestyle. Estelle's plan also included stashing away reserve money for old age; she knew an annuity alone was not enough with increasing inflation. She had seen over and over during the Great Depression how old people, black and white, were mistreated by their children when their money ran out; and the elderly did not have the ability to take care of themselves.

She thought of her father and how unprepared he was for old age, having to rely on the child he mistreated most. Her father's poor health and old age forced Harrison Jr. to enter the military to send money to their father for subsistence. Estelle did not want to find herself in the same predicament. At last, she had a secure job, and she planned to work hard to keep it.

CHAPTER TWENTY-THREE

Getting Even

After Anise ran away to Baltimore and Estelle followed, Harrison Sr. and Harrison Jr. were now living together and were no longer working for the Astors. The two men fought like cats and dogs. After completing his enlistment, Harrison Jr. was in the best physical shape ever. He procured a federal civilian job. He saved some money for himself, even after sending an allotment to his father for three years.

After having the time away in the military, he reflected on his life and all the years he had spent in church as a child and decided he no longer believed in God or in organized religion. He wondered why God would give him such a mean and hateful father.

He decided, as a working adult, he was no longer putting up with his father's physical and emotional abuse or his father's lack of appreciation of his working alongside his sisters contributing to the maintenance of the family. Upon his return from the military, he found his father had not changed during the years he was away. He remained outspoken and cruel.

Harrison Jr. took a stand and said to his father, "Got dammit! I am taking care of you, nigger! You are no longer going to talk to me that way!" He was angry. He spewed hatred and contempt for his father and said again, "You don't talk to me that way, old man! I am taking care of you! Understand?"

The hatred filled the room with Harrison Jr.'s words. As his eyes bulged, he continued shouting to his father. He recounted all the times his father forced him to wear dresses for not being as smart as Estelle and Anise. He recounted how his father had placed him and his sisters out to work as child laborers and stealing their earned money to support his lazy ass. He spoke of how hard it was for him to get a job decent enough to support himself because his father did not allow him to finish high school. "I hate you, old man. And I want you to know I hate you! You are an old, mean, sick bastard! That's what you are!"

In his younger days, Harrison Sr. would have never tolerated such insolence and disrespect from any of his children and would have whipped them within an inch of their lives—both day and night if necessary—for punishment. However, the tide had taken a decisive turn, and Harrison Jr. inflicted on his father the same abuse that his father inflicted on him as well as Estelle and Anise.

There was nothing that Harrison Sr. could say or do. He was too old now to defend himself from the verbal assaults of his son.

Harrison Jr. continued to support him and take care of him in his old age, but he never let his father forget how despicable he was as a father. When he visited Anise and Estelle in their respective homes, he bragged and gloated about how good he felt at expressing his rage, cursing his father for himself and in behalf of his sisters. He felt proud, and he felt manly for the first time toward his father. He was no longer a child and vulnerable to his father, and he let off a lifetime of rage toward his father.

Estelle was appalled. She agreed wholeheartedly that her father had mistreated his children, but nobody deserved to be mistreated so harshly. Harrison Jr. cared liked his sister, but he cared less as to what she had to say on the topic of their father. Harrison Jr. did not realize that what he was doing to his father had become a lifestyle. He had become the person he most hated. Their relationship was irreparable.

Harrison Jr. was never able to marry or have children. He was so bitter with God and his father. He became a very unpleasant person to be around. In his childhood, he had been born the most kind and sensitive human being, his mother. He thought he was getting even with his father but had destroyed himself in the process.

Chapter Twenty-Four

First Burn, Brother Hate

Estelle could feel the toll of her new job and her ability to care for the house and children as she once had, but she and Albrecht were making the adjustments. After a year or two of pouting about Estelle working, he eventually succumbed to giving Estelle a ride to work with him in the morning and picking her up in the evenings. Occasionally, the two of them would go out for an evening together, to a cabaret or house party. They both loved each other and tried to keep the marriage alive.

They could not afford—nor did they believe in—babysitters coming into their home. They instead tried to teach responsibility to the children and leave them alone for three or four hours, providing delicatessen submarines, french fries, and Coca-Colas to eat in their absence along with a telephone number of their whereabouts, trusting they would not kill each other or destroy the house. The foods they left were an incentive for the children to behave themselves until they returned. It was a treat for them because Estelle never purchased any of these foods.

Albrecht would leave stern instructions that no one was allowed in the house, no cooking on the gas stove, and there would be no use of the telephone just in case he or Estelle needed to call home. They did not want to find that the line was busy. Seymour was to be in bed at 8:00 PM, and Aries and Claudia were to be in bed by 9:00 PM. Seymour never had to be told to go to bed; he went on his own.

No sooner had Albrecht and Estelle shut the front door to enjoy an evening out with each other, Aries would assert his authority. He would stand in the middle of the living room floor and say in an authoritative voice to Claudia and Seymour, "I am the oldest, and I am in charge of the two of you, and you will do everything I tell you to do!" He would imitate the behavior of Harrison Sr. (his grandfather), which Estelle used on him. His victims were Claudia and Seymour. Claudia was one year younger and would ignore Aries's boisterousness, but it inevitably would lead to physical violence on her. She would try hard to defend herself from her older brother, but she was no match for his brutish force. She would try and try again, only to lose.

Seymour, seven years old, was defenseless to both his brother and sister. They were teenagers, and the thought of their fighting frightened him. He had seen Aries push Claudia through a sheetrock wall that led to Claudia crying from hitting her head on the wall and the abrasions on her back. She also had welts on her arms from where he grabbed her to shove her into a wall. She tried hard not to cry. Seymour was terrified from observing this violence toward Claudia. He could not defend his sister, and he did not know if he was next on Aries's violent streak if he had defended her. Aries was a very broad and strong teen.

One Saturday evening, Albrecht and Estelle were out for a few hours, never more than a few blocks away. Claudia was boiling water for hot tea—a small pleasure she enjoyed. As the water was coming to a rapid boil, Aries stormed into the kitchen, scaring the hell out of everybody, and told Claudia she was not allowed to light the stove. He demanded that she discontinue boiling the water for her tea. When Claudia refused, he proceeded to turn off the gas range. Claudia reached to turn it back on. Aries grabbed her hard as he could and told her, "Cut off the got dam stove like I told you! I told you to turn it off, and I mean for you to turn it off! You are going to do what I tell you to do!"

Seymour heard the threatening commotion from the living room and ran to Claudia's aid. He tried to get between the two of them to prevent Aries from fighting Claudia and to keep it from escalating to a full-blown brawl between them. In Seymour's attempt to rescue Claudia from Aries's attack, the pot of boiling water got knocked off the gas stove and the scalding water burned Seymour's entire back. Without a second's hesitation, Seymour let out a scream that the entire neighborhood could hear, and the next-door neighbors contacted Albrecht and Estelle to tell them to come home immediately because Seymour was screaming endlessly.

Seymour was the most innocent and good-natured of Albrecht and Estelle's children, and the least deserving of mistreatment. When they returned home, they were outraged at what they saw. Estelle commenced into a screaming fit and proceeded to lecture both Aries and Claudia, knowing full well that if it was not Aries's fault—at the very least, he had something to do with it and was the most likely culprit. This was his pattern. She said, "The older you children get, the dumber you get!"

Under the usual circumstances, Estelle yelled and screamed at her children as their discipline and punishment; but when she saw the extent of Seymour's burns, she eventually went mute to keep from exploding. She thought to herself, *I did not want to have this child, but I never wanted anything to happen to him.* This thought was never transmitted to Aries and Claudia because they assumed, from listening to their mother's lamenting about having this child, it was okay for them to not like him too. They cared nothing of Seymour. Similar to Estelle, they never talked to him, read him a book, played a game with him, or showed him any interest.

Estelle dutifully nursed Seymour's burned back with gauze and Vaseline every four hours as the scabs formed on his back, leaving permanent burn marks. She would gently smooth a stick of butter over the pus-filled scabs to even out the coloring of his brown skin and further remove the stubborn gauze. Seymour cried with each application and continuously cried even when it did not hurt too bad just to illuminate the vile nature of Aries toward his siblings. He had always feared his brother, but now, wounded and helpless, his fears escalated, never knowing when the next episode would erupt. His brother was always angry. It appeared to Seymour nobody had the time or took the time to figure out what was wrong with this child.

After each dressing of Seymour's burned back, Estelle thought, *This is why I did not want another child.* She was sick and tired of wrestling with the first two children. She had practically raised Anise and Harrison Jr. Albrecht was of no help when it came to caring for the sick. He had a weak stomach and could not look at Seymour's burns. He historically said old people and sick people made him sick to his stomach. As good as he was as a person, caring for the sick was not his strong suit. Estelle did not want to ask her supervisor if she could take leave from work to nurse Seymour back to health since she had not completed her probationary period, but she did. Seymour had to miss school, and she did not want that to happen either. Ms. Albright was already upset with Estelle for not properly prepping the child for first grade. But this is how it all played out. She just thought, *Well, isn't this a fine how-do-you do!*

After things had settled down and everybody got their nerves back together, Claudia supported Aries in his violence toward her and reported to Albrecht and Estelle it was an accident. She was fearful of being abused later by Aries for not taking his side of the situation. Aries got away scot-free. In addition, she was just as guilty of lighting the kitchen stove to make tea, so she had to save her neck too. They were in cahoots and lied together.

Seymour heard Estelle say to Aries in a calm voice, "I think you owe Seymour an apology. Go in there [bedroom] and apologize."

Fear swept through Seymour as he heard his brother enter the room. Aries was a bully and never apologized to anyone, including his mother and father; but he followed Estelle's directive and did what he was told. This time, he knew he screwed up big time, if for no other reason than he felt Albrecht favored Seymour. Aries did not know if it was because Seymour was the baby or because this was Albrecht's favorite child. He knew it was something special about Seymour that neither he, Estelle, nor Claudia had with Albrecht.

This was an apology Seymour knew his brother would not want to make, but due to the magnitude of the trouble he was in, he slowly approached the top of the bunk bed and said, "I am sorry." No introduction, no salutation, or sincerity—just "I am sorry."

Seymour was mute, and whether the apology was sincere or not, he vowed to hate his brother forever. He thought, *How many times does a person have to be forgiven—when you have forgiven and forgiven again—before you cut ties?*

Seymour also vowed to never have children for fear they would be like his brother. He thought in his young mind, if he had been a father to a teenager like Aries, his heart would always be broken.

CHAPTER TWENTY-FIVE

Second Burn, Deeper Hate

As Estelle continued to nurse Seymour's burned back, she was still fuming in her mind about Aries and his association with the incident. She knew her child's behaviors were bad, but this time, he had taken it too far and she did not like it. She loved Aries because he was her first child and she could see so much of her father and herself in him. It was a mystery to her how traits from one generation were passed on to the next generation. On the other side of the coin, he was a difficult child to rear. She would say in sadness, "That child got the worst of both sides of the family."

As part of her ongoing punishment of Aries, she forced him to take Seymour for a walk to get him out of the house and to get some fresh air after being cooped up for days. She knew this was something Aries hated, so as punishment, she ordered him to take Seymour for a walk. Seymour was not completely healed and did not want to go with Aries any more than Aries wanted to go with him. But when Estelle spoke this time, he did what she asked. He could feel her withdrawal from him, and he did not like the feeling of not being loved by his mother.

Once Aries was out of the front door, he grabbed Seymour by the hand and started walking at a pace that was too difficult for Seymour to keep up with. Frustrated, Aries proceeded to quicken his pace and dragged Seymour along the street, and he said, "I hate you, boy! I don't see why Mother makes me take you with me all the time. You are not my child, and I shouldn't have to take care of you!"

Scared to death of his brother and hoping his sore back did not get reinjured, he said nothing. He started to cry, wishing his mother could have punished Aries in a way that did not involve him. Any other way would have been fine with Seymour.

Instead of Aries taking Seymour for a walk, Aries took Seymour to his friend's house to see if he could come out and play football. His friend's house was heated by an open-flame gas heater. As Aries dragged Seymour across the threshold of the front door, Seymour got his little feet tangled in an extension cord and fell into the open flames of the burning heater. Seymour screamed at the top of his voice and cried, "I want to go home! I want to go home!" Aries grabbed Seymour by the hand and dragged him back home on the same route he started. Seymour was screaming at the top of his lungs. He screamed all the way home from the pain of his inflamed arm, disappointment with his mother, and the hatred he felt for Aries. This was anger that he could not fight back. He was helpless.

Albrecht and Estelle heard Seymour screaming from down the street, and before he got to her, she said, "What on earth has happened now?" When they took a look at Seymour's burned arm, she started screaming and chastising Aries. He tried to explain what happened when Albrecht interjected and acidly declared, "Shut your mouth, Aries! There is no excuse for this! Just shut your mouth before I punch you in it!"

Estelle rushed to examine Seymour and immediately started to treat and bandage his badly burned arm. Once she could get Seymour to quiet down, she thought, *Now here I go again tending this child again. He is missing school, and I am missing work.* Seymour was feeling no amore for his mother at this moment or his hateful brother. She knew "good and well" just how much Aries hated to be bothered with him. Seymour felt he had been put in harm's way because of Estelle's need to further punish Aries, and he had been used in the process.

After this second incident, Estelle concluded that she had no choice but to take Seymour with her everywhere she went because when she entrusted him to Aries and Claudia, hoping they would show some signs of their brotherly and sisterly love toward their baby brother, there was none. There were no signs of adulation for Seymour, her child, the one she did not want to have. She was deflated, never knowing she had sparked some of their dislike for this child.

CHAPTER TWENTY-SIX

Deed to a House

Estelle was industrious at her new job and was elevated to the next steps and grades in government service. Eventually, her income disqualified Albrecht from the subsidized housing where they were living. Estelle did not mind that they were being forced out of subsidized housing. It was never the house of her dreams. She thought that now was a good time to try and soften Albrecht into her dream of home ownership.

Estelle was far more comfortable with her present accommodations than her past. She was living better than she had ever lived on her own. She did not like the stigma of subsidized housing. She had tired of the apartment and had saved enough money for a down payment on a house. With her salary, she and Albrecht could afford to buy a house. The voice of her father reverberated in her ear: "Daughter, get yourself the title to a car and a deed to a house, and you will be successful." She had the title to a car. The deed to a house she still needed to feel successful as her father had prescribed.

When Estelle broached the subject of home ownership to Albrecht, he flatly refused. "But, Albrecht?" she said. But he would reply, "Estelle, I said no! You are just trying to henpeck me. You think that now that you have a job, we can keep up with the Joneses. No!"

Estelle figured her timing was not right for the subject and, though disappointed, she would bide her time and wait until she could soften Albrecht on another occasion. She accepted his rejection and restrained her frustration. She only had thirty days to change his mind because, otherwise, they would be put out of their current quarters.

Albrecht was still under the conviction that Estelle had gotten a job knowing full well he never wanted her to work. He was not materialistic and did not aspire for things. He felt that since she had a roof over her head and food in her stomach, why couldn't she be content? He knew he had manipulated her into getting pregnant with Seymour, but he thought she should be over it after all this time. She had always wanted more in life compared to him. He did not understand why she could not be content with what he was providing as a man. Regardless of her feelings, he was not going to budge. When Estelle returned home from work a few days later, the apartment was vacant. Albrecht had moved the entire household, along with Aries and Claudia, to another apartment without discussion with Estelle.

Seymour stayed behind until his mother came home from work. Albrecht said to Seymour, "Well, you can wait here and show your mother where we are now living." Since entering first grade, Seymour always sat on the front steps of the old apartment to await his mother's arrival from work. He would not go to the playground or interact with other children. He always waited for his mother to ascend the dusty path at the top of the hill, and with lightning speed, he would run to her beaming with joy and so happy to greet her.

Although the old apartment was vacant, this day was no different for Seymour. He walked his mother through the woods that separated the subsidized housing from the civilian housing to their new apartment. Estelle had surmised what had happened but was too tired from work that day to react. She looked at Seymour said, "You waited here for me? You mean you know where it is? You are a big boy!"

The new apartment was one of six units in one colonial-styled building. It was all red brick, slate roof, and adorned with fake Corinthian columns. Albrecht knew his tone to Estelle was rough when he rejected the idea of buying a house, but he did not like being forced into a decision on short notice. As he looked for new housing for his family, he softened some—but not enough to buy a house. He selected a state-of-the-art unit considering it was civilian housing. There was a spacious combined living and dining area with a huge walk-in closet for coats and storage. The kitchen was furnished with white enamel, knobless upper and lower wall cabinets, new appliances, and a tiled kitchen floor; and there was light from the spacious windows and room for a dining table and chairs for seating six. There were three large bedrooms and a bath with black and white ceramic tile on the walls and floors. This apartment was a step up to anything either of them had ever known, but it was not home ownership.

When Seymour escorted Estelle to the new apartment, she had no choice but to acknowledge that it was very nice. In her thinking, she thought it was foolish to spend this amount monthly on rent when, with the down payment she had saved, they could have purchased a small home, accumulated equity, and owned a piece of property at the end of twenty years. To Estelle, it just did not make any sense to live in an apartment, regardless of how nice, when you could afford a house. It really rubbed against her wishes and what Harrison Sr. had taught her. In her hometown, she was seeing blacks move up in the world, and she wanted to be in that crowd. Apartment living was just not what she wanted.

Seymour liked the improved living environment but could discern his mother's dissatisfaction. However, she could not afford to purchase a house on her own. After reconciling within herself, Estelle decided she would make use of the new space. She would use this time to furnish the apartment with things she could later use in a new home she eventually planned to get. She thought to herself, *Well, it is going to take longer than expected get Albrecht to understand the value of home ownership.* She was going to have to start building her case as time moved along; and for the time being, she was just going to have to make herself content. But she was not giving up on home ownership.

To begin softening Albrecht, she agreed that since she was working, she would assume the responsibility for the food, telephone, and furnishing the house and children. This left Albrecht with paying the rent, car, insurances, maintenance, and gas and electric bills. Estelle received the better end of the stick, but she thought he should be happy with her offer. She thought, *It is better than nothing!*

Albrecht was gleeful with this unexpected windfall of discretionary income. The Catholic Church had always taught him to give to others and sacrifice himself, but this added income to his pocket allowed him to pursue his classical teachings. He enjoyed classical music, reading the classics, Broadway shows, and golf. And he could give up "white lightning" and move up to Gordon's Gin.

In that Estelle was responsible for the food, she would serve him a one-inch-thick sirloin steak once a week. Albrecht's face would light up and shine with joy when she served him a sirloin or T-bone steak. Estelle would look at him glowing because she had pleased him. She would jokingly say, "Coon, what are you grinning about? You know you have never eaten this good in your life." She was feeling assured he was beginning to see the benefit for himself from Estelle's income, and it felt good.

Things were looking up for him too with the additional income. He purchased Lacoste golf shirts and fine leather golf shoes with steel cleats from the finest downtown men's clothier. He never could have afforded any of these luxuries without Estelle's income. He was gradually appreciating Estelle lightening his load. He also began to loosen up on the Catholic belief of self-sacrifice. He thought maybe in the future, he would consider a deed to a house.

CHAPTER TWENTY-SEVEN

Grocery Store

After Seymour suffered from the burns on his back and arms, he never let Estelle out of his sight. Aries and Claudia were galvanized and supported each other—right or wrong, good or bad—and they were not going to include Seymour in their teenage activities.

Estelle thought that everybody deserved time to themselves, and she enjoyed food shopping and getting her hair coiffed. She liked to use her grocery-shopping days, hairdresser appointments, and personal shopping as her personal time away from her family. As circumstances stood for her now, she would not get any free time to herself because she said Seymour stuck to her "like white on rice."

On Friday evening, every two weeks, Estelle went grocery shopping. She could kill two birds with one stone by taking Seymour along because she could drop him off at the barbershop and instruct him to meet her at the grocery store when the barbers finished cutting his hair.

Estelle would always go into the barbershop before going grocery shopping. She would walk in the door of the barbershop dressed fancy and tell the barber, "Take some hair off of this boy's head and cut it close, because I can't be running back and forth to the barbershop getting haircuts for this child and keeping you barbers rich!"

The barbers loved to see Estelle come into the all-men's barbershop and chatting as if she had no fears of the men at all. Most women of the rural town would never be seen in a men's barbershop. They would laugh at Estelle's comments and appreciate her gift of gab and sense of humor. They would respond to her, saying, "Ms. Rose, we will take care of him, but we are not getting rich!"

Estelle enjoyed giving, and the barbers loved receiving. Estelle's made advanced payment for Seymour's haircut and gave a more-than-generous tip. As she left the shop, she would say to the barbers, "Now you send my child to the grocery store when you get finished, and don't keep him here all night! I have roads to go down!"

The barbers all stopped what they were doing and laughed. She would then look at Seymour and say, "You hear me, Seymour? Don't let these clowns keep you sitting in here all night!"

All the barbers chuckled at Estelle as she made her exit.

Seymour was punctual in meeting his mother at the grocery store. When he found her in one of the aisles of the store, he observed closely how she went up one aisle and down the other with her grocery list, checking off the two weeks of groceries. She was in a world of her own. When she turned around and spied Seymour watching her, she would say, "Now you go and get yourself a cart and take this list and get my paper towel, beach, soap powder, and some bluing, then come back and meet me here!"

When Estelle approached the meat counter, she would ring the counter bell to summon the butcher from the refrigerated area. And when he arrived, she would say out loud, "Hey, Ace! You got any ground round back there in the back?"

The butcher would reply, "Yes we do!"

Estelle would say, "Well, grind me up a couple of pounds please, sir."

Seymour would interject, "Mother, there is ground round already in the display case. Why don't you simply pick that up?"

She would reply, "Oh, child, you don't know what they have put in those packages. You get home and it is some old dark meat from a few days ago that they have covered with some fresh meat on the top. Oh no! Always ask them to grind it for you fresh."

Mrs. Astor had always instructed Estelle to do this when shopping for her foods. Estelle knew and had learned from the white lady she worked for how to shop for the best quality.

While Estelle shopped, Seymour would sneak a few snack items and cheap toys in the extra cart he pushed for her. When Estelle arrived at the checkout counter and her bill totaled more than she budgeted, she would double-check the prices again and look to see what mistake she had made. She would take an extra minute to make sure she was not being overcharged and her mathematical calculations were correct. Then she would discover items on the conveyor belt she did not pick up. She stopped and thought a moment. *Seymour must have put these extra items in the cart when I was not looking.*

She would sternly look at Seymour and say out loud, "In the name of the Father, boy! What is all this stuff you have put in my grocery cart, boy? It's not Christmas around here! Do you think money grows on trees?"

Seymour would lower his head with a smile as the cashier would ask, "Would you like me to subtract those items, miss?"

But not wanting to look as if she could not afford them, Estelle said, "No, you can leave them on."

Seymour smiled, but as they exited the store, she said to him, "I am going to leave you at home the next time! Everywhere we go, you are always sticking me up for all my money!"

Estelle was loud and embarrassing, but she wanted to give the impression she was chastising him. Seymour kept his head lowered, knowing that the next time, he would still follow her to the store and could sweet-talk her into something extra for him.

As Estelle drove the Chevy back home, she would think about the child who sat next to her playing quietly with his little toys and how helpful he was going through the store, picking up all the heavy items she needed. When they got to the car, he would agreeably struggle to get all the bags in the trunk of the car while she stood under the parking lot lamppost, checking her grocery bill to ensure she did not pay too much for what she got. She reminded herself how good-natured this child was—the child she never wanted. She reflected with regret on the scolding she had given him in the store and thought to herself, *Seldom does he cause me a minute's trouble.*

Although a mother's boy, he was helpful to her; and on his own volition, he was unloading the grocery bags from the car when they returned home. She would summon Aries, but he was so lazy he would deliberately wait until Seymour had unloaded all the bags before he showed his head.

So if the child wants a few extra things, he deserved them, she thought, to reconcile her feelings toward Seymour and the extra money spent over her allotted budget.

CHAPTER TWENTY-EIGHT

Scalp Scorcher's

On Saturday mornings at ten o'clock, every two weeks, Estelle had scheduled hairdresser appointments with her dear friend Sadie. She would say to Albrecht, "I am taking the car and going to the scalp scorchers."

Sadie had been coifing Estelle's hair since she had left Washington and moved to Baltimore, and every Saturday, that God-sent Seymour wanted to go with her. And she would ask, "But why do you want to go to the beauty parlor with me? It is a place for ladies to go, not boys. And besides that, I am coming right back."

Seymour would look at her with dejected eyes, and this always weakened her heart. She would look at Seymour and say, "Nobody wants you, boy, and you won't let me get a minute to myself. Well, okay then! Hurry up now and get dressed. And don't take too long because I am ready to hit the road." She would yell to Seymour from the hallway, "And make yourself presentable!"

She thought, *I just can't get rid of this child! He just wants to stick to me everywhere I go!*

When Seymour was ten to twelve years old, Sadie was getting sick of Seymour sitting in a beauty salon full of ladies, waiting for his mother to get her hair done. Sadie chastised Estelle for continuing to bring him to her salon. She did not think it good training for boys. She thought Seymour should be traveling with his father by now. "Estelle, he is not a baby!" Sadie would say. "Estelle, you have to stop bringing that child to the beauty salon. You are just spoiling him! He needs to be playing with children his own age."

Estelle would reply, "Sadie, I have done everything I can to get that boy to play with children his age. He just won't cut me loose! He sticks with me like white on rice!"

In Estelle's mind, she knew Sadie had a point to what she had said, but she did not like someone who had no husband or children telling her how to raise her child. And furthermore, Sadie did not know the ins and outs of what was going on in Estelle's household. Though she agreed in principle that Seymour should be playing with other children—on the other hand, Seymour also brought her a child's love that her other children had never done. She privately thought it was somewhat cute that he wanted to stick to his mother. Estelle felt guiltless about Seymour's choices to be with her because she had given him every opportunity to play with other children or go with his father, and he continued to choose her. He was still her child, and somebody needed to watch over him.

Sadie was not finished chastising Estelle. "Well, you tell him that 'I' said he is not allowed in here anymore!"

But sure enough, two weeks later, Seymour persuaded Estelle to let him come along, knowing Sadie would not let him in the beauty salon. She asked, "But, Seymour, what are you going to do while I am in the hair salon?"

Estelle thought that maybe this would be his deal breaker, but Seymour replied, "I will wait for you in the car."

Estelle said, "But, Seymour, that is three hours. What are you going to do sitting in the car for three hours?"

And Seymour simply replied, "Waiting for you."

This melted Estelle's heart, and it was getting late. She needed to get on the road. Silently, Estelle thought, *Lord, child! What am I going to with you?* Then she said, "Okay then, just come on."

Seymour would smile, and Estelle would say, "Okay now. Stop smiling like a Cheshire cat and let's go!"

After three hours of Seymour sitting in the car in the hot sun waiting for his mother, she would come out of the salon looking very good, happy, and would jokingly say to Seymour, "Are you still here, boy? Mother's child, I guess you must be hungry now. I will take us to get something to eat. Let's go to a nice cafeteria and have lunch. I have a taste for a chicken salad sandwich on toast with lettuce tomato and mayonnaise. What about you?"

Seymour always ordered whatever his mother ordered. He knew that whatever she ordered, he could not go wrong.

Sadie would look out the window of her salon and say to the remaining ladies, "Estelle is just going to ruin that child!"

CHAPTER TWENTY-NINE

Shopping Mall

The local clothing stores discriminated against Negros; but with her new income, Estelle was not moved by discrimination. She would speak out, "If one store won't take my money, another one will." She opened charge accounts at three of the largest department stores in the area. There was one other large department store that was the last to integrate, and as time went on, it was the first of the large department stores to go out of business. Estelle never shopped in the stores that discriminated. Her attitude was "My money will be spent elsewhere."

The nearby shopping center was hailed as America's first open-air shopping center located on the East Coast. Estelle shopped at the two anchor stores. She would drive there almost every week with Seymour seated in the front seat beside her. She found shopping for Christmas and Easter holidays, birthdays, and back-to-school days was something she enjoyed and found pleasurable.

Estelle tried to dress Aries and Claudia in department store clothes so that they looked like polished children, but they were not materialistic and had no interest in conservative fashion. They instead preferred to dress like the children where they lived and attended school. Like Albrecht, they just wanted to blend into the community. Her city ideas were just not appropriate for the setting. Seymour, on the other hand, loved the department stores. He could differentiate the quality of the fabric in his clothing: how they fit and how they felt to his skin. He enjoyed learning his mother's cosmopolitan taste in fashion. He enjoyed food shopping with his mother also. He learned so much about foods, prices, brand names, and most of all, the good-tasting foods. Seymour always managed to see something he wanted in either of the two environments and would persuade his mother into purchasing this for him. Estelle was often happy that he was learning to differentiate quality, but she chastised him for selecting the most expensive thing in the store. He thoroughly enjoyed his new clothing and looked forward to wearing them to school and church; but just as in elementary school, he stood out from his peers. In Seymour's thinking, the high-quality fashion compensated for all the ridicule he received for being effeminate. He was labeled a mother's boy and a sissy.

In addition to clothes shopping, Estelle enjoyed purchasing furniture for the apartment. In anticipation of the house she someday wanted to own. She liked saying to the sales representatives, "Charge and send." She had witnessed Mrs. Astor saying this many times when she accompanied her shopping for her daughters.

Almost every month, the delivery truck was pulling up to the apartment with a new piece of furniture. Estelle selected a beautiful Duncan Phyfe sofa upholstered in tapestry, one red barrel-back chair, one occasional chair, mahogany and leather-top coffee and step tables, milk glass lamps, and an avocado-green wool area carpet for the living room. These furnishings were her prized possessions. They were very similar in taste to Mrs. Astor's. After she paid down for one piece of furniture, she would select another piece. The apartment was one of the most tastefully appointed by formal standards. On the military base, in a master sergeant's quarters, it looked out of place. It looked closer to the interior of one of the Smithsonian Museum's displays or maybe a room in the White House.

Albrecht did not care how Estelle decorated the house. His concern was her being in debt. Albrecht did not like debt. Aries and Claudia acknowledged their mother's quality and good taste, but they would have preferred something that they could have jumped up and down and played on. Estelle did not want the furniture abused and torn to pieces because it had to last if she ever got a home of her own. She said the children had a room of their own to play with their belongings, and the front of the house was reserved for receiving and entertaining guests.

She would say to the children, "I want at least one room in the house to look presentable. I don't want people to think we live in some kind of a dive! So play in your rooms. There's enough space for you there!"

The children's bedrooms were spacious. She always gave Claudia the largest room and Aries and Seymour the smaller room. Seymour never understood her decision on this matter.

Estelle made herself content with her life in that she had a job and some savings. The family was eating well, and she liked the comfort of her apartment (though she never gave up on her dreams of home ownership). She and Albrecht were accumulating as she thought they should.

Albrecht was sent on numerous temporary-duty assignments for national training in the field of engineering. His skills were utilized to enhance the military's ability to design and prepare for warfare. He excelled and was recognized and promoted for his skills, talents, and devotion to his work. For a Negro, he was doing well and making above-average income, which gave Estelle the status of having married well. She prided herself for selecting a good man as her husband.

She always felt Albrecht possessed the qualities of a good husband and father and was happy they married, though they struggled from difficult beginnings and marital issues. She was accustomed to not getting everything in life she wanted. Her current situation was above satisfactory.

CHAPTER THIRTY

Pregnant by the Mailman

Estelle decreased her visits to her sister. She judged her sister was getting on her feet after her stay at the mental hospital. She now had a good job that allowed her to take care of herself and her son. She was a more fastidious housekeeper than Estelle and had a higher-reaching arch for beautiful residential furnishings than Estelle. She saved no money and stayed deep in debt.

One Saturday afternoon, around two o'clock, Estelle and Seymour visited Anise after her visit to Sadie's beauty salon. Estelle had just gotten her hair done and put on what she called her war paint and was looking pretty stately dressed in a navy linen suit with white underblouse, black patent leather shoes and matching bag, and a good pair of seamless stockings.

Shortly after she and Seymour arrived, Anise summoned Estelle to the small living room that also served as her sleeping quarters. In that she could only afford one bedroom, she had given that to her son. The living room was small and a huge comedown from the plush life with Sequester Toms.

Estelle was feeling pretty good about herself and her life. She and Albrecht had grown in their marriage, overcoming their differences. Her children were healthy, and she, at last, was able to work in a secure setting.

After Estelle was seated in the small room, Anise closed the door. Estelle said, "Anise, what are you going to tell me that you feel the door needs to be shut?"

Anise paused and held her head down, and she had the most pathetic facial expression when she announced to Estelle that she was pregnant.

Estelle could not control her shock and disbelief. She yelled, "Pregnant? By who?"

"By Morris," she replied.

"Well, who in the Sam Hill is Morris?" Estelle asked. "Well, does he have a last name?" she chided.

"He is the mailman, and he comes by with the mail every day, and we talk just about every day. And he said he would leave his wife and marry me if I had a baby for him. He said his wife could not have children, and he wanted a child, and so I believed him and slept with him."

Estelle could feel blood and heat rising in her veins, but she calmly said, "Well, Anise, you can't believe every word that comes out of a man's mouth! All he wanted was to have sex with you! I thought you had more sense than that. I know Father was mean to us, but he did not teach us to do all the things you are doing. I mean, hasn't it been enough with Toms leaving you with a child and no money? Then you turn around and have a nervous breakdown. You are barely making ends meet now with one child, and you mean to tell me you are pregnant with another child—and by a married man too? I can understand one mistake like this—but two? How are you going to make it? I can't ask Albrecht to take care of you, Antwan, and a new baby."

Anise said in a beaten-down and timid voice, "Well, he said he loved me, Estelle. And he was leaving his wife."

Estelle lost her composure again and retorted, "Ain't no man leaving his wife, even if he thinks he is leaving, because his wife has something to say about it too. Well, all I can say now is that you are grown. It is water over the dam. You and what's-his-name will have to work this out, but 'Mother' is through! I can't help you."

Estelle was now frustrated, and the happy good mood that she had when she arrived was shot. She grabbed her patent leather bag, opened the living room door, and grabbed Seymour by the hand and said her goodbyes to her sister and her sister's son. Antwan cried every time his aunt Estelle got ready to leave their home because he always remembered how kind Estelle was to him when he lived with her for six months. He remembered that whatever Estelle did for her children, she did for him. She never discriminated or spoke unkindly to him. She gave him plenty of food and purchased very nice clothing and toys for him. In his heart, he loved Estelle more than his biological mother.

As Estelle drove her Chevy home, she was thinking hard about her sister's newest predicament. Seymour heard her say to herself, "That man ain't gonna marry no Anise. Um, um, um in the name of the Father!" Snarling and shaking her head, she said, "How stupid can you be for god's sake?"

CHAPTER THIRTY-ONE

No Love Lost

Harrison Jr. telephoned Estelle to inform her that their father had died. He died in his sleep on Labor Day. Now that she had moved away, married and had three children, she rarely got to see her father. She and Seymour had taken the train to visit her father a few times, to give Seymour the experience of a train ride and to visit him too. In her heart, she had never gotten over how harsh her father had been to her growing up. She felt he had redeeming qualities, like sending them to church and allowing them to go to school; but overall, he was not a nice father, and thus the news of his death did not generate any deep sense of grief for her. His death was more of a relief, and to think he died on Labor Day.

"Ain't that a joke?" she said. He was not a hard-working man. He made his children perform most of the work, and he kept their money.

It was unfortunate that Harrison Jr. had to give up the best part of his life to take care of their father, but she was giving as much time and money as possible to help get Anise on her feet and would say, "If it is not one thing with her, it is another!"

Considering how Seymour trailed behind his mother with every step she took, on the day of the funeral, he looked at his mother and said, "Do I have go?"

Estelle was perplexed and said, "Well, no. If you don't want to go, you don't have to go. But I want you to know you will be at home all by yourself until we get back."

Seymour accepted his mother's terms and stayed at home alone.

He remembered—on the day of his grandfather's funeral—the two times that he met him and how vehemently he disliked him after the first meeting. He was talkative, loud, domineering, and arrogant. Seymour remembered how fearful Estelle became when in the presence of her father. As with the burn on his back that Aries had caused, Seymour was resolved that he hated his grandfather too. How can you grieve someone you are fearful of? It didn't help Seymour's opinion of his grandfather when he ridiculed Harrison Jr. for being a mother's boy, laughing as he recounted the stories of making Harrison Jr. wear a dress and making him stand in the bay window on the front of the house for all his schoolmates to see. Seymour could see himself in Harrison Jr.'s place and knew he would never want to have a father like him, whereby he was afraid all of the time. In many ways, Aries was just as bad—if not worse—than the grandfather.

Seymour did not see himself in school as the brightest star in the firmament, but he never wanted to imagine the horror of being forced to put on a dress and stand in a bay window for his classmates to see. *Noooooo*, he thought in his young mind. This did not rest well with him. A fear was generated in his brain with the slightest thought of this happening to him. He was fully aware that he too was a mother's boy, and his grandfather would have persecuted him in the same way he did his son. Seymour did not like the thought of just being in his presence, dead or alive. It generated fear in his soul. He held the same staunch feeling for Aries as he did for his grandfather. They were too much alike.

For Estelle, she felt a sense of relief with her father dying; and for Seymour, there was no love lost.

CHAPTER THIRTY-TWO

Teenagers

With the death of her father, Estelle thought this was one less thing on her plate to worry about, and she hoped that it was not too late for Harrison Jr. to get married and have children, if he wanted, and have a happy life.

Estelle's next biggest concern now was for Aries. Claudia was no trouble but was distant most of the time. Both were now teens. Different from Seymour, Aries and Claudia had grown up differently and made lives of their own. Neither of them were mother's children. Aries and Claudia were one year apart. Seymour was ten years younger. Aries loved Claudia, and Claudia loved Aries—and they stuck together against Albrecht, Estelle, and Seymour. They had created a world of their own, taking the good along with the bad.

Since these first two children were so codependent but independent in their personage, it freed Estelle. She only had to care and look after Seymour exclusively. Estelle felt that she had given her children a head start in health by breastfeeding each of them. She was counseled by elder women that breastfeeding was better nutrition for the child and gave the child a sense of connection with the mother. This old adage did not hold true with Aries and Claudia. They got the better nutrition and were healthy children, but they were not bonded to Estelle.

When Estelle gave applause to her children's good health and to honor herself, she would say, "I breast-feed all of my children!" Her children were appalled by their mother's openness and would stutter at the imaginary vision of themselves being in position for such a feeding. When she caught the children frowning at what she had said, she would continue, "I don't know why you children are frowning. That was good nourishment for you! You children have more food, clothing, and shelter than I ever had as a child! I don't know what is wrong with you!" She dismissed their conversation as pure immaturity and would say, "I am not thinking about you children. What do you know about anything? You must be sick!"

Estelle saw to it that her children had good moral training by taking them to church every Sunday, which was a sacrifice for her because she hated getting out of bed every day of the week, and Sunday was no different. She also hated the ceremony and pageantry of the Catholic Church. She was familiar and more comfortable in the all-colored church she attended as a child. Estelle made sure her children received all the sacraments of the Catholic Church and that they had everything they needed for school. They had new shoes, clothes, pencil and paper for school—yet it felt to her that Aries and Claudia were ungrateful because they showed no signs of appreciation. She could barely get them to say "thank you" or "please." When she insisted that they say "thank you" for the things she had done, they would say to her, "If I have to say 'thank you,' then I don't want it!"

Aries and Claudia thought Estelle was a fish in the wrong bowl. They thought the white lady she worked for as a child laborer taught her to be white when she was black. They wanted to fit in the environment where they lived and had no desires to imitate a white woman when they learned in their one-room-school American History classes how whites had notoriously enslaved Negros. Aries and Claudia both harbored resentment and hatred toward white folk.

Estelle did not see history as her teens had, academically or morally. Estelle and Albrecht did not believe in hatred and petty revenge as a solution to the Negro heritage. Instead, they wanted to take advantage of the opportunities they had for building a life of their own and not blaming someone else for their shortcomings. Limited opportunities were offered by benevolent whites if they saw Negros working hard. Albrecht and Estelle considered themselves hard workers, and over time, they were rewarded. They knew that neither they nor their children were heirs to a privileged place in society. Hard work was all that was available to anybody in their situation, white or black.

Albrecht and Estelle believed if their children did not achieve, it was not their fault. In unison, Albrecht and Estelle agreed their children had more than they ever dreamed of having when they were teens. Estelle was raising her mother's children and working outside of the home as a teen, and Albrecht was working outside of the home too. He was also sent to the farm for the summers to bring food in the house for Bessie and Albrecht. They did not use their Negro heritage as an excuse for not building their lives. They did not feel like hostages by their two angry teenagers.

Aries remained Estelle's biggest concern because he was the most ungovernable of the three children. He always managed to get himself in some difficulty, whether at home or school. Estelle could see herself in Aries, but more of her father. She thought her father would have disciplined Aries far more sternly than she could, but she also felt her father was too hard on his children. She did not know what a happy medium could have been for Aries.

*   *   *

One Saturday afternoon, Estelle received a call from one of the neighborhood children instructing her to send someone to come and get Aries. He had been in a fight with one of the boys. "He was kicked in the balls, Ms. Estelle!" the caller said.

Estelle was flabbergasted to have been informed in such common terms by the young teenage girl. When she hung up the telephone, she immediately called for Albrecht. "Go get that boy. He has been in a fight again, and this time, he got kicked in his private parts. Now you know I don't know anything about that! Just go get him and bring him home! The way these children talk today just about sets me crazy. Such nasty talking! And, Albrecht, you have to take care of that because I don't know how to treat something like that! Go ahead now and get him!"

*   *   *

Estelle wanted her children to have music instruction, as Mrs. Astor had done for her daughters. She purchased a clarinet and trumpet for Aries to play in the school band. She wanted him to learn the value of having extracurricular interest since he showed no interest in academics—and possibly, the music would keep him out of the neighborhood fights. Estelle thought he was a smart child but restless and lazy. "He is just like my father!" Estelle would repeatedly say.

After weeks of musical rehearsals for a school closing performance, Aries deliberately played the very last two notes of a perfect performance off key just to make the perfect performance imperfect. Aries laughed when everybody looked at him for playing the wrong notes. The administration, faculty, and students laughed because they knew Aries had deliberately made a mockery of the music teacher, whom Aries believed to be a musical perfectionist. Aries thought the music did not need to be perfect and the teacher was just going overboard with musical perfection.

At the conclusion of the performance and in great fury, the music teacher—who was indeed a perfectionist when it came to his music—made his move. He had a statewide reputation for playing and teaching beautiful music well. He was sick and tired of Aries's deliberate antics over the entire school year. The teacher's eyes flared with red fury through the double-thick magnifying lens in his eyeglasses. He slammed through the crowd with force to find his way through the chorus and the band to get to Aries. And as he was knocking people out of the way and the folding chairs were crashing to the floor and students were trying to get out of the way of the certain attack, he reached Aries, grabbed him by the collar, and punched him in the face, knocking him to the floor. Aries laughed no more.

Estelle was the PTA president, and Albrecht was the chairman of scholarships for the school Aries and Claudia attended. When Estelle got the call from the school principal to explain the inexcusable behavior of the music teacher, Estelle said to the principal, "It was not the teacher's fault! I know my child, and I know he is responsible."

Estelle left her job and rushed to the school and said to the music teacher, "It's not your fault. I just wish you could have knocked some sense into his head!" Estelle and Albrecht were frustrated and apologized to the music teacher.

Seymour witnessed the incident. He was frightened for his brother's life and was embarrassed that his family was associated with such a disgrace. Again!

*   *   *

While riding home from school one day on the military school bus, Aries's teen friend—who also had a younger brother in Seymour's class in elementary school—made a bet that his shorter brother could win a fight against Seymour, who was tall for his age. Most of Seymour's schoolteachers adored him because he did not have a behavioral problem. They thought he received good home training and, though not an A student, he completed all his assignments. He was average in most subjects. He did not earn A's like Claudia, but he was not a nuisance and class clown like Aries. They were delighted that Seymour did not share the same genes with his older brother, whose reputation had preceded him.

However, among his boy classmates, Seymour had the persona of being timid. Aries knew Seymour was much taller and more physically fit than his friend's shorter brother. Aries accepted his friend's bet and walked to the back of the school bus and told Seymour, "When you get off of this school bus today, I want you to kick little Timmy's ass! He is just a short squirt! You can knock him out in just a few punches!"

Seymour had never gotten a stain on his clothing, and the part that Estelle combed in his hair in the morning was still there in the late afternoon. Getting into a fight was not his thing, and he said to Aries, "I am not going to do it!"

Aries stood firm and tall over Seymour, who was seated on the school bus. He fumed and demanded, "Yes you are!"

Seymour replied, "No, I am not!"

Aries then said, "Look, I have bet money on you, and you can do it now. When you get off this got-dam school bus, you are going to kick Timmy's ass!"

When the school bus arrived at its designated stop, half of the children on the school bus got off the bus before their designated stop to see timid Seymour in this fight that had now been advertised throughout the school bus by Aries's loud and forceful commands.

When Seymour got off and proceeded to go home without a fight, Aries grabbed Seymour in the seat of his pants and said, "I told you that you are going to fight, and you are going to fight!" And he proceeded to throw him on top of Timmy.

The two began to fight, and Seymour easily overpowered him and won the fight. Timmy was favored to win. He had a reputation for being the school bully. But after the fight, he never bothered bullying Seymour again.

Seymour was not really fighting Timmy; he was fighting the anger he held for his older brother, whom he hated for making him become someone he did not want to be. Aries forced Seymour to lose his innocence. His depth of hatred for Aries continued to grow. In Seymour's eyes, Aries was a reprehensible brother, unloving and unkind.

When the fight was over, Aries beamed with pride because he had won the bet and the money. Seymour cried all the way home as his brother praised him for winning the fight, saying, "I knew you could whip that little squirt!"

Aries never understood or accepted that Seymour was comfortable with himself and did not need to fight someone to prove he was strong. This was a fight he never wanted to fight, and he felt no sense of victory. He just hated his brother more, and as with everything else, it fell in his emotional buildup pile of his not being wanted by Estelle. Seymour felt his brother had used him just as the local men used chickens in cockfights.

* * *

Claudia was an honor student and was praised by her teachers and the school administrators for her academic acumen. She was selected to represent her school in a regional debate competition and won. Winning the regional competition made her eligible to participate in the statewide competition, which was to be televised on network television, along with other regional winners. Claudia was a superstar in her school, the local community, and mostly in Estelle's eyes. Claudia was very much like Albrecht, and she remained calm and nonchalant about the event and the fanfare surrounding it. For Claudia, it was just another day in her world.

When the final statewide competition was being aired, Claudia was introduced on network television. Classmates, friends, and neighbors gathered around their televisions to watch the program. Within her heart, Estelle knew Claudia was going to win the competition. She had been observing Claudia's ability as a quick leaner since her birth and for the years that followed. Estelle was feeling proud and full in her breast to be the mother of the winning student of the state debate competition.

However, after each of the competing students from other regional schools had a chance to debate, many teams dropped out after the first, second, or third rounds. When the final round was called, Claudia's team lost due to a mistake Claudia made, causing her team to drop out of the final round and lose the statewide championship.

Estelle was totally crestfallen and deflated. Although Claudia was indifferent toward her mother, Estelle had always enjoyed being associated with Claudia's successes in her intellectual pursuits. She had wanted desperately over the year for Albrecht to agree to send her to private schools, to build on her natural abilities—but he denied her every time. What bugged Estelle the most was that as she stood in front of the television looking at Claudia, Estelle could have made the debate team win in the state competition. Estelle knew the first-person affirmative responses better than her daughter. Estelle just could not understand Claudia not having the correct responses that caused the team to lose and took them out of the winner's circle.

Albrecht had driven Claudia to the state competition, but just as soon as they returned home, Estelle could not wait to ask Claudia how she had come to make her mistake. "Claudia," she said, "how come you screwed up the debate? Even I could have gotten that right. Doggone, you should have gotten that right!"

Claudia was hurt by her mother's comment, but she never said a word or made an excuse. She just went to her room and closed the door and fumed that her mother could not come up with anything other than a criticism.

In Estelle's mind she just could not allow herself to understand Claudia's indifference and nonchalant attitude. When Claudia was at the top of her class in almost every subject, she was praised in school in a way Estelle never had. Estelle was an average student. She would have expected Seymour, an average student, to get the debate incorrect—but not Claudia.

Seymour thought Estelle's comment was cold and hurtful, but he knew it was not his mother's intention. Such a comment would have wounded him. If nothing less, it would diminish his desire to achieve above average if it generated this amount of disappointment from a mother who never wanted him. He thought, *Good is good enough for me!*

Estelle thought back to the days when she attended public schools. Her schools were among the best in the country for Negro children. When Estelle was commended by blacks and whites on her command of the English language for a Negro, Estelle consistently bragged and credited her teachers in her hometown.

She had learned through Claudia's experience that her children were not receiving the kind of education she had wanted for them. Aries, she thought, could do better in school but was simply a lazy child. And regardless of ability, a lazy child will never perform to his maximum ability. Seymour struggled to just be average, but this was okay with Estelle. But with Claudia, she held the highest hopes and greatest success for her daughter. With her job, she could send her daughter to a good college, and she could become a world leader. She relished the idea of hitching her wagon to Claudia's star and carrying the parental bragging rights for a child she had produced.

*   *   *

Claudia was smart, respected by her peers, well-groomed, and although nonchalant, the boys from all over the county liked her, and she liked them too. Albrecht and Estelle had reserved conversation time with Aries and Claudia twice per month as teenagers to discuss changes in their development, but mostly to discuss the birds and the bees. Under Estelle's insistence, these discussions were an effort in attempting to dissuade them from premarital sex and the consequences of pregnancy—a mistake she and Albrecht had made. Aries was of lesser concern because he had not matured enough to show interest in girls in that way. He remained more of a holy terror and bully to as many in his path as he could.

Claudia was a concern in this arena because she was a girl. A bigger concern was that the boys came to their front door in numbers. Estelle was delighted that Claudia was popular with the boys. She had recalled memories of how mistreated she was as a teenager because she was poor and unkempt and because her father had put her out to work in the homes of white families. She did not have time for boys because she worked before and after school.

Estelle wanted to befriend her daughter and share in Claudia's delights and sorrows, but Claudia would never confide in her mother. Estelle talked too loud and too much, and this offended Claudia. She did not trust her mother with her personal confidences. If she had, her mother would not have listened but instead would react to what Claudia was saying before she could explain the whole story. Estelle was excitable and felt she had all the right answers.

Claudia could never understand why her mother imitated the white woman she worked for in her childhood. What made her so special? Why didn't she like herself more? Why couldn't she just stay at home and be a mother like all her girlfriends' mothers—remain quiet, demure, and docile. Instead, her mother was loud and mouthy. Claudia saw Estelle as too ambitious for a woman, and she possessed uppity manners like a white woman who looked down on coloreds. She thought her mother should stay in her place and be at home, in a home that was homely and wear homely clothes. But her mother wore suits with hats and gloves, matching shoes, and handbags when none of the other mothers wore those types of clothes, not even in church.

Seymour was a spectator to everything that took place in the home because he never went outside or played on the playground. He adored his mother's stately look; Aries and Claudia did not. It annoyed Seymour that his brother and sister could not see that their mother was striving for something more than mediocre. They did not see the bigger picture: they had urban parents and not rural parents. They just lived in a rural place. Further, he thought all colored people were not the same. Some were ambitious, and some were not. Aries and Claudia were always at each other's throats or in a territorial fight; yet at the same time, they were monolithic.

By this time, though unspoken, Seymour knew he was gay. His young mind was growing into a more accepting attitude toward difference. He knew he was different every day he went to school, but he also wanted to be accepted too. But he knew he would not be accepted in his home. Estelle and Claudia were homophobic.

When Claudia's menstrual cycle started, she suffered severely with painful cramps and cried hard. Her eyes would get red, and the under-eye skin got puffy. She was in misery and suffered. The doctor suggested placing a hot water bottle over her lower waist and hips to bring a modicum of comfort. Estelle would prepare the hot water bottle and attempt to compress it against Claudia, but she would recoil. Even in her agony, Claudia would never let her mother touch her. Through her tears, she would say to Estelle, "Seymour can do it."

Estelle thought, *Well, what does Seymour know about these things?* But again, feeling rejected by her daughter, she just let Claudia have it her way. And Seymour would hold the hot water bottle for his crying sister, not having one clue as to what he was doing or what it was for. At times, Claudia cried so hard, Seymour would cry with her to let his sister know he was sharing her pain. But if he had been asked why he was crying, he would not have known. It was interesting to observe Seymour coming to the aid of his sister in pain because when Seymour was in pain from the burns on his back and arm, Claudia never said a kind word.

Seymour was not sure if Claudia was using the cramps to expel her teenage resentments toward their mother or whether, possibly, the children at school were correct when they viciously promoted that his sister was probably having a botched abortion because they believed Claudia was sexually active. Seymour never knew the correct answer and did not believe what the children were saying was true. By this time, he had learned from his high-pitched voice and feminine mannerisms that children were deadly cruel.

Claudia had so many boys calling her, but it was not considered ladylike for a girl to be anxious when a boy called. Claudia would have Seymour to answer the telephone, and then she would take her sweet time coming to the telephone. Eventually, Seymour believed he was being used as Claudia's flunky. He no longer wanted to be a flunky for his sister, but Estelle could not endure the frequent ringing telephone. She would direct Seymour to answer the telephone, "Go ahead and answer the telephone! You are not doing anything else!" This made him feel like a double funky.

One Friday night, Seymour was feeling fed up with answering the telephone for his sister. The telephone was always ringing, and it was always for her. On this Friday night, he begrudgingly picked up the receiver from its base and angrily jerked it to her and, in doing so, the crocheted doily where the telephone was placed, along with one of Estelle's Limoges figurines, fell crashing to the floor, cracking the telephone base and shattering the figurine.

When Estelle heard and saw the telephone base and her porcelain figurine crashing to the floor with Seymour standing near the scene, she said to Albrecht, "Go beat that boy! Beat him good with a strap!" Seymour ran to his bedroom with fear after hearing Estelle's pronouncement, and he heard Estelle say again, "And whip him good, Albrecht!"

Albrecht had never laid a hand on Seymour, but he slowly followed Seymour to the bedroom with a leather belt and closed the door. Seymour started screaming bloody murder loud enough for Estelle to hear so that she would be convinced Albrecht had severely punished him. Albrecht simply said, "Seymour, you behave yourself." He knew Seymour just as Estelle knew Aries, and whatever the circumstances, it was not Seymour's fault. Seymour continued his convincing screams for a few extra minutes for his mother's sake, but Albrecht never laid a hand him.

When Estelle came charging into the bedroom to make sure Albrecht had whipped Seymour to her satisfaction, he started the crying again just so his mother was convinced that Albrecht had actually laid a heavy hand. Seymour, unknowing, was Albrecht's special child. Seymour never knew what was later said to Estelle or Claudia about the boys calling, but Seymour never had to answer the telephone again for his sister.

*   *   *

After Aries and Claudia became teenagers, they wanted a weekly allowance. Albrecht assigned them chores to earn the money he provided them. Aries's chores were sweeping the kitchen floor after dinner and taking the trash to the dumpster every day. Claudia's chores were washing, drying, and putting away the dishes and peeling five white potatoes every day. Estelle believed in a well-balanced meal, and each day, the family was served a meat, a vegetable, and a starch; but most days, the starch was a serving of boiled white potatoes. She learned from Mrs. Astor the importance of a balanced meal and that boiled white potatoes did not contain the butter and salt as mashed white potatoes.

Up until the time Estelle went to work for the government, she assumed full responsibility for food preparation. She felt it saved her time to do it herself than to constantly teach Claudia, who was slow and had distanced herself from Estelle. If Estelle attempted to teach her domestic skills, she would then have to go behind her to correct whatever she had assigned. Claudia did not like domestic work of any kind and saw domestic work for poor colored and uneducated women. She wanted to be educated and have someone else assume these low-level skills.

"It just saves me a little time to just do it myself," Estelle would moan. "I just don't have the time to be fooling around with you children! Mothers are sorry creatures."

Estelle could have used the help, but she thought back on her days as a child when she assumed the bulk of the household responsibilities after her mother died. She remembered her sister, Anise, was frail, and it took Estelle more time to teach her housework than to simply go ahead and do it herself. Aries and Claudia were not frail, but they did not want to perform their chores, and the effort she had to put into forcing them to do it was not worth it to her now that she was working outside of the home too. Estelle thought she must have spoiled her children in an effort to give them more than she had as a child. She was assured, however, that if they lived in this world, they would learn how to take care of themselves or be dead out of luck.

Truthfully, Estelle did not really like anybody in the kitchen with her at the same time anyway. It was Albrecht's idea to have Claudia peel potatoes while in the kitchen with her mother. This idea did not settle well for Estelle because she thought the kitchen too small to have two full-sized women working side by side. Estelle re-instructs Claudia to peel the potatoes after school and leave them in a pot of cold water. When she returned from work, the kitchen would be cleared, and then she would prepare them herself.

To defy Estelle for overriding her father's instructions, Claudia waited until the last minute to peel the five potatoes. Thus, when Estelle got home from work, Claudia was still in the kitchen slowly peeling potatoes, preventing her from getting started with cooking dinner.

When Estelle walked into the kitchen and found the potatoes were not peeled, she scolded Claudia, saying, "I told you before I left home this morning that I wanted these potatoes peeled by the time I got home. And here it is five o'clock, and you are just getting started peeling my potatoes." She repeated, "When I told you to peel them this morning! Listen to me, child. When I tell you to do something, I expect you to do it! I don't care what your father said to you."

Claudia, clearly insulted for being chastised, spoke up and said, "Well, I thought Daddy was the head of the household."

Without a breath of air, Estelle slashed back, "Yes, he is the head of this household. But I am the head of YOU! I run this kitchen, and I run you!" Estelle was too tired to deal with any back talk, so she was short and sharp with Claudia.

Claudia was shot down by Estelle's attitude toward her but proceeded to cut the potatoes, but by the time Estelle changes her clothes from work and returned to the kitchen to get the dinner started, she saw that Claudia had cut the potatoes into the size of small marbles. Then she saw stars. She was hot and tired from working all day, only to come home to a child who had not followed her directions and who had a resentful attitude.

She quickly picked up the closest thing to her, which was a wooden spoon, and forcefully slammed it as hard as she could into Claudia's shoulder and said, "Just get out of here. I will do it myself!"

Claudia ran out of the kitchen and to her bedroom and closed the door.

Estelle enjoyed the income her job produced, but her patience when she returned home each day was thin, and she wanted to get her task done as soon as possible so that she could get a minute to herself before getting herself ready for the next workday and the children ready for school. She did not have time for pussyfooting around in the kitchen. She was organized and expected her instructions to be carried out.

When Albrecht came to the kitchen to see what all the commotion was about, Estelle said, "I asked that child to peel these potatoes before I got home so I could go ahead and get dinner cooked, and just look, Albrecht, what she did. She cut my potatoes up into little marbles. There is not enough potato here to fill a cavity. I don't have any food around this house to waste!"

Growing up poor, neither Albrecht nor Estelle believed in wasting food. From then on, Albrecht ensured that Claudia peeled the potatoes each day, resentful or not, before they got home from work. Seymour witnessed Estelle's attack on her daughter and ran to his room crying for his sister and the pain she endured, but he could not understand why Claudia was insolent. *You know how she* [Estelle] *is. Why not just do as you were told?* he thought.

Seymour felt sorry for Claudia when she was chastised by Albrecht and Estelle, but he never felt sorry for Aries. He found it too difficult to feel sorry for someone when they had been less than just to you. He would have been happy if Aries was chastised more. From both of his siblings, he learned how to satisfy and please Albrecht and Estelle, and he proved it each day. In a way, they were gifts to him and his learning. He was his mother's unwanted child, and he wanted to be wanted. Pleasing his parents became his expertise, and this gained him many rewards, considering to whom he was being compared.

*   *   *

Every evening after dinner, one of Aries's chores was sweeping the kitchen floor. He was the laziest of Albrecht and Estelle's three children. Albrecht was constantly on him to perform his chores as instructed, usually military style. Albrecht, having seven years of military training, could control his son; but it was a constant battle that he did not mind doing because he knew what he said was going to be enforced. When it came to sweeping the kitchen floor, Albrecht would instruct Aries to pull the kitchen table and four chairs away from the kitchen wall to get all the crumbs and any food that may have dropped to the floor from the kitchen table while they all ate. Aries resented taking orders, period—but from his father, he hated it even more because his father never let up on him.

Aries was happier when his father was away in the military. He saw himself as the head of the household. With Albrecht's return from overseas, he was usurped. He did not like it for one minute, although he was just a young teen. He was accustomed to getting one over on his mother most of the time, but his father was a different story. He constantly challenged his father, and he decided he was going to do as little as possible of what his father instructed him to do. Albrecht, on the other hand, was determined his son was going to obey his orders. This created a male testosterone tension between the two of them.

Every day, Albrecht would wait until Aries had settled himself down in front of the television; then he would ask Aries if he had swept the kitchen floor. Aries would reply with a "why are you questioning me?" attitude, saying, "Yeah, I swept the kitchen floor."

Albrecht would then go to the kitchen and inspect the floor to see if it was done to his satisfaction. When he finished his inspection, he would then interrupt Aries from his television program and say, "Go back and sweep the kitchen floor. And the next time, pull out the table and chairs from the wall as I asked you to do."

Aries would reply, "But I just swept the kitchen floor!"

Albrecht would say, "But I asked you to pull the table and chairs from the wall, and you did not do as I asked you to do."

Angry and belligerent, Aries would jump up from the television program, knowing he had only done a half-assed job at sweeping the kitchen floor the first time. In a hurry to get back to his television program, he swept the floor half-assed the second time too. When his father inspected the kitchen floor for the second time, he again interrupted Aries and asked for the third time to sweep the floor. Aries, now missing twenty minutes of his television program and sulking, finally pulls the table and chairs from the wall and sweeps the floor as he was instructed the first time. For the life of him, Aries simply could not figure out for years how his father—who was not present in the kitchen when he swept the floor—knew he had not pulled the table and chairs from the wall.

What Albrecht had never told anybody was that each day after dinner, he would place a matchstick under one leg of the kitchen table. If Aries pulled the table from the wall, the matchstick would have been swept up along with the table crumbs. But since Aries did not pull the table from the wall, his father always knew he had not moved the table because the matchstick remained.

After missing his entire television program, he pouted in sadness. On the way back to his bedroom, he could hear his father saying to him from the hallway, "Aries, it will always take you three times as long to do your chores when you don't do them right the first time!"

This situation occurred time and time again. Aries never knew his father's secret, and it annoyed Aries when he could not outwit his father, especially when he was in a hurry to go somewhere or do something he really wanted to do.

*   *   *

One of Albrecht's younger brothers had been a juvenile delinquent. Theopolis and Bessie sent him to reform school to see if they could get him to turn his life around. The reform school was good for him, and when he completed his stint with the school, he enlisted in the military for four years. He traveled the world and met many women in Spain, France, and Italy who taught him their language. In preparation for his discharge from the military, he had decided to use his GI Bill benefits to attend college and study foreign languages. He had completed his GED equivalency while in reform school and was accepted to college.

While in the military, he sent an allotment to his mother and father to save for a down payment to eventually use for the purchase of a family house. Up to this time, his parents still lived in the apartment they had raised their eight children in.

A few weeks prior to his discharge, he purchased a new car for use to commute to and from college. He looked up to his older brother Albrecht because, of all the Rose siblings, he had made the most of his life. He asked Albrecht and Estelle if he could park his new car at their house for a few weeks until his discharge was final, and they agreed. He figured since they lived on military property, it would be safer than parking it in the city, where it could be subjected to vandalism or even stolen.

Aries was approaching age sixteen, at which time he would be eligible to apply for a driver's permit. Albrecht had no enthusiasm for getting his son a driver's license because, throughout his childhood, he was a problem child. However, he made a promise to his son that if he got a job after school and saved his money to purchase his car insurance, he would let him apply for a driver's permit and allow him privileges to use the family car occasionally.

With great joy, Aries got a small job and hustled to save his money. He made a shoe box and started shining shoes for the military and civilian men on the base. He got a little job after school emptying trash cans at the gas station. All his earnings were saved religiously for his car insurance. Up to this point, a driver's permit was the only thing in his life he ever got serious with. His grades even improved in a small measure. Estelle was pleased to see this change in her son. He had actually taken steps to maturity, and Aries saved far more than he needed. This change was temporary for about six months until Aries ruined it.

At this same time, Bessie was proud of her young son for being able to turn his life around—first by completing his GED and, second, for serving in the military for four years. However, with her youngest son, she was also having problems. He had been drafted in the army a few years earlier but was honorably discharged with a disability after being shell shocked during the war. He was her most good-natured son before he went into the military. But when he returned, he was an alcoholic, and she could not control him.

Theopolis and Bessie also imposed on Albrecht and Estelle, asking if the very youngest son could stay with them for a few weeks, to get him dried out. Since being discharged from the military, all he would do with his disability check was to hang out until all hours in the morning, drinking wine with the local bums in the city. Albrecht and Estelle agreed to let him move in with them for a few weeks. Estelle felt her plate was full, but there was really nothing she could say because Albrecht had accepted Anise's son for six months while she was in the mental hospital. In addition, she and Albrecht had lived with Bessie and Theopolis when they got married.

After Albrecht's youngest brother arrived, Aries got the bright idea that he was going to teach his twenty-one-year-old shell shocked, alcoholic uncle how to drive. Aries was so anxious to get out of the house, he thought if he taught his uncle, he could be viewed as a good son, and he could get out of the house officially and justifiably for performing a good deed for his uncle.

Aries thought he was being welcoming and helpful to his uncle's recovery if he taught him how to drive. At this point, Aries had already taken driving lessons. In preparation for his driving test the following week, he felt like he would share his new skill with his uncle.

On the first Saturday night of his uncle's arrival, Aries sneaked into Albrecht and Estelle's bedroom (which was off limits to all the children), and without authorization, he took the keys to the brand-new car.

Aries unlocked the car and had his uncle sit in the driver's seat. He instructed his uncle on how to start the car. After the car was started, he told his uncle to step on the clutch to put the car in reverse. His uncle did as he instructed. Then Aries told him to step softly on the gas pedal to back the car out of the tiny parking space. But never having any experience driving a car, his uncle pressed the gas pedal too hard and crashed into the car parked in the rear, tearing out the front bumper, grill, and headlights.

Aries panicked and said, "Ahhhh, man, we have got to get out of here. Put the car in drive and step on the gas." His uncle did just as he was told, but Aries did not tell him to turn the steering wheel, and he crashed into the car in front of him, tearing out the bumper, grill, and headlights on the brand-new car and tearing out the bumper, taillights, and trunk of the car in front of him. Three cars were severely damaged in five minutes.

On the military base, you could leave the doors to your house open. In the middle of the night, Seymour was awakened by a female neighbor who asked him, "Where are your mother and father?" She needed the telephone number because Aries had wrecked three cars in front of her house.

Seymour recited the number to the neighbor lady. She said "thank you" to Seymour, but Seymour dropped his head on his pillow and fell back to sleep. Seymour had no feelings about his brother being in a car crash.

The neighbor lady interrupted Seymour and said, "Well, aren't you upset about your brother?"

Seymour replied "No, he deserves what he is going to get!" and went back to sleep.

The neighbor lady laughed and told everyone in the neighborhood what Seymour had said. They too saw the humor and honesty because they knew it was all true.

When Albrecht returned home and found out what had happened to the three cars, all he said to Aries was "Give me your passbook saving account." Aries, with Estelle standing by his side, knew instantly what Albrecht was going to do—and that was to take every penny that Aries had saved for car insurance and more to pay for the damage to the cars, and there was to be no driving test for Aries the following week. That was Aries's punishment.

The entire family was mute for a week. Aries had once again disrupted the Rose family.

And, as anticipated, Albrecht made Aries pay for all the damages, forcing him to continue working after school and handing his entire paycheck over until all the damages were paid. Albrecht also prevented him from getting his driver's license until the following year. It took well over a year for Aries to pay for all the damages.

Estelle thought the punishment was too severe and said, "But, Albrecht, the punishment is too severe!"

Albrecht replied, "Estelle, the boy has got to learn. My decision is final, and don't talk about this anymore!"

Estelle did all she could to console Aries, but there was nothing she could say or do to console him.

Seymour, who shared a bedroom with Aries, had no sympathy. His heart had still not softened toward his brother. There was too much negative history, and Aries kept making more. This was just another of his numerous infractions, and there was never enough justice for all who came in contact with Aries. And—with the exception of this incident—Aries always laughed at his own toxic behavior, which made it hard for Seymour to digest such thoughtlessness.

*   *   *

By the following year, Aries had paid the damages for the three wrecked cars. Albrecht allowed Aries to get his driver's license but never gave him permission to use the family car. By June, his high school held its annual senior prom event. Estelle knew that Albrecht held animosity toward Aries for being such a consistently disobedient child. Albrecht felt, at the very least, children should be obedient. He worked hard every day, and none of his children wanted for anything. In Albrecht's mind, obedience was an absolute minimum requirement. If they disobeyed, they had consequences. That was all there was to it.

Estelle saw Aries's prom night as a once-in-a-lifetime thing, and for two weeks prior to Aries's prom, Estelle tried as hard as she could to get Albrecht, just this one time, to let Aries use the family car. And Albrecht said, "No!"

On the night of the prom, Estelle pressed Albrecht so hard, he finally snapped and, in total disgust for being pressured, said, "Okay, Estelle, you want the boy to have the car? Here are the keys. You tell him to take the car! Here are the keys, just take the car!"

Estelle, pleased with her victory, took the keys and rushed to Aries at the last hour, saying, "Here are the keys. Your father said you could take the car. But I want you to have the car back home by midnight."

Aries hated Albrecht's punishments and paid Estelle no mind about the time. He thought midnight was too early, and she did not know anything about proms of the current day. In his mind, he felt cocksure that his mother was going to get the keys for him. He knew she had a compassionate heart, not knowing she had enabled the behavior she received from him. He took the keys to the car and quickly left the house.

Estelle knew she had stuck her neck out too far with Albrecht, pressuring him to let Aries have the car, so she stayed awake to make sure Aries brought the car back home by midnight and in one piece. Then at midnight, it would be over, and Aries would have gone to his prom and she could rest in peace. Estelle felt sure that since Aries knew she had broken a blood vessel to get the car for him, the least he could do for her was to return the car as she had asked.

Aries felt that since he had been punished for so long by his father, he thought he would get even with Albrecht and keep the car as long as he pleased. No punishment would hurt as much as being denied his driver's license. When midnight arrived, there was no car and there was no Aries. When one, two, and three o'clock arrived, there was still no Aries. Estelle was sleepless and now in a panic.

As she tiptoed into the bedroom to awaken Albrecht to let him know that Aries had not returned the car, Albrecht opened his eyes, still salty with Estelle for pressuring him into letting Aries take the car and knowing full well the child was not going to follow their directions. He said to Estelle in a huff, "You wanted him to have the car. Now he has the car, and I don't want to hear nothing about it!"

He laid his head back down on the pillow and went back to sleep. Estelle bit her nails, talked to herself, and cried as she waited for Aries to return.

*   *   *

Estelle wanted Claudia to be a debutante. She reflected on the years she had assisted Mrs. Astor's daughters getting dressed in and out of their gowns for their coming-out parties. Estelle knew her days were over for participating in such activities, but she wanted these same things for her daughter. Although Albrecht and Estelle, as parents, did not have the credentials to sponsor Claudia in the prestigious black cotillions of society, Estelle had made friends with her physician and asked if he would be willing to sponsor her daughter since she and her husband could not. Her physician said yes, he would be happy to sponsor Claudia. He had delivered all of Estelle's children and had been kept up to date by Estelle as to their growth and progress. He knew that Aries was a bit unruly; but to his satisfaction, he knew Claudia to be polished, well-mannered, modest, and an honor student. He also knew she was not a virgin but never revealed this to Estelle.

After Estelle had set the stage for Claudia to be become a debutante and introduced to society, she presented her idea to Albrecht and he flatly refused, stating, "Estelle, we are not in that class of people, and I don't want to be around them anyway. They are the snobby kinds of people who say "Well, how do you do, and what do you do?" Those kinds of people. It is horseshit! No. I want no part of it. We are not college graduates, and we cannot sponsor her anyway."

Estelle heard Albrecht's rebuff and desperately replied, "I have asked Dr. Evans, and he said he would sponsor her for us."

"No, Estelle! I don't want some other man sponsoring my daughter. It makes us appear as if we are not good enough to belong. Claudia would be considered a second choice to those young men," he said.

"But, Albrecht, how do you ever move up in the world if someone doesn't help you? Benevolent whites taught the slaves to read and write. You are not making any sense."

Estelle was excited about the idea and knew that Claudia would love the beautiful gowns and accoutrements. She could wear her first makeup and enjoy all the fanfare associated with a coming-out party. Through Estelle's eyes, how could any girl not jump at the chance to be exposed to the most eligible young men in the city who have a college education and opportunities for professional jobs? Estelle knew this would have been her choice if she had been given the opportunity.

Estelle approached Claudia with the thought that if she approached her father, he would say yes to his daughter. She asked, "Now wouldn't you like to be a debutante and meet the most eligible young men in society?"

Claudia looked at her mother and just shook her head and said, "No. I am not interested."

Estelle could not believe her ears. Whoever heard of a young girl not wanting to be a debutante? Estelle did not get it. She was hurt and disappointed, but she concluded Claudia was her father's child, and her attitude toward life was the same as her father's. Shaking her head in disbelief, she said to herself, "I got plenty of nothing, and nothing is plenty for me! Whoever heard of such foolishness?"

Later in the evening, Albrecht could still see the disappointment in Estelle's face and said, "Well, if the child does not want to do it, why would you make her do it?"

Estelle sadly replied, "Well, if you had just encouraged her a little, she would have done it for you. She is just a child, Albrecht, and children don't know what they want. You have got to help guide them along. Our chances are gone, but you could at least encourage your children."

Estelle was exasperated with both of them and could not understand why she was surrounded by a husband and daughter who wanted nothing in life.

*   *   *

Estelle purchased a handsome wool sports jacket for Aries because he and two of his high school friends were going to the sports stadium to see a baseball game. Estelle was so pleased to see Aries neatly dressed for a change, wearing polished shoes, pressed slacks, a freshly ironed starched shirt, and he had his hair freshly cut.

Estelle had, over the years, great hopes for Aries because, though he was a terror to Claudia and Seymour, he tried to get away with murder with Albrecht, but she loved him. She sometimes wondered if Aries was her punishment for sometimes giving her father a hard time when she was a child. She admitted to herself that she disliked her father's abuse and challenged him at every point in the road, but she also thought she was the hardest worker in her family and deserved a little slack, which her father never gave her. Aries was not the hardworking type. He was lazy like her father. *Genes are fascinating*, she thought.

Aries, on the other hand, had both a mother and father, never missed a meal, had plenty of clothing, had a stable roof over his head, and he had not been abused. Yet he never appeared to be grateful or appreciative for any of her kindness toward him. He was selfish and thoughtless.

It was a beautiful summer day, and with so much hope in her heart, Estelle thought that maybe this would be the day that he started to mature and show some signs of straightening himself out and getting on the right track. She had stuck by him and protected him as much as she could, but he was not the child to adjust his attitude, behave, or do the right thing.

After Estelle attempted to hug her child and wish him a wonderful day, Aries did his standard pushback and said, "Ahhh, Ma! You don't have to hug me like that! You always want me to be a gentleman, but I don't want to be a gentleman. I just want to be a man!"

Estelle never gave up on her children; but for the life of her, she could not figure out how she managed to produce two cold children.

So off they went, Aries and his two friends, for a fun day at the stadium. But unbeknownst to Albrecht, Estelle, or his two friends, Aries had illegally purchased a pint of whiskey and placed it in the inside of his sport jacket. He had planned to sneak the whiskey in the stadium as a surprise for the young men as they watched the game. He wanted to impress them. Also unknown to Albrecht and Estelle, a next-door neighbor was also supplying Aries with booze for sport, thinking this was the way to turn boys into men.

When the police department called Albrecht and Estelle to report that Aries was in jail, Estelle became hysterical, wondering what on earth had happened between her front door and the entrance to the stadium. Aries had only left home an hour ago. The officer informed Albrecht that Aries was in possession of alcohol and that it was absolutely prohibited in the stadium—and further, that he was underage. Someone would have to come and post bail for him before he was released. He had forty-eight hours in the holding cell.

Albrecht took a deep breath and said to Estelle, "I am going to kill that boy. He is in jail!"

"Well, come on, Albrecht. Let's go get him!" Estelle said.

He shortly replied, "No! Just let him sit there in jail awhile. Let him cool his heels."

In a whiny voice, Estelle said, "Now, Albrecht! You don't want the child to have this on his record. He will never get a job. You have to get him out!"

Albrecht said, "No!"

Estelle walked the floor night and day for nearly the full forty-eight hours, wondering what was happening to her child. On Monday at noon, Estelle dressed like she was going to a coronation. She and Albrecht went to the court to post bail for Aries.

When Aries was brought into the courtroom, he was so happy to see his parents, but his mother and father said not a word; nor did they crack a smile. Estelle's instincts were to run to Aries and hug him as if he had been away for six years, but Albrecht had coached her to control herself in the courtroom. This was the first time in their marriage that they were both disappointed to the core with Aries and his whole attitude. Aries thought all this was funny once he saw his parents. He knew his parents were going to come and get him.

The judge told Albrecht and Estelle that he was going to let their son go this time because they appeared to be very respectable colored people; but if, under any circumstances, he appeared in this court again, he would be prosecuted and sent to jail for the full duration of his sentence.

On the ride home, neither Albrecht nor Estelle said a word to Aries as he sat in the back seat of the old Chevrolet. Aries sought immediate forgiveness, but forgiveness was not forthcoming. Albrecht was disgusted, and Estelle was relieved and tired, for she had not slept in two days. Just as his father made him responsible for the three damaged cars, he made him responsible for reimbursing them for his bail.

When they arrived home and pulled into the parking lot, Estelle got out of the car, slammed the door shut, and she said out loud, "Children! When they are little, they are on your feet, and when they are grown, they are on your heart! You don't ever get through with them!"

* * *

It was Aries's senior year in high school, and Estelle had saved money for him to go to college. She did not know how much it was going to cost, but she would borrow additional funds from the bank if necessary. He was going to college in her mind. She had established good credit with the department stores. She created debt but paid on time each month. The stores required the credit be issued in her husband's name, thus her credit cards read "Mrs. Albrecht Rose" rather than "Mrs. Estelle Rose."

Since Albrecht was not interested in paying to send his children to college, Estelle decided years earlier that she would pay to send the first child to college if Albrecht would agree to send the second. As she recovered from paying for Aries, she would then pay for Seymour. It was a more-than-fair arrangement. Albrecht believed the boys should make it on their own, and a girl was supposed to stay home to be wife to her man and mother to his children. He did not think women needed a college education, but he went along with Estelle's scheme, thinking that by the time it was his turn to pay for Claudia, she would already be married or wouldn't want to go to college. Estelle thought in some areas, Albrecht was so archaic and not forward-thinking.

At the last minute, Aries applied and was accepted at a rural western state college. It was not Estelle's first choice for him, but it was somewhere, and she had hopes that the exposure to other young college men would help him to mature and finally show some signs of growing up.

After Aries's arrival at the rural college campus, he considered it nowhere land, and he was not enamored with the location. But after the first year, his grades were not good enough to transfer to another college. During the first semester of his second year, he asked Estelle to buy him a car. He knew his mother tried to support him in all he did. Even when he was wrong, she stood by his side; but in this case, Estelle said flatly and without hesitation, "No, boy! Here I am out here working every day, bursting a blood vessel for you to go to college and have an opportunity I never had, and you want me to buy you a car too? No! That is first of all. And second of all, I cannot afford to buy you a car. And if I could, I wouldn't do it anyway!" She said to him, "You have got a lot of nerve."

Knowing just how important it was to Estelle for her son to go to college, he threatened her by saying, "Well, if I can't have a car, then I will quit college."

Estelle replied, "Then you just have to quit then, because Mother is not buying you a car. If you wish to cut off your nose to spite your face, then so be it. But I am finished with you, boy."

Aries had played his last card with Estelle, and he had lost. Rather than take low and stay in college, he quit. Estelle was disappointed but unmoved.

She told Albrecht, Claudia, and Seymour, "Aries does not know what I am made of, but I was negotiating in the streets of Washington, DC, when I was ten and twelve years old! He must think I am a fool, but you all listen to me. My money will be spent elsewhere! He is on his own from now on, and let's see how far he gets in this world with no college education! I was trying to help the boy!"

Aries could not believe Estelle would not buy him a car. She had, in the past, dug him out of many holes. She had always taken his side and protected him. She even interceded on his behalf when Albrecht had lost hope for his son. He was shocked and could not believe this situation he had created for himself. But on this occasion, he had dug his own hole and was stuck in it! The only thing he could hear Estelle say was "I am finished with you, boy!" Although he had her support in the past, he knew this time, she was really finished with him.

He assumed that after he quit college, he was coming back home to live with Albrecht and Estelle. His father had a different plan for him. Aries was going to get a job and move out, or he could join the military—but under no circumstances was he living at home. Albrecht had instilled in each of his three children that when they reached legal age, he was "breaking their plate." This translated to "I am not feeding you anymore!"

Aries was the first child of his three children, and it was time for him to go out into the world and make his way. Albrecht felt he and Estelle had offered him an opportunity to make a better life for himself with a college education, and he chose not to accept it.

*   *   *

When Aries heard his father's alternatives, he got belligerent and threatened to fight his father. To Albrecht, this was a lack of respect that he was not tolerating from his son. Albrecht said without an ounce of anger or fear, "Well, son, we are going to settle this right here and right now!"

Although Aries had some size on him as a healthy young man, he knew his father was a champion swimmer and had continued his military exercises each morning, and this was not going to be an easy fight. Albrecht could do a hundred push-ups a day and balance himself on his head. He was in good health and great physical shape.

Aries had not expected his father to follow through on his bullying comment because Albrecht had never laid a hand on any of his children. But in this case, he escorted his son to the front yard of the apartment building and said, "Now you take the first punch, son. And when you do, you had better kill me because otherwise, I am going to kill you!" This was Albrecht's threat to his son.

As all the neighbors peeked from windows and doors at the spectacle Aries had created, some of the men and boys ran to the front yard from faraway apartments within the complex to see this father-son fight which no one had ever seen in this stable middle-class community—and on military property too.

Albrecht had tightened his fists and positioned them in the air. He was swinging them in the air and waited for Aries to take the first punch. Estelle, Claudia, and Seymour did not go out of the house from total embarrassment and knowing that this was another situation Aries was not going to get out of, period! Estelle had made peace in her soul that she was finished with worrying about Aries after he dropped out of college. She knew from past experience that Albrecht was at the end of his rope with his son.

Teen boys chanted and urged Aries on. "Hit him! Hit him!"

Albrecht egged the teenagers on too, in an effort to take the opportunity to reduce and humiliate his son before his friends. Albrecht said "What are you waiting for?" with his fists clenched and ready for a quick knockout. "Go ahead. Go ahead and hit me."

Albrecht maintained his stance and clenched fists to knock his son out, and the crowd had gotten larger with each passing minute. Albrecht had enough of Aries's bullying and abuse to Claudia and especially to Seymour. This was going to be the day for him to straighten up and ship out.

The teen boys said again, "Aries! Go ahead, hit him!"

Aries was now totally humiliated and diminished in front of all his friends and the neighbors—men and women and girls too. He knew he did not want to lose this fight or be harmed as he had harmed many others during his elementary and high school years.

Aries, after a few minutes, had tears in his eyes and slowly dropped his fists in defeat and backed down. All the teenage boys booed him and told him he was a coward. "You are a punk, Aries!" they shouted. Those who had been victims of Aries's terror finally saw justice for themselves for the first time. Seymour saw justice for himself too, and although he thought he hated his brother, he was saddened that Aries was so recalcitrant. And after this incident, all the teens reminded Aries that he was nothing more than a scared and frightened coward. He "punked-out."

Aries signed up for the military and was sent to basic training, where his life turned for the worse.

With Aries moved out of the house to join the military, the Rose house was much calmer. Seymour was the happiest with the departure of his brother because he no longer needed to live in fear within the confines of his habitat. Moreover, he did not have to share a bedroom any longer. He was relieved that he no longer had to live in danger, bullying, and fear. He was sorry that things ended the way they did, but Aries was not going to obey when he and Claudia obeyed. It was not fair.

He asked Estelle to take Aries's bed out of the room they shared with the hope that he never returned home again. Estelle said no to the overture. "The bed can be used for a guest."

Seymour was not happy with the reply, and Estelle looked at him and said, "Well, that's tough!"

*   *   *

The following June, it was announced that Claudia was the valedictorian of her high school class. Estelle glowed with pride and instantly assumed parental bragging. She loved to distinguish her children from all the rest. Claudia was not a competitive person. Her becoming valedictorian was an act of her purely going to class every day and doing her homework consistently. Claudia was impervious to how much the faculty and staff adored her and marveled over her aptitude and scholarship. All the attention she received came without a hint of gloating. She received partial scholarships for her college tuition, but the high school did not have funds for a full scholarship for all the honor students. As the scholarship chairman for her school, Albrecht was grateful for what the school was offering to Claudia, but he knew there were other children in greater need than his daughter, so he voted to support a particle or no scholarship for Claudia. This gave the less fortunate honor students a chance to have assistance with their tuition expenses.

It was now Albrecht's turn to pay for his daughter's college education, but instead of paying up front, as Estelle had done for Aries, he made student loans in Claudia's name, which made her responsible for payment if she did not earn a college degree. He agreed that if she stayed in college until she graduated, he would assume responsibility for her student loans. If she decided to quit and waste the loan money, she would be liable for the loans. Albrecht was not as anxious to throw crutches to his spoiled children as Estelle would have done. Albrecht did not care if his children went to college or not. All he wanted of his children were for them to follow the Ten Commandments, obey public laws, grow up, and move out of his house.

Claudia had not been a problem child. Estelle thought it unreasonable for Albrecht to make such an arrangement with his daughter, but in that Claudia was not warm toward Estelle, she took the position of just staying out of it. Claudia understood and agreed to the terms, so there was little else Estelle could do. She had gone that route with her cotillion dreams for Claudia, and that route did not work. Estelle was still repaying tuition loans for Aries's fiasco, and she still had to prepare for Seymour if he decided to go to college. She took a hands-off approach to Albrecht and Claudia's agreement.

Estelle, with Seymour in tow, visited Claudia on her private college campus just as religiously as she did when Anise was in the mental hospital. She brought shopping bags of new clothes, new bedding for her dormitory room, and gave Claudia above-average spending money. She even gave Claudia a credit card to charge her incidentals at the nearby shopping center.

Estelle bent over backward to help Claudia. She was no fool in giving Claudia her credit card. She knew Claudia would not take advantage of her or go overboard. Claudia was a flawlessly responsible and trustworthy girl. In normal fashion, she was nonchalant and dismissive toward her mother's offerings and rarely—if ever—used the credit card, saying she didn't need anything. Claudia's friends could not believe or understand how she could be so cold toward her mother. They would have grabbed at the opportunity to have their mother's credit card. Claudia did not want anything from her mother.

Claudia majored in European history. She took languages, mathematics, and advanced literature and historical research courses. She had some academic adjustments to make but only had difficulty with calculus. All eyes were on her, from her high school teachers, college professors, her parents—but most of all, Seymour. Claudia's going to college was the biggest inspiration he had ever had from his family. He wanted to be just like her, to attend college and be somebody special. By this time, he had made no identifiable distinguishing marks toward anything but being an average student, a good-natured person, and a mother's boy. Claudia was his light, but she was as distant to him as she was toward her mother.

Like the cotillion, Estelle encouraged Claudia to join a sorority with the thought that she could learn better social skills. She would be exposed to high-end people and no longer be associated with less ambitious teens. But again, Claudia said she did not want to join. But under the peer pressure of her new college dormitory mates and girlfriends, she joined a sorority. She flourished in the sorority as she had in high school. She was hailed and admired by many, but she appeared indifferent toward most people. The people she was closest with were the students who were otherwise shunned by the campus elite. On the other hand, the most handsome young men on the campus asked her out for dates. In her dating, she appeared to date well-endowed men whose genitals pressed favorably through their tight slacks.

When Claudia brought men home from high school and college, Estelle would often say, "Claudia, why do you bring these 'lap-legged' men around here?" Estelle thought it "seedy" that men did not wear support underwear or roomier pants to accommodate their private parts; she thought it ungentlemanly for men to expose themselves in such a common manner.

Claudia had no idea what Estelle was talking about when she referred to men with lapped legs, and one day, she pulled Seymour aside and asked, "What does Mother mean when she says that?" Claudia knew that Seymour was always around their mother and would probably know what she intended by the remark. Unbeknownst to Claudia, he had made the same observation as their mother. Seymour noticed with interest.

Embarrassed, he whispered to Claudia with his head held downward, "You know, Claudia." As he lowered his head and pointed his index finger to his private parts, he replied, "A big dick!"

Claudia replied with disdain, "Well, I have never!" She thought the remark was obscene and totally inappropriate for a mother to say such a thing to her daughter. She further thought why her mother was checking out her boyfriends' crotches anyway. Estelle never realized that the warmth she wanted from her daughter was denied due to Estelle's raw honesty.

Claudia thought it was a disgusting statement. She looked at Seymour and said, "See, that's why I don't want to have anything to do with her."

Estelle never comprehended that what she said to her children carried a negative and disapproving impact that would affect the quality of her relationship with them. For Estelle, whatever came up came out unfiltered. She never intended any harm—just taking a shortcut to an honest observation. If challenged on any of her comments, her justification was this: "It is no harm in calling a spade a spade." There was a rawness, honesty, and a truth to calling a spade a spade.

Albrecht understood Claudia and Estelle but never corrected or chastised Estelle during these occasions. But he would shake his head and say, "Estelle, you never cease to amaze me."

Estelle's children never could comprehend that their mother had already been a mother to her sister and brother. She was shaving her father when she was ten years old. Estelle was life-schooled before her years, and her time for being delicate and dainty was squat. She needed to get to the point without all the "gentility" that was considered polite manners and social graces. She had too much to do and little time. If she had offended her children, it was just too bad.

The delicate feminine tone her children expected was seldom present. She would say to her children, "I just don't have time with you children for all that malarkey." Estelle had matured long before her years. Elder neighbors and friends often told Estelle she had a lot of wisdom for one so young.

*   *   *

Weeks after Aries enlisted in the military, he learned from a girl he had sex with in a local park that he had a baby on the way. Unlike Claudia, Aries knew little to nothing about the ends and outs of sexuality. Seymour may have known more.

Aries knew for sure that Estelle had preached to all the children, "Now don't you children go out here and have no babies because I will not be rocking them! If you do make one, figure out where you are going to live because no babies are coming in here. And that goes for you too, Seymour! Noooo. I see these teenagers around here having all these babies that they can't take care of then bring them home to Mama to keep! But I have news for you. This mama is not going to do it! I raised my mother's children and my own, so it is just a tough tidy if you want to go out here and make a mistake! And don't be coming up here with some excuse that nobody told you! I am telling you now, and you had better listen to me!"

Again, Estelle was forgetting that she had asked Bessie to take care of Aries so that she could accept a government position. She was offended when Bessie said no to her.

As a teenager in his early years, Aries had been sneaking alcohol and getting pretty glassy-eyed, but learning of this pregnancy accelerated his problem. He did not know what he was going to do, but under no circumstances did he want Estelle to know. After about three years of guilt feelings and his conscience beating him so bad, he wrote to Claudia at her college from his duty station to ask her what he should do. Over the few years of the child's birth, he never sent a penny for child support because he wanted to stay in denial. Further, he had married someone else. When Claudia replied to Aries's letter, she wrote back four simple words: "Just tell the truth."

When Aries returned to the States on furlough, he mustered up the courage to tell Albrecht what had happened some three years ago in the park. Albrecht simply looked at Aries and said, "You have hurt and disappointed your mother enough, and under no circumstances is she to know about this because it would kill her. So you just go about your life. Figure out what you want to do, but keep your mother out of it."

Albrecht convened Claudia and Seymour to inform them that they had a nephew out there, and he said, "But please do not disclose this to your mother because she would not be able to handle the news."

Seymour thought about what Albrecht had said to him and Claudia, but from his Catholic teaching, this was some type of collusion, making him an accessory to the situation. Seymour had a history of standing to support his mother in everything. After a few days of childhood deliberation, he ran and told his mother what had happened. Since Seymour was only twelve years old, she dismissed it, saying out loud, "You don't know what you are talking about, boy! You are too young to know anything like that!"

Seymour did not care if his mother dismissed his message to his ignorance of the subject, but he felt cleansed and resolved from within himself for not holding a secret from his mother or not being loyal. She still reminded him from time to time that he was an unwanted child, and he was still struggling internally with these words from her.

Seymour was too young to know what was really going on with Aries and Claudia. There was no one who took the time to explain to him what was happening. He clearly recognized that whatever it was, it was not making Albrecht very happy. Even though he still held feelings of being unwanted and unloved, a piece of him hurt for Albrecht, whom he thought was a good man.

Seymour cried at almost every crisis that Aries and Claudia ever found themselves. He cried because he was too old to be a baby and too young to understand what was happening in the world around him. Crying in seclusion was his release. More than anything, he felt left out because all his father's and mother's energies were devoted to fishing his siblings out of situations, leaving no time for him. He felt ignored and that the whole family was totally unaware of the impact Aries's and Claudia's behaviors had on him. The only thing he learned was to avoid these blunders when he became a teen.

He also concluded never to marry and to never have children. He knew within himself that he was much too sensitive to have children; and if they turned out like Aries and Claudia, they would break his heart.

CHAPTER THIRTY-THREE

Home Ownership

Albrecht had broken two plates. Aries and Claudia were independent and had moved away from home. Albrecht, Estelle, and Seymour shared the three-bedroom apartment. Albrecht was quite content living there. He liked the simplicity of apartment living, and it was what he had grown accustomed to. He had lived in an apartment all his life. Estelle had grown up poor and lived in a single-family detached house before the Great Depression. While living with Mrs. Astor, her family lived in an English basement. In this situation, she desired and valued home ownership and aspired to have a home someday.

One bright, sunny day, Albrecht went to the post office to check the mailbox. When he opened the mailbox, he pulled out a letter addressed to him that contained a notice that the apartment complex they lived in was being sold to developers. All residents were being required to vacate the premises within ninety days. Almost all the tenants were outraged and were not prepared to uproot and relocate. When Albrecht informed Estelle of the notice, she was as happy as could be and thought, *Well, praise Jesus!* She was approaching forty years old, and she felt they still had time to buy a house. If the house was financed for twenty years, it could be paid off by the time she was sixty, and this would be in keeping with a reasonable age to retire from her government job. *This could happen*, she thought.

After reading the letter, Albrecht made the mistake of asking Estelle what she wanted to do. Estelle had been pouting with him over the years for never buying a house. She felt the last time they were forced to relocate, it was due her salary. This increased household income disqualified them from subsidized housing. She wanted a house then. Over the years, she persisted on the house issue, but Albrecht would not give an inch.

When Albrecht posed the question to Estelle this time, she firmly seized the moment and took full advantage. She started one of her long-winded lectures to him that she knew Albrecht would not want to hear. "Well, don't ask me! If you were concerned with what I wanted to do in the first place, we never would be living in this apartment! It simply does not make sense to continue to pay all this money for an apartment when you get no return on your dollar! I always thought you had more sense than that, Albrecht. My father used to tell me, 'If you make a dollar, save a cent.' And if you get a title to a car and deed to a house, you will have a little something in your old age! You can see how both of our parents ended up in old age with nothing. Is this what you want for yourself? And I sure hope you don't think Aries and Claudia are going to take care of us!"

Estelle wasn't angry; however, she saw this as her last opportunity to get what she wanted. She was frustrated with the amount of time it took to make Albrecht come to his senses.

And furthermore, she continued, "You don't have a dime saved for old age. You are the one who didn't want me to have a job. And now that I have the job, all you want to do is spend your money on wine, women, and song." She repeated, "I hope you don't think these children of yours are going to take of you! They are not thinking about you!"

Estelle vented years of her frustrations at this moment, and she did not care how it sounded or who approved. She and Albrecht were now almost forty years old, and this was her last-ditch effort to get a house. Otherwise, it would be too late.

"When I wanted to move to a college town, you said you didn't want to live there. So now it is on you to figure it out where you want to live!"

When Estelle finished her lecture, he dryly replied, "I am sorry I asked."

Albrecht did not make sense to Estelle, and she did not make sense to Albrecht. He associated home ownership with hoity-toity, upwardly mobile middle-class colored folk. He felt these were the same elitists who ridiculed him when he was a child going to Catholic school. When he came in contact with this element, he would simply say "horseshit!"

When socializing with Estelle's friends and acquaintances, he hated it when the colored ladies and gentlemen who thought they were of pedigree would say to Albrecht in voices of fake superiority, "And how do you do? And what do you do?" Albrecht thought all colored folk were struggling with and without a college education and homeownership. He felt discrimination was discrimination no matter where you lived. He did not see the need for coloreds to further divide and subdivide themselves by social and educational classes.

So annoyed with their pretentiousness, Albrecht, at these gatherings, would announce for all to hear, "I am a laborer!" At which time Estelle would swiftly kick him under the table and correct him by informing her friends that her husband was a chemical engineer. Estelle enjoyed putting on French airs around her friends. They would nod to Estelle with faint approval, disbelief, and doubt. They would then follow up in a polite tone with the question, "Yes. And where was he educated, may I ask?"

To save himself from being kicked under the table again by his wife, he politely said to Estelle, "We have to excuse ourselves now." And they excused themselves from the table and returned home.

Albrecht would refer to these occasions as pure horseshit! When they got in the car to proceed home, Estelle would laugh at herself, knowing what Albrecht was saying was true. She knew that these were the same type of smartass children who made fun of her in school too. But she still saw value to the group, whether they were pretending to be something they were not. She just wanted to be exposed to a nicer community and be exposed to a better class of people than the ones she saw in apartment living.

Estelle strived for what she saw in her hometown. She longed to be accepted. Albrecht did not need their acceptance or seek it.

Albrecht deliberates on Estelle's lecture about home ownership. He did not have much time to relocate, but he decided to buy a lot of land in a segregated housing development. He procured a builder and had them break ground on a three-bedroom ranger for Estelle. It meant living in temporary housing for six more months.

Estelle pretended not to be enthused, but she was ecstatic as hell and started a house-shopping frenzy. It was a happy day for her, and Seymour joined in her happiness.

CHAPTER THIRTY-FOUR

Claudia

Claudia had completed her first year of college and was doing well. She had been an honor student in high school, a finalist of a statewide debate contest, valedictorian of her high school senior class, and carried a 3.5 in her first year of college. With coaching from her mother and peers, she pledged and was accepted in an old established Greek sorority. Her accomplishments were stunning for a young country girl who appeared nonchalant and unassuming.

At the conclusion of the second semester of her freshman year, a group of her sorority sisters had decided to work in Martha's Vineyard for the summer. She asked Albrecht and Estelle for permission, and they were elated that she was willing to take on a job to get some work experience and the opportunity to live away from home. Albrecht and Estelle thought it was not too far away from home, and she would have some of her college mates as a support system. This was an opportunity Albrecht and Estelle had never had at that age, and they were both happy for her.

Up to this point, she had only earned a few dollars babysitting for most of the Negro families in the neighborhood. The young wives and mothers thought Claudia was responsible and dependable and trusted her completely with their children. She was an academic model for their children. The husbands and fathers liked her as well, with lesser emphasis on their children. She was tall, slim, poised, graceful, and had style galore.

The young college girls worked for a businessman who had come to Martha's Vineyard from the African continent and had done very well. He owned several small hotels, guesthouses, and bars. He catered to the upwardly mobile Negro community. Negros from New York City, Boston, Philadelphia, Baltimore, and Washington, DC, came to Martha's Vineyard in the summers for the beach and nightlife. Albrecht and Estelle never had the discretionary funds for such trips or vacations. They were familiar with the conversation around Martha's Vineyard and prominent Negro families that traveled there. Other successful businessmen who settled along the eastern seaboard catered to this Martha's Vineyard crowd. The magazines that catered to the Negro communities featured articles on the Negro rich and famous.

Albrecht and Estelle were not worried about Claudia being away. Between Aries and Claudia, she was the most levelheaded of the two. It wasn't until Claudia called home to announce she was getting married that they questioned Claudia's levelheadedness.

When Estelle answered the ringing telephone, she was shocked and had a look of total disbelief on her face. She started asking a battery questions. "Getting married—marrying who? Well, you haven't been gone three weeks and you mean to tell me you are getting married?"

Claudia said, "Yes."

"Well then, Claudia, why are you getting married? Are you pregnant?"

Claudia said, "No."

"Well, what about college and your schooling? Don't you want to finish college first?"

Claudia said, "No."

"Well then tell me this. What is the big hurry? Why can't you wait?"

Estelle could not shake her total disbelief and just could not understand Claudia's rationale. It just made no sense to her. If this had been Aries on the telephone, she could have understood the impetuousness. But with Claudia, she could not.

Eventually, she gave up the conversation since she could not get straight answers from her daughter. In frustration, she shoved the telephone to Albrecht and said to him, "Claudia is on the telephone and says she is getting married." Estelle started stomping through the house in shock, saying, "This cannot be happening!"

Albrecht was listening to Estelle's interrogation of Claudia and knew that Claudia (or anyone else for that matter) did not want to be questioned in the manner and tone Estelle used when she was excited. She had a habit of responding to her children with a litany of questions. He calmly picked up the telephone and said, "Claudia, come home now and tell your mother and me what you are planning to do." Then Albrecht hung up the telephone. He was the opposite of Estelle when it came to being high-strung and raw with emotions. He accepted Estelle the way she was and ignored the intensity of her style of delivery. Albrecht could defuse any situation.

Estelle said, "Albrecht, there is something mighty fishy here. There is no way that child could have gone to Martha's Vineyard and, in a few weeks, meet someone, get engaged, and get a proposal of marriage. You mark my word, there is something mighty wrong, but I don't know what it is."

Albrecht said, "Calm down, Estelle. Let's hear what the girl has to say."

Calming down was not in Estelle's nature. When things did not make sense to her, she flipped out until they made sense.

Claudia, in her fashion, listened to her much calmer father and agreed to come home. She drove her fiancé's car to the ferryboat that would take her to the mainland, and she headed south on Interstate 95 and drove until she arrived home. She was nineteen years old, and when she pulled up to Albrecht and Estelle's new house, she was driving a baby-blue Lincoln Town Car convertible, the exact same year and model the late president John F. Kennedy was assassinated in. Her hair was colored jet black and teased to the hilt. She wore a beautiful pink chiffon scarf to hold her hair in place, large framed sunglasses to cover her attached eyelashes, and light coordinated makeup. From the nonchalant, nonmaterialistic, unassuming person her family knew, this was an entrance beyond recognition. They hardly recognized her. She was as well put together as any Hollywood leading lady.

Seymour thought she looked like a movie star and immediately liked the look—hook, line, and sinker. He did not need to ask any questions as he ran to the car and jumped in. Seymour had never seen such a display of opulence and money, and he thought if going to college introduced you to this life, he was in.

As Claudia exited the car, Albrecht said to Estelle, "Now, Estelle, stay calm and let the girl talk."

But Estelle was a raging tiger within herself and was chomping at the bit to have her questions answered, and she had no intention of staying calm too long if the story did not make sense. She acknowledged that her daughter looked glamorous and was driving a luxury car, but she really cared less about that. She wanted answers to her questions, and they had better not take too long to get out of Claudia's mouth.

Claudia was very direct when she announced she was marrying. She said they were flying to the Caribbean next week to get married.

Estelle tried to stay calm, but it was not in her nature. She asked, "Well, where did you meet him?"

Albrecht jumped in and said, "Estelle, keep quiet and let the girl talk."

Claudia replied tensely, "When my sorority sisters and I got to Martha's Vineyard, I was assigned to the Pearl Hotel as a desk clerk. Every day during my lunch break, I would sit at the pool reading. The owner of the hotel came up to me while I was sitting there and asked me to go out with him. He was my boss and owner of the hotel, so I told him yes."

Estelle was on pins and needles, not wanting to accept what she was hearing from her daughter. She rushed in, "So you are getting married just like that? Do you know anything about him? Does he have a family? And by the way, how old is he?"

Claudia answered the last question first. "Thirty-five."

Estelle, not calm any longer, said, "Thirty-five! Claudia, you can't just up and get married just like that to a man who is sixteen years older than you! Is he into drugs? Where does he get that kind of money?"

"He is the owner of the hotel where I work," Claudia repeated.

"The owner? What Negro do you know who owns a hotel in Martha's Vineyard that is of any repute? This is sounding like some cockamamy tale Anise would tell when she married Toms. There is something fishy here, Claudia. I am just telling you for your sake. There is something not adding up here!" Estelle—fatigued from asking questions and fatigued from the answers she was receiving—said. "Well, are you sure you are not pregnant?" she continued in a calmer voice.

"Yes, I am sure. We have not had sex yet," Claudia answered.

As Estelle pranced through the living room of her new house, she knew she was not making any headway with her daughter, which was not unusual. So she looked at Albrecht to pick up the slack and blurted out, "Albrecht, tell that child that she can't just jump up and get married to a man she doesn't even know. It does not make any sense!"

Albrecht turned his head toward his daughter and said, "Claudia, is there anything that I can do to stop you from marrying this man?"

Claudia replied, "No. I am going to marry him."

Albrecht turned his head back to his wife and said, "Estelle, she is nineteen years old and of legal age. And she said she is going to marry him, whether we like it or not."

In loathing to what she heard Albrecht say to his daughter, she thought of her husband as spineless. She took a breath to accept the sum total of Albrecht's response. She accepted defeat but, in one final plea, said, "But, Albrecht, you have got to do something."

As the baby-blue Lincoln glided over the bumpy country road from Estelle and Albrecht's new home back to up north, Seymour followed the vision of Claudia and the car from his bedroom window until it was no longer in sight. He understood his father's simplicity of thinking but was totally sympathetic to his mother. Seymour valued everything his mother believed in and took her side in all family disputes. But he sure looked forward to driving the Lincoln Town Car if she married.

Albrecht was content with his question and Claudia's reply. He thought his daughter wouldn't be the first woman or man to make a mistake. He believed children had to learn for themselves, make mistakes, and move on. He believed that you really couldn't change anybody—not even your children.

Estelle, on the other hand, drew on her childhood experiences with men and the harsh but wise counsel of her father who, in bachelorhood, was a man of the night. She believed, at the most basic level, men wanted sex and women wanted money out of relationships. Although Claudia said she had not been sexual with this man, she still thought something was up; and for the life of her, she could not figure out the thinking of either her husband or her daughter. Why would a man let his daughter just run off with another man without finding out something about him? Why would a girl blindly trust a man, knowing that it was a man's world and their needs always came before a woman's?

It is pure stupidity, she thought.

After Claudia drove off, Estelle calmed a bit and said to Albrecht, "This is the same thing that happened to my mother—a young, naïve country girl being taken advantage of by some city slicker [her father]. And where did she end up in ten years? Three children and dead. She never even got to see her children grow up. You don't have to listen to me, Albrecht, but you mark my word. There is something up here."

As Claudia drove north on Interstate 95 toward Boston, she heavily considered her mother's words and had braced herself for the emotional interrogation she knew Estelle was going to drop on her. Over her childhood, she had tried to stay out of her mother's way since she could never have a conversation with her. Estelle always claimed to have bad nerves and quickly became impatient, jumping into a loud, argumentative, and chastising argument that she resented. She knew her mother made sense, but this was her chance to get out of this one-horse country town and away from her struggling parents. She was afraid of Aries too, and there were never severe enough consequences for all the hell he put her through when they both lived at home.

She was going to marry and move up in Negro society and play bridge with the wives of businessmen. She did not want to be stuck with a Duncan Phyfe sofa and leather-top tables. She wanted modern furnishings and the fashions of the upwardly mobile.

She thought her father was slow and a foot shuffler and never took an aggressive stand against Estelle to defend the children against her verbal assaults and impatience with his children. She thought all her mother ever wanted was a job and pretty things and did not care about her anyway.

She had figured out in her high school biology class that Estelle was three months pregnant with Aries when she and her father married. She thought, *That was not a planned baby.* She knew from her mother's mouth that "Nobody wanted to see Seymour coming!" And she overheard her mother and her aunts talking about their children at a Christmas dinner table, and she overheard Estelle say to the ladies, "Claudia only got here because the rubber broke."

Claudia came to her own conclusion that her mother really did not want any of her children. It was not just Seymour she did not want. She thought back in time and drove forward, north.

Claudia and her fiancé eloped in the Caribbean, where marriage laws were not honored in the United States. Claudia had no wedding gown, no church bells, no reception, no family or friends, and no sex. There was a diamond cocktail watch for an engagement gift and a ring of no distinction. Claudia did not complain. She had no interest in the trappings of a traditional marriage. She was looking forward to the escape from her parents, love and sex.

Estelle racked her brain, trying to figure out Claudia's reasoning for a quick marriage. *God knows*, she thought, *I tried to give the girl everything a normal girl would want and certainly more than I ever had!* After working all day, Estelle decided to take it upon herself on a weekday to drive to Martha's Vineyard to see for herself what was going on. Seymour was again in tow! This time, she wanted Seymour to go with her to keep her company, and she did not want to be on the highway alone.

Albrecht was not worried at all about Claudia and did not attempt to stop Estelle. He simply felt they both would figure out what was going on between them. If either of them did not like their personal decisions, they were women and entitled and had the prerogative to change their minds.

As Estelle drove the Chevy up US Route 40 over the Susquehanna River and Delaware Memorial Bridges, she was rambling to Seymour all the way, "I hope you are learning from your brother's and sister's mistakes how not to mess up your life. And don't you run out here and get some girl pregnant because you are going to have to get married and take care of her and your child when you don't even have a skill to take care of yourself. You are a sheltered child. If children would only listen to their parents, they wouldn't find themselves in these situations. But they won't listen!

"My children heard me preaching all my life about the lives of my father, my mother, my sister, and my brother. Well! If they were not listening, then they just should have paid attention to me! They just should have listened to me when I was telling them all of these things. It is a cruel world out here, and nobody gives a damn! At least, when my children make their mistakes, my conscience will be clear. I have given them their health and strength and the chance to make it! This is what my father taught us. Your health and strength!" she repeated.

Seymour was accustomed to Estelle's lecture and rambling rants. He would just sit and listen. He was content to be at her side regardless of what she had to say or for how long. He read the street signs along the way and thought of the homework for school he had not done. He did not care. He preferred to be with his mother wherever she was going or whatever she was saying. He found more learning in her than any of the classes he attended at the segregated schools.

When they arrived at the home of Claudia and her new husband, Estelle was mesmerized by the opulence of the house and its appointments. It was not quite her taste or what she aspired to, but she could certainly be comfortable. The house was clean, and fresh floral arrangements were placed nicely around the house. Claudia was unusually receptive, and her husband was more than welcoming to Estelle and Seymour.

Claudia, amazingly, got a cookbook and hosted a lovely dinner. Estelle jumped in to help, but Claudia said she did not need any help. Estelle received this as a rebuff, but she did not want to cause a scene, so she just sat back down and let Claudia do it her way. When the dinner was over, her husband offered an invitation to Estelle and Seymour to stay for the night since it was an incredibly long drive.

Estelle declined and said she just wanted to meet the man who had married her daughter. She still had a long drive back. "Seymour has school in the morning, and I have to go to work tomorrow" was all she said.

As Estelle drove the car another five hours back down the dark road, she told Seymour to place his head on her lap and go to sleep because he had school in the morning. But before he went to sleep, he could hear Estelle say to herself, "That child is not happy."

All of Estelle's girlfriends said to her, "Stop worrying and leave the girl alone! She has been a good child. Just let her make up her own mind!"

Estelle tried her best to let it go, but there was something in her craw that just would not digest. In her head, she had never heard of a woman dating a serious man for a few weeks, getting engaged with a cocktail watch, then getting married with no ceremony in six weeks and it turned out to be anything but pure disaster.

"I have never heard of such a thing," she would tell them.

The last Saturday in July, Claudia called home crying her eyes out. Seymour answered the telephone, and the way Claudia sounded over the telephone, Seymour sarcastically thought, *Well, I guess those fake eyelashes are off now!*

He handed the telephone to Estelle, and when she heard her child sniffling and crying over the telephone in a nearly inaudible voice, she said, "Baby, what on earth is wrong with you?"

Through her tears, Claudia explained, "I don't know why, but he won't have sex with me."

Claudia's demands in life were few, but she enjoyed sex. Sex was something Estelle never wanted to talk about; but trying to be compassionate, she said, "Have you been having disagreements?"

"No," Claudia replied.

"Does he come home at night?"

"Yes," Claudia replied.

"Do you prepare meals for him and keep the house clean?" Estelle inquired.

Claudia replied, "Yes!"

After a battery of questions, Estelle concluded, "Well, Claudia, I don't know what else to ask you. I have never heard of a man not wanting sex with a young woman."

Estelle paused, and in her final attempt to get some understanding of the rationale behind her daughter's distress, she said, "Well, do you think he is gay? I mean, I don't know."

To ask this question was a real stretch for Estelle.

After being on the telephone with Claudia for one hour, Estelle hung up the receiver. She was annoyed by the call and livid with the conversation but, in a small way, victorious that whatever the problem, it was coming to a head. She could finally understand what was happening. Her answers were coming soon.

She looked at Albrecht, who was seated comfortably in the red barrel-back ribbed upholstered chair, and with disdain, she said, "That was Claudia on the telephone. She's up there in Martha's Vineyard snooting and crying because her husband won't have sex with her. I am telling you, it makes me so blame mad! When you are trying to teach these children some sense and trying to put something in their heads, they won't listen to you. But just as soon as they have a problem, then the first thing they want to do is run back home or call you with all their sob stories as if I know what to do. I don't know what to do. I begged her not to marry a man thirty-five years old. She had only known him a few weeks. I begged her!

"Children make these big messes and call me as if I know how to figure it out! Why do they have to call me with this stuff? She wouldn't be honest and tell me the truth, now I am supposed to guess what's wrong?

Well, I don't know what to do. I don't know why or how they get into these predicaments.

"It is just as I told you, Albrecht. I knew it was not going to be hunky-dory. Now it's a mess, she wants me to clean it up! I tell yah! I told her not to marry him, but she had to be so hardheaded and marry him anyway.

"And here you are, Albrecht, wanting to have ten of them [children]. Where is the pope now? When the Catholic Church wants you to have all these children. Where is he when the shit hits the fan? You have not been to see her once! Now I have to go back up there and help her clean up this mess. She wouldn't have been up there anyway if you had just opened your mouth and said something, anything. If you had just said something. She would have listened to you! I am telling you, mothers are sorry creatures!"

Estelle went on arguing for a half hour, walking from one room to another. Albrecht did not say a word. He sat calmly, trying to not hear everything Estelle was saying, but it was not working.

The next day, she said, "Come on, Seymour. We have to drive back up there again to see if we can straighten out this mess!"

Without ever saying a word, Seymour was her only friend in this situation. He felt needed; he felt like Estelle's husband. He wondered if this was his mother's first sign of accepting him as a person. He had never been invited to join his mother. He usually forced himself onto her. She usually tried hard to discourage him from going with her. This time, she had said "Come on, Seymour."

She was silent this time as she drove back north on the highway toward New York. She was thinking hard and gathering her thoughts on what she could possibly say to console her daughter. Seymour knew to listen, should she decide to talk. Keeping quiet or just being there would help provide some comfort to his mother. She did not want him to say anything anyway, because he was too young and would not know from experience what she was talking about.

Seymour thought when Aries and Claudia left home, it would be his turn to get some time and attention from his parents. He had not been a problem child, never was in trouble. But here we go again with another situation with one of the older children. And there was no need for them to be attentive to him because he never did anything. He saw Aries and Claudia as the high-priority children; he was not. He never required the attention from his parents that his siblings received. He was well cared for with food, clothing, and shelter. Estelle kept him in decent clothes, and nobody was concerned about him. He was an average student, so he simply lived his young life in solitude and in waiting. He was waiting to feel as loved as his brother and sister. His brother and sister received all the attention; thus he concluded they were loved the most.

Another three weeks passed, and the situation for Claudia had not changed. This time, when she called home crying, she said her new husband wanted a divorce. This time, Claudia's spirit was broken down. She was hurting. She had been a fool.

When the telephone rang this time, Estelle gave the telephone directly to Albrecht, who was relaxing in the red barrel-back chair. He was having a gin and orange juice and reading the *Razor's Edge* by Somerset Maugham.

Albrecht made his conversation with Claudia short. He said to her, "Leave everything behind, get on a bus, and come home."

Claudia got off the bus, and as she walked down the dusty country road to her parents' new home, she looked pitiful. Claudia composed herself and told her parents that the reason her husband had married her was to have legal reasons for not marrying a physician's daughter that he had gotten pregnant. The physician had pressed charges against him for getting his underage daughter pregnant and wanted to force him to marry her. If not, he was going to jail for raping an underage girl.

Her husband's only way out of the situation was to be married to someone else. Claudia was someone else. When the case was settled, the jail time was expunged. Not only because he was married but, in addition, he had dependent children from a previous marriage, and the judge felt placing him in jail would have punished his dependent children. Claudia knew nothing of this story he was confessing.

In three months, Claudia had met, haughtily got engaged, and married against Estelle's wisdom. Then she was divorced, humiliated, and disgraced—all in one summer.

It was a hot summer.

Albrecht talked Claudia into going back to school so that her mind would not be idle. It was against her wishes. She was too embarrassed and hurt to show her face to her girlfriends, whom she had joined during the earlier part of the summer. She knew she would be the subject of gossip on the campus. She only agreed to return to school if she could live off campus. She could not live in the dormitory and face the girls after she had been such a fool. Her pie in the sky had met its Waterloo.

Theopolis and Bessie, who lived near the college campus, were very welcoming to their granddaughter. They had lived through differing kinds of situations with their ten children. They were forgiving and nonjudgmental. They understood what Claudia was experiencing. Claudia resumed her studies until she graduated. Albrecht paid all of Claudia's student loans—thus, upon graduation, she had no debt. Claudia was not demonstrative to either of her parents, but she thanked Albrecht for repaying the student loans.

Estelle never told Claudia "I told you so," and she never interfered with any of Claudia's future decisions. She told herself, "Claudia is grown. I have discharged my responsibilities as a mother, and if she doesn't want my advice, she will just have to find out for herself that what I was telling her was true. I have been on this earth longer than any of my children, I have had a harder life than any of my children, and I know I have more common sense than any of my children. They just have to learn for themselves and make their own mistakes as I did!"

Estelle further resolved in later years that she loved her children, but in her heart, she had to let them go. Aries she had let go when he asked her to buy him a car while she was struggling to get him a college education. Claudia she had let go after her marriage fiasco. She simply thought, *I cannot save my children. They have to live their own lives.*

She had tried to be closer to them and guide them along the way, but they seemed to reject her every step of the way. She just did not know how to reach them. She thought it curious that she always wanted to have a mother to guide her along the way in life, and her children had a mother they did not seem to want.

Estelle was getting weary with her children and questioning her dreams. She had Seymour as her last hope of having a child who shared her dreams. In Estelle's mind, Seymour treated her as if she was Jesus Christ. She had invested the least amount of time and energy in him, less than in her husband or her other two children. It was hard for her to comprehend that this child she did not want was the one who stood by her the most.

She had achieved her father's dream of having titles to several cars, and she now had a house with an almost clear deed. If she could see Seymour over the hump of high school and college, she could relax and feel that her life's work was done as far as her children were concerned.

When Albrecht decided to build a house for Estelle, he never asked her for a single penny; and though Estelle assumed he had blown all his discretionary money, he had not.

When Albrecht never asked Estelle for the down payment for the house, as she had repeatedly offered, she thought "good!" It was good news. She could use the money for Seymour's college tuition, which was coming up in a few years. Then she could get him out of the way to enjoy any years she had left.

PART FOUR

Seymour in Adulthood

CHAPTER THIRTY-FIVE

Seymour

With Aries in the military and Claudia living with Theopolis and Bessie while finishing college, the Rose household was much calmer, and Seymour was as happy as a lark. Adding to his joy, the segregated junior high school he attended was in walking distance of their new house. It was just across the country road. He no longer needed to ride a bus fifteen miles in each direction to school. And after volunteering to take on household chores and cut the grass, in a short period of time, he earned the smallest of the three bedrooms in the new house, occupying a room to himself. No more Aries! It was a Terry McMillan *Waiting to Exhale* moment.

It especially pleased Albrecht, when he returned home from work, to find that Seymour had cut the grass in the front and back of the house on their large one-acre lot. He would never have given Seymour this chore because the yard was so large, it needed to be cut in two shifts since they did not have a riding lawn mower. Seymour cut the grass with a hand mower. Albrecht actually saw this as heavy work. He had accepted that Seymour was a mother's boy. He had not been groomed for outside work or manual labor.

Albrecht would discuss with the neighborhood men across the white wooden fence, "I just don't understand it! Estelle gives that boy the best of everything. She does not require him to do any hard work!" Albrecht viewed Seymour as the child Estelle had for him. To some extent, he was okay that Estelle spoiled him. He never knew the whole story on why Seymour clung to his mother; nor did he know the frequency of Aries's bullying toward him.

Estelle was more pleased than Albrecht when she too returned home from work. She found Seymour to be a more thorough housekeeper than she had ever been. Seymour was far more detailed. He would clean the oven, defrost and clean the refrigerator, disinfect the bathroom, polish furniture, make up Albrecht and Estelle's bed, and have dinner prepared when they arrived home from work. At the dinner table, Estelle would happily say to her husband, "Albrecht, that boy is paying off like a slot machine! Yes indeed! Just like a slot machine!"

What Albrecht and Estelle both liked about their son was that he would do all these household chores for his parents on his own volition. They never asked him to perform any of these tasks. They would have preferred he spent more time on his studies, but they could not inspire him to take full interest in too much of anything. Aries and Claudia never cleaned their bedrooms and resented having to earn the allowance Albrecht provided them every two weeks. They would not vacuum or dust their bedroom floors, nor would they make up their beds. In comparison to Seymour, they were slobs when it came to domestic work.

Giving a child a bedroom of their own was something neither Albrecht nor Estelle were inclined to do with any of their children, because they never wanted them to get too comfortable and think they never had to move out. Estelle believed that children were like birds that eventually needed to leave the nest, but since Seymour had been placed on the back burner while she and Albrecht were contending with Aries and Claudia through their teen years, and since Seymour was her most devoted child and he did anything she or Albrecht asked, they reconciled in their minds that he deserved some type of reward for good behavior. With these considerations, they let up on their principles and let him get comfortable in a space of his own.

Seymour—who had a space of his own in the new house—regularly relived his childhood years and thought of all the injustices and slights he felt. He recalled boarding the military bus every Saturday to go to the movies and again on Sunday to attend church services. He did these activities on his own just to get out of the house and to entertain himself. Seymour felt he was being scarred when he witnessed the interactions of his mother and father with his older brother and sister. Their being constantly disciplined bothered him.

Estelle never saw the offense of telling everyone she saw that Seymour was the child she never wanted to have. He never had the courage to ask why, but she periodically injected it into almost every casual conversation. When a neighbor or friend complimented Seymour or said an admiring word about how well behaved he was or comment on how cute he was, she would say without intending harm, "Yes, he's the baby and the one I never wanted to have."

Unknown to her, this statement settled deeply in Seymour's emotions and affected his sense of self-esteem. He had never heard of a mother speaking this way about one of her children. It made him continuously analyze what she meant and her need to repeat it over and over again.

He never forgot the burn on his back from scalding water—from Aries's brutality toward their sister. Each day after his morning shower, he looked at his marred back in the bathroom mirror and thought resentfully of his brother. He remembered the shame and disgrace Aries brought to the family by challenging his father to a fight in the front yard of the apartment complex. He could not understand Claudia running off to get engaged, married, and divorced in ten weeks.

Witnessing each of his brother's and sister's interactions with their parents made him feel insecure. He lived in uncertainty and anxiety when Aries and Claudia were around him. He thought the two of them brought trouble to the household. It appeared to Seymour there was always something going on in the house and he could never relax.

Seymour was able to figure out that he had attached himself to his mother for safety; but moreover, he needed to feel wanted and loved by her. He never could understand why she felt no compunction about making remarks about his birth. He did not believe she meant any harm, but it remained tiring to him. But regardless of her motives or reasons, he favored his mother over his father and his siblings. A part of him still felt sympathetic for her childhood and the generations of his family that preceded him.

In Seymour's thinking, his mother's life history was sad. She told him of all her childhood circumstances, her mother's death, and the nice house that she lived in that her father lost during the Great Depression. She told him of how her father put her out to work when she was his age. It was true that Estelle hollered and screamed at her children and could be almost as punitive as her father, but after hearing all her stories of her father's treatment toward her and her life with Mrs. Astor, he excused his mother's bad behavior and tried every day to compensate for what he perceived as her sad life. He considered, in his young mind, from whence his mother had come.

He recalled that his parents' only real concern for him was that he never showed any interest in too much of anything for too long. They never considered that he was too distracted by the lives of the people with whom he lived. He was extremely social and well known throughout the community. Seymour was friendly and had the gift of gab, which he got from spending so much time with his mother.

He concluded his friends remained mostly older ladies whose doors he would knock on. The ladies would invite him into their homes and give him a hot buttered biscuit as they were pulling them out of the oven or a cold slice of watermelon during the hot summer months. He humored and entertained the older ladies. He was a charming and talkative child. The old ladies would later tell Estelle and Albrecht of the wonderful stories their son had told.

On the brighter side, Seymour would get a few laughs when Albrecht would come home and share stories of how the ladies and children in the town center would refer to him as "Seymour's father." He would laugh and say, "I don't have a name of my own. I am just Seymour's father!"

Albrecht's heart swelled when he was referred to in this way. He loved the attention directed at him and having a likable child.

While his brother was away, Seymour thought Aries was also an average student also but took interest in arts and sciences. He was as bright as Claudia, but Estelle would say, "He's just like my father. Lazy!" Claudia excelled academically in all she pursued but was slightly weaker on social skills. Estelle's opinion of her children also affected Seymour's opinion of his sister and brother.

After the move to the new house, Seymour had outgrown going to Sadie's beauty shop with his mother and joining her in her grocery shopping. He continued to prefer his mother's colorful and talkative nature when she was in a good mood. He liked her ambitiousness and personal style. He wanted to stay close to her because he learned so much from her in the ways that she managed money and organized the house. Seymour wanted to manage his life as she had managed her life. She was his only childhood role model. His mother was an acceptable person. People liked her and often spoke of how much she talked. He thought his mother was hard and deliberate at times, mostly with her children. She wanted more in life than living in a segregated military project. He wanted these things too.

Seymour was living through a different generation. He waited every weekday for the Walt Disney *Mickey Mouse Club*, *Leave It to Beaver*, and *Izzy and Harriet*. He discerned from watching these programs that the world was very different than the world he was living or the world as portrayed by *Amos and Andy*. Seymour desired the world he saw on television, where people were nice to each other.

He recalled, at one point in his earlier childhood, he did have one friend who was white. Kenneth had red hair and lots of freckles on his face and arms. Kenneth was a year or two years older and had failed a couple of grades in school. During this time, the public schools were segregated, and thus, Kenneth and Seymour attended different schools. Saturdays were the only times they got to play together. Kenneth's father was in the military. Kenneth was very proud of his father although he was overseas most of the time. His mother was a housewife and took care of his ten sisters and brothers. Their family was one of the few Catholic families who lived on the military property. Kenneth's mother and older sister did not want him to associate with the colored children, but he and Seymour played together regardless.

The real problem between Kenneth and Seymour was Aries. Aries hated Kenneth because he was a nasty-looking white child who always had dried mustard or ketchup around his mouth. His clothes were rough-dried, and his shoes were run over to the sides. These were habits Estelle did not tolerate with her children. Aries thought Kenneth was not good enough to play with Seymour since he had failed a couple of grades in school and because he was unkempt. Aries did not like white people in general as a result of his readings about the treatment of Negros in history.

Each time Kenneth knocked on the door to see if Seymour was home, Aries said no regardless of whether Seymour was at home or not. Sometimes Seymour didn't know Kenneth had visited him, and other times, he would hear Aries say "No he is not here!" Then Aries would slam the door shut in Kenneth's face. Seymour would run to the door and intercept the exchange between Aries and Kenneth. Then he would go outside of the house and walk with Kenneth through the neighborhood. They talked or would go to the playground. Most of the time, if Aries was at home, he forbade Kenneth to come inside the house from pure contempt for the child. No one in the family stopped Kenneth from visiting Seymour but Aries. They were glad that, at last, Seymour had a friend his age. Aries had a strong need to bully and control both Seymour and Kenneth.

Kenneth eventually got tired of Aries's abuse. He stopped coming to visit with Seymour. When Seymour inquired why, Kenneth said, "Because your family are just niggers!" Seymour did not know what he meant, but when he ran home to tell his parents what had transpired, Estelle retorted, "Then you just stay away from him!" The relationship with Seymour and Kenneth ended. Seymour was sad and without a friend because of Aries. Aries liked to be judge and jury to everyone.

Seymour relived and thought of his young life. He thought Aries and Claudia were consistently unkind to him. As close as he was to his mother, he never told her what was happening to him because she had always chided, "Now you don't want to grow up and be a tattletale." Thus he stopped communicating with her the things that Aries and Claudia had done to him. They got away with their ridicule and mockery toward him without repercussions.

When Seymour was much younger, he insisted on traveling with Estelle wherever she was going. It hurt his feelings when she would say, "Well, you can go with me, but you must keep your mouth shut and not cause me a minute's trouble. Otherwise, I will leave you at home the next time!" During the occasions Seymour traveled with Estelle, he kept absolutely still and kept his mouth shut because he knew his mother did not want to be bothered with him, and he did not want to be left with his siblings.

As a result of living in this environment, Seymour never learned to express his thoughts or feelings. Estelle would sometimes double down on her stance with the same words her father used on her: "Children are to be seen and not heard!" and "Speak only when you are spoken to!" These comments offended Seymour as well. He knew Estelle sensed that Seymour disliked his brother and sister; thus her telling him he had to stay at home with them would instill enough fear in him to ensure he would not be the slightest nuisance to her. They did not want to be bothered with him, and she did not want to be bothered with him. Seymour was in between a rock and a hard place. He learned from these dejections that he needed to learn how to become independent and self-sufficient.

In the school setting, he never developed a voice of his own, he never spoke up for himself, and he never had an opinion even if asked a simple question for fear it would be the wrong answer or that he might be condemned for not being smart enough. He was ridiculed at school as well. He had traits similar to his uncle Harrison. As a teen, he became insulated, insecure, and had feelings of not being loved. He was learning to live with himself by himself.

Neither of his parents or his siblings read him a book or took him to a movie, to the park, the zoo, or any other childhood activities. They never spent any time with him. His siblings called him names like "stupid," "dumb and lucky," "jug-head," "head-a-plenty," "temple top," "a greased pig," or "Little Lord Fauntleroy." He remembered all these taunts along with Estelle telling him, "Seymour child, God must have really wanted you to be here, because I never wanted to have you, boy!" This made him feel worthless in ways his department store clothes could not hide.

Albrecht loved Seymour most, but he had to spend most of his time at work or in school for the government to keep up his career credentials and certifications. He continued to work hard to get ahead for the entire family. Estelle also worked out of the home and felt overwhelmed with the roles of wife, mother, and employee. She would say to Seymour if he mentioned that no one spent any time with him, "Listen, Seymour. Trying to please a man, taking care of children, keeping food on the table, and keeping a supervisor happy is a lot of work!"

When Albrecht would overhear Estelle's explanation to Seymour, he would interject, "This is why I never wanted you to work. You could spend more time with your children, and you would not have to keep a supervisor happy."

If there were childhood disputes or injustices between the children, Estelle would simply say, "You children have to learn to get along. I don't want to hear any stories about who struck John! Mother is tired now!"

There simply was not enough time for Seymour. He did not require intervention. Seymour felt some childhood infractions required parental intervention, but Estelle only got involved if there was bloodshed or trouble with the law and the authorities or if there was something that did not make any sense to her. She would dismissively say, "I just can't be worried. You children will have to work things out."

At times, she could be very hands-off with resolving conflict between her children. Albrecht never contradicted Estelle in front of the children. He let her stay in charge unless it involved him.

Seymour was vulnerable either way he looked. When he could not take any more of his family, he would retreat to his bedroom and cry. He knew he was in an inhospitable situation, and he was going to have to wait year after year until he was of age to fend for himself.

The lesser of the evils for his survival was staying close to his mother even if she was not in the happiest of moods. Her tongue could be tart, her scolding harsh, and she could get impatient with his clinging; but he was not giving her an out for not making him safe. When she moved, he moved with her. This is what his childhood life became.

*   *   *

An announcement over the public address system in the segregated school that Seymour attended stated, "Ten years after the *Brown vs The Board of Education* decision, the county school system is being fully integrated. Those black students wishing to attend white schools in their neighborhood can now do so."

Seymour was attending the same school that Aries and Claudia attended years earlier, but since their graduation, Albrecht and Estelle were less active as school leaders by the time Seymour was coming through.

When Seymour announced at the dinner table that evening that he wanted to attend the white school in his county, his parents were aghast since Seymour, up until this time, showed so little interest in anything but being at his mother's side. Albrecht was immediately, but protectively, opposed and felt Seymour would never make it in a white school. He thought they were far more competitive schools. He thought that just because school integration was the law, it did not mean that in the hearts and minds of the people, anything had changed. Albrecht knew, from his military experiences, that the hearts and minds of people in various regions of the county were not in full agreement with civil rights. He thought that Seymour—having been sheltered and protected by Estelle for all of his life—was not prepared for the mistreatment he would face. Albrecht also thought this was a much larger step up for Seymour than he could handle and wanted mostly to protect his son from the racism and discrimination he had experienced throughout his life and especially in the segregated military.

Estelle was as happy as hell that he wanted to get out of the segregated conditions, but in her lukewarm attempt to support Albrecht [a man], she said to Seymour, "Well, you know you have been taking the bus to and from school for ten years. You can walk a short distance to school now. Why would you want to take the bus again when you will graduate in two more years?"

In Estelle's opinion, she thought that if Seymour changed schools, maybe he would be more motivated, and maybe the change in environment would lift his spirits toward a more advanced education. However, she did not want to contradict Albrecht. She hated that women always needed to filter their words to their husbands as head of the household. It was the old joke of the man who has the gold makes the rules. She did not think it very funny. This was her reasoning for wanting a job and money of her own.

Seymour was certain this was what he wanted to do. Albrecht's building the house for Estelle took a big pressure off her, and he no longer had to listen to her complain about wanting a deed to a house. The negativity his siblings had inflicted on him was now gone. And the stigma of being a sissy—that had dated back to first grade when he stood in the group of girls versus the group of boys—could be put to rest. He thought going to the white school would give him a fresh start, and he would be able to escape his childhood history and pay attention in school.

All his life, he had trailed behind the lives of Albrecht and Estelle, who were parent-teacher school leaders. Claudia was the highly favored academic child and valedictorian of her class. Aries the family bully and class clown. Seymour had no trademark of his own, and he wanted one. Integrating the white school would be a historical trademark, and he was willing to take the risk.

After Albrecht and Estelle discussed it a little longer without Seymour's input, she concluded the conversation by saying to Albrecht, "Well, I say let the boy go if he wants to go! If, by chance, he can't make it at the white school, he can come back to the segregated school."

Seymour was Estelle's child in Albrecht's mind, so he succumbed to his wife's wishes. She knew Seymour better than anybody else. Seymour glowed with joy that his mother backed him up and supported his wishes. Albrecht was not pleased; he wanted to protect his sheltered son. For reasons unknown to Estelle, Albrecht was very protective of Seymour, but she never analyzed it.

Seymour was the only black student in his class of five hundred. This made him stand out and gave him the visibility and attention he wanted and needed. This was a bold, brave, and courageous move on his part. The social skills he had learned from hanging around his mother and being able to communicate with older adults paid dividends. He made new school friends for the first time. He learned as many names as he could to personalize his communications with them. Seymour was the exotic student to the white students and teachers.

Estelle continued to keep him stocked in high-quality clothing. She liked to see her children looking good, and although Aries and Claudia could care less, Seymour thrived just getting dressed each morning for school. The white school became a stage for his presence. Seymour not only enjoyed expensive clothing, he enjoyed expensive everything. He continued to pursue an academic diploma, but his grades remained the same with the exception of an "A" or two in elective classes. He took a lot of business classes and did very well. He hated taking physical education during the first period in the mornings, although he liked looking and being physically fit. Aside from it being so cold in the mornings, he did not want to get his clothes wrinkled before his day got started. Teachers and students all marveled over how well he dressed, and they would ask him what his mother and father did for a living. As a black child, his teachers did not think he was supposed to look better than his peers, but Seymour was dressed better than most of his all-white teachers.

The difference between the white and black schools was tremendous; they were separate but not equal by any stretch of the imagination. The black schools struggled and fought for fundamental school supplies and equipment for their students. The textbooks were hand-me-downs from the white schools, as were the science equipment, foreign language tools, and office equipment like typewriters, adding machines, and calculators.

At the white school, there were the state-of-the-art chemistry labs, foreign language labs, new textbooks, physical education equipment, and reams of paper for the typing classes. The focus at the white school was all for student growth. At the black school, more attention was focused on survival. All of this was a big adjustment for Seymour, who was not accustomed to state-of-the-art anything.

At the white school, there was a student parking lot, baseball and football fields, tennis courts, and a swimming pool. There were more student automobiles parked on the lot than there were faculty automobiles. The student cars were nicer than any car Albrecht or Estelle owned.

Albrecht always purchased cars that were at least one year old—lemons that needed constant repairs. He and Estelle never owned a new car until he retired. That only came through Estelle's persistence. She would say, "Look, Albrecht, you can't take the money with you! The children are gone now. Why don't you buy yourself a decent car!"

Albrecht did not want to hear Estelle yapping any longer, so he went to his writing table and signed a blank check and gave it to Estelle and said, "Go get a car."

In Seymour's wrestling classes, he had a hard time not getting an erection when positioned tightly between his teammates and the wrestling mat. It appeared to go unnoticed, and no one said a word to him about it. He had never been touched so closely by anyone. His family was not a touching family. Human touch felt good, even from a white person or a same-sex person. This would have been highly socially unacceptable if he was discovered. Seymour declared himself as nonathletic and refrained from contact sports. He was healthy and strong and excelled in track and field.

It was not all easy for Seymour during the first year he attended the white school. He was assigned a seat in the back of the school bus. He was called a "nigger" by some of the white children, the school principal called him "boy" in the most diminishing tone, and some classmates wanted to touch his hair to see if it felt like steel wool. In gym class, some whites were curious to see if blacks really had tails. All this was not intended to harm, but regardless, he had to figure a way to cope and respond to the idiocies.

He knew these comments and reactions to his attending what they perceived as "their" school were comments they were taught at home. Seymour had been called a nigger by Kenneth, his white friend, and he had been teased at the segregated school for being a sissy, so these racial taunts did not get a rise out of him as the white students intended.

Estelle had taught him to stay above such people—thus he learned to kill them with kindness as Estelle had taught him. He learned not to care or to raise an eyebrow. The one child that stood out most and who was deliberately trying to be hurtful toward Seymour was a white redhead girl. She too was relegated to the back of the school bus with Seymour because she was born with deformed arms and fingers. She felt that her station in life had just been elevated with a "nigger" on the bus, and she would no longer be the butt end of the school-bus taunts and harassment due to her physical birth defects. She was not pretty. She called Seymour a nigger every chance she got, and not one of the students or the bus driver said a word to correct or reprimand her.

Some members of the faculty were equally as punitive as the students. Seymour's geometry teacher had him removed from his class because, he informed the principal, "I simply refuse to teach 'niggras.' They have no business in our white schools." By law, Seymour knew he could have legally fought the issue. Dear god, it was ten years after the judicial decision. But instead, he chose to acquiesce than be in a class with a teacher who announced he didn't want him in his class. He would have found some way to fail or remove him anyway. It was like living with Aries—these kinds of people were going to get you back one way or the other.

Seymour chose to step aside and be removed from his class, and the next teacher he got was a "godsend." It was just like Estelle had taught him: "When one door closes, another one opens!"

Seymour had drawn on Estelle's teachings and remembered the times when similar situations occurred to him and she would ask, "Why would you want to be around anyone who tells you up front that they don't want to be around you?" She would ask, "Now aren't there people you don't want to be around?"

Seymour would reply "Yes!"

"Well!" she would say. "It is the same thing. There are people who don't want to be around you. I want you to turn the page on this, Seymour, and do well with the new math teacher!"

Seymour felt, upon entry into his eleventh-grade homeroom classroom, that his teacher was enamored with him, if not downright loved and protected him almost as much as his father had. He even excused the fact Seymour talked too much in his class while he was teaching world history and was only a fair student. The white teacher saw no wrong in Seymour. It was school policy that teachers never engage in physical contact with their students. He would place his hand around Seymour's shoulder in camaraderie, and Seymour would put his hands around his homeroom teacher's waist in return. The homeroom teacher took Seymour under his wing and tutored and coached this new black student for two years to graduation. Seymour had a guardian angel within the school walls. He was protected against racial hatred and unfair treatment. This teacher was his anchor. Seymour loved the attention and outward protection that he was given.

Occasionally, Seymour returned home from school hurt by what some of the children were saying to him, and he would report it to Estelle on a day she was not in the mood to hear any consternation. She was cooking dinner at the kitchen stove. She stopped what she was doing and looked at him sternly. "Listen, Seymour. Your father and I let you go to this school because this was something you said you wanted to do. So don't think you can come home every day with some tale of woe is me. This is the real world you live in, and we have protected you as much as we could when you were a child, but it is time now for you to grow up and take your punches like everyone else. Now, unless there is some bloodshed in that school, you are going to have to figure a way to work things out for yourself. Mother can't be with you every day anymore."

Spoiled Seymour was put in his place by her lecture but continued to report every injustice of his school year. On some days, Estelle would sneer and look in bewilderment at Seymour and say to herself, "Does that child understand a word I said?"

During Seymour's senior year, his class nominated him the Friendliest Senior of the Year, and he won by an overwhelming majority of his classmates' votes! He was ecstatic. This was Seymour's first distinction at home or at school. He was honored for having a perfect attendance in second grade, but that was the sum total of his public accolades. Recognized for this mention was something good for his self-esteem. He yearned for recognition. He was creating an image for himself at last!

Seymour was featured in the school's newspaper and the town newspaper for all to see. He received telephone calls from all over the county and was applauded as the only black in his class and to receive such recognition. And moreover, he graduated without any major racial conflict, which was a great accomplishment for him and his race.

He graduated on time with an academic diploma. The school principal questioned his getting an academic diploma. He did not think a black child should receive an academic diploma. He recommended a general diploma for Seymour. Teachers who supported civil rights verified and supported Seymour's grades, and his academic diploma was awarded.

Neither Albrecht nor Estelle or members of the Rose extended family thought Seymour would make it out of high school—not to mention a white high school. Judging from the stories he told every day at the dinner table and his mediocre grades, they thought Seymour's move was too bold and too risky and he would be doomed. His family members were old-school Negros who knew their place in American society, and they stayed in it. Seymour was crossing the line, and they were not comfortable with what he was choosing. Seymour was the only person in his family who thought it was possible to graduate and not be killed or lynched. He was gaining confidence in himself now that Aries and Claudia were out of his light.

Albrecht and Estelle were privately shocked and amazed when Seymour graduated without incident. Although they never mentioned to him they worried about him every day, but this also meant they could stop worrying about him being randomly attacked in a historically segregated school system and in a county where racial tensions were high and this change was not welcomed. The tension in the nation was at its peak.

They did not attend Seymour's graduation. He felt the pinch, but he was so happy with himself and that his parents allowed him to make his own decision to go to the white school. Their attendance was not compulsory. He had just made history. He did not care about their not showing up, but he recorded it in his mind that his parents did not show up for his high school graduation.

Attending the white school was an overall happy and broadening academic and social experience for him. Attending college like Claudia was next on his agenda.

*   *   *

Seymour graduated high school and was awarded an academic diploma. His grade-point average was a 2.0, which was the minimum qualification for graduation and acceptance in most state colleges. Estelle had saved bonds and had purchased a few certificates of deposit in preparation for sending this final child to college.

Albrecht remained less enthusiastic about spending more money for college on Seymour after Aries dropped out of college after two years and Claudia so easily quit college and ran off to get married. In his mind, Seymour had barely completed high school, and his potential for finishing a four-year college did not appear realistic.

Estelle once again stepped in for another of her children and convinced Albrecht to stick with her program of educating the children. She said, "In the long run, if these children make a mess of their lives, they can't blame us." She wanted to give them enough preparation so that when they left home, they wouldn't come back.

Estelle said, "Don't you see all these children today coming back home with babies and some sob story to tell their parents: 'If you had only told me!' They blame their parents for their mistakes. Well, I am not giving them a chance to blame me. I have given generously to all of them. And when they leave, I want them to stay gone so I can start enjoying what little life I have left!"

Estelle looked at Seymour, who was listening to every word she said, and she reiterated words from one of her a childhood riddles, "Then birdy leaves the nest and flies—flies far, far away!"

Albrecht and Estelle were both in concert when it came to their children growing up and leaving home and never coming back to live with them. They were doing well, but they had struggled to get where they were. It was not an easy road for them. They wanted to live and enjoy their old age with some peace and freedom.

When they spoke like this in his presence, Seymour never thought his parents were talking to him or about him since he was a dutiful son. He wasn't thinking at all of "birdy flying far, far away!" He was thinking of never leaving home. He would have taken care of his parents in their old age. And somewhere deep within, he knew Albrecht had a soft spot for him. He thought what was said to the other children did not apply to him. Thus he was not worried about his plate being broken.

Albrecht was amused that Seymour was so spoiled and did not see himself as privileged. Albrecht would say to him over and over, "You think you are a privileged character!"

Seymour would tilt his head with certainty and reply to his father, "Yes! I am supposed to be!"

Albrecht would shake his head, smile, and say, "You are just dumb and lucky, boy!" He would smile, shaking his head, and he would walk away. He would not challenge Seymour; he just thought his son was spoiled and naïve. He thought Seymour was innocent, and he had no idea what he was saying.

When it came time for Seymour to apply for and select a college, a big rub arose for Albrecht when Seymour announced he wanted to go to the largest university in the state. A top 10 school. Albrecht had no problem with Seymour going to college at this point, but he was thinking he would perform better at a small historically black college, where he would get some academic tutoring from the black faculty. He did not think Seymour would get the attention needed from white faculty if he attended a white school. Albrecht thought a top 10 university was too large of an institution for a student with Seymour's academic ranking.

Albrecht thought Estelle was lenient with all the children; but Seymour, who came almost a decade later, was the baby and got the lion's share of everything. Seymour paid little attention to his father's rubbed feelings because he was the more soft-spoken of his two parents. If Seymour could survive Estelle, his father was a piece of cake. He also knew that Estelle was footing the tuition bill, and she had said to Seymour in private, "You can go to college anywhere you want to go." Shrewdly, Estelle knew she could make this statement with confidence considering that with Seymour's average grades, he would only be accepted in a limited number of colleges.

When Seymour returned from freshman orientation, he ran up the front sidewalk of the new family house and through the front door to greet and hug his mother. But as usual, she recoiled and said, "My god, child! You have only been away for two days! Where did you get all that hugging from anyway? Our family doesn't go around hugging people!"

Estelle was not a touchy-feely person—ever. But as his mother, he thought on this occasion, she could make an exception and be happy to see him. He had never spent the night away from home; and although he was happy with the orientation, at the same time, he had a slight fear of leaving home too. Completing freshman orientation was a victory for him.

The Rose family was not great at showing affection of any kind toward each other. Seymour had never seen any expression of love between his parents or toward their children. Seymour stepped back from his mother and, for the first time, deeply felt the coldness of his family. In just the short period of time with the young bright talented students in orientation, he could feel a sharp difference in receptivity. He was familiar with this lack of affection, and it made him sad in that he was merely expressing a natural reaction to being away from home. But Estelle did not like such displays, and thus he was rebuffed.

Seymour was conflicted by Estelle. On one hand, she was the most generous person he knew; and on the other hand, she appeared unloving. He could not decipher Estelle's two sides. He learned just how sensitive he was to Estelle's two sides, but he coupled it with her not wanting to have him. This reframe always played in his head, and he could not let go because he could never decipher what she meant. When he combined not feeling loved with not being wanted, it made him feel slighted in his gut.

When the college school year began in September, Albrecht and Estelle dropped Seymour off at his dormitory. This was the first time Seymour was going to be separated from Estelle for any length of time. They had only one experience of separation, and that was when he went to first grade, and it was painful. This had only lasted a primary school day until he returned home the same day. And although now eighteen years old, this was going to be every bit as painful. It was the beginning of another new experience. Whereas most college students were excited and filled with glee to escape their parents, Seymour had mixed emotions now that the time had arrived.

The university was less than fifty miles away, but for Seymour and Estelle, it was far away. This separation was new for both of them. As dysfunctional as his history had been thus far, it was all he knew. After they looked at Seymour's dormitory room, they knew he was going to have a hard time because it was in the oldest dormitory on the campus. It was small and dark, with one set of bunk beds and an adjoining desk for two and a common shower for the floor for all men. Seymour was not used to any such thing, but he made the choice and this was it. It felt like a very sad day.

When Albrecht unloaded his last piece of luggage, Estelle started to cry. Albrecht said, "Okay, Estelle, let's go!" By no means did he want Seymour to come back home that day. He wanted him to finally get started with his independence and grow up and separate from his mother. It was painful to Albrecht too, but differently. He would miss his son, but he wanted him to grow, see the world, and discover what was out there for him.

Estelle had invisibly grown more attached to her son than she had ever realized. Albrecht grabbed her arm and escorted her to the car. Together, they let Seymour go for the first time. Within Albrecht, he regretted not being able to go to college. He also had his doubts that Seymour would make it at this university academically. He too felt conflicted. The university had a larger population than the town they lived in.

As they drove away, Seymour stood at the drop-off parking spot, and his eyes watered; and by the time Estelle had gotten to the driveway, she cried with the loss of her "ace, coon, and boon." She also felt a huge relief that she had gotten her last child in college. She was almost finished with parenting. She took a deep breath at the amount of the stiffer tuition she was going to have to pay for Seymour. It was far more expensive than Aries's or Claudia's. Paying this tuition she could do, but it was going to be hard.

After about two weeks on his own, Seymour had adjusted to campus life. He had nicely set up his room and found his way around the campus with a university map. When his roommate arrived two weeks late from his summer vacation in Europe, he entered his assigned dormitory room only to find Seymour, his black roommate. He was aghast and immediately requested that Seymour be reassigned to another room. He was not living with a colored.

Since Seymour had arrived first to the room and was settled in, he could not understand how the resident assistant decided that he should be reassigned. The very next day, between classes, Seymour was moved to another dormitory. Seymour knew he could have yelled discrimination but did not want to contact his parents, especially since Albrecht had trepidations from the start.

His next roommate was unaware that Seymour was moving in and angrily protested on the grounds that the university was placing two minorities together in the same room as a form of discrimination. He was Jewish, and Seymour was black. He too requested that Seymour be reassigned to another room, but Seymour would not budge. If anyone was going to move, it was going to be the Jewish student—not because he was Jewish but because Seymour did not want to be pushed around again. The Jewish fellow made such a stink, he called the university housing administration to intercede in his behalf since the resident assistant would not put in the request for Seymour to be moved. The housing office called Albrecht and Estelle and said that Seymour needed to be moved.

Albrecht had served in a segregated branch of the military. He fumed when he found out Seymour had been removed from his original room assignment. This was two dormitory rooms in the first semester of his freshman year, all due to race. Albrecht knew all too well the hurt and pain he experienced in the military. He was now reliving it again through this situation Seymour found himself in. There was no one to speak up for Albrecht while he served in the military, but this was his opportunity to speak up for someone, and it was his son.

Albrecht and Estelle had not planned on seeing Seymour again until the Thanksgiving break, but they both took a day of vacation leave to visit with the university housing officer, to find out what was going on and to get Seymour settled in a fair campus housing setting. The housing administrator was not happy to be called on the carpet for the two scenarios. She made the remark that if Seymour had gone to the historically black school, he would not be facing these kinds of problems.

Albrecht replied, "But he has not! You must provide fair housing to my son! And you will!"

Estelle had never, in all of her marriage, see Albrecht assert himself so forcefully. Albrecht could see fumes emanating from the top of the housing officer's head.

After his comments, he stopped talking and he kept quiet but took copious notes as to what the housing officer was saying. She did not know he was building her own losing civil rights case. Legally, she had to do her job as Albrecht informed her.

When he used the word "legally," the housing officer proceeded to give him a copy of all the vacant housing on the campus to allow him to select a room for his son anywhere he wanted to live on campus.

Albrecht said, "Don't give it to me. Give it to my son."

The housing officer underestimated Seymour. She thought, as a first semester freshman, he would not know how to choose a room on the newer housing complex reserved for white students. These rooms were air conditioned with plush lounges and a study hall. The rooms were more spacious than either of the previous two room assignments he had occupied. These rooms had all state-of-the-art amenities, with a separate dining facility and separate student parking lot accommodations for students—but they were reserved for white students.

Seymour read the list carefully and noticed on the list of rooms a single-room vacancy in the new campus complex. This was what Seymour chose. He loved the idea of not having a roommate. Aries had been his roommate experience for thirteen years, and that was enough.

The housing officer tried to steer Seymour to a less desirable campus housing, stating that single rooms did not allow for students to socialize and learn to share with others. But before she finished her statement, Albrecht interceded and said to Seymour, "Is this where you want to be?"

Seymour replied, "Yes!"

Albrecht looked at the housing officer and said, "This is what my son has selected. Please assign him to this room."

And it was done! The housing officer's face turned red. She did not think Seymour had enough time to figure out where the better accommodations were on the campus. She became stiff, resistant, and huffy; but she signed the room assignment order knowing she was legally required to do so. Moreover, she resented being commanded by a person of color.

As Albrecht and Estelle walked in total silence to their car, they said their goodbyes to their son, and the incident was settled. Albrecht said nothing to Estelle, but he was thinking as they drove home that these kinds of situations would occur for Seymour over the next four years. These incidents were the reasons he did not want Seymour to attend a white university. He was happy to have been able to stand up to help his son in this situation. He did not like to interact with non-accepting whites, but serving in the military toughened him enough to deal with situations and occurrences as he chose to address them.

As Albrecht drove home, Estelle thought how she had witnessed, for the first time, that he took action to support and protect Seymour adroitly. She had never seen him go to bat for Aries or Claudia with the same muscle. He did not stand up or intercede when Aries decided to quit college; nor did he stand up or intercede for Claudia when she ran off to get married. Estelle had begged and pleaded with him to intercede, and he would not. But for Seymour, he took a full eight hours off from work and drove fifty miles to help this child. She had not seen anything like this during all of the years they had been married.

Estelle was skilled at choosing the right moment to broach any subject with her husband. She knew he might take offense if her timing was off. This time was no different. She chose a moment as they continued their ride home, and when she thought the dust had settled, she asked Albrecht, "Why did you go to the extent of taking time off from work and speaking with such strength to the housing officer to defend Seymour when I used to beg you to step in for the other children and you would not?"

Albrecht did not like being questioned or called out for his actions, but if put in the situation, he would answer honestly and purely. He simply replied to Estelle's question by saying, "Estelle! Seymour is an obedient child!"

Estelle said no more; she felt the sting of his reply. She also felt a tinge of jealousy.

*　　*　　*

For Seymour, the housing issue was resolved, but there was still the issue of academics. After four years of living on campus, he struggled every semester for academic survival. He found himself on and off of academic probation, adding and dropping courses and changing majors. He had student advisors who were of no help. One advisor suggested he go to a junior college, which really hurt because no one but Seymour believed he would graduate.

Albrecht had given up on Seymour by the third year and said, "He will never make it!"

Seymour was crushed by his father's statement. He returned to the shoulder he had always cried on. That was Estelle's shoulder. He was twenty-one years old and still ran to his mother for comfort. She was all he ever had. Albrecht had wounded his feelings with his remark.

Estelle replied, "Seymour child! Don't pay your father any attention! He does not know what he is talking about! Plus he has been drinking that gin! Just don't pay your father any mind. He doesn't know anything about raising any children."

Estelle had been paying a steep tuition for close to four years. When she asked kindly, politely, and with hope and pride, "Are you coming out [graduating] in June?"

Seymour—now twenty-two years old, wearing a size 13 shoe, and sporting an afro hairstyle—bowed his head down to his mother and said, "Uha! No, I need more credits!"

Estelle was expecting a yes from her son. She fumed at the thought of paying a fifth year of tuition. She knew this child loved the university setting. She could see some growth and change in him. She knew he wanted to graduate, so she looked at him straight in his two eyes, and as sternly as possible, closely pointing her index finger in his face, she said, "Listen, boy! I am giving you one more year to get out of that school because I am tired of paying all this money for you to be clowning 'round down there. So you had better get whatever you need to get done, done— and get out of there! I have covered for you long enough."

Seymour knew from Estelle's tone that she was not joking or playing around this time. She meant business. This time, he did not misread her voice, because she had never used this voice on him in twenty-one years.

Seymour was both scared and grateful. Scared because he knew Estelle was dead serious this time, just as she had been with Aries. He was grateful that his mother was going to give him more time. He did not know just how he was going to get out of the university because he had only earned 65 credits in four years. He needed 55 additional credits within one year. Her comment to Seymour was a threat that she meant to keep. His gravy train at the university was coming to a screeching halt if he did not figure this out!

Seymour immediately made an appointment with the dean of the college. He told her what had transpired between him and his mother and that he must graduate in one year. The dean puffed on an unfiltered cigarette as she reviewed his transcript. When she finally looked up over her arched framed eyeglasses, she said to Seymour in a deep and raspy Mississippi voice, "Well now, Seymour, just tell me. How do you plan to graduate in a year with this transcript I see before me?" She was appalled and serious too.

Seymour naively said, "I don't know. I only know that I have to graduate in one year."

The dean said, "Well, you step out of my office and you sit there in the waiting area with a paper and pencil, and don't come back in here until you can tell me how you are going to accomplish this. I can't help you if you cannot tell me what you want to do. So you go out there and figure it out, then you let me know what you have planned."

When Seymour returned, he presented his plan to the dean. "Well!" he began. "If I take 21 credits first semester, 22 credits the second semester, 6 credits the first half of summer, and 6 credits the second half of summer, I can graduate."

Still puffing on her cigarette, the dean replied, "Well, you know what you have presented to me here is a pretty rigorous schedule. You also know that you will need the dean's approval to take 21 credits. But I will tell you what. If you promise me right now a 3.0 GPA or higher this first semester, then I will approve the 22 credits next semester. But if you do not get a 3.0 or higher, you are out, Seymour! Now I think you can do it, and you had better not disappointment me and, more importantly, your mother—because you have been wasting a lot of time and money at this university at someone else's expense."

The dean signed the approval papers for 21 credits and said, "Now get out of my office and let me get some work done."

Two women had just made a huge difference in his life. His mother was extending an additional year to his college education, and the dean was extending one semester with the condition of a 3.0 GPA, which he had never had in high school or college. He was shaking in his boots when he left the dean's office. When the fresh air hit his face from the top stair of the college and the reality of what his mother and the dean had done set in, within a few hours, he became happy to have these two women give him a break and a chance. He was not going to disappoint them.

Seymour successfully made the dean's list for both semesters. When his mother asked again one year later, "Are you coming out of school in June?" Seymour said, "Yes, but I have to go to summer school."

Estelle flipped and said, "I am not playing with you, Seymour. This is it!"

"But Ma!" Seymour replied. "Look at my transcript and this letter from the dean. I am on the dean's list!"

Estelle burst. "The dean's list? How did you get on the dean's list when you have never been on the dean's list before?"

"You said I had a year, and the academic year is not over until August thirtieth!" Seymour reminded her.

Estelle was still skeptical, so she took the transcripts and the letter from the dean to Albrecht and said, "Look, Albrecht! Can you believe this? The child is on the dean's list at school!"

Albrecht was dumbfounded and speechless. They said to each other, "Maybe he is coming around. Maybe he is just coming around."

At the end of the two summer sessions, Seymour was on the dean's list. At the end of August, he was conferred a bachelor of science degree from one of the top ten state universities. The dean of the college had put pressure on Seymour to prove himself academically, but Estelle was the one who stuck with him to the bitter end. He felt like a true winner for the very first time in his life, and although there were no congratulations, no exclamations of "good job" or "job well done," he was happy with himself.

*   *   *

Seymour was employed within two weeks of his graduation. He did not have time to look for a good job after his fifth year of concentrated studies. He had grown enough during this period to know he had to grow up and live on his own. He had lived off his parents enough, especially Estelle. Reality had set in for him.

He did not land the job of his dreams but, instead, a job to earn an immediate income. He lived at home and paid rent to his parents. He could see in the family home that things had changed over the five years he was away. His parents had gotten accustomed to his not living there and were enjoying an empty nest. The axis of the universe had changed for him, Albrecht, and Estelle.

Within six months, he had purchased a new car and rented a very nice two-bedroom apartment he could not afford. Albrecht wanted him to stay at home a little longer, until he saved enough money to pay cash for his first car, but Seymour wanted to get out on his own as soon as possible. He financed a new car for two years. Estelle was shocked again that Albrecht, of all people, wanted him to stay at home longer to pay for his car in cash. She could not believe what she was hearing, for he never suggested that to either of the other two children.

Seymour had lived the best years of his life in college with all expenses paid by Estelle and Albrecht. In addition to his tuition and room and board, his parents had sent him an allowance every two weeks on their paydays. Estelle was responsible for mailing the two checks: one from Albrecht and one from her. She always sent $1 more biweekly than Albrecht. The envelope would arrive just as regularly as any government check. Seymour could bank on spending the money before it ever arrived; his parents were just that dependable. Now he was on his own; there was no allowance, and life was not as easy. He needed to find a way to apply what he had learned in high school and college to live the best life possible.

Segregated schooling did not help prepare him for the world of work; nor did the years he wasted at the university. He accepted his share of responsibility too for not taking his studies seriously. He was trying as hard as he could, and he realized now why Albrecht wanted him to attend a smaller historically black school.

Up to this point, Seymour had never had a girlfriend or a boyfriend. In junior high school, he loved a girl who lived in the neighborhood, but neither she nor her mother liked him. In college, he loved a straight guy who hung around him all the time, but sex was not part of the picture. There was another guy who really showed a lot of interest in Seymour; however, Seymour was too naive to recognize he was gay. He had no experience with relationships.

He had known, within himself, that he liked boys since the age of four. He was born with a birth defect called hypospadias, which he associated with his mother doing everything she could to abort him during her pregnancy. The physical defect had nothing to do with physical performance, but like the burn on his back and arm caused by his brother, it was a daily reminder that he was an unwelcomed pregnancy. These two events continued to haunt him, greatly strengthening his insecurity. He did not like going to the beach or exposing his body because of his physical markings.

With Seymour's Catholic indoctrination and his paternal grandmother's devoutness to Catholicism, he clearly understood that homosexuality was not acceptable in the church or in his family. As a result of these Christian teachings, he learned to conceal this part of himself that he knew was not acceptable. Estelle, Aries, and Claudia were profoundly homophobic.

Albrecht knew very early on that his son was homosexual and had accepted him unconditionally. His father never discussed the topic with him, but he knew Albrecht had opened the door to allow him to own his gayness when he was ready. Seymour was more afraid to come out to his mother. He did not want to be further rejected by her, and he knew her stance. Estelle was his survival during his youth and developmental years. She did the child rearing, taught the home training, and was very generous toward him. He just did not want to bring further disappointment to her by making his homosexuality known, especially since her first two children did not turn out as she had groomed them.

Estelle knew, somewhere deep inside, that Seymour was the most different of her three children. She never took the time to sit down and discuss with him things that were on either of their minds. His being gay crossed her mind. However, since he had grown into a tall, handsome, and healthy young man, she knew some women would seek him out and turn him around. She was convinced of this. In her mind, he met all the qualifications that a woman would be interested in. He had a college degree, a job, and lived independently. As far as sex was concerned, Estelle thought that even if a man was slow warming to sexuality, there were women who were not and would help them along. She did not want to think of her child as gay. Everything in Seymour's life that she did not want to face, she wrote off as just a "stage." "Seymour is just going through a stage." She was in denial.

When he was a young child, the neighborhood men would whisper to Estelle that her son was showing effeminate behaviors. They suggested to her that she needed to let go of him and encourage him to be exposed to his father more. The same neighborhood men would directly tell Albrecht, "You need to spend more time with Seymour."

Albrecht was a classical man who was a voracious reader; he enjoyed going to libraries, museums, the theater, and listening to his Broadway recordings. He was not a hunter who skinned rabbits, squirrels, and deer. He did not enjoy fishing as many of the men enjoyed on the military base. Albrecht's sport was swimming and golf versus football, basketball, or baseball as most men rallied. Albrecht had exposed his son to the things he liked. He loved and accepted Seymour as he was, whatever his proclivities. He loved his son. He wanted Seymour to use his school time better; but otherwise, he thought his son was all right.

Albrecht would discuss with Estelle what the men shared with him. However, due to her discomfort with the subject of sexuality, whether heterosexual or homosexual, she dismissed it and told Albrecht, "The boy is just going through a phase that boys go through." Estelle was not a man, and she did not have the know-how for discussing the issue of male homosexuality, and the subject required more thought than what she was willing to put into it.

When Seymour would try to bring his homosexuality to Estelle's attention, she would say, "You don't want to be 'one of them,' do you? I would rather you be an alcoholic than 'one of them'!"

With this comment, Estelle validated the fears Seymour had in coming out to his mother. Estelle's comment translated to Seymour as "don't be gay, and don't come out of the closet." Of the number of conversations he had with his mother since his birth, this was one she could not and would not have with him. She did not want to discuss homosexuality, and he independently did not know enough himself to explain or justify who he was or why he felt this way. He just placed it on the back burner. He was simply at a loss for understanding his feelings or to explaining to her who he was.

Seymour knew she worked hard as a wife, parent, employee, and community worker. He did not want to add anything else to burden her heart and soul. This was just something he was going to have to work out on his own. As far as his mother was concerned, she avoided any discussion about his sexuality. He just went to another level of deeper concealment because the only person in the world he ever talked to was his mother, and she was not available on this topic. Estelle had blocked this discussion with her son.

Eventually, concealing was taking a great deal of effort on his part. He was so accustomed to being purely honest with his mother. Concealing was taking away from the honesty of the communications between them. Although she could be abrupt in her comments, he did not like her referring to him as "one of them." He could not understand why his mother—or any mother—would choose to have an alcoholic child rather than a gay child.

He was confident that he was a decent person. He wanted her in his life; but at times, she made no sense. This was the reality for his mother and for him. He could see they were dividing into two different camps on just one issue—an issue that could destroy a perfectly good relationship. All of the good sank to bad.

As a youngster, Seymour had already been fooling around with a couple of boys his age. He explored their anatomy, and they explored his. By the time he was a teenager, a few of the upperclassmen took notice of him and spoke of their desire to be with him. Seymour listened to what he was hearing as interest and devotion. He was hungry to be loved and adored, but they were only interested in sex. They wanted same-sex activity with no commitment and total secrecy. They did not want to be seen in public with Seymour for fear of being called a "queer"! They did not have love and adulation in their minds, just sex and secrecy. By the time Seymour had been taken advantage of a couple of times, he learned their psyche, and he was emotionally hurt to figure out he had been used for their gratification.

Some guys rationalized that if they did not kiss a boy on the lips, this meant they were not gay. Most of the older boys knew he was inexperienced, and all they wanted was to break him in. For Seymour, to reveal a word of these overtures and experiences to his family would have created a disaster for him. He was already suspected by Claudia; she would have detested him even more. She had strong motivation for detesting Seymour because since his birth, she had hated the attention Seymour received from both Estelle and Albrecht. She would have enjoyed him being brought down a notch or two.

Unknown to his homophobic sister, two of the young men she dated had hoisted Seymour to their groin area and grinned on his butt as they waited for her to get dressed for their evening out. Claudia suspected that her younger brother was gay. She did not like it and tried her best to squelch anything she thought was deviant or coming his way. Having lived with his sister, he knew firsthand just how vengeful she could be. If she was certain he was a homosexual, he would have hell to pay. The extent of her hatred toward homosexuals exceeded their mother's. Seymour would never have said a word to her. He avoided her as he did his mother at all costs. Trying to keep himself hidden did not feel good in his soul.

In his high school, there was one flamboyant male student who was on the school's cheerleading squad. He wore a white open-collar shirt, tight white pants, double pairs of white bobby socks, and snow-white canvas tennis shoes for girls. He also wore a pink chiffon scarf around his neck. He jumped up and down, twisting and twirling with all the girls for all the school's athletic events. The male cheerleader was true to himself, but Seymour was not. Most of the teachers and administration honored and supported differences in all students. Seymour was encouraged to join the cheerleading squad, but he declined. He did not want to be on public display, nor was cheerleading his thing anyway. Coming out was too much for him. To manage his home life with his mother and sister was difficult enough; to bring the issue up front at school would have been too much for him to bear alone. He had no support system.

Seymour also recalled, while in high school, he amazingly caught the football for his team but unknowingly ran to the opponent's goalpost, scoring two points for the opposing team. He was ridiculed for the balance of the school year. The guys never forgot that scene and never let up on him. His fine wardrobe did not insulate him from their hilarity. From then on, he was always last to be selected to play on their teams. Becoming a cheerleader would set him up for more jokes. He managed to endure the school year being taunted, but there was no shoulder to cry on.

Seymour was not living at home anymore and wanted to live an adult gay life. He wanted to date men. He wanted to date steady and be identified with one man, just as men and women identified as one. The time had not come for him to expose himself to Estelle. He had narrowed down his concern with the public knowing who he was and did not care what anyone thought of his gayness—except his mother. He needed her, and she was the toughest nut to crack. She was the female version of her father on this one family topic.

He had read about gays that could not cope, and it led to running away, suicides, sexual promiscuity, alcoholism, and drug addiction. Just "one issue" could cause all of these outcomes for gays.

* * *

During the years that Seymour felt he had to maintain a charade for Estelle, he had no problem getting a date for the sweetheart's ball, the prom, or any social event that required a female escort. Most of the time, women old and young would call him to be their escort to cabarets, banquets, and dinner parties. "You cut a dashing image," Estelle would say of her son.

Estelle had taught him every social grace on how to treat a woman. He knew to lead a lady on the dance floor, open and close car doors, bring a corsage or flowers, and she even taught him about condoms. As he left home, she would say from the kitchen, "Don't forget your 'raincoat'!" Part of this comment was to let him know it was okay now to engage with women, and the second part was to ensure he did not produce any babies.

After Seymour turned eighteen years old and she sent him off to college, she stopped attending the Catholic services. She was required to become Catholic as a condition to her marriage to Albrecht. When Seymour left home, she felt her sentence with the Catholic Church had been completed. She returned to the church denomination of her childhood. Many women in the women's auxiliary who attended Estelle's church regularly approached her, urging her to get Seymour to date their daughters. They thought he was a good catch for their daughters. They also suspected he was a little slow with romancing women and would be less likely to get their daughters pregnant.

Many of the so-called "nice girls" that Seymour escorted to school or college events were as forward as some men were with women. While dancing or going to a drive-in movie, they would press themselves against his nature, trying to arouse, stimulate, and generate interest. While seated in the back seat of a drive-in theater, a date would arouse Seymour then raise her dresses and lower her panties in what seemed to him one movement, and then proceeded to impale his erectness. Seymour knew she had been around. There was no resistance upon penetration. It felt, to him, like sinking in quicksand. To Seymour, it was nasty.

A married woman and a single adult woman sexually molested Seymour. When he reported these two incidents to Estelle, she rolled her eyes and was mute. In that Estelle was mute on the subject of someone sexually molesting her child, Seymour felt his mother was happy with what had happened. He thought she did not care what means were necessary— she did not want a gay son. Seymour could feel and see it in her muteness. Had she encouraged these women?

In that Estelle had no response to his stories, for the very first time in his life, he shared his stories with his father. Albrecht hit the ceiling in fury. Seymour had never seen his father so outraged. When Seymour told the whole story of what happened with the two women, his reaction was so violent and out of the ordinary that Seymour was not sure if his father was going to kill the ladies or cause a huge ruckus.

Albrecht met privately with each of the women and threatened them that if they ever put their hands on Seymour again, he was going to expose them to the law. In his faith, he was being kind to the ladies, whom he thought did not deserve kindness. Seymour was relieved the circumstances did not get any further out of hand. Seymour did not want to punish the ladies, but their actions on him were uncalled for, and he did not like it. But he had no voice of his own, and he felt corrupted.

Albrecht was a man who grew up in the streets of the city. He had served in the military. He was exposed to worldly men and women. He had gay friends and felt, under the right circumstance, most men would take the opportunity to release themselves with another man, if women were not around. If a man or woman were born homosexual, his thinking was that all men were under one God. If his son was gay, he wanted him to be who he was and not forced to take part in behavior that he did not consent to; nor did he think men should force themselves on women. On the subject of homosexuality, he disagreed with the teachings and practices of the church and the conflicting passages in the Bible.

*   *   *

On a hot Sunday afternoon in August, Seymour met Christian through a friend. The friend actually had designs on Seymour himself, but Seymour fell head over heels with Christian. He was "lap-legged." The feelings between Seymour and Christian were mutual. Their first meeting took place exactly one year after Seymour moved into his first apartment. He and Christian dated for six months before Seymour and Christian moved in together. Seymour gave up his first apartment that he loved and the single life he did not love for a partner he desperately wanted. He had never had a significant other in high school or college. He finally had someone to call his partner.

His self-esteem was momentarily enhanced having a significant other. After giving up his apartment and living with Christian, he learned that a relationship required a lot of work and commitment. Way more than he had expected or knew how to offer. He was eager to get started with his life. There were men he had held affection for, but his love was unrequited. There were men who held affection for him that he did not love. So he adopted a "what's love got to do with it" attitude. Christian was a good man, just like Albrecht. He was stable, and he was kind.

Before meeting Christian, Seymour had seen and become familiar with the city gay life, mostly through the lens of gay bars. Up to this point, he had never been inside a gay bar, and it took a while for him to adjust to an all-male meeting place. There were a few lesbians and gay-friendly straights, but he had no exposure to either.

Considering Seymour's limited experiences, it was strange for him to see two men dancing with each other. It was a sharp change for him to see more confident, expressive gays who were fully comfortable with themselves in public. They made no bones or apologies for themselves. The newness of what he was experiencing in the gay world created some discomfort and some joy.

Socializing in gay bars led to his drinking too much. He had little experience with alcohol, but drinking was a way for him to feel like he was a part of the crowd. Drinking dissipated the conflicts he felt inside, and it dulled the shock and newness of what he was seeing.

Smartly, Seymour soon learned to set some boundaries for himself. So much of what he was seeing in the bars involved the regular consumption of alcohol, especially on Thursday, Friday, and Saturday nights. Many left church on Sundays and headed to the bars late on Sunday mornings. These gatherings were called "prayer meetings"!

Sometimes Seymour socialized with his new associates on Friday nights. He sometimes would overindulge in alcoholic libations. With the sunrise of Saturday morning, he would swear to himself and the gods in heaven that he would never do this again. However, by Saturday night, he would be recovered, refreshed, and the allure of the gay community drew him back out again to the bar, a house party, or a gay event. He was included by the group, and it felt good to be invited to gatherings where gay men congregated. There was always somewhere to go or something to do.

One night at the hot, crowded, smoke-filled room, he recognized, from across the bar, his homophobic high school art teacher. He was standing at the bar in full drag attire and was holding high court with men, entertaining them in his high glamour. He was wearing a size 13, three-inch-heel Spoletos.

Seymour made it a deliberate point to approach his former teacher to remind him of how bad he made him feel during his high school years. He had made the statement to Seymour many times in the hallways at school in a put-down tone: "Seymour, you need to walk on your heels and not your toes so that you don't switch like a girl." Seymour was embarrassed that his teacher would call him out in the presence of all his classmates. It hurt and embarrassed him deeply.

When he got his teacher's attention, with anger, he respectfully said, "You are such a hypocrite! Do you remember all the times that you ridiculed me in your class for being gay? You were my teacher. You could have helped me understand what I was going through as a teenager. But instead, you chose to belittle me in front of my classmates. By now, I could have been as comfortable with my gayness as you appear tonight. I want you to know you made me feel bad about myself when there was no need. Now look at you! 'Slashhaying' around on your toes in three-inch heels in a gay bar! You are a hypocrite!"

When Seymour finished with his remarks, his teacher downed his drink in one swallow. He was embarrassed to be put down in front of his friends.

Socializing with gays exposed Seymour to inspirational music, arts, and literature that supported gay culture. He was eventually exposed to *La Cage aux Folles* and was fully encouraged to be himself when he heard the song "I Am What I Am." This song, along with "I'm Coming Out" by Diana Ross, "The Need to Be" by Gladys Knight, "Home" by Stephanie Mills, and many others helped Seymour develop his gay identity. Each song enamored Seymour. These songs became his mantra and gave him strength to be himself. All these experiences gave him a beginning to understanding who he was and that his life did not need to be devoted to an outcome of a dark seedy bar. After all, he had been reared by Estelle Rose, and she had taught him deportment and good common sense. He remembered her saying to him as a teenager, "Now don't you go out here and take any wooden nickels!"

Living with Christian grounded and stabilized Seymour like he was at home with his mother and father. Stability was what Seymour wanted from Christian, and he received that. With this new and first-time live-in arrangement with Christian, Seymour informed his parents he was gay. Estelle cried. Seymour cried. And as usual, Albrecht was the anchor for both of them in the most human and compassionate manner.

Initially, Estelle did not like Christian. He was twelve years older, and she erroneously blamed him for bringing Seymour into the gay life. Estelle prayed that Seymour would not take her through the changes she went through when Claudia ran off to get married to an older man. She thought Seymour was "green" and was inexperienced. Seymour knew that his mother did not think it appropriate for this older man to be consorting with someone twelve years his junior. And frankly, she thought he was not good enough for her son.

Seymour continued to have difficulty being disapproved of by his mother. He wanted to be honest with her and align himself with who he was. He had been disapproved of many times. He only cared about the approval of his mother. Although he was not as close with his father, he knew his father was more broad-minded and inclusive. He would support him regardless. He desired to have the whole family support him, but he knew Estelle, Aries, and Claudia were galvanized in anti-gay hatred. After all, she was the mother who had instilled these Christian values into them as Harrison Sr. instilled them into her.

On the other hand, Estelle and Seymour had been together all his life. There was no other. She also felt betrayed and thought some of his attention toward her would be taken away. Her religious upbringing was embedded in her. Homosexuality was wrong. Seymour had never reconciled that if he was the child she did not want to have, then why was his relationship with Christian important to her? He had told her his truth, and now was her chance to get rid of him. With Christian, he was again in a secure environment.

In the transition of Estelle and Seymour reconciling, it became obvious to Seymour that the gay life and culture alone was not enough for him to be happy. He had been dependent on his mother, and he needed her to "want" him before he would feel contentment in his soul. He did not want to hurt his mother, but he did not want to live a lie to make her happy. It infuriated him that she was invested in materialism, but she would not pick up a book to read about her son's sexual orientation.

He needed to find a way of becoming self-sustaining within himself, loving himself and taking ownership of his self-esteem and not allowing someone else to control who he was. He had not found it yet. To lose his mother left him feeling empty, isolated, and alone. He needed to find the strength to stand up and speak up for who he was and who he wanted to be regardless of who he chose as a partner. It was tough for him.

* * *

After changing full-time jobs every year for the first three years after his college graduation, Seymour was trying to not only define himself as a gay black man but also as a career professional. He had spent no time during his last year at the university looking for a job or taking advantage of the opportunities available for finding employment. His job, at that point, was to graduate and get out of Estelle's purse.

In addition to full-time employment, he kept part-time employment because he was living beyond his means trying to maintain the lifestyle his mother and father had provided. He also applied for admission to graduate school. Since his undergraduate grade-point average was only a 2.5, he was accepted in a program with the condition he earn a 3.0 grade-point average in his first two classes. Upon completion of these classes, he would be fully accepted without conditions. He majored in liberal studies. Attending graduate school had nothing to do with enhancing his career but more to find a passion and earn an above average salary.

His undergraduate degree was in economics with a concentration in architecture. He had done very well with his studies in this field. He had changed his major three times, but he was unsuccessful in finding professional employment in economics or architecture that would support the lifestyle he sought. In reality, he had worked as a glorified administrative assistant. He loved the architectural aspects of his field but hated the marketing aspects. He also worked with the store planning department as a draftsman, but there were was no creative work. All the chain stores were engineered by prototypes.

Seymour's first professional break came after meeting a precocious public school department head who fell in love with Seymour's creative talents, ambition, and enthusiasm. It was her intention to get him hired and bring him into her department as a teacher. She contacted her deputy superintendent and twisted her arm to hire Seymour. Seymour was interviewed and, within a few weeks, was hired as a teacher; but he was assigned to the administrative offices with the deputy superintendent since the school principal did not want any gays on his staff.

After hiring Seymour, his immediate supervisor recommended that he earn nine graduate credits of education to qualify for certification within the State Department of Education. She granted him early release time from his duties to take the necessary classes. On his own, he was already enrolled in a graduate program he did not want to quit. He enrolled at another nearby university and started a second master's degree program to earn the education credits his supervisor had recommended. Since Seymour was Catholic, the Jesuit College accepted Seymour unconditionally. Since he was enrolled at a neighboring university, there was a collaborative partnership. This was great for Seymour because both universities were in close proximity, making his commute between the two campuses easier.

With his existing debt, he was now paying tuition to two universities with his credit cards. His supervisor and the deputy superintendent were impressed with Seymour's ambitiousness. He placed an innovative and creative spin on his assignments. They supported him every step of the way. Seymour had mastered studying during his last year of college. He had sharpened his study skills while working toward these two master's degrees simultaneously.

Seymour's job functions were increasing as well as his salary. At the completion of his first master's degree, he was conducting teacher education workshops for seasoned teachers who had been in the school system for ten, twenty, and thirty years. This was a huge leap for his career.

Seymour recognized that although he had studied at a predominantly white high school and university, it was not enough just to attend. He also needed to have something to bring to the table. The name of the institution on his résumé alone was not enough. He felt, after his parents had sacrificed so much for him to go to college, the least he could do was to make use of the investment they had put into him. He was not spoiled, but he was indeed sheltered by his parents. It did not help him at all to be so lackadaisical with his studies in high school and in college—thus he needed a vision adjustment.

He learned, while working in the public school system, he was behind his peers, who were getting better jobs and better pay. He had even wasted the first three years after his bachelor's by not conducting a top-notch job search or employing an employment search firm to help him land a good job from the start of his career. He needed to take aggressive action to move forward. More education was his answer.

He also learned that most of Estelle's teachings and lectures about gays were correct. Living an open gay lifestyle was of no help to his career in most settings. His decision to be out of the closet to align himself with who he was had restricted his job growth.

Living with Christian helped Seymour accomplish his educational ambition since all their household expenses were divided by two. He took advantage of this opportunity since he did not know how long his gay relationship would last. They were not married and did not have the benefit of clergy. Christian's mother was deeply upset with his departure from the family home. He was the breadwinner of his mother's household. She relied on him to supplement her income with the things her husband could not.

Seymour worked full-time, weekdays for the city school system; he worked part-time selling commercial designs on Tuesdays, Thursdays, and weekends and took six credits on Monday, Wednesday, and Friday evenings. Saturday mornings he taught part-time at the community college. All this was to pay dual tuitions that were mounting, and they were tacked on to his existing debt. He was hustling, utilizing all his energy and every waking minute for money to pay for his anticipated career advancement.

Time and organization became supreme. There was no room for error. He was buckling down on himself. He carefully managed his time and his money, as he had seen Estelle do throughout her life. He checked and double-checked every expenditure and was punctual in every payment. He continued to maintain the savings and checking accounts Estelle had helped him to establish when he was a child and had continued to deposit his biweekly allowance while in college. He worked hard and saved. He could hear Estelle's father say to her, "Daughter, if you make a nickel, save a cent!" This translated into 20 percent—not 10 percent as had become the new standard for saving.

During this time, no one in his family was paying Seymour any attention. Seymour had a long demonstrated track record of having little to no interest in anything and had mediocre grades in school. Success was not forecasted in his future by his family. He was now unharnessed from his family situation and felt he could move forward without the internal blockades family members can cause.

Albrecht and Estelle were happy empty-nesters, paying off their new house in preparation for retirement.

Aries was out of the military and had married and remarried. He had seven additional children. His alcohol consumption had increased. He was a functional alcoholic. In adulthood, he continued to intimidate as many people as he could. Seymour thought back to the statement Estelle had made to him: "I would rather you be an alcoholic than 'one of them.'" Now she had one, and she was seriously not happy. As Seymour had cried on her shoulder as a child, Estelle now used Seymour's shoulder to express her displeasures with Aries's alcoholism.

Claudia had graduated college, had married for the second time after her Martha's Vineyard disappointment, and was expecting her first child from revenge sex. So no one noticed that Seymour had cracked down on himself to build his self-esteem and rid himself of his insecurities generated in his family.

After working three years in the public school system and earning two master's degrees, administrators saw Seymour as a rising star and tracked his career: teacher, department head, vice principal, principal, and school superintendent. This was his career ladder to success in this setting. All he had to do was continue to perform well, serve his time, and follow the path. Seymour had never known so much support could be given to one person. He was mentored by the best education leaders, coached by his immediate superiors, and professionally nurtured as he had never been before. He was admired and commended for his energy and up-to-date teaching methods. He proved that his planning, implementation, and evaluation skills were stellar.

He felt good about himself for the first time. He was featured in the city newspapers. He paid membership dues and joined all the affiliated professional associations and had received nationwide recognition for his professional and educational achievements working with limited-income students.

Through his part-time work as a store manager, he unknowingly received an added bonus to his career achievements. He worked with and met the wealthiest African American businessman in the city, who was openly gay. He allowed Seymour to call him by his first name. He was thirty-five years older than Seymour, but they shared mutual interest and they became fast friends.

The businessman was the shining light and inspiration Seymour wanted in his life. The businessman knew that Seymour—like himself in his day—was confused, conflicted, and emotionally beaten up in his youth by family and society in general around their blackness and homosexual identities. He also knew the struggles of maintaining separate personal and professional personas.

On the brighter side of their friendship, the businessman, as elder, saw in Seymour a sense of difference. He discerned unusually good manners and good home training. He did not want to take Seymour on as a full-time project because he knew he was too old. He did want to work with Seymour to help him develop his sense of self-esteem and self-worth. He knew how to help Seymour in this area, and he did so at every opportunity that he could. He generously exposed Seymour to the renowned private clubs, golf resorts, five-star restaurants, and fine men's haberdasheries in Baltimore, Philadelphia, and New York. He had been married in the past and introduced Seymour to his ex-wife and his four children and their families. He extended invitations to Seymour to attend the city's finest grand balls and galas.

In a far more elementary way, Seymour reciprocated as often as he could by inviting the businessman to meet Albrecht, Estelle, and Christian. He also invited him to political fund-raisers he hosted for city elected officials and other social gatherings at his home.

Seymour loved his association and the exposure they both shared. He absorbed as much as he could of these exposures and opportunities as he could. He continued his education and his career. With everything he was engaged in, it meant less and less time for Christian, who did not appear to mind at all. Seymour was getting the drift of becoming a good professional administrative educator.

*   *   *

Seymour became bored with Christian and the stable life they lived. Like many couples who try to hold an unfulfilling marriage together by having a baby, Seymour thought if he and Christian purchased a house, it would take the boredom away. Christian showed no interest in having a home. He was very much like Albrecht in this regard. He did not want to make a commitment of this nature. He had had multiple same-sex relationships in his past, and he did not want to risk comingling of property ownership for fear the relationship did not work. He was content with apartment living but went along with Seymour's grandiose idea.

Seymour canvassed many neighborhoods and settled on a four-bedroom split foyer plan. They, together, had the house built in a nice suburban community. Having watched Albrecht have a house built for Estelle, he knew the entire scope of work to be considered. His formal education in architecture helped him too.

Seymour and Christian lived together as a gay couple in the suburban home. For Seymour, home ownership was a dream come true, but it did not compensate for the lack of fulfillment in the bedroom. He did not know himself when he ventured into this relationship with Christian. In retrospect, this is what he should have done first. He had actually discerned, in the first six months into the relationship with Christian, that he was not happy in the arrangement, yet he so desperately wanted a relationship with someone. He was confused and conflicted. The second occasion he knew he was unhappy was when he stuck the key into the door of the new house they had just settled. His heart just sank, knowing the house alone was not going to make the relationship work. It was done now, and he tried and tried to make things work as he had seen Estelle do time and time again.

He thought if he worked hard enough, he could change Christian. He learned the hard way you cannot change a person. Christian loved Seymour, but he did not know how to make love to Seymour. This was the principal reason for Seymour's malcontent.

It was stupid to think a new house would make any difference in an unfulfilling relationship. Seymour wanted a long-lasting relationship like his mother and father's. Theirs was the only model for the kind of relationship he wanted. His mother and father were a team, and they built their lives together. Of course, they had many disagreements, but there was a glue that they possessed that Seymour and Christian did not. Christian took a hands-off approach to the relationship and allowed Seymour to run everything because he was not interested in the relationship in the first place. Christian was also an "I got plenty of nothing" kind of guy! He was similar to Albrecht in this regard as well.

Seymour led the entire construction process for building their new home. Christian took little interest. He permitted Seymour to do whatever he wanted. After they moved into the house, Seymour did the bulk of the housecleaning, all the yard work, and arranged car maintenance for the two cars. Seymour arranged all of their doctor's and dental appointments. He made sure they both kept their barber appointments. Seymour managed their money with a slant to squeezing the most out of every dollar. Seymour wanted to someday be rich. Seymour assumed most of these responsibilities because he was the partner who most wanted the house, and he wanted to keep it in tip-top shape. He was twelve years younger than Christian, but like his mother, he also liked controlling the money and the house.

Seymour and Christian had a beautiful home. Their family and friends raved over how well they lived. Estelle was impressed and visited with her elder friends to show off the house and furnishings. Every room was impeccably designed. They each had new cars and traveled the world. Christian worked in the private sector, and Seymour worked in the public sector. They had dual professional incomes. They settled on their new home in May, and in June, Seymour started a PhD program at his undergraduate alma mater. The university's Office of Financial Aid personally called and offered Seymour a full fellowship. He was exhausted to the core from working multiple jobs, working on two master's degrees, and building a house. He really did not have the energy to focus on getting another degree. The full fellowship was a once-in-a-lifetime offer. To be both black and gay and to receive this offer was a miracle. He accepted the offer and resolved in himself to dig up more energy to earn this terminal degree.

While living at home with his parents, Seymour had never developed a voice of his own to speak his mind or express to others his displeasures. As far as they were concerned, if a child had food, clothing, shelter, and no job, they should have no displeasures. He was taught as a son—and especially as a person who was black—to learn to keep your mouth shut at all times and especially when in contact with whites. It was a white man's world, and if you wanted to survive in the world, you must control your temper and your tongue. The same rule applied in the Rose household as well. Estelle yelled and screamed to get her point across. Seymour did neither; nor was he allowed or taught to do so either. These circumstances attributed to his poor communication skills in his relationship with Christian. The other factors were that Christian was established in his career and earned more money. If Seymour wanted to retain the lifestyle he was living, he once again had to keep his mouth shut as Christian had once suggested.

After Christian went along with Seymour's program of buying the house, he had made up his mind this was all he was going to do in the relationship. He showed little interest in discussions of Seymour's feelings, needs, or emotions. Seymour was beginning to see that Christian was similar to Albrecht. He was content with what he had and had few aspirations of attaining more.

After a few years had passed, Seymour's earnings had exceeded Christian's. He eventually tired of initiating and taking the lead in running the relationship and the house. He felt that Christian had gotten too comfortable with the status quo. He had no appreciation for all Seymour was contributing in running their affairs. Their intimacy had always been a drawback, thus Seymour stopped initiating intimacy and began caring less about the relationship too.

Another rub for Seymour was that he learned, after living with Christian for many years, that he was not a college graduate. Christian had completed four and one-half years of a five-year MBA program. Seymour was disappointed with himself for being so naive in assuming Christian had graduated college when he had only asked where he had attended college. When Seymour made this discovery years into the relationship, he discussed it with his friends, and they all told him it should not make any difference. But for Seymour, it did. Seymour was ambitious like Estelle, and he strived to be upwardly mobile like the students in his academic environs, and he looked forward to accomplishing the aspirations his mother had aspired to and the ones she had instilled in him.

Christian had always been a person who was as quiet as a tomb. Seymour thought his college graduation was an important piece of information that should have been revealed in the dating period of their relationship. Seymour felt somehow deceived because had he known up front he was dating a man who had not finished college, he might have made a different decision. Christian's secrecy felt sneaky. This was just another example of Seymour's inability to communicate and to ask questions. He had lived under two generations of sayings like "Children are to be seen and not heard!"

Seymour had read in one of his college psychology textbooks that offspring usually married, for the first time, a mate who is very close in type to one of their parents. Seymour felt he married a man like Albrecht the first time. Unfortunately, Seymour witnessed Estelle's hunger for romance and affection from Albrecht and never received it. There is a difference between romance and affection, and sex.

Seymour had continued to shop in the nicer department stores. This was indeed a replication of what Estelle had done as a substitution for affection. Every weekend and some weekdays, he shopped for something he thought he wanted or the house needed. He purchased shoes from

Switzerland and men's suits from Chicago, Washington, and New York clothiers. He purchased sterling flatware, oxford bone china, Irish crystal, Irish linen table coverings, napkins, and all the accompanying accessories for entertaining. All materialistic consumption as a substitute for intimacy.

As Seymour's income increased, he would call Estelle and say, "Hey, Ma! Let's go shopping. I just discovered how to get to a new department store in Philadelphia or Chevy Chase." Once or twice, they hopped a train to New York City to shop at a few designer shops. Estelle would reply to Seymour's invitations by saying, "Boy, you must be sick! I can't afford to spend that kind of money!" But for a change of scenery and to get out of the house, she would cave in to Seymour's invitations. Seymour would drive or they would take the train to their shopping destination. They would enjoy lunch out and return home with a small bag each.

Each month, Seymour hosted parties at the home he and Christian had built. He would celebrate almost anything: birthdays, retirements, anniversaries, and going-away parties for the family and extended family. He would entertain to add glitter to his life.

When the house was saturated with the finest of every home furnishing and wardrobe labels and the grand parties had been held, Seymour wanted a newer house in a more upscale community. Christian would not agree. He did not know where Seymour was getting all his ideas from, but he held no interest. He was fatigued from the over-the-top shopping and entertainment, just as Albrecht had with Estelle. Most of the time, Christian would just disappear to the master bedroom to read a magazine and view a television show while the house was full of Seymour's family and friends. It was the exact type of behavior Albrecht exhibited with Estelle. For Seymour, it was just as if he had married his father—a perfectly good man but with no social interest. Christian would have been just as content with Seymour without all the fanfare. Albrecht felt the same toward Estelle.

Christian did not smoke or drink, and he never said a word to anyone unless spoken to; and then it would be a smile, a nod, or a friendly grin. Seymour's family and friends were the opposite. They smoked, drank, or talked—if not all three. After ten to fifteen years of living this kind of life with Christian, he became disheartened. He was starved for affection that the materialism did not give. After a while, Seymour was just going through the motions of maintaining a lifestyle he loved but could not sustain on his own. The man he chose to spend his life with simply did not share his dreams.

His college textbook was correct. He married one of his parents the first time around; and a new house, furnishings, and clothing did not compensate for intimacy. His relationship with Christian was a similar repeat of what he saw with his parents. He was Estelle's child. He wanted everything, and Christian wanted nothing. Both Albrecht and Christian could both sing "I got plenty of nothing" and be joyous.

*   *   *

After the nationwide media attention Seymour received from his three-year success in the field of education, an urban university in Washington, DC, recruited Seymour for a job that paid significantly more annually. Although he worked for only ten months in the public school system, the university paid for twelve months. The benefits were outstanding.

He had been saving his money as Estelle had taught him, but his savings were offset by credit card debts. Estelle would tell him, "Seymour, you are not saving anything if you owe somebody." With the anticipated increased salary, he could pay off his tuition bills, car, and home mortgage sooner.

There was a price Seymour would pay for the increased income. The commute time doubled when compared to living and working in the same city. The novelty of the new house he and Christian had built had not worn off, and he wanted to be at home more to enjoy it; but mostly, he would be missing dinners with Christian due to evening meetings, activities, or events. He was drawn to the happy hours at the new DC—the gay bars. This attraction would not help him to return home any sooner. He needed to try to spend more time with Christian, but there was something lost, and the relationship was off track.

When Seymour resigned from the public school system, he left behind the highest level of personal and professional coaching he had ever known. His self-esteem was more intact than it had ever been. It made him feel good. The good treatment from the school leadership made him a little overconfident professionally. The school leaders had placed him with a great team, excellent mentorship, the road map to a career path, and a very nice office with a window view.

When he drove to interview for the new job at the university, the supervisor-to-be was a no-show. Seymour was furious. He had been raised in a military environment where business was conducted on time. Not showing up on time in the military setting was not acceptable. He had taken vacation leave to accept the interview, and for the interviewer not call or show up was an insult to him. She called the same evening and begged Seymour to come back the following week at the same time. Seymour accepted the apology and returned for the following week. In his gut, he maintained his disgust with the lady not showing up the first time.

Seymour took a second day of vacation leave for the interview. His supervisor-to-be showed up late. When she arrived, he noticed she was a gargantuan woman who wore a thick knotty afro-style hairdo. It looked uncombed and totally foreign to anything Seymour had ever seen before on a woman or a man. She wore an American version of African attire. Stacks of papers and files surrounded her as she sat behind her desk and attached credenza. Her office looked hideous and totally disorganized. As she asked Seymour a series of interview questions, she chewed and sucked with her hands and lips on a hot, freshly fried fish sandwich with bones. It made her office smell fishy. He was offended and registered this image in his head as a warning not to accept this position.

Seymour had purchased a new navy-blue blazer, white shirt, and rep stripe tie for the interview. He was still carrying the disgust from being stood up the week before. He felt overqualified to work with someone like her. She was pitifully unattractive. He cut short all his interview answers because he could hear Estelle talking in his ear, saying, "It is a sin and a shame!" Estelle had groomed Seymour differently, and he could see and feel the difference Estelle referred to in this woman's attire and her housekeeping. He did not like it. The public school system had treated him much better. He thought anybody deserved better professionalism when being considered for a new job.

When Seymour left the interview, he assured himself that he would not accept the position. He did not like this lady, and she would have been the person responsible for his performance evaluation. He disliked her disorganization, and she appeared uncouth. He was not accustomed to behavior he thought to be unprofessional. "Ain't no way!" he thought. Just as soon as he returned home, he called the university and declined the offer.

Approximately a month later, the director of the organization placed a call to Seymour at his home with a new offer. The new offer included a high five-figure increase in salary. The money was too good to refuse, and Seymour accepted the position and reported to the disorganized, uncouth woman. He made a promise to himself and the Lord that with the increased salary, he would pay off every debt, including the house, in fifteen years instead of thirty years, as the house was originally financed.

Seymour dug right in at the university and continued to make a name for himself, as he had done in the public school system. He conducted a wide range of workshops throughout the city, he wrote articles for the local newspapers, and he hosted a radio show and television show, all to advance and further the mission of the university. But unlike his experiences in the public schools, his colleagues were envious. They did not support the quantity or quality of work he was producing and delivering. They tried to make it difficult for him to achieve success. Seymour possessed an air of confidence and a manner of deportment that distinguished him from his colleagues. He could hear them whisper "Who does he think he is?"

It did not help that he came to work every day dressed from head to toe in first-class business attire, including his underwear. His fashion was over-the-top for a college campus. Seymour was Estelle's child when it came to wardrobe and fashion. Estelle preached to all her children, "Make yourself look presentable! Don't go out of here looking like you were just born yesterday! Get a haircut! Polish your shoes! A man is judged by his neck and collar!" Seymour was in Washington, DC, now, and he took Estelle's words to the overachievement level. He also thought the way he looked to his students was a model for them to aspire to in the business world. Most of his colleagues could not live up to Seymour's exceedingly high standards, so they pooh-poohed him.

Seymour had both experience and education qualifications for the university position. Race was not as much a deterrent to his upward mobility, but his being gay and out was a long-time detriment. Many of his colleagues overtly and covertly sabotaged his career. He was denied numerous promotions and university recognitions because he was gay and overly confident. He needed his confidence and wardrobe as a way of insulating himself from their displeasure with him. Staff members vocally stated that they refused to report to a gay supervisor.

A female employee was convinced that if Seymour had sex with her, he would never be gay again. She was thinking this would solve his professional image issues. To persuade Seymour into dating her, she would take her two index fingers and point them to her private area, saying, "Once you get some of this, you won't be gay anymore." After being repeatedly rebuffed, she changed from seductive to vindictive. Out of nowhere, she rushed through the doors of Seymour's office, slugged him in the face, then she screamed as she ran out of the office and proceeded to the civil rights office, reporting that Seymour had sexually assaulted her.

After police arrived on the scene and the young lady admitted to punching Seymour in the face first and could not tell a consistent story of what happened, the incident was dropped. No report was filed by the police in her behalf. However, the police did give Seymour an opportunity to file assault charges against the employee since she admitted she slugged him in the face. Seymour did not press charges. He found it interesting that women employees were crueler in their actions toward him than men. Seymour also wondered why some of the least attractive women attempted to seduce him when he would have never held interest in these women even if he were straight.

Estelle did not like Seymour being gay and out in the workplace. She foresaw this type of incidence as a liability for his career chances. She would say to him, "Why get all this education if you are not going to follow protocol?" She had chastised Seymour over and over about being out of the closet at home and at work. She yelled at him, "Just keep your mouth shut! There are plenty of men just like you in the workforce, but they keep their business to themselves! They are not running around telling all of their business. Furthermore, nobody needs to know what you are doing in your bedroom anyway!"

Seymour was fearless and had made up his mind that he was not going to live up to someone else's standard of who he should be. He accepted who he was and believed the universal axes would change in time. He was who he was. He felt better this way.

Estelle and his siblings had persecuted him at home for years. He was on his own time and money now, and he wanted to be himself. He did not like living out of alignment with himself or the guilt of lying to protect someone else's feelings. Seymour thought it was deceitful and too difficult to live the life his family wanted for him. Claudia would roll her eyes and remark, "You sure are brave!" This was not a compliment.

In addition to being persecuted by his family members and coworkers, there was the Catholic Church too. He asked himself, "How does one reconcile their gay life with church law? It is too daunting for me." He did not have the constitution to lie to himself. He eventually got to the point where he simply vowed, *To hell with everyone who does not accept me for who I am.* His family's and friends' lives were not beyond reproach. Most of his family and friends who were pointing fingers had their own human condition too, and he had not judged them!

There were women, in and out of the workplace, who pursued him constantly because they did not see him as married, and for some women, sex was not the most important thing. Maybe his mother was in this camp too, he thought. To be dishonest with the women was not right for Seymour, and the offers for love, sex, and marriage were not what he wanted. He defied Estelle's counsel and paid the price in spades for years.

Estelle sensed Seymour's change in attitude and determination to do as he damn well pleased. In her mind, this was the real world Seymour lived in, and he needed to learn, if he wanted to survive in the workplace, that his truth and honesty did not apply in every circumstance. She watched Seymour suffer disappointment after disappointment. She even outed some of the men who lived in the neighborhood where Seymour was raised. She reported that these men were gay, married, and had children. She said they just put up a front, but their wives knew what was going on.

Seymour thought, *Is this what Christianity is teaching you?* He wondered how his mother could remotely make a suggestion that he should live like one of those types of men. He knew the men she referred to. He thought it was they who helped him know who he did not want to be. It was so absurd and a charade. He was not doing it!

Seymour had not attended Catholic church in years, but sometimes his heart was heavy. He would, at times, stand from his desk, leave his office, and go to a church and pray. He was seeking understanding. He thought if he prayed, God would hear him better. With all he had and all he had accomplished, he still did not feel secure within himself. He had never stopped praying and giving thanks for what he had, but he had not unlocked the secret to happiness within himself. He knew, long ago, things were going to get better for gay men and women. He did not know when or how.

CHAPTER THIRTY-SIX

Chance Meeting

Meeting a man like Hans was the day Seymour had dreamed of. He was handsome, smart, and a sparking conversationalist. Hans was of average height compared to Seymour's six-foot-four, and he had curly black hair, clear blue eyes, a perfectly built similar to Michelangelo's David with a larger center focal point. He had a PhD and was employed in a top leadership position in a health research firm. He, like Seymour, was gay and out of the closet. Hans liked having money too.

At a *Gone with the Wind* cookout hosted by a colleague of Seymour's, Hans was present with his gay partner, and Seymour was in attendance with Christian. From the start of the party, there was a powerful magnetism between Seymour and Hans. As the two of them mingled throughout the party, they always found themselves together at the punch bowl, the hors d'oeuvre trays, or standing on the deck overlooking the beautifully landscaped grounds, conversing. They seemed to find each other frequently when their respective partners were not at their sides. From the way it appeared, Hans started this heated little flirtation. It took little time for Seymour to pick up on the vibe, but he consented with a discreet smile of endorsement. Lovemaking between him and Christian was not fulfilling, and he longed to move past the "turtle-doving" of which they engaged. Heat rose in Seymour's crotch, and it felt good to him in that it had been some time since he and Christian had indulged. Seymour also felt a rising in his center section that was beginning to present itself through his hard-pressed slacks. Hans noticed.

To be elegantly dressed and eye-catching at all times was the persona of Seymour. He especially liked the compliments and attention of a desirable male counterpart. As the afternoon continued, and after sip after sip of champagne, both Hans and Seymour became a little nervy and downright bold, staring at each other up and down, disregarding the chances of their partners or other guests taking note of their behavior.

As the party ended, they walked to their respective automobiles, and they both took crotch stares for good measure then proceeded home with their respective partners never knowing if they would see each other again.

The feelings were intense for Seymour. He harbored the feelings for five years. He had images of Hans on the streets of DC that were not real. He kept his eyes open in bars and clubs with hopes of reigniting the feeling he thought they both shared and hoped a freak accident would reunite them again. But it never happened, and after five years, the memory of a few precious hours at a gay *Gone with the Wind* party faded and then disappeared from his spirit.

CHAPTER THIRTY-SEVEN

Last Legs

After twenty years of living with Christian, building a house together, and living as a couple economically co-joined, the relationship was fatally ending. When Seymour had worked all day, made the long commute for fifteen years, he had continued to do the bulk of the house and yard work, as well as maintain a schedule of all their appointments. He was dead tired when he returned home.

He came home from work one hot summer day, wiped out, only to discover Christian had moved his eighty-five-year-old mother into their house without notice. It was bad enough not to have fullfilling intimacy with him for all these years, but to move his mother in without notice? Seymour thought it was too much. In Seymour's head, without a word—with Christian, it was the end! It was curtains!

Seymour and Lena, Christian's mother, had a mutual dislike for each other soon after the blossoming of the relationship between her son and Seymour. Christian had lived at home with his parents until the age of thirty-six. Lena had carved Christian into the role of her surrogate husband. He was the most dependable and the breadwinner of her five children. Lena made him the head of her household although he was the youngest child. He was kindhearted and soft. Lena manipulated him and depended on Christian for financial support for all her needs and a great portion of her wants. Christian was a malleable man, and in Seymour's eyes, Lena took advantage of her child.

Lena was the daughter of a sharecropper and the middle child of eleven children. The family worked hard in the fields of a South Carolina plantation every day but remained an economically depressed farm family.

She married to get away from home and the laborious work of farm life. She did not love her husband, but together, they made five children, none of which were worth a quarter except Christian. He was her crowning glory.

When Christian and his friend visited Seymour on a hot August afternoon at his spacious two-bedroom apartment, Christian was so impressed that Seymour, who was twelve years younger, was able to acquire and manage such a nice place on his own. He said to Seymour during that Sunday visit, "I sure wish I could have an apartment like this!" Seymour was thinking how pitiful the voice. Seymour thought, *Christian is thirty-five years old and has a better-paying job than me. Why shouldn't he have an apartment if he wanted one?* In that Seymour viewed Christian's living circumstances as a trap, he encouraged and helped Christian get independently established.

It was a huge mistake! From that moment forward, Lena did not like Seymour.

Christian selected a nice suburban community not too far from his mother and the beltway, to make it accessible for him to get to work in the morning. Seymour industriously handmade the living room, dining room, and bedroom draperies and under sheers for Christian's new apartment. Christian purchased carpets for the whole apartment from a friend. He and Seymour wallpapered the living room, dining room, and kitchen walls and together. They had fun shopping together and selecting kitchen and bathroom accessories very similar to Seymour's. Christian was very happy and very grateful for all Seymour had contributed to his getting established in his first apartment.

Seymour was still living in his apartment. Periodically, Christian would spend the night with Seymour. One Saturday night, after they had attended a house party, he and Christian were awakened by hard pounding on Seymour's apartment door. Seymour had alcohol in his system, so he did not hear the pounding on the door. The hard pounding was coming from the fire department. The complex that housed Seymour's apartment was engulfed in flames, and they had to evacuate immediately. In pajamas and robe, the firemen grabbed them from the apartment and hurriedly escorted them outside to a clearing. They sat in Seymour's new car in the morning, cold, as the firemen fought to put out the frightening flames. After the fire was contained, the management of the apartment relocated Seymour to a nearby hotel room for the night. The very next morning, they called Seymour to inform him that the fire of the night before was so extensive, the building was declared condemned and that he would no longer be able to live there anymore.

Seymour's tenant insurance picked up the cost of his living in the hotel until he could find new housing, but after several weeks of working all day and going to graduate school at night, he had little time to look for new housing. He continued utilizing the hotel room as his residence. After one month, Christian invited Seymour to move in with him. Seymour did not want to give up the independence he had established for himself, but Christian's offer certainly would help him financially to get back on his feet, so he accepted the invitation. This was mistake number 2 because in Lena's eyes, she thought she was losing control over her son with Seymour now living in his space.

Christian had never come out of the closet to his mother, but after she saw the sleeping arrangements they had, she drew her own conclusions about her son and Seymour. Seymour continued to look for apartments for himself. He wanted to regain his independence, but he and Christian got along tremendously well. Christian wanted Seymour to continue their new living arrangement. In that Seymour's life was work and school, he continued his residency with Christian. He assumed one half of their joint expenses. They were happy, and the reduced economic cost helped each of them to enjoy a better life. They were partners.

When Lena learned about her son and Seymour living together permanently, she cried. She threw a tantrum as if she and her son were getting a divorce. She was angry and hurt. This was when deeper resentments arose between Lena and Seymour. Lena was jealous and felt threatened by what she felt was Seymour's control over her son's malleable nature. This new situation, in her head, was depriving her of the benefits she had been receiving from her son for years. She planned to break this situation up. She would whisper under her breath to Seymour, "I will always be his mother!"

Lena's message hit Seymour in the gut, which is where she intended it to land. The message implied that the relationship between Seymour and her son may or may not last, but she would always reign as his mother. She felt this placed her in a stronger position to manipulate and control her son. In Seymour's mind, her message meant there was a competition between the two for the control of her son. Seymour accepted her statement as a fact. She was correct and ridiculous. He was only there by the request of her son.

Over the time that followed, she interfered each and every day. It was a mistake for Seymour to interrupt what appeared to him as a happy pathological situation between mother and son. It took her twenty years of constant interference, but when her husband died, she convinced her son that she was getting older and should not live alone. Seymour returned from work to discover Christian had moved Lena into their home with no discussion. Seymour was furious, and before long, Lena was sleeping in Seymour's space of the king-sized bed that he and Christian had shared. Her eighty-five-year-old eyes glowed of victory: "I will always be his mother."

Chapter Thirty-Eight

Divine Intervention

Seymour returned from a business meeting held in Los Angeles, California, and his plane landed in Baltimore, where he lived with Christian and Lena. After he picked up his luggage and retrieved his car, shortly after starting the ignition, he decided to drive to a gay piano bar he loved. He was depressed after Christian had moved his mother into their home without notice. He had not figured out how he was going to handle new accommodations for himself because now he felt he had to move out of the home that he had invested every penny he made.

He definitely had no plans to continue living in the situation he found himself in. He was torn about giving up the lifestyle he had so richly enjoyed with Christian. At this point, he thought back as to how he landed in this situation. At the beginning, when he moved in with Christian, he had not planned to fall in love with him. He wanted to finish graduate school and get his career launched, and a roommate did not seem like a bad idea at the time. This current decision was difficult for him because he was now forty-two years old. On the evening he returned from Los Angles, he simply did not want to go home. He needed a break from reflecting on his unhappy situation, and the gay piano bar would have been a great place to unwind.

Albrecht had exposed Seymour to Broadway soundtracks from well-known Broadway plays, and this bar was a safe location in DuPont Circle to socialize with other gay men and sing along with the tunes. He held a glass of scotch and water in his hand. When he entered the bar, the room was lively, softly lit, and warm with the mix of body heat and assorted perfumes and colognes. As his eyes became accustomed to the room, a very handsome man with blue eyes and a very healthy basket—the type Estelle would have called "lap-legged"—was standing at the bar on the other side of the room.

Seymour could not help but notice a sexual chemistry for the man. He visually cruised the man between parting glances. A short while later, the man left his comfortable space along the bar rail and approached Seymour. He confidently said, "I know you." Seymour, totally caught off guard by this Caucasian man, nervously replied, "Well, I don't think so. Because anyone who is as handsome as you, I think I would have remembered."

This reply did not go over well with the man, and he angrily retorted, "I met you ten years ago at a *Gone with the Wind* party. You were wearing a royal-blue shirt with a gold logo, long white pants, a red belt, and boat shoes."

When Seymour processed the response, he froze. It was Hans, the man of his dreams from ten years earlier. The chance meeting.

Seymour said, "Oh my god! I looked all over the city for you for five years and could never find you. What are you doing out tonight?"

"My partner of ten years left me three months ago, and this is my first night out of the house other than work for three months," Hans replied. He continued, "Where is your partner?"

Seymour was totally enamored with the possibility of reconnecting with Hans, and for some reason, he did not want to acknowledge he had a partner. So he dismissively replied, "At home I guess."

Hans was sensitive from his recent breakup. He did not like jive talk from men whom he thought did not have serious intentions in a bar but to get laid. He could quickly saw through Seymour's facade and furiously retorted, "Then why are you out here flirting with me if you have a partner at home?" Hans was angry.

Knowing of his error, Seymour said as kindly as possible, "You have to know that just because a person is in a relationship, it does not mean that they are happy." Seymour was vainly attempting to soften the situation quickly and intelligently, but he failed miserably.

Seymour had set some emotions off in Hans that generated anger and fury. Hans said, "Well, it doesn't matter. I am going home."

Seymour, not wanting Hans to get away this time, says, "No, wait! I am so sorry!"

Hans said, "No, I have had it for tonight!"

Seymour replied, "Well, can I give you a ride home?"

"No!" Hans furiously replied.

The memory of the *Gone with the Wind* party, a chance meeting, was becoming clearer and clearer as Seymour was scrambling to make things right. Seymour did not want this opportunity to escape him. Whatever feelings and disappointments in his life that Hans was holding, Seymour felt he was holding as well with the situation around Christian and Lena.

At the same time, Seymour was actually getting pleasure from the resistance Hans was putting up. He was determined that this time, he was not letting this man get away without some kind of a test run or a trial. He was willing to risk everything he had to be with this man, if just for one happy minute. Seymour wanted to understand and satisfy what was going on within them at the *Gone with the Wind* party that had created such a strong magmatism.

Seymour was willing to beg, plead, or whatever it took, but he was not giving up so easy. He said politely and gently once more, "May I please give you a ride home?"

Hans again replied, "No!"

"May I buy you a drink?" Seymour asked.

Hans replied, "No!"

Seymour was getting desperate and followed Hans to the exit of the bar. From out of nowhere, sheets of rain descended from the October sky to the extent of almost no visibility, and Seymour asked for a third time, "Please let me give you a ride home. My car is parked right in front of the door."

Hans finally relented and said, "Well, okay!"

As Seymour drove his automobile, Seymour thought what a firecracker this man was—how stubborn, how angry and bitter Hans was this evening. He did not whisper a word as they rode together to Hans's townhouse. Seymour was going to figure out that night what was so painful to this blued man, and Seymour was going to correct it that night and make it right.

As Seymour pulled his car to the front door of Hans's townhouse, he parked the car and cut off the ignition. He said to Hans with a very slight victorious smile on his face, "Are you going to invite me in to see your etchings?"

Hans could not help but laugh at the silliness of the question and replied, "Do you drink tea?"

Seymour said, "Yes!"

"Well, just as long as you know we are only having tea!"

Seymour was happy.

After a cup of tea and some introductory conversation, Seymour was getting hot and hungry for more. He wanted to have a deeper conversation and get to the root of what was troubling this man, but he knew it was late and suggested that they exchange telephone numbers to stay in touch. When Seymour stood to depart the townhouse, Hans remained seated.

Seymour deliberately reached for Hans's arms and said, "Are you going to show me to the door?"

As he gently pulled Hans from his ice-cream-parlor chair, he added an extra tug so that Hans was snugly in his arms. He took advantage of that moment and pulled Hans's face to his and kissed him deeply on the lips, and soon their saliva was intermingling and they both longed for human touch.

After only a few moments of passionate face sucking, Hans stepped back and pulled Seymour toward the staircase that led to his third-floor bedroom. Seymour was deeply pleased with himself for breaking down Hans's tension and resistance. It was the best night of bliss Seymour had ever known. And from that moment, with the exception of business travel, Seymour and Hans were never apart. Seymour thought the gods had performed a divine intervention for him.

CHAPTER THIRTY-NINE

A Chance on Happiness

After twenty years of living with Christian and doing his part to make the relationship work, it was just not working. What burned him most was Lena sleeping in his space of their king-sized bed. Seymour thought how all the years of caring, struggling, and building together were just shot to hell. Christian showed no interest in completing his bachelor's degree, investing in moving to a more desirable community, or socializing with aspiring people. His interest in sexuality had diminished since he could not restart the flames of passion. Seymour had no interest in Christian's controlling and deliberately interfering mother, who saw nothing wrong with sleeping in the same bed with her fifty-seven-year-old son. Just thinking about it was more than Seymour could handle.

He recalled the restless and sleepless nights of unfulfilling intimacy. They did not share unified goals. Seymour felt he was living with an ambitionless man who worked and enjoyed looking at television day and night. It was not the life Seymour wanted to live anymore.

The universe placed Hans back in his life for a second time, and he was going to take a risk on happiness and fulfillment. Seymour decided to leave a relationship he had invested over twenty years of his life in. Emotionally, it was the hardest thing he had ever done, but he had to take the step because he was not happy. It was as difficult for him now as it was when he was separated from Estelle when going to first grade. Separations were hard for him. It had been a long time in the making.

Christian had eight promising relationships with men before Seymour. Lena interfered in all of them except one. And that one man was motherless and had adored and appreciated Lena. But none of these men or Lena had celebrated Christian as much as Seymour. Seymour was the person Christian chose, and he accepted Christian's proposal of living together. Over the years, Christian no longer wanted to keep up with what he considered Seymour's overambitious goals.

Christian was the first relationship Seymour had ever had, and he was grateful to simply have a relationship; but he learned a relationship in and of itself is not enough to sustain it. It needed to have intimacy and shared common interest. He was aware the relationship had issues from the very beginning, but he wanted it to work out in spite of the differences.

Lena was a controlling mother. Like a dog you push away and abuse, it still keeps coming back. Seymour could not break the cycle, and he was sure he could not continue to resent anybody's mother. It was not healthy for him.

Christian was saddened by Seymour's desire to break up the relationship. He wanted to keep both his mother and Seymour happy; but between the three of them, they could not figure it out. Seymour wanted . . . needed to be number one in someone's life. It was unhealthy to stay in Seymour's eyes. There was too much family history on both sides. They were both in a hole they could not dig themselves out of. Divine intervention brought Hans to Seymour for a second time. Seymour packed only his clothes and left all the materialism behind and moved with Hans to start anew at age forty-three.

Meeting Hans for the second time was a chance meeting. To leave Christian was a risky. He was not happy with Christian and wanted to take a chance on happiness. He knew from the start that a new relationship with Hans might not last and he would end up with nothing. But he was taking a chance on himself—a chance on happiness.

*   *   *

Hans had set up the perfect life for Seymour and himself and ruled the household as if he were the matriarch. Hans selected their friends and planned small and elegant dinner parties using china and crystal collections. With the exception of working hours, he organized the entire week from Sunday to Saturday.

Sunday was a light breakfast at home, then they strolled to a popular coffee shop on Connecticut Avenue for lattes and to read the *Post* and the *Times*. Then they would return home to get dressed for the opera matinee at the Kennedy Center. Monday and Tuesday evening they were at home as Hans prepared dinner and Seymour washed the dishes; no wine or libation was served other than water. Wednesday evening was the theater and a light meal at a local café; Thursday was dinner and home and wine night, but not to exceed two glasses each. But for a really bad workday, no more than a bottle between them. Friday was the Scotch and water night with dinner at home and a fire in the fireplace; and Saturday was housecleaning day and lattes and reading the *Post*, followed by a matinee at a local stage. Hans purchased season tickets for each of the theater venues and gave them to Seymour for his birthday each year. The lovemaking in between activities made the week all worthwhile to Seymour. He was making up for lost time.

Thanksgiving was the beginning of the holiday seasons blending Christmas and ending on New Year's Day. Hans prepared elaborate holiday foods from his Swedish heritage. The aromas of banana nut bread, cranberry bread, and pumpkin pies filled the house with wonderful holiday spirits. Seymour baked Estelle's fruitcake, pineapple upside-down cake, and sweet potato pies. They both would sit for hours, writing holiday cards and letters. The telephone would ring, and there would be endless long-distance telephone conversations from distant relatives and friends. Hans played classical holiday music to celebrate the birth of Christ. Handmade Christmas stockings were filled to the top and hung over the fireplace. And each season, Hans would pay a small fortune for a perfectly shaped fresh Douglas Fir Christmas tree purchased on upper Massachusetts Avenue NW. The tree salesmen would securely tie the tree on the roof of Hans's seventeen-year-old Nissan. When he and Seymour arrived home and sawed off a few inches of the tree base, they struggled to quickly get it in the house and erected in the tree stand and watered. On New Year's Eve, they never went to parties with friends but enjoyed dinner for two at a small Greek restaurant on Thomas Place. And before New Year's Day, the holiday festivities ended and the Christmas tree came down and they resumed their normal schedule. With the love and affection that Seymour and Hans had for each other, these were the most wonderful Christmas holidays Seymour had ever known.

After the Christmas and New Year's festivities, Hans planned a January or February cruise to a warmer climate. He would arrange the dates after the opening or closing of school to avoid too many children on the ship. During the months of September and October, Hans planned another cruise for the two of them to celebrate their anniversary. They each paid for one cruise per year.

Lovemaking was over the top! There was not an inch of Hans's body Seymour was not completely familiar with. There was mutual willingness, energy, and collaboration in their lovemaking. Hans loved Seymour, and

Seymour loved Hans. Hans and Seymour enjoyed their lovemaking, which was as frequent as the next recovery. They were happily exhausted.

As Seymour explained to Estelle when she inquired why he left Christian, he replied, "Mother, it is the first time I experienced love and sex at the same time." Life for Seymour and Hans was great, and the risk that Seymour thought he was taking at the onset was now a smart risk.

As close as Seymour and Estelle were, he never revealed to her the changes his heart and soul were enduring during the transition from Christian to Hans.

Chapter Forty

Father's Day Revelation

Albrecht was a quiet man and required little attention from anyone. He loved Estelle in his way and admired her commonsense approach to life and running the family household. In his soul, he was a Professor Henry Higgins (from *My Fair Lady*) type of man. He was content with his books, reading poetry, and enjoying good music. He rarely needed anyone to complete him. And the only problem in his marriage to Estelle was that she needed him to complete her. His philosophy was that every person must find contentment within themselves. He could not give contentment to someone.

Seymour never saw the two of them holding hands or engaging in an affectionate embrace, a kiss on the cheek, or a light pat on the butt. Yet through all the mayhem of marriage and raising children, the rent was consistently paid on time, heat and lights were never turned off, and the family had all they needed with a little to spare. Albrecht was content with the provisions he provided for his family and regularly told them, "You have food, clothing, and shelter. You should be grateful for what you have."

Almost every weekend of his adulthood, Seymour would visit his parents; but the conversations were always dominated by Estelle, and he was her cheerleader. When Albrecht was asked why he didn't say anything or contribute to the conversation, he would say, "I can't get a word in edgewise!" But the real issue was that Estelle and Seymour had common interest and dominated the conversations with idle talk of fashion, home furnishings, and people. These were the same things they discussed when riding along in the car going to and from the grocery store or Sadie's beauty parlor.

Albrecht would have preferred talking about public affairs, the news, books, his favorite Broadway musicals, and current events, which held only a slight interest for Estelle or Seymour. Seymour joined in the conversations of whatever Estelle chose. Seymour recognized Estelle's emotional neediness and always allowed her to be the center of attention. Albrecht would, however, submit to what he considered Estelle and Seymour's nonsense while sipping on his regular gin-and-orange-juice cocktail. According to Estelle, he drank gin and orange ever since she had met him.

On Father's Day, Seymour insisted that he and Estelle give Albrecht his day of honor and a chance to talk on any topic he wanted for as long as he liked. It was the very least they could do on this one day of the year dedicated to fathers. They had habitually dominated all the other conversations throughout the year, so this day was dedicated to him.

Albrecht accepted and enjoyed this opportunity to celebrate himself. He would always talk slowly—too slow for Estelle—and carefully with sentences that had commas and periods. Estelle and Seymour spoke in run-on paragraphs with no commas or periods. They often rambled.

Albrecht began telling the story of why he wanted Estelle to give birth to Seymour. Never having heard such a story in his entire life, Seymour sat up straight and took note of what Albrecht was about to say. As Albrecht continued to sip on his gin and orange juice, he told Seymour a story from his childhood.

Seymour had heard a thousand family tales over all the annual holiday gatherings, but he had never heard the story he was about to hear. Albrecht began to tell the story of his mother planning a birthday party for herself. During her preparation, she remembered that she failed to pick up sweet relish, mayonnaise, and a couple of onions she needed for the potato salad that she was preparing for her party. In her hurry to get to Lexington Market and return home to continue her preparations, she swiftly walked to the back door and quietly told Albrecht, who was playing marbles in the backyard, to keep an eye on things because she was leaving the house to pick up a few items from the store.

Her message was concise, informal, and somber. This was Bessie's nature. Albrecht, at the time, was ten years old. He did not pay much attention to what his mother was saying and continued to play marbles in the backyard with his friends. Sleeping in her crib on the third floor was Albrecht's baby sister, Stella.

Of all Albrecht's sisters and brothers, Stella was the one sibling who loved and adored Albrecht most. It was a love that warmed Albrecht's heart. His family was rather stoic and unaffectionate. Stella was a warm and loving child. She was just a toddler but loved Albrecht and would grab his leg as he walked through the house. She would not release him until Albrecht picked her up off the floor. When he picked up his baby sister, she would just grin and smile with pure happiness, as if he were the only person in the world. Albrecht would pick her up and swing her around, and Stella would just coo. Stella melted the tender spot in Albrecht's heart. It was pure sibling love between the two of them.

Bessie and Theopolis never publicly displayed love and affection toward each other or their ten children. Albrecht longed for love and affection, and within his heart, he cooed toward little Stella's pure childhood affection that only an innocent child can give.

In Bessie's rush to get to the market and return, she did not say that Stella was napping in her crib on the third floor; nor did she say that she had left a pot of potatoes slowly cooking on the back burner of the gas stove. She had hoped they would be completely cooked by the time she returned home.

Albrecht did not know that Stella was napping or that the potatoes were on the stove cooking, so he continued to play marbles with his buddies in the backyard. Soon after Bessie departed the house, the water evaporated from the pot of potatoes. The pot eventually got so hot it melted and sent sparks of flame throughout the kitchen, and in no time, the house was engulfed in fire. Stella died in the house fire.

When Bessie returned home to find that the house had burned down and her child was dead, she never said a word to Albrecht, who was paralyzed with fear. She said nothing to console him or to ask what had happened. She said nothing. Cold as steel was Bessie; she said nothing.

Before Albrecht could finish telling his story, Seymour interrupted and sharply said, "Daddy! You know this was not your fault, don't you?"

Albrecht replied, "Ma never said."

Seymour was horrified and sad for his father. Never having physically touched his father in his life, his inclination was to jump up from his chair and hug his father as tight as he could to console him for the pain he had been enduring all these years. He needed consolation. He was a child when this all happened. Bessie never said a word to Albrecht, one way or the other, to release him from his guilt, sorrow, and pain.

Seymour had seen for the first time in his father's face anguish and tears. He did not know how to reach his father to console him and insulate him from what he had been feeling for decades. Seymour was taught that men did not hug or touch. Estelle was present, listening to the story. Seymour was not sure what she would think of her gay son hugging his father and her husband. Seymour was torn between respecting the anti-gay feeling of his mother and the compassion he felt for his father. Uncertainty swept through his heart.

Albrecht concluded his Father's Day story by saying, "I wanted your mother to have you, Seymour, because I thought you would be my child. The child who would replace Stella."

Seymour's heart came to a complete standstill, and his mind raced through all the years he felt so unloved and so unwanted by Estelle. He thought, *For all of these years, my father has carried the guilt and responsibility for the death of his baby sister, Stella.*

For four decades, Seymour felt unwanted because his mother kept telling him she never wanted to have him. On this Father's Day, he learned he was wanted by his father and what an honor it would have been for him to have been a symbol for a deceased aunt whom he had never met. This aunt was his dad's favorite sister. He was his father's favorite child. Seymour could feel a dark cloud of grief for himself and his father. He felt elation fill his heart that someone really wanted him. The understanding of his birth was not as Estelle had portrayed it or the way he interpreted Estelle's messages.

Estelle had known this story, and for as much time as she and Seymour had spent together, she kept this story from him. All his life, Seymour had self-esteem issues and worked every day to earn Estelle's love when he was loved by his father. Everyone in the family could sense that Albrecht had special feelings toward Seymour, but no one ever knew why, most of all Seymour. This was a valuable piece of information in the mosaic of his life. It had never been expressed to him. Not feeling loved had been his life's preoccupation, and to learn on this Father's Day that his dad had a motivation for wanting Estelle to get pregnant, and it was to love and be loved by Seymour.

Seymour felt sad because he had favored his mother all his life. He neglected his father when his father had the same need for love as Seymour.

Estelle's contention was that if she made the sacrifice to have a child she did not want for Albrecht, he would have been more loving and affectionate to her. Instead, when Seymour was born, Albrecht gave all his affection to Seymour. In her hurt and disappointment, she deliberately kept father and son separated. She could not bear to see Seymour getting the affection she wanted.

Estelle was counting on Albrecht to fill the hole in her heart after the death of her mother and the cruelty she endured under her father's regime. Since she could not get the affection she desired from Albrecht, she wanted Albrecht to feel as unloved as she felt. The whole family was a casualty of this life-changing event. Neither Albrecht, Estelle, Aries, Claudia, nor

Seymour felt loved. If Albrecht did not have time to be affectionate to Estelle, then there would be no time for him to love Seymour. Hearing this story floored Seymour, and he was in mental and emotional knots trying to decipher this Father's Day bombshell.

As Seymour drove his car back to Washington, DC, to rejoin Hans, he thought back over the years and remembered how Albrecht never said no to anything he had ever asked. He remembered the toy truck his father had given him, which was an expensive collector's item, and the bookcase he asked his father to build for him when he was in first grade, and the English racer his father gave him on his tenth birthday. He remembered Aries pitching a fit when he heard that Albrecht had paid for an airplane ticket, motel, and rental car for Seymour to attend the NCAA basketball tournament while in college. He thought of all the times Albrecht, in his quiet manner, had reached out to him. Seymour's only obsession was to be loved by his mother, and he never paid attention to these overtures from his father. His soul was overwhelmed with regret. He thought, *How can I ever make up all of these years to a father who loved and wanted me so desperately and who received little in return?*

Seymour chose to spend all of his childhood with Estelle. He had spent all of his life seeking love from his mother, whom he thought never wanted to have him. The love Albrecht showered on Seymour, though unrequited, was the love Estelle thought she was entitled to receive from her husband. After all, she was the one who gave Albrecht something he wanted. Estelle thought some concessions should be made for all she went through giving birth to Seymour, all the way up to the night he was born. This was one of the worst days of her life. She was the one who never wanted another child. Estelle did not realize her attitude was very similar to that of her father, who punished her mother's sisters by refusing to allow them to see their nieces and nephew as punishment for not assuming responsibility for all three of his children after she died. Similarly, Estelle punished Albrecht for not loving her more, and she punished Seymour by keeping him away from his father. She never wanted to turn Seymour over to his father as all of their family, friends, and neighbors suggested—so that he would be less effeminate. When she saw that Seymour was a good-natured child and chose to spend so much time with her, she accepted his love in lieu of Albrecht's.

Thoughts and reflections swam around in Seymour's head as he drove across the Baltimore Washington Parkway. His upbringing was beginning to make sense, but so many years had passed. Estelle had done the bulk of his rearing. But he summarized that Albrecht loved him unconditionally, and Estelle did not.

CHAPTER FORTY-ONE

Finding His Voice

By this time, Seymour was forty-two years old. He had managed to graduate, the only black in his high school, along with the racism and hatred associated with school integration. He graduated from a top-ten predominately white university. He had poor academic preparation, poor study habits, and poor university advisement. He suffered the setback of his father telling him he would never make it. Throughout his life, he coped with the ridicule and taunting from being gay. Within eight years, he earned two master's degrees and a PhD from predominately white institutions. He obsessively nursed his emotional scar tissue that resulted each time Estelle said "I never wanted to have you." And he miraculously lived to transcend his brother, Aries.

He did the hard work of overcoming ill feelings of not being wanted along with Estelle's transmission of those feelings to his older brother and sister, Aries and Claudia. Seymour had been hurt by many of the circumstances he had faced.

Over his young adult years, Seymour voraciously read every new self-improvement book that was on the market. He learned that happiness was a choice. He also learned to have a personal relationship with God versus accepting the laws of organized religion that had also discriminated against him by race and sexual orientation. With his readings and the adoption of a personal relationship with God, he came to a point of happiness. He always wanted to remember those situations in life that caused him hurt and pain because he wanted to always keep in mind how close to danger he had been. He had learned to move along, but he never forgot.

Seymour never shared with Estelle that he was leaving his home of twenty years with Christian to live and start anew with Hans. He was grown now, and he did not want to be lectured by her. At this point, he had made up his mind just as Claudia had when she ran off to Martha's Vineyard to marry. When Estelle found out that Seymour had left Christian, she could not believe her ears, and he got lectured regardless of whether he wanted to hear it or not.

"But why—after twenty years—would you leave your relationship and start all over again at age forty-two? It doesn't make any sense. You have a new home, two new cars, a house full of new furniture, a man who pays his share of the bills. He does not smoke, drink, or abuse you! Why, at this stage of your life, would you do something like this? Seymour?" Estelle chided, "Child, you have everything most women would love to have! When I think about it, I am jealous myself!"

Estelle thought to herself, *Seymour seems to get everything I wanted. He is on a high horse now and is getting just a little too big for his britches!*

Seymour did not understand his mother's reactions. For the duration of his relationship with Christian, she had accused him of introducing Seymour to the gay life. With this new revelation of his move to Hans, she now aligns her sympathies with Christian. Now in her eyes, Seymour had become the villain. Seymour endured his mother's scolding. He did not want to hear it, but he patiently listened. He thought with a smile what a turncoat she was. Seymour the villain.

Seymour politely, respectfully, and in a controlled voice, says to Estelle, "Mother, I am happy to answer your questions. I have been unhappy with Christian for a long time. In my new relationship with Hans, it is the first time in my life I have had love and sex at the same time. I have loved others who did not love me. I have had a few who loved me but I did not love. At this stage in my life, I needed to decide if I wanted to live the rest of my life unhappy with every imaginable material possession or take a risk on being happy and loved."

Estelle was inflamed with the control and coolness of Seymour's tone, and she blurted out, "Well, ain't that a crying shame! I have never had love and sex at the same time. I have been married for over fifty years! Most people in the world don't get that, so I don't know why you think you are so supposed to have it!"

In their discussion, Estelle deduced when the word *sex* was used in his reply that there was some pre-relationship sexuality. She hated to discuss sex, but with a disgusted tone, she said, "Well, don't you go out there and get yourself AIDS because I am not going to take care of you!" Estelle had never liked the idea of Seymour being gay, and she never thought Christian was good enough for her son because he was too old. Now she was running to the aid of the relationship and two people she never approved of from the start.

Withholding as much rage as he could, Seymour spoke up to his mother for the first time in his entire life and firmly said, "Mother, I cannot promise you that I won't have sex again. But I will promise you that if I get AIDS, I will not ask you to take care of me! And furthermore, if you should have a blood transfusion and contract AIDS, you need to think about who you are going to ask to take care of you!"

A hush fell over them and nothing else was said. For the very first time, Estelle was silenced by her son.

Estelle was unhappy learning the child whom she could once rule with the stroke of a finger was no longer a child; nor could he be ruled. Her bargaining tools to leverage over Seymour were gone now that he was grown and independent.

Seymour was sorry to have used a strong voice with his mother. He had been persecuted by her for a long time. All this dissention was generated by her hatred and distaste for gays and the HIV-AIDS epidemic. Seymour was tired of being judged by Estelle, especially when she would not read a book or magazine to read the facts about parents with gay children. Within Seymour's soul, he was feeling a scene from *Torch Song Trilogy*, where Harvey Fierstein said to his mother, "All I ask from you now is respect!"

Seymour, at last, had found his voice.

CHAPTER FORTY-TWO

Senior Appointment

Over a period of years and as times changed, Seymour was eventually promoted in the university setting. He continued to perform his assignments, earning superior and outstanding ratings. He was invited to serve on almost every university committee and to serve in leadership roles with university professional societies. He received honors and recognitions for his leadership. Estelle was not happy with Seymour working in the university setting and still felt he was being penalized for being out of the closet. In Estelle's judgment, Seymour deserved more.

Seymour had no idea what his mother was seeking from him, but she saw something in him that he did not see in himself. He thought, *Will she ever be satisfied with me? Will I ever be enough? Will she ever want me?*

After twenty-two years of working in a university setting, Seymour was recruited for a senior appointment with the federal government. When he called Estelle to tell her about the offer, she said, "Well, dear god, someone has finally been merciful to my child!" Up to this moment, Seymour had never known that his mother held such disdain for his university positions or any past positions. Estelle had listened over the years of how her son had been mistreated in the university workplace. For Seymour, it was a good job that paid his bills; but once again, she implored, "Now when you get this federal job, keep your damn mouth shut! You can be fired in the government for being homosexual!"

Seymour accepted the job and announced his sexual orientation in the interview. He never wanted it said later down the road that he had concealed information about his personal life as a justification for his being terminated. He was totally up-front about who he was. After he was hired, he found that Estelle was correct that there was no federal protection for lesbian, gay, bisexual, and transgender (LGBT) employees; but he declined Estelle's attempts to save him by putting him in the closet. He was determined to be who he was born to be.

I am who I am, he thought. *La Cage Aux Follies* still echoed in his soul from his early years of coming to terms with being gay.

As collateral duties to his job in the policy section, he was assigned the roles of diversity officer and LGBT program manager. Claudia had noticed on one of his correspondence his title including "LGBTQ program manager." She wrote to him, stating, "You sure have a lot of nerve!" After two decades, Claudia's barometer had not moved on the issue of homosexuality; however, in all of her conversations with Seymour, she informed him she was a Christian. Seymour would have preferred Claudia live a Christian life rather than have the need to tell him she was a Christian.

Claudia and her third husband had become born-again Christians and were yoked in mockery, ridicule, and anti-gay advocacy. Rather than take a supportive role in Seymour's good fortune, his mother, brother, and sister were disgraced. "Indeed I don't want any brother of mine being gay!" Claudia would say at the dinner table at family gatherings.

Although there were no federal protections for Seymour in his new job in the federal sector, he was responsible for leading change for LGBT employees. His being gay was an influential reason for his employment. His having a stable relationship with a white man didn't hurt him either.

Seymour could not be more excited with these collateral appointments. He was making a significant impact not only for his agency but the entire LGBTQ population. His sexual orientation was at last rewarding him for not staying in the closet as his mother had sharply advised throughout her life.

As diversity officer for his agency, he came across *Maya Angelou's Collection of Poems*; and from the collection, Seymour read "John J." It was a poem of a woman who never wanted her son. The thread was this: "(His momma didn't want him.) (But his momma didn't want him.) (But his momma didn't want him.) (She didn't want him.)"

Seymour had never heard of a mother who did not want her child and found it hard to believe, but there were such mothers on the face of this earth. He couldn't help himself, but he got so full while reading the poem, he began to cry while reading at his desk, at work, at his senior position. For some reason, the words still hurt.

CHAPTER FORTY-THREE

Motherly Love

By the time Seymour had reached the age of sixty, he had tried everything in his power to get his mother to be nurturing and affectionate toward him and to accept the fact that he was born gay. He had taken her on several of his out-of-state business trips where they resided in luxury hotels. He took her to the some of the finest five-star restaurants in the Baltimore and Washington areas. He purchased for her a Persian lamb and mink coat that she had worshiped. He had given her fine jewelry and occasionally took time off from work to take her on a day trip. He had even given her thousands of dollars for the deposit for a luxury retirement community where she desired to live. Nothing stimulated her to say endearing words to him. She never thought her telling Seymour he was not a wanted chld had caused any harm. If Seymour attempted to broach the subject of how bitter her remark came across to him, her reply was simple: "If any of my children are unhappy with me after all I have done for them, then it is just tough! They all had more than I ever got!" He just could not get through to her. She barricaded any subject that was uncomfortable for her to discuss, even if the attempt was to provide helping support and improve the quality of communications.

For the most part, Seymour had worked his way through the agony of his mother berating him, dismissing him, and for being totally disrespectful toward him behind his back and to his face. He knew she was not happy with his being an average Joe; nor did she like his homosexuality or his choices of mates.

It was hard for Seymour to observe how she showered love and affection on Claudia, who had married three times and had a revenge baby. A daughter who had no respect for her and, for all practical purposes, had rejected her. Aries was an alcoholic, had married three times, and had fathered a child that he never accepted full responsibility for. Neither Aries nor Claudia were as generous, kind, or spent as much time with her as Seymour. But Estelle saw them as normal children. In her heart, Estelle thought of Seymour as abnormal, and she would say to him, "You are my child. Your being gay is just like having a handicapped child! But you are my child. I own you!" Estelle could not see the destruction of her remarks on Seymour.

Estelle was generous and compassionate to the less fortunate. This was a position she held throughout childhood and her formative and young adult years. Christmas and birthdays were her traditional times to give most generously. All other holidays were omitted from her holiday-planned giving.

For Valentine's Day, a holiday which she was never known to recognize, she sent Seymour a Valentine's Day card. Seymour opened the card and read what Estelle had written inside: "I never wanted to have you, but I am glad I did." Seymour broke down and cried at age sixty. The assault was so painful to him, he assumed a fetal position and boo-hooed in his master bedroom walk-in closet. His tears were not of joy but from the constant, persistent harping and reminders of his not being wanted. *What is wrong with her?* He was offended by the card. It had been a great day up until this point. He just did not get it.

He had had enough and did not want to hear it anymore—mother or no mother. Although he had severed his childhood attachment to his mother, she was still his mother. He had just never heard of a mother who would say such a thing for so often and for so long. It was too much for him to bear. Was this card some kind of apology? Was he an illegitimate child? Was she raped? What was her problem with this child? He just could not figure it out.

He had come across hundreds of mothers who said out loud and in public how they loved their child. They would do anything for them, and they were proud of them and accepted them for who they were. Estelle, on the other hand, would say to her friends, "I accept Seymour's homosexuality. It is just like any other birth defect!"

With all this, he could not bring himself to hate his mother; but he surely did not understand her and tried hard to accept her for who she was. But he had a need for motherly love that she had no capacity to give. It appeared that both love and hate could come from the same temple and from the ones we try to love most.

Chapter Forty-Four

Heart Attacks

Albrecht had suffered his first heart attack at the age of fifty-five. After his recovery, he applied for immediate retirement. With his military service and his accumulated civilian years, he had enough time to get out of the workforce. Estelle protested his retirement because she thought age fifty-five was too young to retire. The children had grown and left home, and the house she wanted for years was paid in full. In Estelle's mind, this was the last opportunity to stash more money away for retirement. The doctors gave Albrecht a clean bill of health and informed him he could return to work full time, but he would not entertain the thought. The heart attack scared Albrecht, and he just did not want to take a chance on another medical ordeal. He was firm on this position.

Estelle tried to talk Albrecht into working a little longer but to no avail. Just as he had said no to Estelle on everything she wanted from buying a car, buying a house, Catholic school for Claudia, and all her aspirations, he remained staunch. He retired to live the Professor Henry Higgins lifestyle he had dreamed of living all his life—a quiet life of literature, classical music, sirloin steaks, and gin with orange juice at four o'clock every day.

Early in his retirement, Albrecht built the perfect little man cave for himself in the basement of the house and equipped it with all the things he loved. He added a double car garage to the house with a separate entrance to his man cave. This gave Estelle full rein with the main level of the house.

Albrecht even found a girlfriend from Seymour's high school class. Albrecht was having his midlife crisis. He still wanted to have sex with Estelle, but she had no interest. He told her, "If you don't want to fulfill my needs, then I will go somewhere else." Estelle replied, "Well, go ahead, man! Shake your business, man. If that is what you want to do, my conscience is clear."

Estelle had never experienced an orgasm until well after Seymour was born. She was frigid to the idea of sex. It was all such a nuisance to her. She knew what it meant when Albrecht's hand reached over to her in the middle of the night. She grudgingly thought of the preparation a woman makes to engage in sex and the messy cleanup afterward. All the while, the man turns over and, within moments, is sound asleep. The snoring sounds and the smell of bad breath mixed with gin was awful to her. For a woman, she thought it was no foreplay and no afterglow. So if he wanted to get his jollies somewhere else, it was a relief for her. She thought men at fifty-five were on a decline, and after all the fumbling around for their arousal, they weren't doing anything anyway. "Yeah! Go shake your business, man!" she would say.

Albrecht's announcement of a girlfriend stung just a little, but she comforted herself with thinking, *I know I am not going anywhere, and I know he is not going anywhere. And one thing is certain and two things are for sure. I can look up longer than he can look down, and eventually, men have to give it up and come in.* She was tired from the life she had lived and did not care.

One night at 1:00 AM, a state policeman called Estelle to let her know that Albrecht had been in an automobile accident. He was in the hospital, and she should come immediately. Panic set in, and she got out of bed, quickly dressed, and drove to the hospital, which was about fifteen miles away, in the middle of the night. It was autumn, the air was damp, and the windshield had dew as the wipers flip-flopped back and forth across the windshield.

In the fifty years they had been married, Albrecht had never had one traffic violation of any type. She sat in the waiting room until he was out of recovery and placed in a room. Before she entered Albrecht's hospital room, she spoke with the doctors to find out what had happened to cause him to have an accident since, up until this point, he had a perfect driving record. She also needed to brace herself for she did not know what she was going to see.

The doctors pulled her aside and said, "Mrs. Rose, I regret to inform you. But when the emergency vehicles arrived at the scene of the accident, it was obvious to us that your husband was behind the wheel with a young woman in his company at the time he suffered the heart attack."

"Well, in the name of the Father, what on earth? This is why I say all of the time women are sorry creatures. Now here he is, out with some other woman, and who gets called? The wife! And now I am going to be viewed as the dirty dog because I won't be happy about taking care of my husband! Well, I swear! All right, doctors, thank you! But I want you to know all of you men are just alike!"

Estelle composed herself and walked in the hospital room. She approached the bed where Albrecht was resting quietly with an oxygen mask attached to his face. This man was the reason she left her hometown, which she dearly loved. She was pregnant at age twenty-one. Up until that time, she had no contact with a man. She loved Albrecht. They had three children. They had struggled to make a life for themselves and raise their children. They gave the children a chance for a good education. She knew Albrecht was scared to death to awaken and find himself in the hospital again. She looked at him with tears in her eyes and thought of just how much she loved him and how totally exasperating he could be.

When Albrecht was discharged from the hospital, Estelle assumed her duties as wife and took care of him. She thought if he had continued to work as she had suggested, he would not have had time for such foolishness with someone else. She was ashamed of Albrecht for acting like an old coon fool and told him so.

Albrecht was mute. He knew he was wrong, but getting caught in public was even more embarrassing for him because the local newspaper wrote: "Local Man Has Heart Attack While Driving from Nearby Hotel."

Albrecht had a second heart attack, and his recovery from the second heart attack was much slower than the first since he had not been taking his prescribed medications and continued to drink his gin. This time, he needed quadruple bypass heart surgery.

Estelle called Seymour to help nurse him back to health. Seymour would get up early every morning of Albrecht's hospitalization and dress in a suit and tie to go to the hospital to check on his condition. He would talk to the doctors and nurses. He would tell them all to "take good care of my father." Then he would visit with Albrecht for an hour then depart for work. He would work all day and come back to the hospital after work to make sure Albrecht was being treated with unquestionable care.

Seymour was formally educated and had earned several degrees, and he referred to himself in the hospital as "doctor." He knew that hospitals were not as kind to black patients as they were to white, and he wanted them to know that they were not dealing with an uneducated black man that they could perceive as run-of-the-mill. Seymour was generally mild mannered, but he was serious when it came to Albrecht's health, especially after the revelation that he was a wanted child by his father.

Albrecht never wanted to have the surgery. He told Estelle and Seymour to let him die. Seymour asserted, "No! You have to stay here and finish raising me!" Seymour was well into his sixties, but once he had discovered Albrecht was the parent who really wanted him, he poured just as much time and affection into his father as he did his mother.

When Estelle and Seymour walked beside Albrecht as the medical team rolled him to the operating room, Estelle broke down and cried. After the surgery, as they rolled Albrecht to intensive care, then Seymour cried. He had never seen a person wrapped and bandaged after open-heart surgery. The sight alone of his post-surgery father made him tremble to his core. Within, Estelle held her full level of frustration with Albrecht and his indiscreet actions. She had prepared the house for his return home from the hospital, but rather than pick him up herself, she delegated this responsibility to Seymour.

The doctors had given Seymour specific instructions on how to care for Albrecht when he returned home. Through Estelle's insistence and Seymour's oversight, Albrecht received the very best care during his stay in the hospital. Other than his two heart attacks, Albrecht had never been in the hospital a day in his life. He never went to the doctor for anything. He continued his regular consumption of his favorite gin-and-orange-juice libation after the first heart attack. His overindulgence of this sport caused the second heart attack along with the excitement his young girlfriend provided while he was driving. Along with the second heart attack came an array of medications that he disliked taking. These medications—with his determination to resume his four o'clock gin and orange juice—did not fare well with his blood thinners. He eventually needed long-term care.

Aries, still a functional alcoholic, brought a half pint of gin to the long-term facility and shared it with Albrecht. Aries believed Albrecht was going to die. He thought he should give him whatever he wanted at this point if it made him happy. The gin he gave Albrecht caused a violent reaction. Albrecht got so out of control, the nurses and orderlies had to force him into a straitjacket and ankle straps.

The long-term facility called Estelle and threatened to put Albrecht out of the facility if she did not keep Aries away from Albrecht. Estelle was so upset and dead tired from nursing Albrecht, she became ill. She called Seymour and instructed him to go to the facility to see what all the uproar was about.

When Seymour arrived at the long-term care facility and saw his father in a straitjacket, he shouted at the top of his voice, "What the hell is this?" Albrecht was one of the most calm and gentle people Seymour had ever known. He was purely honest to the core and would not harm a soul. Under no circumstance would he have behaved in a manner that required him to be placed in a straitjacket. Seymour summoned the nurses and implored they take Albrecht out of the straitjacket immediately.

He looked in his father's eyes with the purest love and said, "Daddy, they are going to take you out of this straitjacket, but you have got to stay calm and in control of yourself. Do you understand? I am going to stay here with you."

Albrecht was heavily medicated, but with tears of gratefulness, he nodded his head in agreement just as if he were a child.

When Seymour learned from the hospital administration what Aries, as the last visitor, had done, the intensity of his dislike for his brother's actions rose to orbit levels. He thought it was impossible to intensely dislike his brother any more than he already had, but he managed to take it up a notch.

Medical science classified alcoholism as a disease, but Aries was a buffoon and a clown in his early childhood long before he became an alcoholic. Seymour had no regard for his brother at this point. He had no sympathy for him and refused to acknowledge him as a good human being. For Seymour, Aries was a zero. Aries was too self-centered to recognize and accept that Albrecht and Estelle were both too old and sick to manage his silliness. Seymour found it impossible to make sense with a drunk. He said nothing to Aries. He needed to reserve his energy for the care of their mother and father.

Albrecht was deeply appreciative of Seymour's daily visits to the nursing home. On one of his visits to the facility to visit his father, Seymour used a wheelchair and took his father outside to get some fresh air. The grounds of the facility were lined with beautiful oak trees, and the leaves were bursting with the coming of spring. The flowerpots were filled with yellow and purple pansies, and the air smelled from the mulch that had been spread around the base of the trees. The weather was mild with low humidity, making it a wonderful spring day.

Albrecht, by nature, was a quiet man. Seymour was quiet too as he pushed the wheelchair. They both enjoyed the wonderful combinations of nature. In a low voice, Albrecht broke the silence and said to Seymour, "Seymour, my life is over."

As he did on that one Father's Day, Albrecht began to tell Seymour stories of his life. He told of his impoverished childhood, the Christmases as a child with no gifts, his cold mother and loving father, his altar-boy experiences at Catholic school, his military experiences, and his love and marriage with Estelle.

As Seymour listened and continued to push the wheelchair along the flowered flagstone walkway, Albrecht cleared the congestion in his throat.

He slightly elevated his voice to ensure Seymour could hear what he was about to say. "Seymour I have three children. I love all of my children. But, Seymour, you are the best one."

Tears popped uncontrolled from Seymour's eyes. The emotion he felt was beyond his ability to contain. After so many years of wanting to be validated as a good person by his family, Albrecht made it known to his son his deep affection while the sun, air, trees, and flowers listened. He could not muster a word to his father but never lost a step as he pushed the wheelchair. Albrecht never saw Seymour crying and with a runny nose.

As Seymour drove across the Baltimore Washington Parkway, he prayed to God to take his father. When he told Seymour he was ready to go, Seymour knew it was time. Seymour had seen him suffer long enough.

After Albrecht's first heart attack, he begged his father to have the necessary quadruple bypass heart surgery. Against his father's wishes, he told his father, "You must have the surgery because you have not finished raising me yet." Seymour was sixty years old and his father had finished raising him, but he still wanted to hear his father tell him he was loved. He had never heard these words from either of his parents.

His father had just then given him what he needed. Albrecht's message to him was so powerful, Seymour felt he was prepared to walk the rest of his life with his father in his heart. Albrecht had suffered enough, and he had expressed his love in a way Seymour could feel. Seymour could release his father to God, knowing this was the most unconditional love he had ever known. Seymour also was aware he had spent most of his time with his mother; but on this day, he felt complete with his father.

When Albrecht had returned back home with Estelle, Seymour took Albrecht on a car trip to Atlantic City. After his retirement, Albrecht entertained himself by playing the slot machines. Among Albrecht's favorite operas was *Tannhauser*. After Seymour got his infirm father situated in the car, he headed north on Interstate 95 to New Jersey. Seymour said, "Dad, I know you think that over all the years that I was not paying any attention to all of the classical music you played for us. I want to play for you one of your all-time favorites." After Seymour popped a CD into the player, the car filled with the music from *Tannhauser*. Albrecht broke down and cried.

Seymour was not prepared for the tears. He wanted his father to be happy. Albrecht reached into his back pocket and pulled out a clean white handkerchief. Estelle had continued to iron his clothes for over sixty years. He blew his noise and wiped his eyes. Seymour had never seen his father display such emotion.

When the opera ended, Seymour and his father conversed as they never had before. Seymour had willingly become Albrecht's baby sister, Stella.

He loved his father more than Albrecht could ever know. He regretted all the time he spent with his mother, seeking love, when his father's love was always in his presence.

After a fun day at the slots with Albrecht, Seymour paid the toll on the Delaware Memorial Bridge. As the electric window was rising, Seymour asked Albrecht, "Daddy, did you ever consider divorcing Mother?" In normal fashion, Albrecht took a cerebral moment and replied, "Divorce no! Murder yes!" Seymour laughed merrily because he fully understood.

Estelle, with full support from Seymour, planned and arranged Albrecht's funeral services. The church was packed with family and friends from near and far away. Albrecht was a unique man but was noted as a great provider, husband, father, community worker, and church parishioner. A full listing of his military and community accomplishments were reiterated for the congregation, and the day ended in total exhaustion for Estelle. Sixty-five years of marriage had ended in love and grief.

After Albrecht's death, Estelle made a little memorial for Albrecht on her bedroom dresser. It consisted of one of the few pictures he had ever taken in life. It was an 8×10 from his military years, along with his bone-framed eyeglasses and his wedding band.

After a year of grieving and reflecting, Seymour was visiting Estelle when he noticed the memorial was taken down. He simply commented with no intent, "I see you have taken Daddy's memorial down."

No harm or judgment was intended, but Estelle sharply turned around and said sternly, "Listen, Seymour, everyone does not grieve the way you do. But let me tell you something. When you have been married to a man for sixty-five years, some days you are glad he is gone!"

Seymour burst into laughter. This was his mother's authentic self speaking. He knew her history with Albrecht. He knew what she had gone through in her marriage with her husband, his father. He knew she had every reason to hold on to a bit of her bitterness on some days.

Seymour continued to laugh, saying, "Mother, you are too funny!" But he knew she was dead serious.

Chapter Forty-Five

Hans Dies

With all Seymour did for his elderly parents, Hans was his stable anchor. Hans had loved and supported Seymour through all his family and career stresses and worked around Seymour's life situations to ensure that they still had time for each other. Their love for each other was strong, and they were happy. Han and Seymour understood each other, and it was capped off with lavish intimacy.

Seymour was away for a few days on business travel for the government. Whenever he or Hans were away from each other for business, whether domestic or international, they called each other at 10:00 PM eastern time wherever they were on the globe. Late one March evening, Hans telephoned Seymour. In the conversation, he told Seymour his back was aching and that he did not feel well. He said in the conversation that if he was not feeling better in a couple of days, he was calling the doctor. Hans was never one to complain about health issues, but just to be sure Hans could manage alone, Seymour replied, "Do you want me to come home tonight?" Hans replied, "No. You are coming back tomorrow anyway. Just finish what you are doing."

During that same night, Hans's condition got worse, and he took a cab to the hospital emergency room. They admitted him immediately. When Seymour's plane landed the next day, he left the airport with his luggage in hand. He had a cab take him directly to the hospital where Hans had been admitted. The doctors kept him for three days and tested every organ in his body. Through the process of elimination, they determined Hans had malignant pancreatic cancer.

When the doctor and his team arrived to announce their diagnosis to Hans, Seymour was standing by the bed next to Hans. They asked him to leave the room. Hans interrupted the doctor and his team and said, "Anything you want to say to me, you can say in front of him!" When the doctors gave the prognosis, they reported that Hans had pancreatic cancer. He had three to six months to live, and any final arrangements that needed to be made were to be made now.

Hans and Seymour displayed no emotions in the presence of the attending physicians. When they departed, Hans and Seymour remained silent and emotionless until Hans said to Seymour, "You certainly seem calm about all of this." Seymour replied with strength and confidence, "I just went into autopilot. If I break down now, I will be of no use to you."

Hans understood and was satisfied with Seymour's response.

For the next five weeks, Seymour visited and nursed Hans every day, not missing a single day. The pain in Hans's body increased with each passing day. He eventually required a self-inducing morphine pump. During the first few weeks of Hans's illness, Seymour turned the first floor of the house into a hospital setting. It was set up with the most expensive hospital bed, a multilevel feeding tray, a porta-potty, and every other aid to make Hans as comfortable as possible.

The refrigerator in the summer kitchen was filled with chemotherapy drugs, painkillers, intravenous nutrition, and suppositories—all of which Seymour had to administer. Seymour purchased, online, a large flat screen television and two oversized leather recliners so that Hans could be comfortable and they could spend all of their final time together. Seymour was glad to be useful to Hans, and the time they spent together was the very best time of their lives. He loved Hans.

Home care lasted about two weeks before Hans was readmitted to the hospital and then directly to hospice. The doctors said they had never seen such an aggressive case of pancreatic cancer. Seymour walked Hans up and down the halls of the hospital for twenty minutes twice a day, or until Hans said he had had enough. Seymour rubbed his back every day with lotion to prevent bedsores. He went to the hospital's linen closet to get sheets to change Hans's bed multiple times every day and to replace bath towels and cloths. He emptied the trash can just as soon as the nurses disposed a bandages or disposable wrappings. Seymour would unwrap pink oral sponges and soak them in water then place them on Hans's dried-out tongue and lips. The medications were dehydrating.

Hans responded well to Seymour's attentiveness and was mindful enough to know his life was ending. He told Seymour something very comforting and reassuring, something he had never said before: "You know I love just you." Not prepared to receive Hans's emotionally charged message, Seymour did not want to take himself off of autopilot because there was so much more to do. Seymour had never felt as useful in his life and as deeply loved as he did during this period of his life and their relationship.

Although the hospital staff advised and coached Seymour to prepare for Hans final arrangements, Seymour thought if he personally nursed Hans, he would get well. He was in denial. Seymour said with all his heart to Hans, "When you get to where you are going. Come and get me because I am ready to be with you now wherever you are going." He seriously added, "But take me with you without pain." Hans replied, "No! I want you to have a happy life."

During the final three nights of Hans's life, the doctors on duty informed the night nurses that Hans would be dead by morning. They instructed the nurses to call Seymour two hours before if he wanted to say his final goodbyes.

At 3:00 AM in the morning, the telephone rang, waking Seymour. The night-shift nurse said, "Seymour, I think it is time because Hans's pulse rate and blood pressure are dropping."

In his robe and pajamas, Seymour ran to the car and drove to the hospice center. When he arrived, he told Hans of his arrival and started gently rubbing his arms and legs. He kissed him on the lips, cheeks, and all over his face and neck repeatedly. He got in the bed with Hans to warm his body. Hans's heart rate and blood pressure rose. When the morning doctors arrived and found that Hans was still alive, they could not believe their eyes.

On the second night, Seymour thought he had kept Hans alive the night before by talking to him constantly and warming his body. He thought he could do again on the second night. This time, he sang to Hans. Hans's heart rate and blood pressure rose again. When the morning doctors arrived on the second day, they once again could not believe their eyes. Hans was still alive.

Later in the morning, the day nurse came into the room and Seymour was lying in the bed with Hans, and she sharply said, "What is going on in here? Is this your father?"

"No," Seymour said. And he added, "This is the best friend I have ever had in the world."

The nurse calmed down and said, "Well, I sure wish I had a friend like you." She left the room as the two men—one white and one black—lay in the bed together.

On the third day, the attending doctor at the hospice called Seymour early in the day and said to him, "Seymour, sometimes a person wants to die alone. It is because they do not want their death to be the last memory for the loved one." Seymour took the message as a warning to not stimulate Hans back to life again but let him die in peace.

When the night nurse called at 3:00 AM to let Seymour know it was time to come see Hans, he rose from the bed and—in robe and pajamas—got in his Nissan Maxima and started to drive down the alley behind the townhouse he and Hans shared. At the end of the alley, there was a large black delivery truck, with a large "X" painted on the rear doors, that blocked the driveway. Seymour then placed the car in reverse and backed the car the entire length of the alley to get out to Fifteenth Street. After arriving at Fifteenth Street, there was a down power line at Sixteenth Street that created a huge traffic backup. These delays were making Seymour anxious and taking minutes off his drive time. When he arrived at the hospice, Hans had died.

When Seymour looked at Hans's deceased body, he was overtaken with grief. He walked to Hans's bed and got into the bed with him. Seymour gently hugged the corpse and cried. The hospice nurses allowed him to lie there for two hours and then said to Seymour, "The limousine has arrived, and you must get up."

As Hans's body was wheeled to the hearse, the drivers pulled the zipper of the black body bag over Hans's face. When Seymour observed this, he said, "No! Stop! I know you may think I am crazy, but please allow his head to be exposed to the sunlight." The driver unzipped the bag, and as the limousine slowly moved down the drive of the hospice facility, Seymour's auto pilot snapped off, and he screamed and cried uncontrollably.

Since Hans wanted to be cremated, Seymour delayed the memorial service for six weeks so that it would be held on Hans's birthday. Seymour had planned the service just as if it was his wedding day; no expense was spared. The most expensive funeral home in upper northwest Washington, DC, was selected, two life-sized sprays of red roses banked the cremated ashes, and three-piece strings with harp accompaniment played for the prelude and conclusion.

The service was one hour sharp from start to finish. A large invitational reception was held for family and friends after the services. Seymour was alone but knew he was completely loved at least one time in his life.

CHAPTER FORTY-SIX

Estelle's Gentleman Friend

After Albrecht's death, Estelle sold the family house. She moved into a plush retirement community that she and Albrecht had planned to move into together. It was a cutting-edge retirement community that featured everything from independent living to memory and long-term care until death. She had a retirement annuity of her own, Albrecht had left her the maximum benefit from his military and civilian annuities, she had the proceeds from the sale of the family home they had built, and the 20 percent she had saved from the perpetual memory of her father saying to her, "Daughter, if you make a nickel, save a cent!" Estelle was sitting pretty and would say, "I am living like a queen!" She was, at last, Mrs. Astor—her mother model figure.

A gentleman who knew Estelle's mother's family from the South learned of Albrecht's death. He asked Estelle out on a date, but she said that not until a year had passed would she consider going out with anyone. A year had passed when the gentleman drove twice a month for six months to date Estelle, but eventually, she broke it off.

Seymour asked his mother, "Why did you give up on your gentleman friend?"

"He's cheap!" she snapped back.

"What do you mean 'he is cheap'?" Seymour challenged.

"Well, he takes me out to dinner and then expects me to pay half," she replied.

"Well, what's wrong with that? You can afford it," Seymour asked.

"Seymour, going Dutch treat is for your generation. In my generation, a man takes a woman out to dinner. There was no Dutch treat in my generation. Besides that, I need my money to look and smell good. You know how you men are. You are always looking for a younger woman anyway. No! I need to hold on to my money!

"And another thing. He likes to play the slot machines at the casino, and he will pay the tolls going and wants me to pay the tolls coming back. And you know, child, I am not up for all that foolishness. So after I chastised him about the going Dutch, he paid for the dinner. But then he wanted me to cook breakfast for him with my food. No! I am not getting ahead with him, so I had to let him go! I did it as kindly as I could. At this stage in my life, I am not taking care of or sponsoring any man. For years, women couldn't work. And when we were allowed, we weren't paid fairly. No! If these young girls out here today want to take care of a man, then that is on them. But I think it is a sin and a shame that a woman has to take care of a man when they own and control everything and want to control us too!" Estelle lectured.

Seymour was on the floor, laughing at his mother's views on men. Estelle was right on! Seymour blurted out, "Well, I wasn't having a stepfather anyway!"

"Shut up, boy. You don't tell me who I can and who I cannot go out with! Men are so arrogant!" Estelle shouted!

Seymour was hysterical with laughter. He was egging his mother on, but she was correct. Even as a gay man, he had more privilege than a woman in current society.

CHAPTER FORTY-SEVEN

Judgments of Her Children

As Estelle continued to age, she determined in her mind that she was not really happy with the outcomes of her three children. Aries, her firstborn— she could see the worst of her father and herself in him. He was a functional alcoholic. He had gotten some girl she was never introduced to pregnant. She must not have been from good stock because Aries never introduced her to anyone in the family. He had little to nothing to do with their child after the birth. Estelle frowned upon this situation. He married for the first time and had four children. Estelle thought he loved his children born to marriage but discriminated mercilessly toward the child not born in marriage. Estelle thought Aries was dogmatic and subordinating to his wife. His wife was far more naive than her sister, Anise. She agreed the wife was not perfect, but she thought women did not need to be chastised as she had witnessed him doing often. She thought she would never have tolerated or put up with a man like Aries.

He married a second time—a divorcee with five children. And with his four, there was a total of nine children. *What kind of sense does that make?* Estelle thought. She thought, *You can never get ahead with nine children.* Aries had a bass voice and was outspoken and sometimes boisterous. He was lazy and cheap. He would do anything to get out of a task if he could pin it on someone else. He spent a disproportionate amount of his money on alcohol, cars, and chasing women. He admitted that he was never faithful to either of his wives. She was happy that at age fifty-five, he finished college. In her mind, at age fifty-five, it was much too late in his life for him to gain the kind of professional growth she hoped for him years earlier when he was in high school. She thought that if he had graduated college when she had begged him not to quit, his professional life would have produced a larger salary. She was happy that he would at least pop in to visit her in the retirement community.

She reconciled that his visits were important to her, and at least she could say all her children visited, although he came at lunchtime, and shortly thereafter, she nodded off. When she opened her eyes, he was gone.

She always paid him a little tip for his time and effort if she had him run an errand. One day, she requested that he go to the grocery store and pick up a good cut of steak. She had a taste for a good steak, a baked potato, and a garden salad for her dinner. She told him before he left that he could keep the change from the one-hundred-dollar bill she had given him. She knew in her heart that he was the child that was never going to do the right thing; but today, she hoped so because she was now old and infirmed. She had hoped that, with the more-than-generous tip, he would fulfill her request and do as she asked.

When he returned from the store with the steak, he slipped it in her refrigerator. He sat and chatted a moment and then said he had to leave to pick up his grandson. Estelle had set her hopes on enjoying a wonderful dinner. When dinnertime arrived and she was prepared to cook the steak, she opened the package and saw the steak Aries had purchased. She shouted, "Son of a bench hook! The boy bought me the last piece of meat jumping across the fence! I swear to my rest! I should have known better! Aries will not get it right for love or money!" She was hurt that her own child, at seventy years old, was still selfish and thoughtless to his old and infirmed mother. She was really disappointed too that her meal was ruined.

Claudia was the child she always wanted to shower with all the things that she never had as a girl growing up. Estelle had witnessed Mrs. Astor being kind and generous to her daughters. Estelle wanted so much for Claudia—to have a close relationship with her and to give her all those things most girls dreamed of having. Claudia showed little interest in things like buying dresses, suits, hats, and shoes with matching handbags. She showed no interest being a debutante, being in a sorority, and she was nonchalant about attending college after her marriage fiasco. Claudia was a different kind of girl, and Estelle described her as being just like Albrecht.

Estelle was proud that she was an honor student and showed great potential for being a leading African American woman. Estelle wanted to boast about Claudia's achievements. Instead, she stubbornly decided to marry some man she had only known for a few weeks. Estelle felt, with that decision, she had ruined her self-esteem and her life. When Claudia married for the third time, she married a successful businessman, but she was not happy. She cried all the time with no reason that was ever mentioned. Eventually, she became a born-again Christian. Estelle was a believer in Jesus Christ, but she nor Albrecht believed everything in the Bible. She thought some Christians took organized religion too far.

Estelle felt defeated by Claudia. Estelle had hoped for a more inspired and ambitious daughter who would someday make huge contributions to the world. Estelle's dreams for Claudia were lost. In Estelle's mind, she saw her daughter as having similar ideals as Albrecht.

Seymour was the child that she never wanted to have. But after his arrival, he was her last chance of having one child who would model the type of child she would have desired. He indeed was the closest to her of her three children. He was good-natured and generous. She had taught him how to be a gentleman to young ladies. He showed the greatest interest in fashions for men that she approved. And although he struggled to graduate from high school and college, with determination and courage, he graduated. He continued to a terminal degree. Through trials and tribulations, he eventually earned a six-figure income. He lived well.

Estelle thought, *But why did he turn out to be gay?* She thought this was a birth defect. As far as she was concerned, his gay life did not qualify him as a normal child.

CHAPTER FORTY-EIGHT

Old Stomping Ground

Estelle was ninety-six years old. Seymour was now sixty-six years old. Both are retired. Both had worked long years and inherited greatly from their spouses. They were sitting pretty. Nothing had changed their relationship with each other—the love or the hate. Overriding everything they had gone through regarding his gay life, she was still his mother and he was still her son. He was still a mother's boy, although his feelings of not being wanted had subsided knowing Albrecht had made his revelation about his wanting Estelle to get pregnant with him. This gave him comfort in his heart.

Estelle was a dutiful and generous mother to him. Neither Estelle nor Albrecht deprived him of anything. Seymour never deprived Estelle or Albrecht of anything after he became independent. He gave generously and looked after them in their old age.

One weekday morning, Estelle called Seymour and asked him to spend the day with her. She wanted to take a ride over her old stomping ground. Seymour arranged his day to take Estelle for a ride through both Washington and Baltimore so she could see her old stomping grounds and the remains of her life.

It was a beautiful sunny morning when they got started. The sky was clear and the temperature was pleasant. They both agreed to have their breakfast at home. They stopped to pick up coffee to sip and a scone to munch on as they drove along their route. Seymour picked her up at the lobby of her plush retirement condominium. She was smartly dressed in a platinum-colored top-designer knit suit. She had, for years, smelled of world-class fragrances. Estelle loved the fragrances and selected one perfumer and used that collection exclusively.

Seymour wore a custom-made navy-blue blazer, gray slacks, white open-collar shirt, and black leather shoes with a black leather belt and black socks. Estelle had groomed him to dress elegantly, and he was comfortable. They both looked their best.

Seymour drove from his home to Estelle's plush apartment lobby then to Washington, DC—her birth city. First, they drove by the location of the women's hospital where Estelle was born. Estelle gave directions to Seymour to the streets where she once lived and played ninety years earlier. Seymour was just as thrilled to see the city and the monuments that adorned the city of his mother's birth. They enjoyed the locations of the primary, junior high, and high schools Estelle, Anise, and Harrison Jr. attended. She pointed out the streets where she lived and routes she and Anise would take to shop for groceries.

They drove by the house where Mrs. Astor lived, and she pointed to the basement apartment where Harrison Sr. raised his family after Anna had died. She said the house looked so much larger to her as a child. The beautiful green shrubbery that served as a backdrop to the scarlet, pink, and white azaleas all brought back memories of her childhood—both the good memories and the bad memories. The forsythia and the tulips were evenly woven into the landscape of the private homes that housed Washington's elite. As Seymour drove the car, she gave detailed descriptions of the trials and tribulations she experienced as a child; but in her heart, she had missed the beauty of her hometown.

She thought Washington, DC, was a more beautiful city than Baltimore; and within herself, she felt that love and romance blinds you to choices you make in life. She had loved Christopher Hudson as a teenager. His mother was her reason for leaving Washington, DC, and not returning. Most of all, she remembered Sundays after church when her mother would allow the children to play on the steps of the capitol grounds. Anna would allow them to play in their Sunday-school clothes. Estelle said it was the only time she felt pretty as a child. Then Anna died and the Great Depression came along, and they became destitute.

As Seymour drove by the schools she attended, Estelle would sing all the songs she used to sing in elementary school and recite the poems she had memorized in her classes. These memories brought bittersweet feelings for Estelle and Seymour.

Seymour took a break from his driving by noon. They had a nice lunch on Connecticut Avenue. Estelle commented that places like these were not integrated when she was a child. "You are living high off the hog,

Seymour, if you can eat on Connecticut Avenue, child!" she would say. Estelle conversed over lunch and thanked Seymour for taking her on this excursion. She said she was enjoying herself.

As Seymour made the return trip to Baltimore, to take her back to her home, he asked if she was up to riding a while longer in the city of Baltimore. She said yes.

Seymour chose random streets in Baltimore where she and Albrecht had their beginnings. She directed Seymour to drive by the street where she and Albrecht lived with Bessie and Theopolis. They drove past the bakery where she worked before Aries was born. They drove by the hospital where she gave birth to Aries and Claudia.

Then Seymour drove her by the street where he was born. Estelle saw the once beautiful street and noticed the house where Anise once lived. "This is where Seymour was born," Estelle said in a *Ms. Jane Pitman* voice. "Pull over and stop the car, son." She intensely looked out the car window toward the house. She focused on the apartment building as she reflected on what she was remembering about her life and the time she spent there.

As in the days when he would ride along with his mother to the grocery store, Sadie's beauty salon, and the shopping mall, Seymour was content and at peace to be with his mother. He had no idea what she was thinking because he was not born yet, and thus he let her contemplate her thoughts.

After a few moments, Estelle broke the silence and said, "Seymour, these were difficult years for me. I was nine months pregnant with you. Your father had broken his leg two days before you were born. When I went into labor, we were living out there on the military base. The hospitals were segregated. I had to pack up Aries and Claudia and take them to a neighbor, then get on a bus, in labor, to transport myself to the hospital. When I got to the hospital, I was turned away because of a polio outbreak in the maternity ward. There was no such thing as a private room for Negros in those days. I had to take a cab to your grandmother's house, and she turned me away. She felt Anise was living as well as any white woman, so she had your aunt and uncle walk me over there to deliver you."

She digressed for a moment and interjected, "When Aries got the chickenpox, Claudia got them, and then I got them. It settled in my left eye, and I have been blind in my left eye ever since. It was dark outside, and it was getting late. I was scared with no place to go, no husband to help, and no doctor around. It was awful."

Seymour was becoming hot and warm listening to his mother tell her story. Traffic was moving along in the busy city streets. Children were getting out of school and playing along the sidewalks. Employers were letting employees off from work.

Seymour locked the car door so he could concentrate on what his mother was saying as Estelle continued, "It was not enough that my mother died. The Depression came and wiped out all we had. My father had worked me like a mule. Christopher Hudson was the only man in the world who expressed any kindness toward me. His mother interfered with that. Your father, who didn't like birth control, got me pregnant with first one, then the other of the two children. Then he runs off to the military, saying he does not feel man enough. He leaves me with the two children. He writes to me from overseas, telling me about the women he was socializing with and that he was going to be a better lover when he returned home. When you were born, I thought I would get some consolation prize for having you since he was the one who said he wanted you. Instead, he showers you with love. I was his wife, but he adored you."

Seymour thought his was mother was blaming him for her not being loved by her husband. He said nothing and tried to concentrate and listen.

Estelle continued, "You have never been married. You have never had children, and you don't know what it is like to be a woman. As I have watched you mature, you have gotten everything. You were my child, but you were a boy. Boys don't need to be pampered. Women do! But you were a man, and you got everything I wanted. You were loved by Christian and Hans too! For me, nobody had time for love."

When Estelle finally finished her story, she came out of her daze. To Seymour, his mother had the same look on her face as he had when he felt relieved. She had a brain dump.

In a low, sad voice, she said, "You can take me home now."

After Seymour dropped her off at home, he asked if he should walk her to the door. He did not know what to say or think after listening to his mother's story.

She said, "No. I am all right."

As Seymour drove back across the interstate, he tried to decipher what his mother was telling him in the day they had spent together. His first thought was that his life was 100 percent better than her life. His life was better because of her. At that moment, he stopped judging her.

The following Christmas, she sent Seymour a special card for a son. It read, "I love you."

Seymour knew, at this point, that she had no capacity to speak the words "I love you" to him. He thought of his mother's life. She had loved and cared for everyone around her all her life—her father, sister, brother, husband, sons, and daughter. He concluded that the perfect mother that he had been searching for in Estelle, he already had for a lifetime. She really had no time to love, but she loved.

And most of all, she loved him.

Epilogue

After Estelle's sermon to Seymour, she lived to be one hundred years old. She had over a half million dollars in savings, several mink coats, and she wore expensive clothing and accessories. She drove a large Buick Park Avenue. She had worked her way out of poverty and lived her dream.

Unbeknownst to her children, she changed the original will that she and Albrecht had prepared when Albrecht had the house built for Estelle. It was his desire that everything first go to the surviving spouse, and the last remaining spouse was to divide the remaining estate equally among the three children. Since Claudia was the brightest and the only girl, she would have been the executor.

After living as a widow for twenty years, she made judgments about her children. She changed the original will. In her mind, she did not think it fair that the child who had done the most for her and Albrecht should only have an equal portion of her estate. She thought the child who had done the most should be recognized with a larger portion of the estate. Thus she divided everything that was left from Albrecht's estate equally between the three children. Her personal annuity and personal savings she left to Seymour. She named him executor. The only person who had a problem with her decision was Aries.

Estelle's father, Harrison Sr., had always taught her when discerning who and who not to keep in her life. He would say to her, "Daughter, always stick with the bridge that takes you safely across. That's how you choose your friends in this world." Of her children, she judged that Seymour was the child that was the bridge that had taken her safely across when she needed it.

Aries, at eighty years old, had never taken her out to dinner or purchased one rose for her on Mother's Day. Claudia was nonchalant toward her since childhood. Seymour, she thought, did not have any more time than her other two children. He lived the greatest distance from her, but he made the time to see her and Albrecht. He spent time and money on them, even during the days when he could least afford to do so. In her mind, her father was correct. She thought that even if she had given Aries a greater share of her money, he would only have more libations. Claudia wanted to lead her life without her mother's engagement. Estelle could not justify why they deserved more.

On the day of Estelle's funeral, Aries arrived late and smelled of alcohol. The pastor of the church gave an electrifying account of Estelle's life. He spoke of how her mother died when she was ten years old, leaving her an orphan, and how Estelle, at ten years old, became the matriarch of the house, tending to her father's needs while raising her sister and brother. The pastor went on to tell of how she was married to Albrecht for seventy-five years and raised two children alone while he was in the military. He told of her three children. He stated that all of them were college graduates, and one earned a PhD. He told of how she worked in the government system for over thirty years and maintained a perfect attendance record for the last fifteen years of her career. The pastor told the story of what a good sister Estelle had been to her sister, Anise, and how she took her nephew in when her sister was hospitalized. The pastor said Estelle's road had not been easy, but he believed that Jesus had forgiven her for any transgressions and that she would sit at the hands of the Lord.

Her father and mother, Harrison and Anna Cory, were deceased. Her sister, Anise, could not attend the funeral because she was in a nursing home. Her son, Antwan, whom Estelle and Albrecht had taken in as a child, had a massive heart attack and died mountain-climbing ten years earlier. He loved his Aunt Estelle more than his mother. The mailman's wife would not give him a divorce, and thus he never married Anise. Her brother, Harrison Jr., died without a friend in the world due to the hatred he held in his soul for his father. Albrecht died after two heart attacks and open-heart surgery. Aries remained a functional alcoholic and father of nine. Claudia had three husbands and three children. She became a born-again Christian.

And Seymour, the child whom she dreaded, having reconciled and accepted that he was a product of his mother and father, and he was also a product of himself. He made sense out of his confused feelings. He learned from his grandfather, whom he disliked after his first meeting, "to stick with the bridge that takes you safely across" and "if you make a nickel, to save a cent." In three generations of family history, he finally knew from whence he had come and loved.

The End

Printed in the United States
By Bookmasters